HE WAS SUSPENDED SOME FIVE METERS ABOVE THE FLOOR

The night before he had warned himself of the dangers of apathy. Now, for one awful instant—all the time he had—he recognized that overconfidence extracted an equally bitter price. The sharp *twang* of released springs filled his enhanced hearing, and the servos within his arms snapped his fingertip lasers into position faster than his brain could register the black wall hurtling itself toward him. The flying wall reached him, and he had just enough time to notice it was actually a net before it hit, wrapping itself around him like a giant cocoon. A split second later he was jerked sharply off his original path as unnoticed suspension lines reached their limit, snapping him back to hang more or less upside down in the middle of the room.

And Jonny was captured . . . which, since he was a Cobra, meant that he was dead.

TIMOTHY ZAHN

COBRA

science fiction

COBRA

Copyright © 1985 by Timothy Zahn

The chapters "Veteran" and "Loyalist" appeared in slightly different form in *Analog Science Fiction/Science Fact*, © 1981 and 1983 by Timothy Zahn.

A Baen Book

Baen Enterprises
260 Fifth Avenue
New York, N.Y. 10001

First printing, May 1985
Second printing, November 1985

ISBN: 0-671-65560-4

Cover art by Vincent DiFate

Printed in the United States of America

Distributed by
SIMON & SCHUSTER
MASS MERCHANDISE SALES COMPANY
1230 Avenue of the Americas
New York, N.Y. 10020

Trainee: 2403

The music all that morning had been of the militant type that had dominated the airwaves for the past few weeks; but to the discerning ear there was a grim undertone to it that hadn't been there since the very start of the alien invasion. So when the music abruptly stopped and the light-show patterns on the plate were replaced by the face of Horizon's top news reporter, Jonny Moreau clicked off his laser welder and, with a feeling of dread, leaned closer to listen.

The bulletin was brief and as bad as Jonny had feared. "The Dominion Joint Military Command on Asgard has announced that, as of four days ago, Adirondack has been occupied by the invading Troft forces." A holosim map appeared over the reporter's right shoulder, showing the seventy white dots of the Dominion of Man bordered by the red haze of the Troft Empire to the left and the green of the Minthisti to the top and right. Two of the leftmost dots now flashed red. "Dominion Star Forces are reportedly consolidating new positions near Palm and Iberiand, and the ground troops already on Adirondack are expected to continue guerrilla activity against the occupation units. A full report—

including official statements by the Central Committee and Military Command—will be presented on our regular newscast at six tonight."

The music and light pattern resumed, and as Jonny slowly straightened up, a hand came to rest on his shoulder. "They got Adirondack, Dader," Jonny said without turning around.

"I heard," Pearce Moreau said quietly.

"And it only took them three weeks." Jonny squeezed the laser he still held. "Three weeks."

"You can't extrapolate the progress of a war from its first stages," Pearce said, reaching over to take the laser from his son's hand. "The Trofts will learn that controlling a world is considerably more difficult than taking it in the first place. And we *were* caught by surprise, don't forget. As the Star Forces call up the reserves and shift to full war status, the Trofts will find it increasingly hard to push them back. I'd guess we might lose either Palm or Iberiand as well, but I think it'll stop there."

Jonny shook his head. There was something unreal about discussing the capture of billions of people as if they were only pawns in some cosmic chess game. "And then what?" he asked, with more bitterness than his father deserved. "How do we get the Trofts off our worlds without killing half the populations in the process? What if they decide to stage a 'scorched earth' withdrawal when they go? Suppose—"

"Hey; hey," Pearce interrupted, stepping around in front of Jonny and locking eyes with him. "You're getting yourself worked up for no good reason. The war's barely three months old, and the Dominion's a long way from being in trouble yet. Really. So put the whole thing out of your mind and get back to work, okay? I need this hood plate finished before you head for home and homework." He held out the laser welder.

"Yeah." Jonny accepted the instrument with a sigh and adjusted his de-contrast goggles back over his eyes. Leaning back over the half-finished seam, he tried to put the invasion out of his mind . . . and if his father hadn't made one last comment, he might have succeeded in doing so.

"Besides," Pearce shrugged as he started back to his own workbench, "whatever's going to happen, there's not a thing in the universe we can do about it from here."

Jonny was quiet at dinner that evening, but in the Moreau household one more or less silent person wasn't enough to change the noise level significantly. Seven-year-old Gwen, as usual, dominated the conversation, alternating news of school and friends with questions on every subject from how weathermen damp out tornadoes to how butchers get the back-blades out of a breaff hump roast. Jame, five years Jonny's junior, contributed the latest on teen-age/high school social intrigue, a labyrinth of status and unspoken rules that Jame was more at home with than Jonny had ever been. Pearce and Irena managed the whole verbal circus with the skill of long practice, answering Gwen's questions with parental patience and generally keeping conversational friction at a minimum. Whether by tacit mutual consent or from lack of interest, no one mentioned the war.

Jonny waited until the table was being cleared before dropping in his studiously casual request. "Dader, can I borrow the car tonight to go into Horizon City?"

"What, there isn't another game there this evening, is there?" the other frowned.

"No," Jonny said. "I wanted to look at some stuff out there, that's all."

" 'Stuff'?"

Jonny felt his face growing warm. He didn't

want to lie, but he knew that a fully truthful answer would automatically be followed by a family discussion, and he wasn't prepared for a confrontation just yet. "Yeah. Just ... things I want to check out."

"Like the Military Command recruitment center?" Pearce asked quietly.

The background clatter of dishes being moved and stacked cut off abruptly, and in the silence Jonny heard his mother's sharp intake of air. "Jonny?" she asked.

He sighed and braced himself for the now inevitable discussion. "I wouldn't have enlisted without talking to all of you first," he said. "I just wanted to go get some information—procedures, requirements; that sort of thing."

"Jonny, the war is a long way away—" Irena began.

"I know, Momer," Jonny interrupted. "But there are people *dying* out there—"

"All the more reason to stay here."

"—not just soldiers, but civilians, too," he continued doggedly. "I just think—well, Dader said today that there wasn't anything I could do to help." He shifted his attention to Pearce. "Maybe not ... but maybe I shouldn't give up to statistical generalities quite so quickly."

A smile twitched briefly at Pearce's lip without touching the rest of his face. "I remember when the full gist of your arguments could be boiled down to 'because I said so, that's why.'"

"Must be college that's doing it," Jame murmured from the kitchen door. "I think they're also teaching him a little about fixing computers in between the argument seminars."

Jonny sent a quick frown in his brother's direction, annoyed at the apparent attempt to sidetrack the discussion. But Irena wasn't about to be distracted. "What *about* college, now that we're on that topic?" she asked. "You've got a year to go before you get your certificate. You'd at least stay that long, wouldn't you?"

Jonny shook his head. "I don't see how I can. A whole *year*—look at what the Trofts have done in just three months."

"But your education is important, too—"

"All right, Jonny," Pearce cut off his wife quietly. "Go to Horizon City if you'd like and talk to the recruiters."

"Pearce!" Irena turned stunned eyes on him.

Pearce shook his head heavily. "We can't stand in his way," he told her. "Can't you hear how he's talking? He's already ninety percent decided on this. He's an adult now, with the right and responsibility of his own decisions." He shifted his gaze to Jonny. "Go see the recruiters; but promise me you'll talk with us again before you make your final decision. Deal?"

"Deal," Jonny nodded, feeling the tension within him draining away. Volunteering to go fight a war was one thing: scary, but on a remote and almost abstract level. The battle for his family's support had loomed far more terrifyingly before him, with potential costs he hadn't wanted to contemplate. "I'll be back in a few hours," he said, taking the keys from his father and heading for the door.

The Joint Military Command recruiting office had been in the same city hall office for over three decades, and it occurred to Jonny as he approached it that he was likely following the same path his father had taken to his own enlistment some twenty-eight years previously. Then, the enemy had been the Minthisti, and Pearce Moreau had fought from the torpedo deck of a Star Force dreadnaught.

This war was different, though; and while Jonny had always admired the romance of the Star Forces,

he had already decided to choose a less glamorous—
but perhaps more effective—position.

"Army, eh?" the recruiter repeated, cocking an
eyebrow as she studied Jonny from behind her
desk. "Excuse my surprise, but we don't get a lot
of volunteers for Army service here. Most kids your
age would rather fly around in star ships or air
fighters. Mind if I ask your reasons?"

Jonny nodded, trying not to let the recruiter's
faintly condescending manner get to him. Chances
were good it was a standard part of the interview,
designed to get a first approximation of the appli-
cant's irritation threshold. "It seems to me that if
the Troft advance continues to push the Star Forces
back, we're going to lose more planets to them.
That's going to leave the civilians there pretty
much at their mercy ... unless the Army already
has guerrilla units in place to coordinate resistance.
That's the sort of thing I'm hoping to do."

The recruiter nodded thoughtfully. "So you want
to be a guerrilla fighter?"

"I want to help the people," Jonny corrected.

"Um." Reaching for her terminal, she tapped in
Jonny's name and ID code; and as she skimmed
the information that printed out, she again cocked
an eyebrow. "Impressive," she said, without any
sarcasm Jonny could hear. "Grade point high
school, grade point college, personality index ...
you have any interest in officer training?"

Jonny shrugged. "Not that much, but I'll take it
if that's where I can do the most good. I don't
mind just being an ordinary soldier, though, if
that's what you're getting at."

Her eyes studied his face for a moment. "Uh-
huh. Well, I'll tell you what, Moreau." Her fingers
jabbed buttons and she swiveled the plate around
for his scrutiny. "As far as I know, there aren't any
specific plans at present to set up guerrilla networks on threatened planets. But if that *is* done—

and I agree it's a reasonable move—then one or more of these special units will probably be spearheading it."

Jonny studied the list. *Alpha Command, Interrorum, Marines, Rangers*—names familiar and highly respected. "How do I sign up for one of these?"

"You don't. You sign up for the Army and take a small mountain of tests—and if you show the qualities they want they'll issue you an invitation."

"And if not, I'm still in the Army?"

"Provided you don't crusk out of normal basic training, yes."

Jonny glanced around the room, the colorful holosim posters seeming to leap out at him with their star ships, atmosphere fighters, and missile tanks; their green, blue, and black uniforms. "Thank you for your time," he told the recruiter, fingering the information magcard he'd been given. "I'll be back when I've made up my mind."

He expected to return home to a dark house, but found his parents and Jame waiting quietly for him in the living room. Their discussion lasted long into the night, and when it was over Jonny had convinced both himself and them of what he had to do.

The next evening, after dinner, they all drove to Horizon City and watched as Jonny signed the necessary magforms.

"So . . . tomorrow's the big day."

Johnny glanced up from his packing to meet his brother's eyes. Jame, lounging on his bed across the room, was making a reasonably good effort to look calm and relaxed. But his restless fiddling with a corner of the blanket gave away his underlying tension. "Yep," Jonny nodded. "Horizon City Port, *Skylark Lines 407* to Aerie, military transport to Asgard. Nothing like travel to give you a real perspective on the universe."

Jame smiled faintly. "I hope to get down to New Persius some day myself. A hundred twenty whole kilometers. Any word yet on the tests?"

"Only that my headache's supposed to go away in a couple more hours." The past three days had been genuine killers, with back-to-back tests running from seven in the morning to nine at night. General knowledge, military and political knowledge, psychological, attitudinal, physical, deep physical, biochemical—they'd given him the works. "I was told they usually run these tests over a two-week period," he added, a bit of information he hadn't been given until it was all over. Probably fortunately. "I guess the Army's anxious to get new recruits trained and in service."

"Uh-huh. So . . . you've said your good-byes and all? Everything settled there?"

Jonny tossed a pair of socks into his suitcase and sat down beside it on his bed. "Jame, I'm too tired to play tag around the mountain. What exactly is on your mind?"

Jame sighed. "Well, to put it bluntly . . . Alyse Carne is kind of upset that you didn't discuss this whole thing with her before you went ahead and did it."

Jonny frowned, searching his memory. He hadn't seen Alyse since the tests began, of course, but she'd seemed all right the last time they'd been together. "Well, if she is, she didn't say anything to *me* about it. Who'd you find out from?"

"Mona Biehl," Jame said. "And of course Alyse wouldn't have told you directly—it's too late for you to change things now."

"So why are *you* telling me?"

"Because I think you ought to make an effort to go see her tonight. To show that you still care about her before you run off to save the rest of humanity."

Something in his brother's voice made Jonny

pause, the planned retort dying in his throat. "You disapprove of what I'm doing, don't you?" he asked quietly.

Jame shook his head. "No, not at all. I'm just worried that you're going into this without really understanding what you're getting into."

"I'm twenty-one years old, Jame—"

"And have lived all your life in a medium-sized town on a frontier-class world. Face it, Jonny—you function well enough here, but you're about to tackle three unknowns at the same time: mainstream Dominion society, the Army, and war itself. That's a pretty potent set of opponents."

Jonny sighed. Coming from anyone else, words like that would have been grounds for a strong denial ... but Jame had an innate understanding of people that Jonny had long since come to trust. "The only alternative to facing unknowns is to stay in this room the rest of my life," he pointed out.

"I know—and I don't have any great suggestions for you, either." Jame waved helplessly. "I guess I just wanted to make sure you at least were leaving here with your eyes open."

"Yeah. Thanks." Jonny sent his gaze slowly around the room, seeing things that he'd stopped noticing years ago. Now, almost a week after his decision, it was finally starting to sink in that he was leaving all this.

Possibly forever.

"You think Alyse would like to see me, huh?" he asked, bringing his eyes back to Jame.

The other nodded. "I'm sure it would make her feel a little better, yeah. Besides which—" He hesitated. "This may sound silly, but I also think that the more ties you have here in Cedar Lake the easier it'll be to hold onto your ethics out there."

Jonny snorted. "You mean out among the decadence of the big worlds? Come on, Jame, you don't really believe that sophistication implies depravity, do you?"

"Of course not. But someone's bound to try and convince you that depravity implies sophistication."

Jonny waved his hands in a gesture of surrender. "Okay; that's it. I've warned you before: the point where you start with the aphorisms is the point where I bail out of the discussion." Standing up, he scooped an armful of shirts from the dresser drawer and dumped them beside his suitcase. "Here— make yourself useful for a change, huh? Pack these and my cassettes for me, if you don't mind."

"Sure." Jame got up and gave Jonny a lopsided smile. "Take your time; you'll have plenty of chances to catch up on your sleep on the way to Asgard."

Jonny shook his head in mock exasperation. "One thing I'm *not* going to miss about this place is having my own live-in advice service."

It wasn't true, of course . . . but then, both of them knew that.

The farewells at the Horizon City Port the next morning were as painful as Jonny had expected them to be, and it was with an almost bittersweet sense of relief that he watched the city fall away beneath the ground-to-orbit shuttle that would take him to the liner waiting above. Never before had he faced such a long separation from family, friends, and home, and as the blue sky outside the viewport gradually faded to black, he wondered if Jame had been right about too many shocks spaced too closely together. Still . . . in a way, it seemed almost easier to be changing everything about his life at once, rather than to have to graft smaller pieces onto a structure that wasn't designed for them. An old saying about new wine in old wineskins brushed at his memory; the moral, he remembered, being that a person too set in his ways was unable to accept anything at all that was outside his previous experience.

Overhead, the first stars were beginning to appear, and Jonny smiled at the sight. His way of life on Horizon had certainly been comfortable, but at twenty-one he had no intention of becoming rigidly attached to it. For the first time since enlisting, a wave of exhilaration swept through him. Jame, stuck at home, could choose to see Jonny's upcoming experiences as uncomfortable shocks if he wanted to ... but Jonny was going to treat them instead as high adventure.

And with that attitude firmly settled in his mind, he gave his full attention to the viewport, eagerly awaiting his first glimpse of a real star ship.

Skylark 407 was a commercial liner, the majority of its three hundred passengers business professionals and tourists. A handful, though, were new recruits like Jonny; and as the ship made stops over the next few days at Rajput, Zimbwe, and Blue Haven, that number rapidly went up. By the time they reached Aerie, fully a third of the passengers were transfered to the huge military transport orbiting there. Jonny's group was apparently the last batch to arrive, and they were barely aboard before the ship shifted into hyperspace. Someone, clearly, was in a hurry.

For Jonny, the next five days were ones of awkward—and not totally successful—cultural adjustment. Jammed together in communal rooms, with less privacy than even the liner had afforded, the recruits formed a bewildering mosaic of attitudes, habits, and accents, and getting used to all of it proved harder than Jonny had anticipated. Many of the others apparently felt the same way, and within a day of their arrival Jonny noticed that his former shipmates were following the example of those who'd arrived here earlier and were clumping in small, relatively homogenous groups. Jonny made a few halfhearted attempts to bridge the social gaps, but eventually he gave up and spent the remainder of the trip with others of the Horizon contingent. The Dominion of Man, clearly, wasn't nearly as culturally uniform as he'd always believed, and he finally had to console himself with the reasonable expectation that the Army must have figured out how to handle this kind of barrier a long time ago. When they reached the training camps of Asgard, he knew, things would change, and they'd all be simply soldiers together.

In a way he was right . . . but in another way, he was very wrong.

The registration foyer was a room as large as the Horizon City Concert Hall, and it was almost literally packed with people. At the far end, past the dotted line of sergeants at terminals, the slowly-moving mass changed abruptly to a roiling stream as the recruits hurried to their assigned orientation meetings. Drifting along, oblivious to the flood passing him on both sides, Jonny frowned down at his own card with a surprise that was edging rapidly into disappointment.

JONNY MOREAU
HORIZON: HN-89927-238-2825p
ASSIGNED ROOM: AA-315 FREYR COMPLEX
UNIT: COBRAS
UNIT ORIENTATION: C-662 FREYR COMPLEX:
1530 HOURS

Cobras. The transport had included a generous selection of military reference material, and Jonny had spent several hours reading all he could about the Army's Special Forces. Nowhere had anything called the Cobras been so much as hinted at.

Cobras. What could a unit named after a poisonous Earth snake be assigned to do? Decontamination procedures, perhaps, or else something having to do with antipersonnel mines? Whatever it was, it wasn't likely to live up to the expectations of the past weeks.

Someone slammed into his back, nearly knocking the card out of his hand. "Get the phrij out of the road," a lanky man snarled, pushing past him. Neither the expletive nor the other's accent were familiar. "You want to infiloop, do it out of the phrijing *way*."

"Sorry," Jonny muttered as the man disappeared into the flow. Gritting his teeth, he sped up, glancing up at the glowing direction indicators lining the walls. Whatever this Cobra unit was, he'd better get going and find the meeting room. The local-time clocks were showing 1512 already, and it was unlikely *any* Army officer would appreciate tardiness.

Room C-662 was his first indication that perhaps he'd jumped to the wrong conclusion. Instead of the battalion-sized auditorium he'd expected, the room was barely adequate to handle the forty-odd men already seated there. Two men in red and black diamond-patterned tunics faced the group from a low dais, and as Jonny slipped into a vacant chair the younger of them caught Jonny's eye. "Name?"

"Jonny Moreau, sir," Jonny told him, glancing quickly at the wall clock. But it was still only 1528, and the other merely nodded and made a notation on a comboard on his lap. Looking furtively around the room, Jonny spent the next two minutes listening to his heart beat and letting his imagination have free rein.

Exactly at 1530 the older of the uniformed men stood up. "Good afternoon, gentlemen," he nodded. "I'm Cee-two Rand Mendro, Cobra Unit Commander, and I'd like to welcome you to Asgard. We build men and women into soldiers here—as well as flyers, sailors, Star Forcers, and a few other specialties. Here in Freyr Complex, we're exclusively soldiers . . . and you forty-five have had the honor of being chosen for the newest and—in my opinion—most elite force the Dominion has to offer. *If* you want to join." He looked around, his eyes seeming to touch each of them in turn. "If you do, you'll draw the most dangerous assignment we've got: to go to Troft-occupied worlds and engage the enemy in a guerrilla war."

He paused, and Jonny felt his stomach curling into a knot. An elite unit—as he'd wanted—and the chance to help civilian populations—as he'd also wanted. But to be dropped in where the Trofts already had control sounded a lot more like suicide than service. From the faint stirrings around the room he gathered his reaction wasn't unique.

"Of course," Mendro continued, "we aren't exactly talking about space-chuting you in with a laser rifle in one hand and a radio in the other. If you choose to join up you'll receive some of the most extensive training and *the* absolute top-of-the-line weaponry available." He gestured to the man seated beside him. "Cee-three Shri Bai will be the chief training instructor for this unit. He'll now demonstrate a little of what you, as Cobras, will be able to do."

Bai laid his comboard beside his chair and started to stand up—and halfway through the motion he shot toward the ceiling.

Caught by surprise, Jonny saw only the blur as Bai leaped—but the twin thunderclaps from above and behind him were the gut-wrenching signs of a rocket-assisted flight gone horribly bad. He spun around in his seat, bracing for the sight of Bai's broken body—

Bai was standing calmly by the door, a hint of a smile on his face as he looked around at what must have been some pretty stunned expressions.

"I'm sure all of you know," he said, "that using either a lift pack or exoskeleton muscle enhancers would be foolhardy in such a confined room. Um? So watch again."

His knees bent a few degrees, and with the same *thump-thump* he was back on the dais. "All right," he said. "Who saw what I did?"

Silence . . . and then a hand went tentatively up. "You bounced off the ceiling, I think," the recruit said, a bit uncertainly. "Uh . . . your shoulders took the impact?"

"In other words, you didn't really see," Bai nodded. "I actually flipped halfway over on the way up, took the impact with my feet, and continued around to be upright when I landed."

Jonny's mouth felt a little dry. The ceiling was no more than five meters up. To have done that much maneuvering in that small a space . . .

"The point, aside from the power and precision of the jump itself," Mendro said, "is that even you, who knew what was going to happen, couldn't follow Bai's movement. Consider how it would work against a roomful of Trofts who *weren't* expecting it. Next—"

He broke off as the door opened and one more recruit came in. "Viljo?" Bai asked, retrieving the comboard at his feet.

"Yes, sir," the newcomer nodded. "Sorry I'm late, sir—the registration people were running slow."

"Oh?" Bai waved the comboard. "Says here you went through the line at 1450. That's—let's see— seventeen minutes *before* Moreau, who got here seven minutes earlier than you did. Um?"

Viljo turned a bright red. "I . . . guess maybe I got a little lost. Sir."

"With all the signs posted around the complex? Not to mention all the regular Army personnel wandering around? Um?"

Viljo was beginning to look like a hunted animal. "I . . . I stopped to look at the exhibits in the entry corridor, sir. I thought this room was closer than it was."

"I see." Bai gave him a long, chilly look. "Punctuality, Viljo, is a mark of a good soldier—and if you plan to be a Cobra it's going to be an absolute necessity. But even more important are honesty and integrity in front of your teammates. Specifically, it means that when you crusk up, you damn well better not try to push the blame onto someone else. Got that?"

"Yes, sir."

"All right. Now come up here; I need an assistant for this next demonstration."

Swallowing visibly, Viljo unglued himself from the floor and threaded his way through the chairs to the dais. "What I showed you a minute ago," Bai said, once again addressing the entire room, "was essentially a party trick, though with some obvious military applications. This, now, I think you'll find along more practical lines."

From his tunic, he produced two metal disks, each ten centimeters in diameter with a small black inset in the center. "Hold the one in your left hand sideways," Bai instructed Viljo, "and when I give the word, throw the other toward the back of the room."

Mendro had meantime gone to one of the room's back corners. Taking a few steps off to the side, Bai checked positions and bent his knees slightly. "All right: *now.*"

Viljo lofted the disk toward the door. Behind him, Jonny sensed Mendro's leap and catch, and an instant later the disk was shooting back toward Bai. In a smooth motion that was again too fast to follow, Bai fell to the side, out of the disk's path . . . and as he rolled again to one knee, two needles of light flashed in opposite directions from his outstretched hands. Viljo's surprised yelp was almost covered up by the crash of the flying disk against the wall.

"Good," Bai said briskly, getting to his feet and heading over to retrieve the first disk. "Viljo, show them yours."

Even from his distance Jonny could see the small hole just barely off-center through the black inset. "Impressive, um?" Bai said, stepping back up on the dais and presenting the other target. "Of course, you can't always expect the enemy to hold still for you."

This shot hadn't been nearly as clean. Only the very edge of the black showed the laser's mark, and when the light hit it right Jonny could see that the adjacent metal was rippled with the heat. Still, it was an impressive performance—especially as Jonny had no idea where Bai had been hiding his weapons.

Or where they were now, for that matter.

"That gives you an idea of what a Cobra can do," Mendro said, returning to the front of the room and sending Viljo back to find a seat. "Now I'd like to show you a little of the nuts and bolts involved." Retrieving the comboard, he keyed in an instruction, and a full-sized image of a man appeared beside him. "From the outside a Cobra is virtually indistinguishable from any normal civilian. However, from the *inside*—" The hologram's exterior faded to a blue skeleton with oddly-shaped white spots scattered randomly around. "The blue is a ceramic laminae which makes all the major and most of the minor bones unbreakable, for all practical purposes. That, along with some strategic ligament strengthening, is half the reason Cee-three Bai was able to pull off those ceiling jumps without killing himself. The non-laminated areas you can see are there to allow the bone marrow to continue putting red blood cells into the system."

Another touch on the comboard and the piebald skeleton faded to dull gray, forming a contrast to the small yellow ovoids that appeared at joints all over the hologram. "Servomotors," Mendro identified them. "The other half of the ceiling jump. They act as strength multipliers, just like the ones in standard exoskeletons and fighting suits, except that these are particularly hard to detect. The power supply is a little nuclear goody here—" he pointed to an asymmetric object situated somewhere in the vicinity of the stomach"—and I'm not going to explain it because I don't understand it myself. Suffice it to say the thing works and works well."

Jonny thought back to Bai's incredible jumps and felt his stomach tighten. Servos and bone laminae were all well and good, but a trick like that could hardly be learned overnight. Either this Cobra training was going to take months at the minimum, or else Bai was an exceptionally athletic man ... and if there was one thing Jonny knew for certain, it was that he himself hadn't been selected for this group because of any innate gymnastic abilities. Apparently the Army was getting set for a long, drawn-out conflict.

On the dais, the hologram had again changed, this time marking several sections in red. "Cobra offensive and defensive equipment," Mendro said. "Small lasers in the tips of both little fingers, one of which also contains the discharge electrodes for an arcthrower—capacitor in the body cavity here. In the left calf is an antiarmor laser; here are the speakers for two different types of sonic weapons; and up by the eyes and ears are a set of optical and auditory enhancers. Yes—question?"

"Recruit MacDonald, sir," the other said with military correctness, a slight accent burring his words. "Are these optical enhancers like the targeting lenses of a fighting suit, where you're given a range/scale image in front of your eyes?"

Mendro shook his head. "That sort of thing is fine for medium- and long-range work, but pretty useless for the infighting you may have to do. Which brings us to the real key of the whole Cobra project." The red faded, and inside the skull a green walnut-sized object appeared, situated apparently directly beneath the brain. From it snaked dozens of slender filaments, most of them paralleling the spinal column before separating off to go their individual ways. Looking at it, Jonny's thoughts flashed back to a picture from his old fourth-grade biology text: a diagram showing the major structures of the human nervous system. . . .

"This," Mendro said, wagging a finger through the green walnut, "is a computer—probably the most powerful computer of its size ever developed. These optical fibers—" he indicated the filament network—"run to all the servos and weapons and to a set of kinesthetic sensors implanted directly in the bone laminae. Your targeting lenses, MacDonald, still require you to do the actual aiming and firing. This nanocomputer gives you the option of having the whole operation done automatically."

Jonny glanced at MacDonald, saw the other nodding slowly. It wasn't a new idea, certainly—computerized weaponry had been standard on star ships and atmosphere fighters for centuries—but to give an individual soldier that kind of control was indeed a technological breakthrough.

And Mendro wasn't even finished with his surprises. "In addition to fire control," he said, "the computer will have a set of combat reflexes programmed into it—reflexes that will not only include evasive movements but such tricks as were demonstrated a few minutes ago. Put it all together—" the hologram became a colorful puzzle as all the overlays reappeared—"and you have the most deadly guerrilla warriors mankind has ever produced."

He let the image stand a few seconds before switching it off and laying the comboard back on one of the chairs. "As Cobras you'll be on the leading edge of the counteroffensive strategy that I expect will ultimately push the Trofts out of Dominion territory . . . but there'll be a definite cost included. I've already mentioned the military dangers you'll be facing; at this point we can't even guess at what kind of casualty percentages there'll be, but I can assure you they'll be high. We'll need to do a lot of surgery on you, and surgery is never very pleasant; on top of that, a lot of what we put inside you will be there to stay. The laminae, for example, won't be removable, which requires you to keep the servos and nanocomputer, as well. There'll undoubtedly also be problems we haven't even thought about yet, and as part of the first wave of Cobras you'll take the full brunt of any design glitches that may have slipped by."

He paused and looked around the room. "Having said all that, though, I'd like to remind you that you're here because we need you. Every one of you has tested out with the intelligence, courage, and emotional stability that mark you as Cobra material—and I'll tell you frankly that there aren't a hell of a lot of you out there. The more of you that join up, the faster we can start shoving this war down the Trofts' throat bladders where it belongs.

"So. The rest of the day is yours to get settled in your rooms, get acquainted with Freyr Complex—" he glanced in Viljo's direction—"and perhaps look through the exhibit halls. Tomorrow morning you're to come back here whenever each of you is ready to give me your decision." Sweeping his gaze one last time around the room, he nodded. "Until then; dismissed."

Jonny spent the day as Mendro had suggested, meeting his roommates—there were five of them—

and walking through the buildings and open-air sections of Freyr Complex. The Cobra group seemed to have an entire barracks floor to themselves, and every time Jonny passed the lounge area there seemed to be a different collection of them sitting around arguing the pros and cons of joining up. Occasionally, he paused to listen, but most of the time he simply continued on his way, knowing down deep that none of their uncertainties applied to him. True, the decision ahead wasn't one to be taken lightly . . . but Jonny had gone into this in the first place in order to help the people on threatened planets. He could hardly back down simply because it was going to cost a little more than he'd expected.

Besides which—he was honest enough to admit— the whole Cobra concept smacked of the superhero books and shows that had thrilled him as a kid, and the chance to actually become someone with such powers was a potent enticement even to the more sophisticated college student he was now.

The discussions in his room later that evening went on until lights-out, but Jonny managed to tune them out and get a head start on the night's sleep. When reveille sounded, he was the only one of the six who didn't mutter curses at the ungodly hour involved, but quickly got dressed and went down to the mess hall. By the time he returned, the others—except for Viljo, who was still in bed— had gone for their own breakfasts. Heading upstairs to Room C-662, he discovered that he was the third of the group to officially join the Cobras. Mendro congratulated him, gave him a standard-sounding pep talk, and issued him a genuinely intimidating surgery schedule. He left for the medical wing with a nervous flutter in his stomach but with the confident feeling that he'd made the right decision.

Several times in the next two weeks that confidence was severely strained.

*   *   *

"All right, Cobras, listen up!"

Bai's voice was a rumble of thunder in the half-light of Asgard dawn, and Jonny suppressed a spasm of nausea that the sound and the chilly air sent through what was left of his stomach. Shivering had never made him feel sick before ... but then his body had never undergone such massive physical trauma before. What pain remained was little more than a dull ache extending from his eyes all the way down to his toes, and in the absence of that outlet his system had come up with these other quirks to show its displeasure. Shifting uncomfortably as he stood in line with the other thirty-five trainees, he felt the odd stresses and strains where his organs squeezed up against the new equipment and supports in his body cavity. The nausea flared again at the thought of all that inside him; quickly, he turned his attention back to Bai.

"—rough for you, but from personal experience I can assure you all the postoperative symptoms will be gone in another couple of days. In the meantime, there's nothing that says you can't start getting used to your new bodies.

"Now, I know you're all wondering why you're wearing your computers around your necks instead of inside your skulls. Um? Well, you're all supposed to be smart, and you haven't had much to do the last two weeks except think about things like that. Anyone want to trot out their pet theory?"

Jonny glanced around, feeling the soft collar-like computer rub gently against his neck as he turned his head. He was pretty sure he'd figured it out, but didn't want to be the first one to say anything.

"Recruit Noffke, sir," Parr Noffke, one of Jonny's roommates, spoke up. "Is it because you don't want our weapons systems operational until we're off Asgard?"

"Close," Bai nodded. "Moreau? You care to amplify on that?"

Startled, Jonny looked back at Bai. "Uh, would it be because you want to phase in access to our equipment—weapons and other capabilities—gradually instead of all at once?"

"You need to learn how to give answers more clearly, Moreau, but that's essentially it," Bai said. "Once the final computer is implanted its programming is fixed, so you'll wear the programmable ones until there's no danger of you slagging yourselves or each other. All right: first lesson is getting the feel of your bodies. Behind me about five klicks is the old ordnance range observation tower. Interworld contenders can run that in twelve minutes or so; we're going to do it in ten. *Move.*"

He turned and set off toward the distant tower at a fast run, the trainees forming a ragged mass in his wake. Jonny wound up somewhere in the middle of the pack, striving to keep his steps rhythmic as he fought the self-contradictory feeling of being both too heavy and too light. Five kilometers was twice as far as he'd ever run in his life—at *any* speed—and by the time he reached the tower his breath was coming in short gasps, his vision flickering with the exertion.

Bai was waiting as he stumbled to a stop. "Hold your breath for a thirty-count," the instructor ordered him briefly, moving immediately to the side to repeat the command to someone else. Strangely enough, Jonny found he could do it, and by the time those behind had caught up, both his lungs and eyes seemed all right again. "Now: that was lesson one point five," Bai growled. "About half of you let your bodies hyperventilate themselves for no better reason than habit. At the speed you were doing your servos should have been doing fifty to seventy percent of the work for you. Eventually, your autonomic systems will adjust, but until then

you're going to have to consciously pay attention
to all these little details.

"Okay. Lesson two: jumping. We'll start with
jumping straight up to various heights; and *you'll*
start by watching *me*. You haven't got your combat reflexes programmed in yet, and while you
won't be able to break your ankles, if you come
down off-balance and hit your heads it *will* hurt.
So watch and learn."

For the next hour they learned how to jump,
how to right themselves in mid-air when necessary,
and how to fall safely when the righting methods
weren't adequate. After that Bai switched their
focus to the observation tower looming over them,
and they learned a dozen different ways of climbing the outside of a building. By the time Bai
called lunch break they had each made the precari-
ous journey up the side and through an unlocked
window in the main observation level; and at Bai's
order they returned to the walls to eat, wolfing
down their field rations while clinging as best they
could ten meters above the ground.

The afternoon was spent practicing with their
arm servos, with emphasis on learning how to
hold heavy objects so as to put minimal stress on
skin and blood vessels. It wasn't nearly as trivial a
problem as it looked at first blush, and though
Jonny got away with only a few pressure bruises,
others wound up with more serious subcutaneous
bleeding or severely abraded skin. The worst cases
Bai sent immediately off to the infirmary; the rest
continued training until the sun was brushing the
horizon. Another brisk five-klick run brought them
back to the central complex building where, after
a quick dinner, they assembled once more in C-662
for an evening of lectures on guerrilla tactics and
strategy.

And finally, sore in both mind and body, they
were sent back to their rooms.

*   *   *

It was the first time Jonny had been in his room
since his two-week stint in surgery had begun, but
it looked about as he remembered. Heading straight
for his bunk, he collapsed gratefully into it, wincing at the unexpectedly loud protest from the bed's
springs. Pure imagination, of course—he wasn't
that much heavier, despite all the new hardware he was carrying around. Stretching his sore
muscles, he gingerly probed the bruises on his
arms, wondering if he could survive four more
weeks of this.

His five roommates arrived a minute or so behind him, coming in as a group and obviously in
the middle of comparing notes on the day. "—tell
you *all* Army trainers act like assembly robots,"
Cally Halloran was saying as they filed through
the door. "It's part of the toughening-up process
for the recruits. Psychology, troops, psychology."

"Phrij on psychology," Parr Noffke opined, leaning over the end of his bunk and doing some halfhearted stretching exercises. "That whole farrago
about eating lunch ten meters up?—you call that
toughening up? I tell you, Bai just likes making us
sweat."

"It proved you could hang on without devoting
your entire attention to your fingers, didn't it?"
Imel Deutsch countered dryly.

"Like I said," Halloran nodded. "Psychology."

Noffke snorted and abandoned his exercises.
"Hey, Druma; Rolon? Get in here and join the
party. We've got just enough time for a round
hand of King's Bluff."

"In a minute," Druma Singh's soft voice called
from the bathroom, where he and Rolon Viljo had
vanished. Jonny had noticed the pale blue of heal-
quick bandages on Singh's hands when they entered, and guessed Viljo was helping the other
change the dressings.

"You, too, Mr. Answer Man," Noffke said, looking in Jonny's direction. "You know how to play King's Bluff?"

Answer Man? "I know a version of the game, but it may be just a local one," he told Noffke.

"Well, let's find out," the other shrugged, stepping to the room's circular table and pulling a deck of cards from a satchel sitting there. "Come on; Reginine rules say you can't turn down a card game when it's not for money."

"Since when do Reginine rules apply on Asgard?" Viljo demanded as he strolled in from the bathroom. "Why not play Earth rules, which state that all games *are* for money?"

"Aerie rules are that you play for real estate," Halloran offered from his bunk.

"Horizon rules—" Jonny began.

"Let's not reach *too* far into the Dominion backwaters, eh?" Viljo cut him off.

"Perhaps we should just go to sleep," Singh said, rejoining the group. "We'll undoubtedly have a busy day tomorrow."

"Come on," Deutsch beckoned, joining Noffke at the table. "A game will help us all settle down. Besides, it's these little things that help mold people into a team. Psychology, Cally. Right?"

Halloran chuckled, rolling out of bed and back onto his feet. "Unfair. All right, I'm in. Come on, Jonny; up. Druma, Rolon—Reginine rules, like the man said. One round only."

The game that Noffke described turned out to be almost identical to the King's Bluff Jonny was familiar with, and he felt reasonably confident as they launched into the first hand. Winning was completely unimportant to him, but he very much wanted to play without making any foolish mistakes. Viljo's gibe about the Dominion backwaters had finally crystallized for him exactly why he felt uncomfortable with this group: with the exception

of Deutsch, all the others came from worlds older
and more distinguished than Horizon—and Deutsch,
as the only Cobra trainee from Adirondack, had
obvious status as native authority on one of the
two worlds the Trofts had captured. Most of the
others weren't as blatant in their condescension as
Viljo, but Jonny could sense traces of it in all of
them. Proving he could play a competent game of
cards might be a first step toward breaking down
whatever stereotypes they had of frontier planets
in general and Jonny in particular.

Perhaps it was his indifference toward winning
aiding his merely average tactical skills, or perhaps it was small differences in body language
giving his bluffs an unexpected edge . . . whatever
the reason, the round hand wound up being the
best he'd ever played. Out of six games he won one
outright, bluff-won two others, and lost another
only when Noffke stubbornly stayed with a hand
that by all rights should have died young. Viljo
suggested a second round—virtually demanded one,
in fact—but Singh reminded them of the agreed-
upon limit, and the game dissolved into a quiet
flurry of bedtime preparations.

For several minutes after lights-out, Jonny replayed the game in his mind, searching every remembered nuance of speech and manner for signs
that the social barriers were at least beginning to
crack. But he was too tired to make much head-
way and soon gave up the effort. Still, they *could*
have left him out of the game entirely; and his last
thought before drifting off was that the next four
weeks might be survivable, after all.

The first week of training saw a great deal of
practice with the servo system, activation of the
optical and auditory enhancers, and the first experience with weapons. The small lasers built into
their little fingers, the trainees were told, were

designed chiefly to be used on metals, but would be equally effective in short-range antipersonnel applications. Bai emphasized that, for the moment, the power outputs were being held far below lethal levels, but Jonny found that of limited comfort as he practiced against the easily melted solder targets. With anywhere up to seventy-two lasers being fired across the range at any given time, it didn't take much imagination to picture what a careless, servo-supplemented twitch of someone's wrist could do. The semiautomatic targeting capabilities, when added, just made things worse: it was all too easy to shift one's gaze with the variable/visual lock activated and wind up firing at the wrong target entirely. But luck—or Bai's training—proved adequate, and by the time the last of those sessions was over, Jonny could stand amid the flickering lights without wincing. At least not much.

At the beginning of the second week, they began putting all of it together.

"Listen up, Cobras, because today'll be your first chance to get yourselves slagged," Bai announced, apparently oblivious to the steady rain coming down on all of them. Standing at attention, Jonny tried to achieve a similar indifference; but the trickles working under his collar were far too cold for him to succeed. "A hundred meters behind me you'll see a wall," Bai continued. "It's part of a quadrangle containing a courtyard and a small inner building. Running along the top of the wall is a photoelectric beam simulating a defense laser; inside the courtyard are some remotes simulating Troft guards. Your objective is a small red box inside the building, which you are to obtain— *quietly*— and escape with."

"Great," Jonny muttered under his breath. Already his stomach was starting to churn.

"Be thankful we're not invading Reginine," Noffke

murmured from beside him. "We set *our* wall lasers pointing *up* instead of across."

"Shh!"

"Now, the remotes are programmed with the best estimates of Troft sensory and reflexive capabilities," Bai was saying, "and the operators running them are the best, so don't count on *them* making stupid mistakes. They're carrying dye-pellet guns, and if they get you, you're officially slagged. If you hit the wall photo beam, you're also slagged. If you make too much noise—as defined by the sound pick-ups we've set up—you'll not only lose points, but probably also bring the remotes down on you and get slagged. On top of all that, there are likely to be various automatics and *reasonable* booby-traps in the building you'll need to avoid— and don't bother asking what kind, 'cause I'm not telling. Questions? Um? All right. Aldred, front and center; everyone else to that canvas shelter to your left.

One by one, the trainees moved to Bai's side and headed across the muddy field. Bai had failed to mention that a kill was announced by an alarm horn, and as each man's disappearance over the wall was followed sooner or later by that sardonic bleat the quiet conversation in the shelter took on an increasingly nervous flavor. When the eighth trainee across—Deutsch, as it happened—reappeared over the wall without triggering the alarm, the collective sigh of relief was as eloquent as a standing ovation.

All too soon, it was Jonny's turn. "Okay, Moreau, everything's been reset," Bai told him. "Remember, you're being judged on stealth and observation, *not* speed. Take your time and remember all the stuff I've been lecturing you about the past couple of evenings and you should be okay. Um? Okay; *go.*"

Jonny took off across the mud, running hunched-over to give any hypothetical optical sensors a smaller target to work with. Ten meters from the wall he slowed, splitting his attention to search for trip wires, wall-mounted sensors, and possible climbing routes. Nothing hazardous caught his attention; on the debit side, the wall had no obvious handholds, either. At the base Jonny gave the wall one final scan. Then, hoping his height estimate was close enough, he bent his knees and jumped. If anything, he erred on the short side, and at the very peak of his arc, his curved fingers slid neatly over the top of the wall.

So far, so good. From his new vantage point, Jonny could see the photoelectric apparatus, from which he could tell that he would need to clear a maximum of twenty centimeters in getting over. A relatively easy task ... provided he didn't bring the pseudo-Trofts down on him in the process.

Clicking his back teeth together, he activated his auditory enhancers; clicked three times more to run them to max. The sound of impacting rain reached frequency saturation and leveled out at a dull roar; beneath it, fainter noises became audible. None of them, he decided, sounded like remotes slogging through mud. Mentally crossing his fingers, he eased his head above the wall, switching off his super-hearing as he did so.

The inner building was smaller than he'd expected, a single-story structure covering perhaps a tenth of the walled-in area. No guards were visible near it; shifting his attention, he gave the rest of the courtyard a quick sweep.

Empty.

Either he'd been incredibly lucky and all the guards were momentarily on the far side of the building, or else they were all inside, perhaps watching through the darkened windows. Either way, he had little choice but to grab the opportunity. Pulling hard with his right arm, he sent his legs and torso up and over the wall, vaulting horse style, tucking his arms to his chest as he did so to clear the photobeam. Beneath him, he got his first glimpse of the area where he would land—

And of the dull metallic sheen of the remote standing there.

The single thought *unfair!* was all he had time for. Kicking in his targeting lock, he snapped his hands into firing position and gave the remote a double blast. His attention on his shooting, his landing a second later was embarrassingly clumsy; but he had the satisfaction of seeing the guard hit the ground the same time he did.

But there was no reason yet for self-congratulation, and almost before he had his balance back Jonny was running toward the building. Wherever the rest of the remotes were, they would be bound to discover their downed colleague before too long, and he had to move while there was still something left of his initiative. Reaching the nearest wall, he sidled to the corner and took a quick look around it. No one in sight, but he could see the steps leading to an entrance door. Breaking into a run again, he headed for it—

Even without his auditory enhancers on, the buzzer that went off beside him was deafening. Jonny cursed under his breath; obviously, he'd hit one of the automatics Bai had warned them about. In a hurry or not, he still should have taken the time for a careful search. Now, it was too late, and there was nothing to do but prepare for combat. If he could get inside before the remotes reacted to the alarm there might still be a chance . . . he was at the door, aiming his laser at the solder lock, when a remote came around the far corner.

Jonny hurled himself from the building in a flat dive, arm swinging around as he targeted the guard. But even as he squeezed off the shot, the door to his side slammed open; and before he could do more than twist his head to see, he felt the dull punch of a dye-pellet against his ribs.

And, announcing his failure to the world, the alarm horn hooted from the wall. Feeling like an idiot, Jonny got to his feet and looked around for the way out.

"Let that be a lesson to you," someone said from the building, and Jonny turned to see a man with a *Cobra Operations* patch on his coveralls standing behind the remote who'd shot him. "When you've got two or more targets it can actually be faster to slag the first one visually, without the targeting lock."

"Thanks, sir," Jonny sighed. "How do I get out?"

"Right over there—you can head back and get cleaned up. And if it helps, a lot of the others did worse."

Swallowing, Jonny nodded and set off in the indicated direction. It wasn't much comfort to know that others would have died sooner. Dead is still dead.

"So, the great Horizon hope finally crusked one," Viljo said, setting his tray down at the far end of the table and favoring Jonny with an off-cordial smile.

Jonny dropped his eyes to his own lunch and said nothing, concentrating instead on the last few bites of his meal as the blood rushed to his face. Viljo's snide comments had become more and more frequent the past couple of days, and though Jonny was trying hard not to let the other get to him, the tension of the whole thing was becoming increasingly difficult to ignore. Afraid of doing anything that would brand him as overly sensitive or—worse— that would emphasize his frontier origins, he could only sit on his anger and hope Viljo would get tired of his verbal target practice.

Though if he wasn't, possibly others were. Across

from Jonny, Halloran hunched over the table to eye Viljo. "I didn't notice you walking away with high honors, either," he said. "Matter of fact, except for Imel, I think we *all* got our egos nicely trimmed for show out there."

"Sure—but Jonny's the one Bai always holds up like he was the ideal trainee. Haven't you noticed? I just wondered if he liked being demoted to mortal."

Beside Viljo, Singh stirred in his seat. "You're exaggerating rather badly, Rolon; and even if you weren't, it would hardly be Jonny's fault."

"Oh, wouldn't it?" Viljo snorted. "Come on—you know as well as I do how this sort of favoritism works. Jonny's family's probably got some fix in with Bai or even Mendro, and Bai's making sure they're getting their money's worth."

And with that, the insults crossed a fine line . . . and Jonny abruptly had had enough.

In a single smooth motion, he stood up and leaped over the table, dimly aware of his chair slamming backwards into the next table as he did so. He landed directly behind Viljo who, apparently caught by surprise, was still seated. Jonny didn't wait for the other to respond; grabbing a fistfull of shirt, he hauled Viljo upright and spun him around. "That's it, Viljo—that's the last breaff dropping I'm going to take from you. Now *back off*—understand?"

Viljo eyed him calmly. "My, my; so you have a temper after all. I suppose 'breaff dropping' is just one of those colorful expressions you use out there in the backwaters?"

That final smirk was too much. Letting go of Viljo's shirt, Jonny threw a punch at the other's face.

It was a disaster. Not only did Viljo duck successfully out of the way, but with his servos providing unaccustomed speed to his swing, Jonny was thrown completely off balance and rammed his thigh hard into the table before he could recover. The pain fanned his anger into something white-hot, and with a snarl he twisted around and hurled another blow at Viljo. Again he missed; but even as his arm cocked for a third try, something pinioned it in midair. He shoved against the grip, succeeded only in losing his balance again. "Easy, Jonny; *easy*," a voice murmured in his ear.

And with that the red haze abruptly vanished from his brain and he found himself standing in a roomful of silent Cobra trainees, his arms gripped solidly by Deutsch and Noffke, facing Viljo who—completely unmarked—looked altogether too self-satisfied.

He was still trying to sort it all out when the room's intercom/monitor ordered him to report to Mendro's office.

The interview was short, but excruciatingly painful, and by the time Jonny left he was feeling like one of the solder targets on the laser range. The thought of having to go back out on the practice field—of having to *face* everyone—was a knot of tension in his stomach, and as he walked across Mendro's outer office, he seriously considered turning back and asking for a transfer to a different branch of service. At least then he wouldn't have to endure the other trainees' eyes. . . . But as he debated the decision, his feet kept walking; and outside the office the whole question of hiding suddenly became academic.

Deutsch and Halloran peeled themselves from the wall where they'd been leaning as Jonny closed the door behind him. "You okay?" Deutsch asked, the concern in his face echoed in his voice.

"Oh, sure," Jonny snorted, unreasonably irked by this unexpected invasion of his private shame. "I just got verbally skinned alive, that's all."

"Well, at least it *was* all verbal," Halloran pointed out. "Don't forget, all of *Mendro's* weapons are functional. Hey, lighten up, Jonny. You're still in the unit, aren't you?"

"Yeah," Jonny said, the hard lump starting to dissolve a bit. "At least as far as I know. Though Bai will probably have something to say about that when he hears what happened."

"Oh, Bai already knows—he's the one who told us to wait here for you," Halloran said. "He said to bring you out to the practice range when you were ready. Are you?"

Grimacing, Jonny nodded. "I suppose so. Might as well get it over with."

"What, facing Bai?" Deutsch asked as they set off down the hall. "Don't worry; he understands what that was all about. So do Parr and Druma, for that matter."

"I wish *I* did," Jonny shook his head. "What has Viljo got against me, anyway?"

Halloran glanced at him, and Jonny caught the other's frown. "You really don't know?"

"I just said that, didn't I? What, he doesn't like anyone who was born more than ten light-years from Earth?"

"He likes them fine ... as long as they don't show they're better at anything than he is."

Jonny stopped abruptly. "What are you talking about? I never did anything like that."

Halloran sighed. "Maybe not in *your* books, but a person like Rolon does his accounting differently. Look, remember our very first orientation meeting, the one he showed up late at? Who was it Bai used to pop his excuse?"

"Well ... me. But that was only because I was the last to arrive before him."

"Probably," Halloran conceded. "But Rolon didn't know that. And then the first evening of our actual training you tore the stuffing out of all of us in that game of King's Bluff. People from Earth have a long history of being successful gamers, and I suspect that really put the icing on the cake as far as Rolon was concerned."

Jonny shook his head in bewilderment. "But I didn't mean to beat him—"

"Of course you did—everyone 'means' to win in a game," Deutsch said. "You didn't mean to humiliate him, of course, but in a way that actually makes it worse. For someone with Rolon's competitive streak, being clobbered by a perceived social inferior who wasn't even trying to do so was more than he could take."

"So what am I supposed to do—roll over and play dead for him?"

"No, you're supposed to just continue doing as well as you can and to hell with his ego," Deutsch said grimly. "Maybe maneuvering you into Mendro's kennel will satisfy his lopsided sense of personal honor. If not—" He hesitated. "Well, if he can't learn to work with *you*, I don't think we're going to want him on Adirondack."

Jonny gave him a quick look. For a brief moment Deutsch's air of calm humor had vanished, showing something much darker beneath it. "You know," Jonny said, striving to sound casual, "a lot of times you don't seem very concerned about what's happening on your world."

"You mean because I laugh and joke around?" Deutsch asked. "Or because I opted to spend a couple of months hanging around Asgard instead of grabbing a laser and rushing back to help?"

"Um . . . when you put it *that* way—"

"I care a lot about Adirondack, Jonny, but I don't see any advantage in tying myself in knots worrying about what the Trofts might be doing to my family and friends. Right now I can help them most by becoming the very best Cobra I can be—

and by nudging the rest of you into doing the same."

"I think that's a hint we should get back to practice," Halloran said with a smile.

"Can't fool a psychologically trained mind," Deutsch replied wryly; and with that the momentary glimpse into his deeper self was over. But it was enough, and for the first time Jonny had a real understanding of the kind of men the Army had chosen for this unit.

The kind of men he'd been deemed worthy to join.

And it put the whole thing with Viljo into a final perspective. To risk washing out of the Cobras over what were essentially emotional fly bites would be the absolute depth of stupidity. From now on, he resolved, he would consider Viljo's gibes to be nothing more than practice in developing patience. If Deutsch could bear up under an invasion of his world, Jonny could surely put up with Viljo.

They'd reached an exit now, and Halloran led them outside. "Wait a second—we're on the wrong side of the building," Jonny said, stopping and looking around. "The practice field's that way, isn't it?"

"Yep," Halloran nodded cheerfully. "But for Cobras cross-country's faster than all those hallways."

"Cross-country as in around?" Jonny asked, peering down the eight-story structure heading halfway to infinity in both directions.

"As in over," Halloran corrected. Facing the wall, he flexed his knees. "Last one to the top's a gumbumbler—and any windows you break come out of your pay."

The second week passed as the first had, with long days of Cobra exercises and equally long—or so it seemed—evenings of military theory. Every day or two they received new neckwrap computer modules, each one allowing a new weapon in their arsenals to be brought into play. Jonny learned how to use his sonic weapons and how to retune them in the event that the Trofts turned out to be particularly susceptible to specific frequencies; learned how to trigger his arcthrower, a blast of high voltage traveling down the ionization path burned by his right fingertip laser, and how to efficiently fry electronic gear with it; and, finally, learned how to handle the antiarmor laser in his left calf, simultaneously the most powerful and most awkward of his weapons. Pointing downward along the tibia, its beam was guided through his ankle by optical fibers to emerge through a flexible focusing lens in the bottom of his heel. Special boots were handed out with the computer modules that day, and as he tried to learn how to shoot while standing on one leg, Jonny joined the rest of the trainees in roundly cursing the idiot who'd been responsible for that particular design. Bai claimed they'd find out how versatile the laser was once they had their programmed reflexes, but no one seriously believed him.

But through all the work, practice, and memorization—through the physical and mental fatigue—two unexpected observations managed to penetrate Jonny's consciousness. First, that Viljo's taunts disappeared almost entirely after the mess hall incident, though the other remained cool toward him; and second, that Bai really *did* tend to single Jonny out for special notice.

The latter bothered him more than he cared to admit. Viljo's suggestion that the Moreau family had somehow bribed the instructor was absurd, of course . . . but at least some of the other trainees must have overheard the allegation, and if Jonny could pick up on Bai's pattern so could they. What did they think about it? Did they imagine it implied he was getting special privileges off the training field?

More to the point, why *was* Bai doing it?

He wasn't the best of the trainees, certainly—Deutsch alone proved that. Nor, he thought, was he the worst. The youngest? Oldest? Closest physically to some old friend/enemy? Or—and it was a chilling thought—did Bai secretly share some of Viljo's biases?

But whatever the reason, there was no response he could think of except the one he was already using: to endure with as much outer stoicism and inner calm as he could manage. It proved more effective than he'd expected it to, and by the time the second week drew to a close he was able to face Bai's comments or work alongside Viljo with only the slightest nervousness. How much the other trainees noticed his new attitude he didn't know, but Halloran made at least one comment on it.

And then the third week began; and all that had gone before paled to the relative significance of a quiet summer's stroll . . . because on the first day of that week they began working with their computerized reflexes.

"It's dead simple," Bai told them, gesturing to the ceiling barely two meters above their heads. "You first key your targeting lock on the spot where you intend to hit, and then jump, giving your body a backward motion as you do so." He bent his knees and straightened them, simultaneously arching his back. "Then just relax and let the computer run your servos. Try not to fight it, by the way; you'll just strain your muscles and make it harder for your subconscious to adjust to having something else in charge of your body. Questions? Um? All right. Aldred, target lock: *go.*"

One by one they all performed the ceiling jump that had been their first introduction to Cobra abilities those four long weeks ago. Jonny had thought himself adequately prepared; but when his turn came he found out otherwise. Nothing— not even the now-familiar servo enhancement effect—could quite compare with the essential decoupling of body and mind that the automatic reflexes entailed. Fortunately, the maneuver was over so quickly that he didn't have time to feel more than a very brief panic before his feet were back on the floor and his muscles returned to his control. Only later did he realize that Bai had probably started them with the ceiling jump for precisely that reason.

They went through the exercise five times each, and with each flawless jump Jonny's anxiety and general feeling of weirdness eased, until he was feeling almost comfortable with his new copilot.

As he should have expected, though, he wasn't allowed to feel comfortable for long.

They stood atop a five-story building, looking over the edge at the ground below and the rein- forced wall facing them about fifteen meters away. "He's *got* to be kidding," Halloran murmured at Jonny's side.

Jonny nodded wordlessly, his eyes shifting to Bai as the instructor finished his verbal descrip- tion of the maneuver and stepped to the edge to demonstrate. "As always," Bai said, "you start with a targeting lock to give your computer the range. Then you just . . . jump."

His legs straightened convulsively, and an in- stant later he was arcing toward the facing wall. He hit it feet first about five meters down, his shoes scraping loudly as they slid a short distance further down along it. The combination of that friction plus the impact-absorbing bending of his knees flipped him partly over; and when his legs straightened again an instant later, the push sent him back toward the original building in a heels-over-head flip that somehow managed to have him feet forward when he struck the side, another five meters closer to the ground. Again he shoved off, and with one final bounce-and-flip off the far wall, he landed safely on the ground at the base of their building. "Nothing to it," his voice drifted up to the waiting trainees. "I'll be up in a minute, then we'll all try it."

He disappeared inside. "I think I'd rather take my chances with a straight jump," Noffke said to no one in particular.

"That's fine for a five-story building, but you'd never make it with anything really tall," Deutsch shook his head. "We *do* have some real cities on Adirondack, you know."

"I'll bet the Great Horizon Hope could give you a dozen more reasons why this is a good maneuver," Viljo put in, smiling sardonically at Jonny.

"Would you settle for two?" Jonny asked calmly. "One: you're never in free fall for very long this way, and besides making for a softer landing that'll play havoc with any manual *or* autotarget weapon they try shooting at you. And two: with your legs pointing up most of the time, your antiarmor laser's in good position to fire at whatever you were escaping from on the roof."

He had the satisfaction of seeing some of the other trainees nodding in agreement, and of watching Viljo's smirk sour into a grimace.

There was more—much more—and for ten days Bai put them through their paces. Gradually, the daily computer modules began to remove the restraints set onto their most dangerous equipment; just as gradually, the scorch-lasers and dye-pellets used by their metallic opponents were replaced by genuine weapons. Half a dozen of the trainees picked up minor burns and pellet wounds, and a new seriousness began to pervade the general attitude. Only Deutsch retained his bantering manner, and Jonny suspected it was simply because he was already as serious beneath the facade as the man could possibly be. The evening lectures were replaced by extra training sessions, giving them the chance to practice with their enhanced night vision the techniques they had so far used only in daylight and dusk. All of it seemed to be building to a head ... and then, almost unexpectedly—though they all knew the schedule—it was over.

Almost.

"There comes a time, Cobras," Bai told them that final afternoon, "when training reaches a saturation point; where drills and practice don't hone so much as fine-polish. Fine-polishing is okay if you're a gemstone or an athlete, but you're neither: you're warriors. And for warriors there's no substitute for genuine combat experience.

"So, starting tomorrow morning, combat is what you're going to get. Four days of it: two solitaire and two in units. You'll be up against the same remotes you've been training with; your own weapons and abilities will be identical to what you'll have when your combat nanocomputers are implanted in you five days from now. So. It's sixteen hundred hours now, and you're all officially off-duty until oh-eight-hundred tomorrow, when you'll be taken by transport to the test site. I suggest you eat tonight as if you'll be on field rations for four days—which you will be—and get a good night's sleep. Questions? Unit dismissed."

It was a somber group that gathered in Jonny's room that evening after dinner. "I wonder what it's going to be like," Noffke said, sitting at the table shuffling his cards restlessly.

"Not easy, that's for sure," Singh sighed. "We've already had minor injuries when everyone knew what he and his opponents were doing. We could very well lose someone out there."

"Or several someones," Halloran agreed. He was standing at the window, staring out. Past his shoulder Jonny could see a sprinkling of lights from other parts of Freyr Complex and, further away, the lights from Farnesee, the nearest civilian town. Somehow, it reminded him of his home and family, a thought that added to his gloom.

"They wouldn't make it dangerous enough to actually *kill* us, would they?" Noffke asked, though his tight expression indicated he already knew the answer.

"Why not?" Halloran retorted. "Sure, they've spent a lot on us—but there's no sense letting marginal ones go on to get killed the minute they land on Adirondack. Why do you think they put off implanting our computers until *after* the test?"

"To save some money where possible," Jonny grunted. "Parr, stop shuffling those cards—either deal them or put them away."

"You know what we need?" Vilo spoke up abruptly. "A night out of this place. A few drinks, some music, a little conversation with real people—especially of the female sort—"

"And how exactly do you expect to persuade Mendro to let us out for this little sortie?" Deutsch snorted.

"Actually, I wasn't planning to ask him," Viljo said calmly.

"I think that qualifies as going A.W.O.L.," Halloran pointed out. "There are lots of easier ways to get ourselves crusked."

"Nonsense. Bai said we were off-duty, didn't he? Anyway, has anyone ever *explicitly* told us we were confined to Freyr Complex?"

There was a short silence. "Well, no, now that you mention it," Halloran admitted. "But—"

"But nothing. We can sneak out of here easily

enough—this place isn't even guarded as well as a regular military base would be. Come on—none of us is going to sleep well tonight anyway. We might as well have some fun.''

Because tomorrow we might die. No one said those words aloud, but from the shifting of feet it was clear everyone was thinking variations of them . . . and after another brief silence Halloran got to his feet. "Sure. Why not?"

"I'm in," Noffke nodded quickly. "I hear there's good card games to be had in the pleasure centers in town."

"Along with lots of other stuff," Deutsch nodded. "Druma; Jonny? How about it?"

Jonny hesitated, his brother's words about decadence and holding onto his ethics flashing through his mind. Still, Viljo was right: nowhere in their verbal or written orders had there been anything about not leaving the complex.

"Come on, Jonny," Viljo said, using his first name for the first time in days. "If you can't justify it as relaxation, think of it as practice infiltrating an enemy-occupied city."

"All right," Jonny said. After all, he wouldn't have to do anything in town he didn't feel right about. "Just let me change into my other fatigues—"

"Phrij on that," Viljo interrupted. "Those look fine. Quit stalling and let's go. Druma?"

"Oh, I guess so," Singh agreed. "But only for a little while."

"You'll be able to leave whenever you want to," Halloran assured him. "Once we're in town everyone's on his own timetable. Well. Out the window?"

"Out and up," Viljo nodded. "Lights out . . . here goes."

It proved far easier to leave the complex grounds than Jonny had expected. From the roof of their wing they dropped to a darkened drill field used by the regular Army recruits in Freyr; crossing it, they arrived at an easily-negotiated perimeter wall. Avoiding the simple photobeam alarms at the top, they went over. "That's it," Deutsch said cheerfully. "Nothing but ten klicks of field and suburb between us and fun. Race you!"

Even with having to slow down once they hit populated areas, the trip took only half an hour . . . and Jonny got his first taste of what a real city could be.

Afterwards, he wouldn't remember much about that first plunge into mainstream Dominion recreational life. Deutsch took the lead, guiding them on a giddy and tortuous path among the shows, night spots, restaurants, and pleasure centers that he'd become familiar with in the weeks between his arrival from an Iberiand university and his final enlistment in the Cobras. More people than Jonny had ever seen at once in his life seemed to be crowded into the district—civilians in oddly cut, luminescent clothing; other civilians whose focus of ornamentation was wild facial makeup, and military personnel of every branch and rank. It was too festive an atmosphere for Jonny to feel uneasy, but by the same token it was too outlandish for him to truly relax and enjoy, either. It made for a lousy compromise, and within a couple of hours he had had enough. Excusing himself from Deutsch and Singh—all that were still together of the original six—he worked his way back through the crowds to the soothing darkness surrounding the town. Getting back into the complex was no harder than sneaking out had been, and soon he was sliding back through the window into their dark and deserted room. Leaving the lights off, he quickly prepared for bed.

He'd been lying in his bunk for perhaps half an hour, trying to will his overactive mind to sleep, when a noise at the window made him open his eyes. "Who's there?" he stage-whispered as the figure eased into the room.

"Viljo," the other murmured tightly. "You alone?"

"Yes," Jonny said, swinging his legs out of bed. Something in Viljo's voice was distinctly off-key. "What's wrong?"

"I thought Mendro and the MP's might be here by now," Viljo said distractedly, flopping onto his back on his own bunk. "I'm not sure, but I think I'm in trouble."

"What?" Jonny bumped his vision enhancers up a notch. In the amplified background light Viljo's expression was tight, but he didn't seem hurt. "What kind of trouble?"

"Oh, I had a little argument with some phrijeater behind one of the bars. Had to bounce him around a bit." Abruptly, Viljo levered himself off the bunk and headed for the bathroom. "Go back to bed," he told Jonny over his shoulder. "If the guy makes trouble we'd both better be innocently asleep when the investigations start."

"Will he recognize you again? I mean—"

"I don't think he was blind or illiterate, no."

"I *meant* was it light enough to read your name off your fatigues?"

"Yeah, it was light enough . . . if he had time to pay attention. Go to bed, will you?"

Heart pounding, Jonny crawled back under his blanket. *Bounced him around a bit.* What did that mean? Had Viljo hurt the other—perhaps even badly? He opened his mouth to ask . . . and then closed it again. Did he really want to know all the details? "What are you going to do?" he asked instead.

"Get undressed and go to bed—what did you think?"

"No, I mean about . . . reporting it."

The sound of running water stopped and Viljo reemerged. "I'm sure as hell not telling anyone else about this. You think I'm crazy?"

"But the guy could be badly hurt—"

"He got away under his own power. Besides, he's hardly the sort of phrijeater worth risking your career over. That goes for *your* career, too."

"I—what?"

"You know what. You go blabbing about this to Mendro and you'll have to admit you were out of Freyr tonight, too." He paused, studying Jonny's face. "Besides which, it'd be a lousy demonstration of team unity for you to turn me in over something this trivial."

"Trivial? What was he armed with, a laser cannon? You could've gotten away without fighting. Why'd you stick around?"

"You wouldn't understand." Viljo climbed into his bunk. "Look, I didn't really hurt him; and if I overreacted, it's too late to change things now. So let's just forget it, huh? Chances are he won't even report it."

"But what if he does? If you don't report it first, it'll look like you're trying to cover it up."

"Yeah, well, I'll play the odds—and since it's *my* risk, you're invited to stay out of it."

Jonny didn't answer. Silence again returned to the room, and after a few minutes Viljo's breathing slipped into the slow, steady pattern of sleep. The mark of a clear conscience, Jonny's father would have said, but in this case that hardly seemed likely. For Jonny, though, the immediate problem was not Viljo's conscience but his own.

What *was* the proper thing to do here? If he kept quiet he was technically an accessory after the fact, and if the civilian's injuries turned out to be severe, that could mean real trouble. On the other hand, Viljo's point about team loyalty was well taken. Jonny remembered Bai saying something about such things at the orientation meeting, and if Viljo had in fact simply put a bully in his place, forgetting the incident *would* seem the best course.

Point, counterpoint; and with the limited information he had the two arguments could chase each other around his brain all night.

They made a good try at doing just that, keeping him uselessly awake for the next hour and a half. One by one his other four roommates came in the open window, performed their bedtime preparations, and went to sleep. At least none of them had gotten caught; and with that particular worry out of the way Jonny was finally able to force the rest of it far enough back in his mind to fall asleep himself. But his dreams were violent, tension-ridden things, and when reveille put an end to them, he felt worse than if he'd been awake all night.

Somehow, he managed to dress, grab his pre-packed combat bag, and head down to the mess hall with the others without his groggy eyes drawing any special comment. No MP's arrived while they were eating, nor was anyone waiting by the transport as they crowded in with the rest of the trainees; and with each kilometer they flew Jonny's load eased a little more. Surely the authorities wouldn't have let them leave if there'd been any complaints of Cobra misbehavior in town. Apparently the other participant in Viljo's fight had indeed decided to let the whole matter slide.

They reached the hundred-thousand-hectare test site an hour later, and after giving them new computer modules, extra equipment, and final instructions, Bai turned them loose on their individual objectives. Putting the entire previous night out of his mind, Jonny set to work surviving the exam.

It was therefore something of a surprise when, returning to field HQ from his first successful exercise, he found an MP transport waiting. It was even more of a shock to find it was waiting for *him*.

The young man fidgeting in his chair next to Mendro's desk certainly looked like he'd been in a fight. Heal-quick bandages covered one cheek and his jaw, and his left arm and shoulder were wrapped in the kind of ribbed plastic cast used to speed broken bone repair. What was visible of his expression looked nervous but determined.

Mendro's expression was merely determined. "Is this the man?" he asked the other as Jonny sat down in the chair his MP guard indicated.

The civilian's eyes flicked once over Jonny's face, then settled onto his fatigue tunic. "It was too dark to see his face well enough, Commander," he said. "But that's the name, all right."

"I see." Mendro's eyes bored into Jonny's. "Moreau, Mr. P'alit here claims you attacked him last night behind the Thasser Eya Bar in Farnesee. True or false?"

"False," Jonny managed through dry lips. Through the haze of unreality filling the room a nasty suspicion was beginning to take shape.

"Were you *in* Farnesee last night?" Mendro persisted.

"Yes, sir, I was. I ... sneaked out to try and relax before the final exam started today. I was only there for a couple of hours—" he glanced at P'alit—"and I most certainly didn't fight with anyone."

"He's lying," P'alit spoke up. "He was—"

Mendro's gesture silenced him. "Did you go alone?"

Jonny hesitated. "No, sir. All of us in my room went. We split up in town, though, so I don't have any alibi. But . . ."

"But what?"

Jonny took a deep breath. "About a half hour after I got back one of the others came in and told me he'd—well, he said he'd bounced someone around a little behind one of the bars in Farnesee."

Mendro's eyes were hard, unbelieving. "And you didn't report it?"

"He indicated it was a minor argument. Certainly nothing so . . . serious." He looked again at P'alit; only then did the sophistication of the frame-up sink in. No wonder Viljo hadn't wanted Jonny to change clothes before they all left. "I can only conclude that he was wearing my spare tunic at the time."

"Uh-huh. Who was it who told you all this?"

"Rolon Viljo, sir."

"Viljo. The one you attacked in the mess hall awhile back?"

Jonny gritted his teeth. "Yes, sir."

"Obviously just trying to put the blame on someone else," P'alit spoke up scornfully.

"Perhaps. How did the fight start, Mr. P'alit?"

The other shrugged with his free shoulder. "Oh, I made some snide comment about the outer provinces—I don't even know how the topic came up. He took it personally and shoved me out the back door where a bunch of us were standing."

"Isn't that what you targeted Viljo over, Moreau?" Mendro asked.

"Yes, sir." Jonny resisted the almost overwhelming urge to again explain that incident. "I don't suppose any of your companions might have gotten a clear look at your assailant, Mr. P'alit?"

"No, no one saw you clearly—but I don't think that's going to be necessary." P'alit looked back at Mendro. "I think this story's pretty well lost its factory finish, Commander. Are you going to take action on this or not?"

"The Army always disciplines its own," Mendro said, tapping a button on his desk console. "Thank you for bringing this matter to our attention." Behind Jonny, the door opened and another MP appeared. "Sergeant Costas will escort you out."

"Thank you." Standing up, P'alit nodded to Mendro and followed the MP out. Catching the eye of Jonny's guard, Mendro gestured minutely, and the other joined the exodus. The door closed and Jonny and Mendro were alone.

"Anything you'd like to say?" Mendro asked mildly.

"Nothing that would do any good, sir," Jonny told him bitterly. All the work, all the sweat . . . and it was about to come crashing down on top of him. "I didn't do it, but I don't know any way to prove that."

"Um." Mendro gave him a long, searching gaze and then shrugged. "Well . . . you'd better get back to the testing, I suppose, before you get any further behind schedule."

"You're not dropping me from the unit, sir?" Jonny asked, a spark of hope struggling to pierce the rubble of his collapsed future.

"Do you think this sort of misbehavior rates that?" Mendro countered.

"I really don't know." Jonny shook his head. "I know we're needed for the war, but . . . on Horizon, at least, picking on someone weaker than you are is considered cowardly."

"It's considered that way on Asgard, too." Mendro sighed. "It may very well come to expulsion, Moreau; at this point I don't know. But until that decision's made there's no point in depriving your team of your help in the group operations."

In other words, they were going to give him the chance to risk his life—and possibly lose it—and *then* decide whether that risk had any real meaning or not. "Yes, sir," Jonny said, standing up. "I'll do my best."

"I expect nothing less." Mendro touched a button and the MP reappeared. "Dismissed."

It wasn't as hard as Jonny had expected to forget his new troubles as the testing continued. The defenses he faced were devilishly tight, and it took every milligram of his concentration to handle his assigned missions. But his luck and skill held out, and he completed the solitaire exercises with nothing more serious than skinned hands and an impressive collection of bruises.

And then he joined his roommates for the group tests . . . and there the disasters began.

Facing Viljo again—working and fighting alongside him—brought out thoughts and feelings that even their danger couldn't suppress . . . and that distraction quickly manifested itself in reduced competence. Twice Jonny got himself into situations that only his computerized reflexes were able to get him out of; more often than that a failure to do his part of the job wound up putting one of the others in unnecessary danger. Singh took a laser burn that had him operating under the sluggishness of heavy pain-killers, while only quick action by Jonny and Deutsch pulled Noffke out of a pincer trap that would almost certainly have left him dead.

A hundred times during those two days Jonny considered having it out with Viljo, either verbally or physically; of letting the others know the kind of vermin they were working with and at least eliminating the lie he was being forced to live. But each time the opportunity arose he choked his anger back down and said nothing. They were all just barely surviving with one of their number under an emotional handicap; to multiply that burden and spread it around would be not only unfair but likely lethal as well.

The other logical alternative occurred to him only once, and for an hour afterward he actually regretted the fact that his ethical training forbade him to simply shoot Viljo in the back.

The missions went on, oblivious to Jonny's internal turmoil. Together the six of them broke into a fortified ten-story building; penetrated and destroyed a twenty-man garrison; disabled the booby-

traps around an underground bunker and blew up
its entrance; and successfully rescued four remotes
simulating civilian prisoners from a Troft jail. They
camped overnight in a Troft-patrolled wasteland
area, picked up the characteristics of an off-center
group of civilians quickly enough and accurately
enough to avoid being identified as strangers an
hour afterwards, and led a group of Resistance
remotes on a simple mission that succeeded despite the often dangerous errors the remotes' operators allowed their machines to make.

They did it all, they did it well, and they lived
through it . . . and as the transport flew them back
toward Freyr, Jonny decided it had been worth the
risk. Whatever discipline Mendro chose to ad-
minister, he knew now that he indeed had what it
took to be a Cobra. Whether he was ever allowed
to serve as one or not, that inner knowledge was
something they could never take from him.

When they reached Freyr and found the MP's
waiting, he was almost glad. Whatever Mendro
had decided, apparently it was going to be over
quickly.

And it was. What he wasn't expecting was that
the commander would invite an audience to watch.

"Cee-three Bai reports you did extremely well,"
Mendro commented, looking around at the six
grimy trainees seated in a semicircle in front of his
desk. "Given you're all alive and relatively unscathed, I would tend to agree. Any immediate
reactions to the missions that spring to mind?"

"Yes, sir," Deutsch spoke up after a moment of
thoughtful silence. "We had some major problems
leading that Resistance team—their mistakes were
very hard to compensate for. Was that simulation
realistic?"

Mendro nodded. "Unfortunately, yes. Civilians
are always going to make what are—to you—

incredibly stupid mistakes. About all you can do is try and minimize that effect while maintaining an attitude of patience. Other comments? No? Then I suppose we'd better move on to the reason I called you here: the charges outstanding against Trainee Moreau."

The abrupt change of subject sent a rustle of surprise through the group. "Charges, sir?" Deutsch asked carefully.

"Yes. He's been accused of attacking a civilian during your unauthorized trip into town four nights ago." Mendro gave them a capsule summary of P'alit's story. "Moreau claims he didn't do it," he concluded. "Comments?"

"I don't believe it, sir," Halloran said flatly. "I'm not calling this character a liar, but I think he must've misread the name."

"Or else saw Jonny that night, got into a fight later, and is trying to stick the Army for his medical costs," Noffke suggested.

"Perhaps," Mendro nodded. "But suppose for the moment it's true. Do you think I would be justified in that event in transfering Moreau out of the Cobras?"

An uncomfortable silence descended on the room. Jonny watched the play of emotion across their faces, but while he clearly had their sympathy, it was also clear which way they were leaning. He hardly blamed them; in their places he knew which answer he would choose.

It was Deutsch who eventually put the common thought into words. "I don't think you'd have any choice, sir. Misuse of our equipment would essentially pit us against the civilian population, certainly in their minds. Speaking as a citizen of Adirondack, we've already got all the opponents we need right now."

Mendro nodded. "I'm glad you agree. Well. For the next couple of days you'll be off-duty again.

After that we'll be running through a detailed analysis of your exam performance with each of you, showing you where and how your equipment could have been utilized more effectively." He paused ... and something in his face abruptly broke through the deadness surrounding Jonny's mind. "That's one of the things we had to keep secret, to avoid excessive self-consciousness," the commander went on. "With the relatively large amount of space available in those neckwrap computers we were able to keep records of all your equipment usage." Almost lazily, he shifted his gaze. "That alley behind the Thasser Eya Bar was dark, Trainee Viljo. You had to use your vision enhancers while you fought that civilian."

The color drained from Viljo's face. His mouth opened ... but then his eyes flicked around the group, and whatever protest or excuse he was preparing died unsaid.

"If you have an explanation, I'll hear it now," Mendro added.

"No explanation, sir," Viljo said through stiff lips.

Mendro nodded. "Halloran, Noffke, Singh, Deutsch: you'll escort your former teammate to the surgical wing; they already have their instructions. Dismissed."

Slowly, Viljo stood up. He looked once at Jonny with empty eyes, then walked to the door with the remnants of his dignity wrapped almost visibly around him. The others, their own expressions cast in iron, followed.

The brittle silence in the room remained for several seconds after the door closed behind them. "You knew all along I didn't do it," Jonny said at last.

Mendro shrugged minutely. "Not conclusively, but we were ninety percent sure. The computer doesn't record a complete film every time the vision enhancers are used, you know. We had to correlate that usage with servo movements to know whether you'd done it or not—and until you identified Viljo as the probable culprit, we didn't know whose records we also needed to pull."

"You still could've told me then that I wasn't really under suspicion."

"I could've," Mendro acknowledged. "But it seemed like a good opportunity to get a little more data on your emotional makeup."

"You wanted to see if I'd be too preoccupied to function in combat? Or whether I'd just slag Viljo and be done with it?"

"And losing control either way would've had you out of the unit instantly," Mendro said, his voice hardening. "And before you complain about being unfairly singled out, remember that we're preparing you for *war* here, not playing some game with fixed rules. We do what's necessary, and if some people bear a little more of the burden than others, well, that's just the way it goes. Life is like that, and you'd better get used to it." The commander grunted. "Sorry—didn't mean to lecture. I won't apologize for running you an extra turn around the squirrel cage, but having come through the test as well as you did I don't think you've got real grounds for complaint."

"No, sir. But it wasn't just a single turn around the cage. Cee-three Bai's been holding me up for special notice ever since the training began—and if he hadn't done that Viljo might not have gotten irritated enough to try tarnishing my image like he did."

"Which let us learn something important about him, didn't it?" Mendro countered coolly.

"Yes, sir. But—"

"Let me put it this way, then," Mendro interrupted. "In all of human history people from one part of a region, country, planet, or system have tended to look down on people from another. It's simple human nature. In today's Dominion of Man this manifests itself as a faintly condescending attitude foward the frontier planets. Worlds like Horizon, Rajput, even Zimbwe . . . and Adirondack.

"It's a small thing and not at all important culturally, and it's therefore damned hard to test for its influence on a given trainee's personality. So without useful theory, we fall back on experiment: we raise someone from one of those worlds as the shining example of what a good Cobra should be and then watch to see who can't stand that. Viljo obviously couldn't. Neither, I'm sorry to say, could some of the others."

"I see." A week ago, Jonny thought, he'd probably have been angry to learn he'd been used like that. But now . . . *he* had passed his test, and would be remaining a Cobra. They hadn't, and would be becoming . . . what? "What's going to happen to them? I remember you saying that some of our equipment wouldn't be removable. Will you have to . . . ?"

"Kill them?" Mendro smiled faintly, bitterly, and shook his head. "No. The equipment isn't removable, but at this stage it can be rendered essentially useless." There was something like pain in the other's eyes, Jonny noticed suddenly. How many times, he wondered, and for how many large or small reasons, had the commander had to tell one of his carefully chosen trainees that the suffering and sacrifice was all going to be for nothing? "The nanocomputer they'll be fitted with will be a pale imitation of the one you'll be receiving soon. It'll disconnect the power pack from all remaining weapons and put a moderate upper limit on servo power. To all intents and purposes they'll leave Asgard as nothing more than normal men with unbreakable bones."

"And some bitter memories."

Mendro gave him a long, steady look. "We all have those, Moreau. Memories are what ultimately spell the difference between a trainee and a soldier. When you've got memories of things that haven't worked—of things you could have done better, or differently, or not done at all—when you've got all that behind your eyes but can still do what has to be done . . . *then* you'll be a soldier."

A week later Jonny, Halloran, Deutsch, Noffke, and Singh—now designated Cobra Team 2/03—left with the other newly-commissioned Cobras on a heavily protected skip-transport for the war zone. Penetrating the Troft battle perimeter, the teams were space-chuted into an eight-hundred-kilometer stretch of Adirondack's strategic Essek District.

The landing was a disaster. Reacting far quicker than anyone had expected them to, the Troft ground forces intercepted Jonny's team right on the edge of the city Deutsch had been steering them toward. The Cobras were able to escape the encirclement with nothing more than minor flesh wounds . . . but in the blistering crossfire of that battle three civilians, caught in the wrong place at the wrong time, were killed. For days afterward their faces haunted Jonny's memories, and it was only as the team settled into their cover identities and began planning their first raid that he realized Mendro had been right.

And he was well on his way to collecting a soldier's memories.

Interlude

Halfway around Asgard from Freyr Complex—removed both in distance and philosophical outlook from the centers of military strength—lay the sprawling city known simply as Dome. Periodic attempts had been made in the past two centuries to give it a more elegant name; but those efforts had been as doomed to failure as would have been a movement to rename Earth itself. The city—and the geodesic dome that dominated its skyline—were as fixed in the minds of Dominion citizens as were their own names ... because it was from here that the Central Committee sent out the orders, laws, and verdicts that ultimately affected the lives of each one of those citizens. From here could be reversed the decisions of mayors, syndics, and even planetary governor-generals; and as all were equal under the law, so in theory could any citizen's complaint or petition be brought to the Committee's attention.

In practice, of course, that was pure myth, and everyone who worked in the dome's shadow knew it. Small, relatively local matters were the province of the lower levels of government, and that was where they generally stayed. Seldom did any matter not directly affecting billions of people come to even a single Committé's attention.

But it *did* happen.

Committé Sarkiis H'orme's office was about average for one of the thirty most powerful men in the Dominion. Plush carpet, rare-wood paneling, a large desk inlaid with artifacts from dozens of worlds—a quiet sort of luxury, as such things went. Beyond the side doors lay his eight-room personal apartment and the miniature haiku garden where he often went to think and plan. Some Committés used their dome apartments but rarely, prefering to leave their work behind in the evening and fly out to their larger country estates. H'orme was not one of those. Conscientious and hard-working by nature, he often worked late into the night ... and at his age, the strain too often showed.

It was showing now, Vanis D'arl thought, running a critical eye over H'orme as the Committé skimmed through the report he'd prepared. Soon now—probably sooner than either had expected— H'orme would drive himself to an early death or retirement, and D'arl would take his place on the Committee. The ultimate success the Dominion had to offer; but one that carried a twinge of uneasiness along with it. D'arl had been with H'orme for nineteen years—the last eight as chief aide and chosen successor—and if he'd learned one thing in that time, it was that running the Dominion properly took infinite knowledge and infinite wisdom. The fact that no one else possessed those qualities either was irrelevant; the philosophy of excellence under which he'd been raised demanded he strive for the closest approximations possible. H'orme, also born and raised on Asgard, shared that background ... and D'arl therefore knew how much work those goals entailed.

Pushing the "page" button one last time, H'orme laid down his comboard and raised his eyes to

D'arl's. "Thirty percent. After all the preliminary testing thirty percent of the Cobra warrior trainees are still being deemed unfit. I presume you noticed the primary reason listed?"

D'arl nodded. " 'Unsuitability for close work with civilian populations.' It's a catch-all category, I'm afraid, but I couldn't get the numbers broken down any further. I'm still trying."

"You see what this implies, though, don't you? For the tests to have missed that badly, *something* must have changed between the prelims and the final cut; and what *that* means is that we're sending fully-activated Cobra warriors to Silvern and Adirondack without truly understanding their psychological state. On general principles alone that's poor policy."

D'arl pursed his lips. "Well ... it may just be a temporary feeling of power induced by their new abilities," he suggested. "A taste of warfare might make them realize that they're as fallible as any other mortals. Bring any conceit back down to normal."

"Perhaps. But perhaps not." H'orme flipped to the report directory, found an item. "Three hundred of them sent out in the first landing wave; six hundred more in training. Hmmm. I suppose it *could* just be a reflection of the poor statistics available. Any indication the Army's adjusting its prelim testing screen?"

"Too soon to tell," D'arl shook his head.

For a moment the other was silent. D'arl let his attention drift to the triangular windows at H'orme's back and the panoramic view of Dome it provided. Some Committés had the windows permanently blanked in favor of more picturesque holos, and he'd often thought H'orme's choice indicated a firmer commitment to seeking out truth and reality. "If you'd like, sir," he spoke up, "I could place a cancellation order for the whole project on the Considerations List. At the very least it would alert the rest of the Committee that there were potential problems with it."

"Hm." H'orme gazed at his comboard again. "Three hundred already in action. No. No, the reasons the Committee gave its approval in the first place are still valid: we're in a war for Dominion territory and we've got to use every weapon that could possibly help us. Besides, cutting things off now would essentially doom the Cobra warriors already fighting to a losing war of attrition. Still ..." He tapped his fingers on his desk. "I want you to start gleaning all military intelligence coming from Silvern and Adirondack for data on how they're interacting both with each other and the local civilian populations. If any problems start developing, I want to know about it right away."

"Yes, sir," D'arl nodded. "It might help if I knew exactly what you were looking for."

H'orme waved a hand vaguely. "Oh, call it a . . . a *Titan complex*, I suppose. The belief that one is so powerful that one is above normal laws and standards. The Cobra warriors have been given a great deal of physical power and that *can* be a dangerous thing."

D'arl had to smile at that. Imagine, a Committé of the Dominion worried about too much power in a single individual! Still, he saw the other's point. The Cobra warriors had been handed their power all at once, instead of having to acquire and use it in small increments, which essentially sidestepped the usual adjustment mechanisms. "I understand," he told H'orme. "Do you want me to file that report in the main system?"

"No, I'll do it later. I want to study the numbers more closely first."

"Yes, sir." The unspoken implication being that some of those figures might wind up in H'orme's personal database rather than in the more accessible main Dome system. One of the bases of power, D'arl had long ago learned, was in not letting potential opponents know everything you did. "Shall I have someone bring up dinner for you?"

"Please. And add in an extra pot of cahve; I expect I'll be working late this evening."

"Yes, sir." D'arl got to his feet. "I'll probably also be in my office until later if you need me."

H'orme grunted acknowledgment, already engrossed in the comboard again. Walking silently on the thick carpet, D'arl crossed to the inlaid grafwood door. The Cobra warriors were certainly no danger while occupied in a war; but H'orme wasn't one to jump at sudden noises, and if he was becoming concerned, it was time D'arl did likewise. First step would be a call around the planet to the Cobra training center in Freyr Complex to see about shaking loose some more numbers.

And after that . . . it would probably be best to have the dining service send up two dinners instead of just one. It looked like this could be a long evening for him, too.

Warrior: *2406*

The apartment living room was small and cluttered, with the kind of sad dinginess that comes more from lack of time and materials rather than from lack of interest in housekeeping. Seated at the scarred table in the room's center, Jonny let his eyes drift across the far wall, finding an echo of his own weariness in the faded blue paint there. A map of his own soul, he'd frequently thought of it, with its small cracks and chips echoing the effects of nearly three years of warfare on Jonny's psyche. *But it's still standing,* he told himself firmly, as he always did at this point in his contemplation. *The explosions and sonic booms can strain the surface, but beneath it the wall remains solid. And if a stupid wall can do it, so can I.*

"Like this?" a tentative voice asked from beside him.

Jonny looked down at the rumpled piece of paper and the lines and numbers the child had written there. "Well, the first three are right," he nodded. "But the last one should be—"

"I'll get it," Danice interrupted, attacking the geometry problem with renewed vigor. "Don't tell me."

Jonny smiled, gazing fondly at the girl's tangled red hair and determined frown as she redid her work. Danice was ten years old, the same age that Jonny's sister was now, and though Jonny hadn't heard from his family since arriving on Adirondack, he sometimes imagined that Gwen had grown to be a dark-haired version of the girl now sitting beside him. Certainly Gwen's spunk and common-sense stubborness were here in abundance. Certainly too Danice's ability to treat Jonny as a good friend—despite her parents' quiet reservations over the Cobra's temporary presence in their household—showed the independent streak Jonny had often seen in his sister.

But Danice was growing up in a war zone, and no strength of character could get her through that entirely unscathed. So far she'd been lucky: though crowded into a small apartment with too many people, the simmering guerrilla war outside had otherwise touched her life only indirectly.

Given sufficient time, though, that was bound to change, especially if the Cobras overstayed their welcome in this part of Cranach and brought the Trofts down on the neighborhood. On the negative side, it gave Jonny one more thing to worry about; on the positive side, it was an extra incentive to do his job right and end the war as quickly as possible.

Through the open window came the dull thump of a distant thunderclap. "What was that?" Danice asked, her pencil pausing on the paper.

"Sonic boom," Jonny said promptly. He'd cut in his auditory enhancers halfway through the sound and caught the distinctive whine of Troft thrusters beneath the shock wave. "Probably a couple of kilometers away."

"Oh." The pencil resumed its movement.

Standing up, Jonny stepped to the window and looked out. The apartment was six stories up, but even so there wasn't much of a view. Cranach was a tall city, forced by the soft ground around it to go up instead of out as most of Adirondack's cities had done. Directly across the street was a solid wall of six-story buildings; beyond them only the tops of Cranach's central-city skyrisers were visible. Clicking for image magnification, he scanned what was visible of the sky for the trails of falling space-chutes. The pulse-code message last night from off-planet had sparked a desperate flurry of activity as the underground tried to prepare for their new Cobras—Cobras who, with lousy planning, would be landing virtually in the lap of the Troft buildup going on in and around Cranach. Jonny's jaw tightened at the thought, but there'd been nothing anyone had been able to do about it. Receiving a coded signal that in essence blanketed half a continent was one thing; signaling back again, even if the courier ship could afford to stick around that long, was a whole lot dicier. Jonny knew a round dozen ways of outsmarting radio, laser, and pulse-code direction finders—and each one had worked a maximum of four times before the Trofts came up with a way to locate the transmitter anyway. The underground had one method in reserve for emergencies; the Cobra landing had been deemed not to qualify as such.

"See anything?" Danice asked from the table.

Jonny shook his head. "Blue sky, skyrisers—and a little girl who's not doing her homework," he added, turning back to give her a mock glare.

Danice grinned, the very childlike expression not touching the more adult seriousness in her eyes. Jonny had often wondered how much she knew of her parents' activities out in Adirondack's shifting and impromptu battlefields. Did she know, for example, that they were at this moment on a hastily thrown together diversionary raid?

He didn't know. But if she didn't need a distraction from what was happening out there, *he* certainly did. Seating himself beside her again, he gave his mind over as fully as he could to the arcane mysteries of fifth-grade mathematics.

It was nearly three hours later before the click of a key in a lock came from the outer door. Jonny, his hands automatically curled into fingertip laser firing position, watched with muted anxiety as the six people filed silently into the apartment, his eyes flicking from faces to bodies as he searched for signs of injuries. The survey, as usual, yielded results both better than his fears and worse than his hopes. On the plus side, all those who'd left the apartment at dawn—two Cobras, four civilians— had returned under their own power. On the minus side—

He was across the room before Danice's mother was two steps inside the door, taking her unbandaged left arm from her husband's tired-looking grip. "What got you?" he asked quietly, steering her over to the couch.

"Hornet," Marja Tolan said, her voice heavy with pain-killers. Two of the civilians brushed Jonny aside and got to work with the apartment's bulky medical kit.

"Locked in on the click of her popcorn gun's firing mechanism, we think," Marja's husband Kem added tiredly from the table and Jonny's former chair. Fatigued or not, Jonny noted, he'd made it a point immediately to go over and reassure his daughter.

Jonny nodded grimly. Popcorn guns had hitherto been remarkably safe weapons to use, as such things went. Their tiny inertially guided missiles emitted no radar, sonar, or infrared-reflection that could be picked up by any of the Trofts' myriad detectors and response weapons. The missiles were furthermore blasted inert out of the gun barrels by a solid kick of compressed air, their inboard rockets not firing until they were ten to fifteen meters from the gunner. A lot of the missiles themselves had been destroyed in flight by Troft hornets and laser-locks, but until now the aliens hadn't had a way to backtrack to the gunner himself. Unless Marja had simply suffered a lucky hit . . . ?

Jonny looked at Cally Halloran, raised his eyebrows in a question so common now that he didn't even need to vocalize it. And Halloran understood. "We won't know for sure until popcorn gunners start dropping en masse," the Cobra said wearily. "But it was really too clear a shot to be pure chance. I think we can safely assume popcorn guns are out for the duration."

"For all the good the damn things have done so far," Imel Deutsch growled. Stalking to a window, he stood there facing out, his hands clasped in a rigid parade rest behind his back.

The room was suddenly quiet. Stomach churning, Jonny looked back at Halloran. "What happened?"

"Cobra casualty," Halloran sighed. "One of MacDonald's team, we think, though visibility was pretty poor. The people who were supposed to be guarding one of the approaches to their position apparently lost it and about a dozen Trofts got inside. We got a warning off but were too far away to help."

Jonny nodded, feeling an echo of the bitterness Deutsch was almost visibly radiating . . . of the bitterness he himself had nearly choked on twice since their arrival on Adirondack. Parr Noffke and Druma Singh—both of their team's own casualties had come about through the same kind of civilian incompetence. It had taken Jonny a long time to get over each of the deaths; Halloran, with marginally less tolerance for frontier people, had taken somewhat longer.

Deutsch, born and raised on Adirondack, hadn't gotten over it at all.

"Any idea of casualties generally?" Jonny asked Halloran.

"Low, I think, except for the Cobra," the other said. Jonny winced at the unspoken implication— more common lately than he liked—that Cobra lives were intrinsically more valuable than those of their underground allies. "Of course, we weren't really *trying* to take that stockpile, so no one had to take any unusual chances. Did the fresh troops make it down okay?"

"No idea," Jonny shook his head. "Nothing's come in on the pulse receiver from off-world confirming it."

"It'd be just like those phrijpushers to put a last-minute hold in the drop without telling us."

Jonny shrugged, turned back to the people working on Marja's arm. "How's it look?"

"Typical hornet injury," one of them said. "Lots of superficial damage, but it'll all heal okay. She's out of action for a while, though."

And for that time, at least, Danice would have one parent out of the immediate fray.

If that mattered. Jonny had already seen far too many uninvolved civilians lying dead in the middle of cross fires.

The next few minutes were quiet ones. The two civilians finished with Marja's arm and left, taking the group's small supply of combat equipment with them for concealment. Kem and Danice accompanied Marja to one of the apartment's three bedrooms, ostensibly to put her to bed but mainly— Jonny suspected—to give the three Cobras some privacy to discuss the operation and plan future strategy before the rest of the apartment's occupants returned home from work.

In the first few months, Jonny reflected, they might have done just that. But after three years most of the words had already been said, most of the plans already discussed, and gestures of hand

and eyebrow now sufficed where conversations had once been necessary.

For now, the gestures merely indicated fatigue. "Tomorrow," Jonny reminded them of the next high-level tactical meeting as they headed for the door and their own crowded apartments.

Halloran nodded. Deutsch merely twitched a corner of his lip.

And another wonderful day on Adirondack was drawing to a close. *If the wall can stand it*, Jonny repeated to himself, *so can I.*

The three people seated at the table looked very much like everyone else in Cranach these days: tired, vaguely dirty, and more than a little scared. It was hard sometimes to remember that they were among the best underground leaders Adirondack had to offer.

It was even harder, in the face of Cobra and civilian casualties, to admit that they really *were* reasonably good at their jobs.

"The first news is that, despite some crossed signals, the latest Cobra drop was successful," Borg Weissmann told the silent Central Sector underground team leaders seated around the room. Short and stocky, with lingering traces of concrete dust in hair and fingernails, Weissmann looked indeed like the civilian building contractor he actually was. But he'd retired from the Army twenty years previously as a Chief Tactics Programmer, and he'd been proving for nearly a year now that he'd learned more than computers in that post.

"How many did we get?" someone sitting against the side wall asked.

"Cranach's share is thirty: six new teams," Weissmann said. "Most of those will go to North Sector to replace those that got lost in the airstrip attack a month ago."

Jonny glanced at Deutsch, saw the other grimace at the memory. Their team hadn't been involved in that one at all, but details like that didn't appear to affect Deutsch's reaction. If *anyone* from Adirondack was involved, he seemed to react as if he personally had let his fellow Cobras down. Jonny wondered if he himself would feel similarly if the war was being fought on Horizon; decided he probably would.

"We'll also be getting one of the teams here," Weissmann continued. "Ama's already made arrangements for their living quarters, identity backgrounds, and all. But given the heightened Troft activity these past few weeks, I think it might be a good idea to create a little breathing space while they're settling in."

"In other words, a raid." The tone of Halloran's voice made it clear it wasn't a question.

Weissmann hesitated, then nodded. "I know you don't like to run operations so closely together, but I think it's something we ought to do."

" 'We'?" Deutsch spoke up from his usual corner seat. "You mean 'you,' don't you?"

Weissmann licked his lips, a brief flicker of tongue that advertised his discomfort. Deutsch had once been a sort of social buffer zone between the Cobras and Adirondack forces, his dual citizenship—as it were—enabling him to short-circuit misunderstandings and cultural differences. Now, in his current state of disillusionment, he was hell for *anyone* to deal with. "I—uh—assumed you'd want a squad or two along to assist you," Weissmann suggested. "We're certainly willing to carry our part of—"

"*Not* carrying your part is what got another Cobra killed yesterday," Deutsch said quietly. "Maybe we'd better do this one ourselves."

Ama Nunki shifted in her seat. "You, of all people, should know better than to expect too much from us, Imel. This is Adirondack, not Earth or Centauri—

we haven't got any history of warfare here to draw on."

"What do you call the past three years—?" Deutsch began hotly.

"On the other hand," Jonny interjected, "Imel may be right on this one. We want a short, tight punch that'll make the Trofts drop door-to-door searches lower on the priority list, not a big operation that may have them calling up support from the Dannimor garrison. A quick Cobra strike would fit the bill perfectly."

Weissmann visibly let out a breath, and Jonny felt an easing of tension throughout the room. More and more lately he seemed to be taking Deutsch's old peacekeeper role in these meetings, a position he neither especially wanted nor felt he was all that good at. But *someone* had to do it, and Halloran had far less empathy for frontier-world people than Jonny did. He could only continue as best he could and hope that Deutsch would hurry up and snap out of his low simmer.

"I guess I have to agree with Jonny," Halloran said. "I presume you have some suggestions as to what might be ripe for picking?"

Weissmann turned to Jakob Dane, the third person at the table. "We've come up with four reasonable targets," Dane said. "Of course, we were thinking there'd be a full assault team going with you—"

"Just tell us what they are," Deutsch interrupted.

"Yes, sir." Dane picked up a piece of paper, the flimsy sheet amplifying the slight trembling of his hands, and began to read. All four, it turned out, were essentially minor objectives; Dane, apparently, had as low an opinion of the underground's troops as Deutsch did.

"Not one of those is worth the fuel it'll take to get there," Halloran snorted when he'd finished.

"Perhaps you'd prefer to take out the Ghost Focus?" Ama suggested acidly.

"Not funny," Jonny murmured as Halloran's expression darkened. It'd been certain for months that the Trofts had a major tactical headquarters somewhere in Cranach, but so far the aptly christened Ghost Focus had proved impossible to locate. It was a particular sore spot for Halloran, who'd led at least half a dozen hunting expeditions in search of the place and come up dry each time.

All of which, belatedly, Ama seemed to remember. "You're right, Jonny," she said, ducking her head in a local gesture of apology that even Jonny found provincial. "I'm sorry; it's not really something to make light of."

Halloran grunted a not-quite-mollified acceptance. "Anyone have any *genuine* suggestions?" he asked.

"What about that shipment of electronics spares that was supposed to come in yesterday?" Deutsch spoke up.

"It's here," Dane nodded. "Locked up in the old Wolker Plant. But that won't be easy to get to."

Deutsch caught Halloran's and Jonny's eyes, cocked a questioning eyebrow. "Sure, why not?" Halloran shrugged. "A commandeered plastics factory's bound to have security loopholes the Trofts haven't plugged yet."

"You'd think they'd have learned that by now," Deutsch said, getting to his feet and glancing around the room at the team leaders. "Looks like we won't be needing the rest of you any more today. Thanks for coming."

Technically, none of the Cobras had the authority to close the meeting, but no one seemed eager to mention that fact. With little conversation and even less loitering, the room emptied, leaving only the Cobras and the three civilian leaders.

"Now," Deutsch said, addressing the latter, "let's

see what you've got in the way of blueprints for this plant."

Ama's expression was thunderous, but as it was clear the other two weren't going to make an issue of Deutsch's action, she apparently decided not to do so either. Instead, she stalked to the plate in the corner, bringing both it and a collection of innocuously titled tapes back to the table. Interspersed among the video images were blueprints to major city buildings, sewer and powerline data, and dozens of other handy bits of information the underground had squirrelled away. It turned out that the entry for the Wolker Plastics Plant was remarkably detailed.

The planning session lasted until late afternoon, but Jonny was still able to make it back to the Tolans' apartment before the sundown curfew. Two of the usual occupants—Marja's brother and nephew, refugees from the slagged town of Paris— were away for the night, giving Jonny the unusual luxury of a private sleeping room when the clan went to bed later in the evening. No one had asked about the meeting, but Jonny could sense that they were aware he'd be going on another mission soon. There was a subtle drawing back from him, as if they were building a last-minute emotional shell in case this was the mission from which he didn't return.

Later that night, lying on his thin mattress, Jonny contemplated that possibility himself. Some day, he suspected, he would reach the point where walking into near-certain death wouldn't even bother him. But that day hadn't yet arrived, and he hoped to keep it at bay for a long time. Those who went into battle not caring if they died usually did.

So in the last minutes before drifting off to sleep he mentally listed all the reasons he had to come through this mission alive. Starting, as always, with his family, and ending with the effect it would have on Danice.

The clock circuit built into their nanocomputers was at the same time the simplest and yet one of the most useful bits of equipment in the entire Cobra arsenal. Like the traditional soldier's chronometer it enabled widespread forces to synchronize their movements; going that instrument one better, though, it could be tied directly into the rest of the servo network to permit joint action on a microsecond scale. It opened up possibilities that had hitherto been the sole province of automatics, remotes, and the most elite mechanized line troops.

And in exactly twelve minutes and eighteen seconds the gadget would once again pay for itself. Wriggling down the long vent pipe he'd entered from the Wolker Plant's unguarded south filter station, Jonny periodically checked the remaining time against his progress. He hadn't been wild about using this back door—enclosed spaces were the single most dangerous environment a Cobra could be trapped in—but so far it looked like the gamble was going to pay off. The alarms the Trofts had installed at the far end had been easy enough to circumvent, and according to the blueprints he should very soon be exiting into a vat almost directly beneath the building's main entrance. He would then have until the timer ran down to find a position from which the inside door guards were visible.

At one point the Trofts had relied heavily on portable black box sensors to defend converted civilian buildings like this, a practice the underground had gone to great lengths to discourage. The aliens quickly learned that, no matter what thresholds the triggers were set at, their opponents soon figured out how to set off false alarms through them. After sufficient effort had been wasted chasing canine "intruders" and hunting for slingshot-and-firecracker-equipped harassers, they'd pulled out the automatics in favor of live guards equipped with warning sensors and dead-man switches. The system was harder to fool and almost as safe.

Almost.

Ahead of him Jonny could see a spot of dark gray amid the black. The grille leading into the main building, probably, the faintness of the back-ground light indicating that particular room was probably unoccupied. He hoped so; he didn't want to have to cut down any aliens this early in the mission.

The crucial question, of course, was whether or not all the dead-man switches could be deacti-vated in the microsecond before their owners were wiped out in the synchronized Cobra attack. That task would probably rest on Jonny's shoulders, since any relays for the alarms would be inside. The Trofts had both closed- and open-circuit types of switches, and he would have to determine which kind was being used here before taking action.

He'd reached the grille now. Boosting his optical enhancers, he studied it for alarms and booby-traps. A current detector from his equipment pack located four suspicious wires; jumping them with adjustable-impedance cables, he cut through the mesh with his fingertip lasers and slid through the last two-meter stretch of pipe into an empty vat. There was no provison for releasing its service openings from the inside, but Jonny's lasers took care of that oversight without any trouble. Poking his head out of the opening, he took a careful look around.

He was suspended some five meters above the floor, his vat the largest in a row of similar structures. Four meters away, at eye level, was what looked like the exit from the room, reached from the floor by a set of stairs built into the wall.

Given Troft security thus far, Jonny expected nothing in the way of booby traps to be set up on the floor below. Still, he had just seven minutes to get into position upstairs ... and to a Cobra a four-meter leap was as easy as a stroll down the walkway. Drawing up his feet, he balanced for a moment on the lip of the vat service opening and pushed off.

The night before he had warned himself of the dangers of apathy. Now, for one awful instant—all the time he had—he recognized that overconfidence extracted an equally bitter price. The sharp *twang* of released springs filled his enhanced hearing, and the servos within his arms snapped his fingertip lasers into position faster than his brain could register the black wall hurtling itself toward him. But it was an essentially meaningless gesture, and even as the pencils of light flashed out he realized the Trofts had suckered him masterfully. A major military target, an enticing backdoor entrance with inadquate alarms, and finally a mid-air trap that used his helpless ballistic trajectory to neutralize the speed and strength advantage of his servos.

The flying wall reached him, and he had just enough time to notice it was actually a net before it hit, wrapping itself around him like a giant cocoon. A split second later he was jerked sharply off his original path as unnoticed suspension lines reached their limit, snapping him back to hang more or less upside down in the middle of the room.

And Jonny was captured ... which, since he was a Cobra, meant that he was dead.

His body didn't accept that fact so quickly, of course, and continued to strain cautiously against the sticky mesh digging into his clothing. But the limiting factor wasn't his servos' power, and it was all too clear that before the net would break, its threads would slice through both cloth and flesh, stopping only when it reached bone. Above his left foot his antiarmor laser flashed, vaporizing a small piece of the material and blowing concrete chips from the ceiling, but neither his leg or arms could move far enough to cause any serious damage to the net. If he could hit one or more of the lines holding him off the floor . . . but in the gloom, with his eyes covered by two or three layers of mesh, he couldn't even see them.

Somewhere in the recesses of his mind, a direct neural stimulation alarm went off from the sensor monitoring his heartbeat.

He was falling asleep.

It was the enemy's final stroke, as inevitable as it was fatal. Pressed against the skin of his face, the contact drug mixed with the adhesive on the net was soaking into his bloodstream faster than the emergency stimulant system beneath his heart could compensate. He had bare seconds before the universe was forever closed off . . . and he had one vital task yet to perform.

His tongue was a lump of unresponsive clay pressed against the roof of his mouth. With all the will power remaining to him he forced it to the corner of his mouth . . . forced it through wooden lips . . . touched the tip of the emergency radio trigger curving along his cheek. "Abort," he mumbled. The room was growing darker, but it was far too much effort to click up his optical enhancers. "Abort. Walked . . . trap. . . ."

Somewhere far off he thought he heard a crisp acknowledgment, but it was too much effort to try and understand the words. It was too much effort, in fact, to do anything at all.

The darkness rose and swept gently over him.

*   *   *

The nearest building to the Wolker Plant was an abandoned warehouse a hundred meters due north of the plant's main entrance. Crouched on the roof there, Cally Halloran ground his teeth viciously together as he tried to watch all directions at once. A trap, Jonny had said, with sleep or death already near to claiming him . . . but was it a simple booby trap or something more elaborate? If the latter, then Deutsch too would probably never make it off the plant's grounds alive. If the operation was wide enough, even this backstop position could become a deathtrap.

For the moment the fact of Jonny's death hardly touched his thoughts. Later, perhaps, there would be time to mourn, but for now Halloran's duty lay solely with the living. Easing his leg forward, he made sure the antiarmor laser within it could sweep the area freely and waited.

With his light amplification on at full power the night around him seemed no darker than a heavily overcast afternoon, but even so he didn't spot Deutsch until the other was well on his way back from the patch of deep shadow where he'd been waiting for his part of the gate attack. The guards, it seemed, saw him at about the same time, and for an instant that part of the landscape dimmed as laser flashes cut in his enhancers' overload protection. Answering fire came immediately: Deutsch's antiarmor laser firing backwards as he ran. With the unconscious ease of long experience, Halloran raised his own aim to the plant's roof and windows, areas Deutsch's self-covering fire would have trouble hitting.

The precaution proved unnecessary. Even with ankle-breaking zigzags tangling his path, Deutsch took the intervening distance like a ground-hug missile, and in bare seconds he was around the corner of Halloran's warehouse and out of enemy view.

But it was clear the Trofts weren't going to be content with simply driving the Cobras away. Even as Halloran slipped across the roof and down the far side the Wolker Plant was starting to come alive.

Deutsch was waiting for him on the ground, his face tense in the faint light. "You okay?" Halloran whispered.

"Yeah. You'd better get going—they'll be swarming around like ants in a minute."

"Change that 'you' to 'we' and you've got a deal. Come on." He gripped Deutsch's arm and turned to go.

The other shook off his hand. "No, I'm staying here to—to make sure."

Halloran turned back, studying his partner with new and wary eyes. If Deutsch was unraveling . . . "He's dead, Imel," he explained, as if to a small child. "You heard him going under—"

"His self-destruct hasn't gone off," Deutsch interrupted him harshly. "Even out here we should have heard it or felt the vibrations. And if he's alive . . ."

He left the sentence unfinished, but Halloran understood. The Trofts were already known to have live-dissected at least one captured Cobra. Jonny deserved better than that, if it was within their power to grant. "All right," he sighed, suppressing a shiver. "But don't take chances. Giving Jonny a clean death isn't worth losing your own life over."

"I know. Don't worry; I'm not going to do anything stupid." Deutsch paused for an instant, listening. "You'd better get moving."

"Right. I'll do what I can to draw them away."

"Now don't *you* take chances." Deutsch slapped Halloran's arm and jumped, catching the edge of the warehouse roof and disappearing over the top.

Clicking all audio and visual enhancers to full

power, Halloran turned and began to run, keeping to the shadows as much as possible. The time to mourn was still in the distant future.

The first sensation that emerged as the black fog faded was a strange burning in his cheeks. Gradually, the feeling strengthened and was joined by the awareness of something solid against his back and legs. Thirst showed up next, followed immediately by pressure on his forearms and shins. The sound of whispering air ... the awareness that there was soft light beyond his closed eyelids ... the knowledge that he was lying horizontally ...

Only then did Jonny's mind come awake enough to notice that he was still alive.

Cautiously, he opened his eyes. A meter above him was a featureless white-steel ceiling; tracing along it, he found it ended in four white-steel walls no more than five meters apart. Hidden lights gave a hospital glow to the room; by it he saw that the only visible exit was a steel door in a heavily reinforced frame. In one corner a spigot—water?—protruded from the wall over a ten-centimeter drainage grille that could probably serve as a toilet if absolutely necessary. His equipment pack and armament belt were gone, but his captors had left him his clothes.

As a death cell, it seemed fairly cheerful. As a surgery prep room, it was woefully deficient.

Raising his head, he studied the plates pinning his arms and legs to the table. Not shackles, he decided; more likely a complex set of biomedical sensors with drug-injection capabilities. Which meant the Trofts ought to know by now that he was awake. From which it followed immediately that they'd *allowed* him to wake up.

He was aware, down deep, that not all the fog had yet cleared away; but even so it seemed an incredibly stupid move on their part.

His first impulse was to free himself from the table in a single servo-powered lunge, turn his antiarmor laser on the door hinges, and get the hell out of there. But the sheer irrationality of the whole situation made him pause.

What did the Trofts think they were doing, anyway?

Whatever it was, it was most likely in violation of orders. The underground had intercepted a set of general orders some months ago, one of which was that any captured Cobras were to be immediately killed or kept sedated for live-dissection. Jonny's stomach crawled at the latter thought, but he again resisted the urge to get out before the Troft on monitor duty belatedly noticed his readings. The enemy simply didn't *make* mistakes that blatantly careless. Whatever was happening, contrary to orders or not, it was being done on purpose.

So what could anyone want with a living, fully conscious Cobra?

Interrogation was out. Physical torture above a certain level would trigger a power supply self-destruct; so would the use of certain drugs. Hold him for ransom or trade? Ridiculous. Trofts didn't seem to think along those lines, and even if they'd learned humans did, it wouldn't work. They would need Jonny's cooperation to prove to his friends he was still alive, and he'd blow his self-destruct himself rather than give them that lever. Let him escape and follow him back to his underground contacts? Equally ridiculous. There were dozens of secure, monofilament line phones set up around the city from which he could check in with Borg Weissmann without ever going near an underground member. The Trofts had tried that unsuccessfully with other captured rebels; trying to follow an evasion-trained Cobra would be an exercise in futility. No, giving him even half a chance to escape would gain them nothing but a path of destruction through their building.

A path of destruction. A path of *Cobra* destruction. . . .

Heart beating faster, Jonny turned his attention back to the walls and ceiling. This time, because he was looking for them, he spotted the places where cameras and other sensors could be located. There appeared to be a *lot* of them.

Carefully, he laid his head back on the table, feeling cold all over. So *that's* what this was all about—an attempt to get lab-quality information on Cobra equipment and weaponry in actual use. Which meant that, whatever lay outside that steel door, odds were he'd have an even chance of getting through it alive.

For a long moment temptation tugged at him. If he *could* escape, surely it would be worth letting the Trofts have their data. Most of what they would get must already be known, and even watching his battle reflexes in action would be of only limited use to them. Only a handful of the most intricate patterns were rigidly programmed; the rest had been kept general enough to cover highly varying situations. The Trofts might afterwards be able to predict another Cobra's escape path from this same cell, but that was about it.

But the whole debate was ultimately nothing more than a mental exercise . . . because Jonny knew full well the proposed trade-off was illusory. Somewhere along the Trofts' gauntlet—somewhere near the end—there would be an attack that *would* kill him.

There's no such thing as a foolproof deathtrap. Cee-three Bai had emphasized that point back on Asgard, hammered at it until Jonny had come to believe it. But it was always assumed that the victim had at least *some* idea of what he was up against. Jonny had no idea how the killing attack would come; had no feeling for the layout of this building; had no idea even where on Adirondack he was.

His duty was therefore unfortunately clear. Closing his eyes, he focused his attention on the neural alarm that would signal an attempt to put him back to sleep. If and when that happened he would be forced to break his bonds, trading minimal information for consciousness. Until then . . . he would simply have to wait.

And hope. Irrational though that might be.

They sat and listened, and when Deutsch finished he could tell they were unconvinced.

Ama Nunki put it into words first. "Too big a risk," she said with a slow shake of her head, "for so small a chance of success."

There was a general shifting in chairs by the other underground and Cobra leaders, but no immediate votes of agreement. That meant there was still a chance. . . . "Look," Deutsch said, striving to keep his voice reasonable. "I know it *sounds* crazy, but I tell you it *was* Jonny I saw being taken aboard that aircraft, and it *did* head south. You know as well as I do that there's no reason for them to have taken him anywhere but their hospital if they just wanted to dissect him. They *must* have something else in mind, something that requires he be kept alive—and if he's alive he can be rescued."

"But he's got to be found first," Jakob Dane explained patiently. "Your estimate of where the aircraft landed notwithstanding, the assumption that figuratively beating the bushes will turn up some sign of him is at best a hopeful fiction."

"Why?" Deutsch countered. "Any place the Trofts would be likely to stash him would have to be reasonably big, reasonably attack-resistant, and reasonably unoccupied. All right, all right—I *know* that part of the city has a lot of buildings like that. But we've *got* it narrowed down."

"And what if we *do* find the place?" Kennet MacDonald, a Cobra from Cranach's East Sector, spoke up. "Throw all our forces against it in a raid that could easily end in disaster? All they have to do if they lose is kill Moreau and let his self-destruct take out the whole building, rescuers and all."

"In fact, that could very well be what they *want* us to do," Ama said.

"If they wanted to set up a giant deathtrap, they would've left him right there in the Wolker Plant, where we wouldn't have had to work to track him down," Deutsch argued, fighting hard against the feeling that the battle was slipping through his fingers. He glanced fiercely at Halloran, but the other remained silent. Didn't he *care* that Jonny could be saved if they'd just make the effort?

"I have to agree with Kennet," Pazar Oberton, an underground leader from MacDonald's sector, said. "We've never asked you to rescue one of *our* people, and I don't think we should all go rushing south trying to rescue one of yours."

"This isn't a corporation ledger we're running here—it's a *war*," Deutsch snapped. "And in case you've forgotten, we Cobras are the best chance you've got of winning that war and getting these damned invaders off your planet."

"Off *our* planet?" Dane murmured. "Have you officially emigrated, then?"

Dane would never know how close he came to dying in that instant. Deutsch's teeth clamped tightly together as endless months of heartbreak and frustration threatened to burst out in one massive explosion of laser fire that would have cut the insensitive fool in half. None of them understood—none of them even *tried* to understand—how it felt to watch his own countrymen's failures and stupidities cause the deaths of men he'd come to consider his brothers . . . how it felt to be defending people who often didn't seem willing to put forth the same effort to free their world . . . how it felt to share their blame, because ultimately he too was one of them. . . .

Slowly, the haze cleared, and he saw the fists clenched before him on the table. "Borg?" he said, looking at Weissmann. "You lead this rabble. What do you say?"

An uncomfortable rustle went around the table, but Weissmann's gaze held Deutsch's steadily. "I know you feel especially responsible since you were the one who suggested the Wolker Plant in the first place," he said quietly, "but you *are* talking very poor odds."

"Warfare is a history of poor odds," Deutsch countered. He sent his gaze around the room. "I don't *have* to ask your permission, you know. I could order you to help me rescue Jonny."

Halloran stirred. "Imel, we technically have no authority to—"

"I'm not talking technicalities," Deutsch interrupted, his voice quiet but with an edge to it. "I'm talking the realities of power."

For a long moment the room was deathly still. "Are you threatening us?" Weissmann asked at last.

Deutsch opened his mouth, the words *damn right I am* on his lips . . . but before he could speak, a long-forgotten scene floated up from his memory. Rolon Viljo's face as Commander Mendro ordered him removed from the team and the Cobras . . . and Deutsch's own verdict on Viljo's crime. *Misuse of our equipment would pit us against the civilian population of Adirondack.* "No," he told Weissmann, the word taking incredible strength of will to say. "No, of course not. I just—never mind." He sent one last glance around the room and then stood up. "You can all do as you damn well please. I'm going to go and find Jonny."

The room was still silent as he crossed to the door and left. Briefly, as he started down the stairs, he wondered what they would make of his outburst. But it didn't matter very much. And in a short time, most likely, it wouldn't matter at all.

Stepping outside into the night, senses alert for Troft patrols, he headed south.

"I do believe," Jakob Danc said as the sound of Deutsch's footsteps faded away, "that Adirondack's Self-Appointed Conscience is overdue for some leave time."

"Shut up, Jakob," Halloran advised, making sure to put some steel in his voice. He'd long ago recognized that each of the underground members had to deal with the presence of the Cobras in his own way, but Dane's approach—treating them with a faintly supercilious air—was a dangerous bit of overcompensation. He doubted the other had noticed it, but as Deutsch's hands had curled into fists a few minutes ago there had been the briefest pause with thumb resting against ring finger nail ... the position for firing fingertip lasers at full power. "In case you didn't bother to notice," he added, "just about everything Imel said was right."

"Including the efficacy of a rescue mission?" Dane snorted.

Halloran turned to Weissmann. "*I* notice, Borg, that you haven't given your decision on assigning underground personnel to help locate Jonny. Before you do, let me just point out that there's exactly *one* Troft installation we know exists that we haven't got even a rough locale for."

"You mean the Ghost Focus?" Ama frowned. "That's crazy. Jonny's a ticking bomb—they'd be stupid to put him anywhere that sensitive."

"Depends on what they're planning for him,"

MacDonald rumbled thoughtfully. "As long as he's alive they're safe enough. Besides, our self-destructs aren't all *that* powerful. Any place hardened against, say, tacnuke grenades wouldn't have any trouble with us."

"On top of that," Halloran added, "it's clear from their slow response to Imel and me that they weren't particularly expecting a raid on Wolker tonight. Jonny's booby trap may have been sitting there for months, and it's as reasonable as anything else to assume they weren't really prepared with another place to put him that we didn't already know about. If the Ghost Focus is like their other tactical bases, they'll have it carved into parallel, independently-hardened warrens. They wouldn't be risking more than the one Jonny was actually in."

"I've never heard that about tactical bases," Ama said, her eyes hard on Halloran.

He shrugged. "There are a lot of things you've never heard," he told her bluntly. "You ever volunteer to penetrate a Troft installation with us and maybe we'll tell you what we know about those hellholes. Until then, you'll have to take our word for it." He had the satisfaction of seeing her mouth tighten; to people like Ama the only real power was knowledge. Turning to Weissmann, he cocked an eyebrow. "Well, Borg?"

Weissmann pressed his fingertips tightly against his lips, staring at and through Halloran. "All right," he said with a sigh. "I'll authorize some of our people for search duty and see if I can borrow a few from other sectors. But it'll be passive work only, and won't begin until after sunup. I don't want anyone getting caught violating curfew—and no one's going into combat."

"Fair enough." It was about as much as Halloran could have expected. "Kennet?"

MacDonald steepled his fingers. "I won't risk

my team randomly tearing up the south side of Cranach," he said quietly. "But if you can show me a probable location, we'll help you hit it. Whatever the Trofts want with Jonny, I suspect it's behavior we ought to discourage."

"Agreed. And thank you." Halloran gestured to Ama. "Well, don't just sit there. Pull out the high-resolution maps and let's get to work."

Jonny waited until his thirst was unbearable before finally breaking free of his restraints and going to the spigot in the cell's corner. Without a full analysis kit it was impossible to make sure the water provided was uncontaminated and un-drugged, but it didn't especially worry him. The Trofts had had ample opportunity already to pump chemicals into his system, and exotic bacteria were the least of his worries.

He drank his fill, and then—as long as he was up anyway—gave himself a walking tour of his cell. On the whole it was a dull trip, but it *did* give him the chance to examine the walls more closely for remote monitors. The room was, as he'd earlier surmised, loaded with them.

The cell door, up close, proved an intriguing piece of machinery. There were signs at one edge that both an electronic and a tumbler-type combination lock were being used, complementary possibilities to the temptingly exposed hinges he'd already noticed. The Trofts, it appeared, were offering him sublte as well as brute-force escape options. Each of which would give them useful data on his equipment, unfortunately.

Returning to the table, he moved aside the remnants of the monitor/shackles and lay down again. His internal clock circuit, which he hadn't had time to shut off or reset during his capture, provided him with at least the knowledge of how time was passing in the outside world. He'd been uncon-

scious for three hours; since his awakening another five had passed. That meant it was almost
ten o'clock in the morning out there. The people of
Cranach were out at work in their damaged city,
the children—including Danice Tolan—were at
school, and the underground . . .

The underground had already accepted and
mourned his death and gone on with their business.
His death, and possibly Cally's and Imel's as well.

For a long, painful minute Jonny wondered what
had happened to his teammates. Had his warning
been in time for them to escape? Or had the Trofts
been waiting with a giant trap ready to grab all of
them? Perhaps they were in similar rooms right
now, wondering identical thoughts as they decided
whether or not to make their own escapes. They
might even be next door to his cell; in which case
a burst of antiarmor fire would open a communication hole and let them plan joint action—

He shook his head to clear it of such unlikely
thoughts. No help would be coming for him, and
he might as well face that fact. If Imel and Cally
were alive they would have more sense than to try
something as stupid as a rescue, even if they knew
where to find him. And if they were dead . . . odds
were he'd be joining them soon, anyway.

Unbidden, Danice Tolan's face floated into view.
It looked like, barring a miracle, she was finally
going to lose a close friend to the war.

He hoped she'd be able to handle it.

The human had been in the cell now for nearly
seven *vfohra*, and except for a casual breaking of
its loose restraints two *vfohra* ago had made no
attempt to use its implanted weaponry against its
imprisonment. Resettling his wing-like radiator
membranes against the backs of his arms, the City
Commander gazed at the bank of vision screens
and wondered what he should do.

His ET biologist approached from the left, puffing up his throat bladder in a gesture of subservience. "Speak," the CCom invited.

"The last readings have been thoroughly rechecked," the other said, his voice vaguely flutey in the local atmosphere's unusually high nitrogen content. "The human shows no biochemical evidence of trauma or any of their versions of dreamwalking."

The CCom flapped his arm membranes once in acknowledgment. So it was as he'd already guessed: the prisoner had deliberately chosen not to attempt escape. A ridiculous decision, even for an alien . . . unless it had somehow discerned what it was they had planned for it.

From the CCom's point of view, the alien couldn't have picked a worse time to show its race's stubborn streak. The standing order that these *koubrah*-soldiers were to be killed instantly could be gotten around easily enough, but all the time and effort already invested would be lost unless the creature provided an active demonstration of its capabilities for the hidden sensors.

Which meant the CCom was once more going to have to perform that most distasteful of duties. Seating his arm membranes firmly, he reached deep into his paraconscious mind, touching the mass of hard-won psychological data that had been placed there aboard the demesne-lord's master ship . . . and with great effort he tried to think like a human.

The effort left a taste like copper oxide in his mouth, but by the time the CCom emerged sputtering from his dream-walk he had a plan. "SolLi!" he called to the Soldier Liaison seated at the security board. "One patrol, fully equipped, in Tunnel One immediately."

The SolLi puffed his throat bladder in acknowledgment and bent over his communicator. Spreading out his arm membrances—the dream-walk had left him uncomfortably warm—the CCom watched the dormant human and considered the best way to do this.

It was an hour past noon in the outside world, and Jonny was once more reviewing everything he'd ever been taught about prison escapes, when an abrupt creak of metal from the door sent him rolling off the table. Crouching at the edge of the slab, fingertip lasers aimed, he watched tensely as the door opened a meter and someone leaped into his cell.

He had a targeting lock established and lasers tracking before his conscious mind caught up with two important details: the figure was human, and it had not been traveling under its own power. Looking back at the door, he got just a glimpse of two body-armored Trofts as they slammed the heavy steel plate closed again. The *thud* reverberated like overhead thunder in the tiny room, and a possible shot at escaping his cell was gone. Slowly, Jonny got to his feet and stepped around the table to meet his new cellmate.

She was on her feet when he reached her, bent over slightly as she rubbed an obviously painful kneecap. "Damn chicken-faced strifpitchers," she grumbled. "They *could've* just let me walk in."

"You all right?" Jonny asked, giving her a quick once-over. A bit shorter than he was and as slender, maybe seven or eight years older, dressed in the mishmash of styles the war had made common. No obvious injuries or blood stains that he could see.

"Oh, sure." Straightening up, she sent a quick look around the cell. "Though I suppose that could change at any time. What's going on here, anyway?"

"Tell me what happened."

"I wish I knew. I was just walking down Strassheim Street, minding my own business, when this Troft patrol turned a corner. They asked me what I was doing there, I essentially told them to go back to hell, and for no particular reason they grabbed me and hauled me in here."

Jonny's lip twitched in a smile. In the early days of the occupation, he'd heard, it had been possible to fire off multiple obscenities at point-blank range, and as long as you kept your face and voice respectful the Trofts had no way of catching on. With the aliens' advances in Anglic translation, though, only the truly imaginative could come up with something they hadn't heard before.

Strassheim Street. There was a Strassheim in Cranach, he remembered, down in the south end of the city where a lot of the light industry had been. "So what *were* you doing there?" he asked the woman. "I thought that area was mostly deserted now."

She gave him a cool, measuring look. "Shall I repeat the answer I gave the Trofts?"

He shrugged. "Don't bother. I was just asking." Turning his back on her, he hopped back up on the table, seating himself cross-legged facing the door. It really *wasn't* any of his business.

Besides which, he was starting to get an uncomfortable feeling as to the reason for her presence here . . . and if he was right, the less contact he had with her, the better. There was no point in getting to know someone you would probably soon be dying with.

For a moment it seemed like she'd come to a similar conclusion. Then, with hesitant footsteps, she came around the edge of the table and into his peripherial vision. "Hey—I'm sorry," she said, the snap still audible in her voice but subdued to a more civil level. "I'm just—I'm starting to get a little scared, that's all, and I tend to bite heads off when I get scared. I was on Strassheim because I was hoping to get into one of the old factories and scrounge some circuit boards or other electronics parts. Okay?''

He pursed his lips and looked at her, feeling his freshly minted resolve tarnishing already. "Those buildings have been picked pretty clean in the past three years," he pointed out.

"Mostly by people who don't know what they're doing," she shrugged. "There's still some stuff left—if you know where and how to find it."

"Are you part of the underground?" Jonny asked—and instantly wished he could call back the thoughtless words. With monitors all around, her answer could lose her what little chance of freedom she had left.

But she merely snorted. "Are you nuts? I'm a struggling burglar, confrere, not a volunteer lunatic." Her eyes widened suddenly. "Say, you're not, uh—hey, wait a minute; they don't think that *I*—oh, great. Great. What'd you do, come calling for Old Tyler with a laser in one hand and a grenade in the other?"

"Old Tyler?" Jonny asked, latching onto the most coherent part of that oral skid. "Who or what is that?"

"We're in his mansion," she frowned. "At least I think so. Didn't you know?"

"I was unconscious when I was brought in. What do you mean, you think so?"

"Well, I was actually taken into an old apartment building a block away and then along an underground tunnel to get here. But I got a glimpse through an unblocked window as I was being brought through the main building, and I think I saw the Tyler Mansion's outer wall. Anyway, even without fancy furniture and all you can tell the rooms up there were designed for someone rich."

The Tyler Mansion. The name was familiar from Ama Nunki's local history/geography seminars: a large house with a sort of pseudo-Reginine-million-aire style, he recalled, built south of the city in the days before industry moved into that area. She'd been vague as to the semi-recluse owner's where-abouts since the Troft invasion, but it was gener-ally believed he was holed up inside somewhere, counting on private stores and the mansion's de-fenses to keep out looters and aliens alike. Jonny remembered thinking at the time that the Trofts were being uncommonly generous to leave the place standing under those conditions, and wondering if perhaps a private deal had been struck. It was starting to look like he'd been right . . . though the deal was possibly more than a little one-sided.

But more interesting than the mansion's recent history were the possibilities inherent in being locked inside such a residence. Unlike a factory, a millionaire's home ought to have an emergency escape route. If he could find it, perhaps he could bypass whatever deathtrap the Trofts had planned for him. "You say you came in through a tunnel," he said to his cellmate. "Did it look new or hastily built? Say, as if the Trofts had dug it in the past three years?"

But she was frowning again, a hard look in her eyes. "Who the hell are you, anyway, that you never heard of Old Tyler? He's been written up more than every other celebrity on Adirondack—even volunteer lunatics can't be *that* ignorant. At least, not those who grew up in Cranach."

Jonny sighed; but she *did* have a right to know on whom her life was probably going to depend. And it certainly wouldn't be giving away any se-crets to the Trofts eavesdropping on them. "You're right—I grew up quite a ways from here. I'm a Cobra."

Her eyes widened, then narrowed again as they swept his frame. "A Cobra, huh? You sure don't look like anything special."

"We're not supposed to," Jonny told her patiently. "Undercover guerrilla fighters—remember?"

"Oh, I know. But I've seen men masquerade as Cobras before to impress or threaten people."

"You want some proof?" He'd been looking for an excuse to do this, anyway. Hopping off the table, he stepped closer to the rear wall and extended his right arm. A group of suspected sensor positions faced him just below eye level. Targeting it, he turned his head to look at the woman. "Watch," he said, and triggered his arcthrower.

A discerning eye might have noticed that there were actually two components to the flash that lit up the room an instant later: the fingertip laser beam, which burned an ionized path through the air, and the high-amperage spark that traveled that path to the wall. But the accompanying thunderclap was the really impressive part, and in the metal-walled cell it was impressive as hell. The woman jumped a meter backwards from a standing start, mouthing something Jonny couldn't hear through the multiple reverberations. "Satisfied?" he asked her when the sound finally faded away.

Staring at him with wide eyes, she bobbed her head quickly. "Oh, yes. Yes indeed. What in heaven's name *was* that?"

"Arcthrower. Designed to fry electronic gear. Works pretty well, usually." In fact, it worked quite well, and Jonny didn't expect to have to worry about that particular sensor cluster again.

"I don't doubt it." She exhaled once, and with that action seemed to get her mind working as well. "A real Cobra. So how come you haven't broken out of here yet?"

For a long moment he stared at her, wondering what to say. If the Trofts knew he was on to their scheme ... but surely her presence here proved they'd already figured that out. Tell her the truth, then?—that the aliens were forcing him to choose between betraying his fellow Cobras and saving her life?

He chose the easier, if temporary, solution of changing the subject. "You were going to tell me about the tunnel," he reminded her.

"Oh. Right. No, it looked like it'd been there a lot longer than three years. There also looked to be spots where gates and defensive equipment had been taken out."

In other words, it looked like Tyler's hoped-for escape hatch. And already in alien hands. "How well were the Trofts guarding it?"

"The place was full of them." She was giving him a wary look. "You're not planning to try and leave that way, are you?"

"What if I am?"

"It'd be suicide—and since I plan to be right behind you it'd leave *me* in a bad spot, too."

He frowned at her, only then realizing that she'd apparently figured out more about what was going on than he'd given her credit for. In her own less than subtle way she was saying he need not burden himself physically with her when he chose to escape. That he shouldn't feel responsible for her safety.

If only it were that simple, he thought bitterly. Would she understand as well if he stayed passively in the cell and thereby sentenced her automatically to death?

Or was that option even open to him anymore? Already, despite his earlier resolve, he realized he could no longer see her as simply a faceless statistic in this war. He'd talked to her, watched her eyes change expression, even gotten a little bit inside her mind. Whatever it cost him—life and data too—he knew now that he would eventually have to make the effort to get her out. The Trofts' gambit had worked.

You'll be proud of me, Jame, if you ever find out,

he thought toward the distant stars. *My Horizon ethics have survived exposure to even war with all their stupid nobility intact.*

On the other hand ... he was now locked up with a professional burglar inside what had to be the most enticing potential target Cranach had to offer. In their eagerness to hang an emotional millstone around his neck, it was just barely possible the Trofts had outsmarted themselves. "My name's Jonny Moreau," he told the woman. "What's yours?"

"Ilona Linder."

He nodded, knowing full well that with an exchange of names he was now committed. "Well, Ilona, if you think the tunnel's a poor choice of exits, let's see what else we can come up with. Why don't you start by telling me everything you know about the Tyler Mansion?"

"This is hopeless," Cally Halloran sighed, gazing across the urban landscape from the vantage point of an eighth-floor window. "We could sneak in and out of deserted buildings for days without finding any leads."

"You can quit whenever you want to," was Deutsch's predictable answer. Sitting on the floor, the other Cobra was poring over a prewar aerial map of southern Cranach.

"Uh-huh. Well, as long as you're being so grateful for all that we're doing to help, I guess I'll stick around awhile longer."

It was Deutsch's turn to sigh. "All right, all right. If it'll ease your smoldering indignation any, I'll admit I went a little overwrought in selling this to Borg and company. Okay? Can you drop the little digs now?"

"I can drop them any time. But eventually you're going to have to face what you're doing to those people, not to mention what you're doing to yourself."

Deutsch snorted. "You mean undermining morale, while driving myself too hard with unrealistic goals and standards?"

"Well, now that you mention it—"

"I'm not pushing myself any harder than I can handle—you know that. As to the underground—" He shrugged, the movement rustling his map. "You just don't understand the position Adirondack's in, Cally. We're a frontier world, looked down on by everyone else in the Dominion—for all I know, by the Trofts as well. We've got to *prove* ourselves to all the rest of you, and the only way to do that is to throw the Trofts off our world."

"Yes, I know that's the theory you're working under," Halloran nodded. "*My* question is whether or not that's the achievement people will remember most."

Again Deutsch snorted. "What else *is* there in a war?"

"Spirit, for one thing. And Adirondack is showing one hell of a fine spirit." He held up a hand and began ticking off fingers. "One: you haven't got a single genuine collaborationist government anywhere on the planet. That forces the Trofts to tie up ridiculous numbers of troops with administrative and policing duties they'd much rather leave to you. Two: the local governments they *have* coerced into place are working very hard to be more trouble than they're worth. Remember when the Trofts tried conscription from Cranach and Dannimor to repair the Leeding Bridge?"

Almost unwillingly, Deutsch smiled. "Multiple conflicting orders, incompatible equipment, and well-hidden deficiencies in materials. Took them twice as long as the Trofts would have if they'd done it themselves."

"And every one of the people responsible for

that fiasco risked their lives to pull it off," Halloran reminded him. "And those are just the things that plain, relatively uninvolved citizens are doing. I haven't even mentioned the sacrifices the underground's shown itself willing to make, the sheer persistence it's demonstrated the past three years. Maybe you're not impressed by your world, but I'll tell you right now that I'd be proud as hell if Aerie did *half* as well under these conditions."

Deutsch pursed his lips, his eyes on the map now folded over his knees. "All right," he said at last. "I'll concede that maybe we're not doing too badly. But potentials and maybes don't matter in this game. If we lose no one's going to care whether we did the best we could or the worst we could, because no one's going to remember us, period. Only the winners make it into the history books."

"Perhaps," Halloran nodded. "But perhaps not. Have you ever heard of Masada?"

"I don't think so. Was it a battle?"

"A siege. Took place in the first century on Earth. The Roman Empire had invaded some country— Israel, I think it's called now. A group of the local defenders—I'm not sure whether they were even regular military or just guerrillas—they took refuge on top of a plateau called Masada. The Romans encircled the place and tried for over a year to take it."

Deutsch's dark eyes were steady on his. "And eventually did?"

"Yes. But the defenders had sworn not to be taken alive . . . and so when the Romans marched into the camp all they found were dead bodies. They'd chosen suicide rather than capture."

Deutsch licked his lips. "I would have tried to take a few more Romans with me."

Halloran shrugged. "So would I. But that's not the point. They lost, but they weren't conquered, if you see the difference; and even though the Romans wound up winning the war, Masada's never been forgotten."

"Um." Deutsch stared off into space for another moment, then abruptly picked up his map again. "Well, I'd still like to come up with a better ending than that for this game," he said briskly. "Anything out there look particularly promising for our next sortie?"

Halloran directed his attention back out the window, wondering if his pep talk had done any good. "Couple of very obviously gutted buildings to the southwest that might make good cover for a guard house or hidden tunnel entrance. And there's a genuine jungle behind a security wall a little further on."

"The Tyler Mansion," Deutsch nodded, marking locations on his map. "Used to be very nice gardens and orchards surrounding the main house before the war. I supose all Tyler's gardeners ran off long ago."

"Looks like you could hide an armor division under all that shrubbery. Any chance the Trofts could have taken the place over?"

"Probably, but it's hard to imagine how they'd do that without an obvious battle. That wall's not just decorative, for starters, and Tyler's bound to have heavier stuff in reserve. Besides, no one's ever seen any Trofts going in or out of the grounds."

"That reminds me—we should find a secure phone and check in before we go anywhere else. See if the spotters have anything in the way of Troft movement correlations yet."

"If they haven't found anything in four months they're not likely to have anything now," Deutsch pointed out, folding his map. "All right, though; we'll be good team players and check in. Then we'll hit your gutted buildings."

"Right." *At least*, Halloran thought, *he's got some-*

thing besides simple win-loss criteria to mull over now. Maybe it'll be enough.

Only as they were heading down the darkened stairway toward the street below did it occur to him that, in his current state, talking to Deutsch about self-sacrifices might not have been the world's smartest thing to do.

Ilona, it turned out, was a walking magcard of information on the Tyler Mansion.

She knew its outer appearance, the prewar layout of its major gardens, and the sizes and approximate locations of some of its rooms. She could sketch the stonework designs on the five-meter-high outer wall, as well as giving the wall's dimensions, and had at least a general idea as to the total area of both house and grounds. It impressed Jonny tremendously until it occurred to him that all her information would have fit quite comfortably in the sort of celebrity-snoop magazines that seemed to exist in one form or another all over the Dominion. The sort of thing both he and an enterprising gate-crasher would have found more useful—security systems, weapons emplacements, and the like—were conspicuous by their absence. Eventually, and regretfully, he decided she was simply one of those avid followers of the Tyler mystique whose existence she'd already hinted at.

Still, he'd been taught how to make inferences from the physical appearance of structures, and even given that his data was second-hand he was able to form a reasonable picture of what Tyler had set up to defend his home.

And the picture wasn't an especially encouraging one.

"The main gate is shaped like this," Ilona said, sketching barely visible lines with her finger on the tabletop. "It's supposed to be electronically locked and made with twenty-centimeter-thick kyrelium steel, same as the interior section of the wall."

Briefly, Jonny tried to calculate how long it would take to punch a hole through that much kyrelium with his antiarmor laser. The number came out on the order of several hours. "Any of the house's fancy stonework on the outer side?"

"Not on the gate itself, but there are two relief carvings flanking it on the wall. About *here* and *here*." She pointed.

Sensor clusters, most likely, and probably weapons as well. Facing inward as well as outward? No way of knowing, but it wasn't likely to matter with twenty centimeters of kyrelium blocking the way. "Well, that only leaves going over the wall," he sighed. "What's he got up there?"

"As far as I know, nothing."

Jonny frowned. "He's got to have *some* defenses up there, Ilona. Five-meter walls haven't been proof against attackers since ladders were invented. Um . . . what about the corners? Any raised stonework or anything there?"

"Nope." She was emphatic. "Nothing but flat wall all the way around the grounds."

Which meant no photoelectric/laser beam setup along the wall. Could Tyler really have left such an obvious loophole in his defenses? Of course, anything coming over the wall could be targeted by the house's lasers, but that approach depended on temperamental and potentially jammable high-speed electronics; and even if they worked properly, a fair amount of the shot was likely to expend its energy on other than the intended target. Sloppy *and* dangerous. No, Tyler must have had something else in mind. But what?

And then a pair of stray facts intersected in Jonny's mind. Tyler had built his mansion along Reginine lines; and Jonny's late teammate, Parr

Noffke, had been from that same world. Had he ever said anything that might provide a clue . . . ?

He had. The day of the trainees' first modest test, the one Jonny had afterward nearly broken Viljo's face over. *Our wall lasers*, Noffke had commented, *point up, not across.*

And then, of course, it was obvious. Obvious and sobering. Instead of four lasers arranged to fire horizontally along the walls, Tyler had literally hundreds of the things lined up together like logs in an old palisade, aiming straight up from inside the wall. A horribly expensive barrier, but one that could defend against low projectiles and ground-hug missiles as well as grappler-equipped intruders. Quick, operationally simple, and virtually foolproof.

And almost undoubtedly the Trofts' planned deathtrap.

Jonny swallowed, the irony of it bitter on his tongue. This was exactly what he'd wanted: some insight into how the aliens expected to stop him . . . and now that he knew, the whole thing looked more hopeless than ever. Unless he could somehow get to the control circuitry for those lasers, there was no way he and Ilona would get beyond the wall without being solidly slagged.

He became aware that Ilona was watching him, a look of strained patience on her face. "Well? Any chance of getting through the gate?"

"I doubt it," Jonny shook his head. "But we won't have to. Up and over is a far better bet."

"Up and over? You mean climb a five-meter wall?"

"I mean jump it. I think I can manage it without too much trouble." In actual fact the wall's height was the least of their troubles, but there was no point telling the hidden listeners that.

"What about the defenses you said might be there?"

"Shouldn't pose any real problem," Jonny lied, again for the Trofts' benefit. He didn't dare appear *too* naive; it might arouse their suspicions. "I suspect Tyler's got his wall lasers built into elevating turrets at the corners. With all that stonework available to hide sensors in, there'd be no problem getting them up in time if someone started to climb in. I haven't seen that sort of arrangement on Adirondack before, but it's a logical extension of your usual defense laser setup, especially for someone with the classical aesthetics Tyler seems to have. Actually, I'm a lot more worried about getting *to* the wall in the first place. I want you to tell me everything you can remember about the route the Trofts used to get you to this room."

She nodded, and as she launched into a listing of rooms, hallways, and staircases, he knew she was satisfied with his spun-sugar theory. Now if only he'd similarly convinced the Trofts to let them get all the way to the deathtrap.

And if he could figure out a way through it.

His internal clock said ten p.m., and it was time to go.

Jonny had been of two minds about choosing a nighttime rather than an afternoon breakout. In the afternoon there would have been people beyond the Tyler Mansion's walls; crowds for the two fugitives to disappear into if they got that far, witnesses perhaps to their deaths—and the mansion's significance—if they didn't. But hiding in crowds made little sense if the Trofts were willing to slaughter civilians in order to get the two of them. Besides, forcing the Trofts' outdoor weaponry to rely on radar, infrared, and light amplification for targeting might prove a minor advantage.

Those were the reasons he gave Ilona. One more—that the aliens might not risk letting them even

get to the wall in broad daylight—he kept to
himself.

He was lying on his back on the table, hands
folded across his chest; Ilona sat beside him, her
knees pulled close to her chest, apparently contem-
plating the door. Ilona's inactivity wasn't an act:
he'd quoted a ten-thirty jump-off time to her.
Whether or not the Trofts could be fooled by so
simple a trick he would probably never know, but
it had certainly been worth a try.

Taking a deep breath, Jonny activated his omni-
directional sonic weapon.

There was a tingle in his gut, a slight vibration
as the buried speakers brushed harmonics of natural body resonances. Straining his ears, he could
almost hear the ultrasonic pitch changing as the
sound dug into the walls, seeking resonances with
the tiny audio and visual sensors open to it. . . .

The full treatment was supposed to require a
minute, but Jonny had no intention of giving the
Trofts that much warning. He didn't need to knock
out the sensors permanently, but just to fog as
many of them as possible while he made his move.
He gave it five seconds; and just as Ilona began
looking around the room with a frown he lifted his
left leg slightly and fired.

The upper hinge of the door literally exploded,
scattering solid and semisolid bits of itself in a
shower to the floor. Beside him, Ilona yelped with
surprise; in a single smooth motion, Jonny slid
forward so that he could target the lower hinge
and fired again. This shot didn't hit the inner sections quite as cleanly, and the explosive vaporiza-
tion that had taken out the upper hinge didn't
occur. Jonny fired three more times, adding his
fingertip lasers to the assault, and within seconds
the hinge was dangling loosely against the wall.
Gripping the edge of the table, he hurled himself
feet-first at the hinge side of the door like a self-

guided battering ram. The door creaked under the
impact, displaced by a centimeter or two. Regaining his balance, Jonny jumped across the room,
turned and tried it again, his hands providing a
last-second boost from the table as he passed it.
The table survived; the door, fortunately, did not.
With a shriek of scraping metal, it popped out of
its frame and sagged at an odd angle, held off the
floor only by its lock mechanism.

"You said ten-*thirty*," Ilona growled. She was
already at the door by the time he got his balance,
peering cautiously outside.

"I got impatient," Jonny returned, joining her.
"Looks clear enough; come on."

Stepping past the ruined door, they headed out
into a dimly lit hallway. Enhancers on full, Jonny
scanned the walls and floor quickly as he led Ilona
in a quick jog. Nothing seemed to be there—

They were nearly on top of it when Jonny spotted the slight discoloration in the wall that indicated a disguised photocell at knee height. "Detector!" he snapped, slowing to let Ilona catch up.
Pointing it out would have taken unnecessary time;
grabbing her upper arms, he swung her over the
invisible beam and then jumped over himself. *Too
easy*, he thought uncomfortably. *Far too easy*. He
knew the Trofts wanted him to get through their
gauntlet alive, but this was ridiculous.

It stopped being ridiculous at the end of the
hall.

Jonny paused there, at the threshold of a large
room; but neither a complete stop nor a full-speed
sprint would have done him a scrap of good. Flanking the hallway exit were two quarter-circles of
armored Trofts.

Stepping back into the hallway would have been
no more than a temporary solution. Shoving Ilona
back into that modest protection, he bent his knees
and jumped.

The ceiling here wasn't as sturdy as the one back in Freyr Complex's Room C-662, the one Bai had first demonstrated on. But it was sturdy enough, and Jonny hit the floor with balance intact and only a minor snowstorm of shattered ceiling tiles accompanying him. Hit the floor, twisted . . . and as the Troft lasers began to track, he threw himself spinning onto his shoulderblades.

Bai had called the maneuver a *break*, for obscure historical reasons; the trainees had privately dubbed it the *backspin*. Curled up in a half-fetal position, knees tucked almost to his chest, Jonny's antiarmor laser swept the line of soldiers, flashing instant death. Only three of the dozen or so soldiers escaped that first salvo, and they died on Jonny's second spin.

The metallic clink of armor-clad bodies hitting floor had barely ceased before Jonny was back in a crouch, eyes darting around. "Ilona!" he stage-whispered. "Come on." Peering into the hall, he saw her leap to her feet and trot toward him.

"Good Lord!" she gasped. "Was all of that *you?*"

"All of it that counted." Which proved all by itself he'd been right about the Trofts' plan. He should at least have picked up some light burns from that exchange. "That door?"

"Right. Remember that it's a stairway."

"Got it."

Like the hallway, the stairs proved to be free of major threats. Probably, Jonny decided, whatever sensors it contained were designed to study his equipment immediately after use, perhaps looking for theoretical limits or emission signatures. Triggering his sonic again, he led Ilona around the two photocells the stairway contained and braced himself for whatever he would find above.

The Trofts' first try had been a straightforward attack. This one was only marginally more subtle. Stretched across the floor, between the fugitives and the room's only exit, was a three-meter-wide black band. Jonny sniffed, caught a wiff of the same smell he remembered from the net at the Wolker Plant. "Glue patch," he warned Ilona, searching the walls with his eyes. A vertical strip of photocells stretched from floor to ceiling at either end of the adhesive; six almost-flat boxes adorned the walls beyond. Unlike the more permanent-looking photocells back in the hall and stairway, this trap had the air of having been hastily set up for the occasion.

Ilona, for a change, was right with him on this one. "So we jump and get hit by something while we're in mid-air?" she murmured tensely.

"Looks like it." Jonny stepped to the side wall near the adhesive and extended his right arm. "I'll try some simple sabotage. Get back into the stairwell, just in case."

His arcthrower flashed even as she obeyed ... and he discovered just how badly he'd underestimated the Troft ability to learn.

Across the room one of the flat boxes abruptly disintegrated before a spinning mass that shot out directly toward him. The mass flattened as it came, its spin unfolding it into a giant mesh net.

He had no time then to regret having demonstrated his arcthrower's range a few hours previously; no time to do anything but get out of the way fast.

And his programmed reflexes did their best. Dropping him toward the floor, his servos threw him in a flat dive at right angles to the net's line of motion. But the room was too small, the net too big; and even as he somersaulted into the wall near the stairway door, the edge of the mesh caught his left shoulder, pinning him to the floor.

Ilona was out of her shelter like a shot. "You all right?" she asked, hurrying toward him.

He waved her away and twisted up on one elbow.

Cutting the mesh would perhaps be simplest, but
if the glue contained a contact soporific again, he
didn't want to risk carrying a patch of it along
with them. Bracing himself, he jerked abruptly,
tearing the trapped sleeve neatly off at the shoulder.

"Now what?" Ilona asked as he scrambled to his
feet.

"We give up on the subtle approach. Get ready
to move." Sequentially targeting the remaining
five wall boxes, he raised his hands and fired.

He was half afraid the attack would trigger the
firing mechanisms instead of destroying them. But
as each box shattered and the briefly lingering
laser beam swept the coiled net behind, it began
to look like the Trofts had missed a bet. Until he
noticed the pale brown smoke rising from the burning nets. . . .

"Hold your breath!" he snapped at Ilona. Stepping to her side, he grabbed her in a shoulder-and-
thigh grip and jumped.

Not simply across the adhesive strip, but all the
way to the door at the other end of the room. A
potentially disastrous maneuver, but the Trofts fortunately had not hooked any more booby-traps to
their photocell strip. The door was closed, but
Jonny had no intention of pausing to see whether
or not it was locked: he landed on his left foot, his
right already snapping out in a servo-powered kick
beside the doorknob. The panel shattered with grati-
fying ease, and—still carrying Ilona—he charged
on through.

The room beyond was much smaller and, like
the others he'd encountered so far, completely bar-
ren of furniture. It would have been nice to pause
at the threshold and check for traps, but with
expanding clouds of unknown gas in the room just
behind, that was a luxury he couldn't afford.
Instead, he took the whole five meters at a dead
run, avoiding a straight-line path to the door oppo-

site but otherwise relying solely on his combat reflexes to get them through safely.

And whatever the Trofts had set up, they apparently were taken by surprise by his maneuver. Reaching the door unscathed, he wrenched it open and slipped through, dropping Ilona back to the floor and slamming the door behind them. They were, as Jonny had expected, in the middle of a long hallway. Snapping his hands into firing position, he gave the place a quick survey, then focused again on Ilona. "You okay?"

"The bruises from this are going to be interesting," she said, reaching around to rub her rear where he'd been gripping her. "Otherwise okay. I came in that way—second door from the end, I think."

"I hope you're right." It wasn't a trivial point; Trofts routinely sealed off interior doors in buildings they took over, and a wrong turn could put them into a section of maze Ilona knew nothing at all about. At least it *was* a hallway, and therefore—if the Trofts kept to their pattern so far—presumably not booby-trapped. The breather would be nice to have. "Okay; let's go."

And with his attention on the walls, his assumptions firmly in mind, he nearly lost it all right there and then.

It started as a humming in his gut, similar to that caused by his own sonic weaponry, and it was pure luck that they were nearly to a node of the standing wave when he finally woke up to what was happening and skidded to an abrupt halt. "What?" Ilona gasped as she bumped into him.

"Infrasonic attack," he snapped. The humming had become a wave of nausea now, and his head was beginning to throb. "Hallway's a resonance cavity. We're standing at a node."

"Can't stay here," she managed, sagging against him and gripping her own stomach.

"I know. Hang on." There were only seconds, he estimated, before they were both too sick to move, and unfortunately the Trofts had left him only one option for a response. He'd hoped to keep at least one weapon out of their view on this trip, but with no indication where their infrasonic generator was located, his lasers were useless. Clutching the unsteady Ilona to his side, out of the direct line of fire, he activated his sonic disruptor and began sweeping the ends of the hallway.

Either he was very lucky or—more likely—the Trofts had again set him up with an easy victory, because in barely four seconds the sonic beam had hit on the resonance frequency for something in the Trofts' generator. Gritting his teeth—fully aware the sonic hadn't been designed for spaces this big— Jonny held the beam steady as his nanocomputer increased amplitude ... and abruptly the nausea began fading. Within a dozen heartbeats all that remained of the attack were weak knees and residual aches throughout his body.

"Come on, we've got to keep going," he told Ilona thickly, stumbling toward the door she'd pointed out earlier.

"Yeah," she agreed, and did her best to comply. He wound up mostly carrying her anyway, a task that would have been impossible without his servos. Reaching the door, he pulled it open.

The Trofts had gone back to being unsubtle. This room, unlike all the previous ones, was almost literally loaded with furniture ... and behind each piece seemed to be an enemy soldier.

It occurred to Jonny in that first frozen millisecond that deviating from Ilona's remembered path might well be disastrous, if for no other reason than panicking the Troft commander. But there was no way he was going to willingly face a roomful of enemies if another possibility existed ... or could be made.

A single, untuned blast from his sonic was all he had time for before slamming the door to; with luck, it would jar them at least enough to slow any pursuit. Grabbing Ilona's arm, he sprinted to the next door, the last one at this end of the hall.

"This isn't the way I came!" she yelped as he let go and tried the door. It was locked, of course.

"No choice. Hit the ground and yell if you see anyone coming." His fingertip lasers were already spitting destruction at the door's edges, tracing a dashed-line pattern that would yield maximum weakening in minimum time. Halfway through he kicked hard at the door; finishing it, he kicked again. With the second kick he felt it give, and four kicks later the panel abruptly shattered. Ilona right behind him, he ducked through.

And it was instantly clear they were off the path so carefully set up for them. No human-style furniture or equipment here—from floor to ceiling the room was jarringly alien. Long, oddly shaped couches lay grouped around what looked like circular tables with hemispherical domes rising from their centers. On the walls were almost archaic-looking murals alternating with smaller bits of gleaming electronics. Across the room Jonny got just a glimpse of a Troft back-jointed leg as the alien beat a hasty retreat . . . and in the relative silence a sound heretofore conspicuous by its absence could be heard: the thin ululating wail of a Troft alarm.

"Dining room?" Ilona asked, glancing around.

"Lounge." A minor disappointment; he'd rather hoped they would wind up somewhere his arc-thrower could be put to use. The control room for the wall defenses, for example.

On the other hand . . .

"Let's get going," Ilona urged, throwing apprehensive glances at the ruined door behind them. "That crowd will be on our backs any minute."

"Just a second," Jonny told her, scanning the walls. Trofts always put lounges and other noncritical facilities on the outer edges of their bases ... and, half-hidden by the murals, he finally spotted what he was looking for: the outline of a window.

Well boarded up, of course. A dark sheet of kyrelium steel, three meters by one, fitted precisely into the opening, leaving only a hairline crack in the otherwise featureless slate-gray wall. Unbreakable with even Cobra weaponry; but if the designer had followed standard Troft building reinforcement procedures, there might be a chance of getting off this treadmill right here. "Get ready to follow," he called to Ilona over his shoulder. Leaning hard into the floor, he charged the window and jumped, turning feet first in midair and hitting the window shield dead center.

The panel popped neatly from its casing and clattered to the ground outside. Jonny, much of his momentum lost, landed considerably closer to the building. Dropping into a crouch, he activated his light amp equipment and looked quickly around him.

He was in what had probably once been an extensive flower bed, extending most of the way out to where the stunted bushes and trees of an elaborate haiku garden began, the latter shifting in turn to a band of full-sized trees near the outer wall. No cover until the trees—Jonny's rangefinder set the distance at about fifty-two meters. The wall itself ... thirty meters further.

Behind him came a noise. He twisted around, vaguely aware that the action hurt, to see Ilona jump lightly to the ground. "That was one beaut of a kick," she hissed as she joined him in his crouch.

"Not really. The edges are beveled against impacts from the outside only. Any idea where we are?"

"West side of the house. Gate's around to the north."

"Never mind the gate—we can go over the wall just as easily here." A corner of Jonny's mind considered the possibility that the Trotts had spy-mikes on them. "First, though," he added for their benefit, "I want to see if the house lasers are set to fire on outgoing targets."

Still no sign of enemy soldiers. Moving to the former window cover, he hefted the metal for a quick examination. Kyrelium steel, all right, about five centimeters thick. He had no idea whether it would do for what he had in mind, but there was no time left to find anything better. Bracing himself firmly, he gripped the panel on either side, raised it over his head like a makeshift umbrella . . . and with everything his servos could manage, he hurled it toward the distant wall.

He'd never gone to the limit in quite this way, and for a long, horrifying moment he was afraid he'd thrown the panel too hard. If it cleared the wall—and in the process ruined his pretense of ignorance as to the defensive lasers there—

But he actually had nothing to fear. The panel arced smoothly into the sky and dropped with a crash of breaking branches into the middle of the distant patch of forest, a good twenty meters in from the wall.

And it made the whole trip without drawing any fire.

Jonny licked his lips. So the automatics would most likely leave them alone. Would the live gunners who were undoubtedly up there abstain as well? There was nothing he could do about that but hope that they were still relying on the wall itself to ultimately stop him. If they were . . . and if his plan worked . . .

"Ready for a run?" he whispered to Ilona.

Her eyes were still on the spot where the kyrelium

plate had ended its flight. "Phrij and a half," she muttered. "Uh—yeah, I'm ready. Toward the wall?"

"Right. As fast as you can. I'll be behind you where I can theoretically handle anyone who tries to stop us." One final look around— "okay; *go*."

She took off like the entire Troft war machine was after her, running in a half-crouched posture that offered at best an illusion of relative safety. Jonny let her lead him by perhaps five meters, enhanced vision and hearing alert for any sound of pursuit. But the Tyler Mansion might have been deserted for all the response they drew from it. *All lined up on the balcony to watch us slag ourselves, no doubt*, he thought, recognizing as he did so that the strain was beginning to affect him. *A few more seconds*, he told himself over and over,the words settling into the quick rhythm of his footsteps. *A few more seconds and it'll be over.*

At the edge of the forest he put on a burst of speed, catching up to Ilona a few steps later. "Wait a second—I have to find that kyrelium plate."

"What?" she gasped. "Why?"

"Don't ask questions. There it is."

Not surprisingly, the heavy metal was undamaged. Jonny picked it up and balanced it like an oversized door in front of him, searching for the best and safest handholds.

"What . . . you . . . doing?"

"Getting us out of here. Come here—stand in front of me. Come *here*."

She obeyed, stepping between him and the plate. "Arms around my neck—hold on tight . . . now wrap your legs around my waist . . . okay. Hold *tight*, whatever happens. Got it?"

"Yeah." Even muffled by his chest, her voice sounded scared. Perhaps she had a glimmering of what was about to happen.

Twenty meters to the wall. Jonny backed up another ten, getting the feel of the extra weight distribution as he gave himself room for a running start. "Here we go," he told Ilona. "Hang on—"

The whine of the servos was louder in his ears than even the thudding of his pulse as his feet dug deeper into the dirt with each step and his speed increased. Eight steps, nine steps—almost fast enough—*ten* steps—

And an instant later his knees straightened to send them soaring upward.

It was a move Jonny had practiced over and over again back on Asgard: a high-jumper's roll, designed to take him horizontally over whatever barrier stood in his way. Horizontal, face downward, he neared both the top of his arc and the deadly wall . . . and an instant before reaching them, he let go of the plate now directly beneath him and wrapped his arms tightly around Ilona.

The flash was incredibly bright, especially considering that all he was seeing was the fraction of laser light reflected from the underside of the kyrelium plate to the surrounding landscape. There was a rapid-fire cracking sound of heat-stressed metal against the brief hiss of explosive ablation— and then they were past the wall, and Jonny was twisting to bring them upright as they arced toward the ground.

He almost made it, hitting at an angle that probably would have ruined both ankles without his bone and ligament reinforcement. Recovering his balance, he tightened his hold on Ilona and started to run.

He got halfway to the nearest building before the Trofts recovered from their surprise and began firing. Laser blasts licked at his sides and heels as he zigzagged across the open ground. *I guess you're going to get one more datapoint,* he thought in their direction; and, again pushing his leg servos to the limit, he took the last twenty meters in an all-out sprint. One second later they were around the building's corner and out of range.

Jonny kept running, aiming for a second deserted factory a short block away. "Any suggestions as to a hiding place?" he called to Ilona over the wind.

She didn't even bother to raise her face from his shoulder. "Just keep going," she said, and even with the jolting of their run, he could feel her violent shiver.

He ran on, changing direction periodically, searching for a section of the city he could recognize. A kilometer or so later he found a familiar intersection and turned north, heading for one of the underground's secure phones. They were still a block away when the sound of approaching aircraft became audible. Jonny estimated distances and speeds, decided not to risk it, and stepped to the nearest doorway. It was locked, of course: but after what they'd just been through, a locked door was hardly worth noticing. Seconds later, they were inside.

"Are we safe here?" Ilona asked as Jonny set her down. Rubbing her ribs, she peered out the mesh-protected front window.

"Not really, but it'll have to do for the moment." Jonny found a chair and sat down, wincing as he did so. With the danger temporarily at arm's length he finally had time to notice the condition of his own body, and it was clear he wasn't as unscathed as he'd thought. At least five minor burns stung spots on arms and torso, evidence of Troft near-misses. His left ankle felt like it was on fire from the heat leakage buildup of his own antiarmor laser—one of the design flaws, he realized, that Bai had warned them to expect. Sore muscles and bruises seemed to be everywhere, and in several places he couldn't tell whether the clammy wetness of his clothing was due to sweat or oozing blood. "We'll have to wait until the aircraft over-head settle into a pattern I can thread, but then I should be able to get to a phone and alert the underground. They'll figure out where to stash you while I go back to the mansion."

"While you *what?*" She spun around to face him, her expression echoing the odd intensity in her voice.

"While I go back," he repeated. "You didn't know it, but the only reason they let us go was to collect data on my equipment in action. I have to try and get hold of those tapes."

"That's suicidal!" she snapped. "The whole phrijing nest of them will be running around by now."

"Running around out *here*, looking for us," he reminded her. "The mansion itself may not be well defended for a while, and if I'm fast enough I may be able to catch them off guard. Anyway, I've got to at least try."

She seemed about to say something, pursed her lips. "In that case . . . you probably can't take the time to go call the underground, either. If you're going back, you'd better do it right away."

Jonny stared at her. No argument, no real pro-test . . . and suddenly it occurred to him he really knew nothing at all about her. "Where did you say you lived?" he asked.

"I didn't say. What does *that* have to do with anything?"

"Nothing, really . . . except that I've just noticed I'm at a distinct disadvantage here. *You* know that I'm a Cobra, and therefore which side I'm on. But I don't know the same about you."

She stared at him for a long moment . . . and when she spoke again the usual sardonic under-tone was gone from her voice. "Are you suggesting I'm a Troft hireling?" she asked quietly.

"You tell me. All I know about you is what you

yourself said—including how exactly you came to be tossed in my cell. Sure, the Trofts *could* have plucked a random citizen off the streets, but they'd have done a lot better to use someone who could be trusted to pressure me if I still refused to perform for them."

"*Did* I pressure you?"

"No, but then that didn't prove necessary. And now you're encouraging me to go back alone, without even calling for underground backup forces."

"If I were a spy, wouldn't I *want* you to get me to the underground?" she encountered. "I imagine the Trofts would like to get a solid line on the resistance. And as to encouraging you to go back alone—well, I admit I'm no expert on tactics, but doesn't it seem likely that before your backup forces got organized the Trofts would be back inside and braced for the attack?"

"You've got an answer for everything, don't you?" he growled. "All right. Let's hear *your* suggestion on what I should do with you."

Her eyes narrowed slightly. "Meaning . . .?"

"If you're a spy I don't want you anywhere near the underground. Nor can I let you loose to tip off the Trofts that I'm coming."

"Well, I'm *not* going back to the mansion with you," she said emphatically.

"I'm not offering. What I guess I'll have to do is tie you up here until I get back."

A muscle twitched in her jaw. "And if you don't?"

"You'll be found by the shop's owner in the morning."

"Or by the Trofts sooner," she said softly. "The patrols looking for us, remember?"

And if she wasn't a spy . . . they'd kill her rather than let word of their mansion HQ get out. "Can you prove you're not a spy?" he asked, feeling new sweat break out on his forehead as he sensed the box closing tightly around his options.

"In the next thirty seconds? Don't be silly." She took a deep breath. "No, Jonny. If you want any chance at all of hitting the mansion tonight, you'll just have to accept my story or reject it on faith alone. If your suspicions are strong enough to justify my death . . . then there's nothing I can really do about it. I suppose it's a question of whether my life's worth risking yours over."

And when put that way, there really wasn't any decision to make. He'd risked his life for her once already . . . and enemy hireling or not, the Trofts had clearly been willing to let her die with him over the wall. "I suggest you find a hiding place before the patrols get here," he growled at her as he moved toward the door. "And watch out for aircraft."

Outside, the sound of thrusters was adequately distant. Without looking back, he slipped out into the night and headed back toward the Tyler Mansion, wondering if he'd just made the last stupid mistake of his life.

It was a much slower trip than before, with aircraft and vehicles forcing him to take cover with increasing frequency the closer he got to his target. Enough so that by the time he finally came within sight of the mansion's outer wall the basic tactical reasoning behind this solo effort was becoming shaky. Nearly three-quarters of an hour had passed since their escape—enough time for the Trofts to begin worrying about a raid and to have drawn their troops back to defensive positions. All around him Jonny's enhanced hearing was starting to pick up a faint background of moving bodies and equipment, all interspersed with the mandible clack of the Trofts' so-called catertalk, as the aliens began barricading the approaches to their base. Forced at last to abandon the ground, Jonny slipped into one of the neighborhood's abandoned buildings, working his way cautiously to an upper floor and a window facing the mansion. With light amps at full power, he studied the scene below.

And knew he'd lost.

The Trofts were everywhere: blocking streets, guarding rooftops and windows, setting up laser emplacements at the base of the wall itself. Beyond them, he could see aircraft drifting over the far wall to join others parked around the mansion. The cordon meant the Trofts were giving up any further hope of disguising their presence in the mansion; the aircraft implied they were preparing to abandon it. A few hours—a day or two at the most—and they would be gone, their tapes of his escape gone with them. Until then—

Until then, the wall's defense lasers would have to be periodically shut down to let the aircraft in and out.

With most of the armed troops *out*side the wall.

An intriguing thought . . . but offhand he couldn't see any way to take advantage of it. With the Troft cordon strengthening almost by the minute, getting to the wall was becoming well-nigh impossible. As a matter of fact, it wasn't even certain anymore that he'd be able to sneak *out* without being spotted and slagged. *I shouldn't have come back*, he thought morosely. *Now I'm stuck here until the ground clutter clears out.*

He was just starting to turn away when a building off to the left emitted a cloud of fire from its base and began collapsing into itself. The thunderclap of the explosion had barely reached him when the streets below abruptly came alive with the stutter-flash of multiple laser weapons.

The unexpectedness of it froze him at the window . . . but for now the *how* of it would keep. He was really too exposed to risk drawing attention with his lasers, but there were other ways he could join the battle.

He watched a few seconds longer, fixing the

layout and specific Troft positions in his mind. Then, moving back from the window, he set about collecting the odd chunks of masonry earlier battles in this region had shaken from the walls. Thrown with Cobra accuracy, they could be almost as deadly as grenades.

He was still busily clearing the street of Trofts when a second explosion lit up the sky. Looking up, he was just in time to see the red afterglow fading from an upper window of the Tyler Mansion.

An hour later, the battle was over.

Swathed in bandages and IV tubes, Halloran looked more like something out of an archeological dig than a living person. But what was visible of his face looked happier than Jonny had seen it in months. As well it might, considering the lousy odds all three Cobras had somehow managed to survive. "When we get off this rock," Jonny told the other, "remind me to have you and Imel sent up for a complete psych exam. You're both genuinely crazy."

"What—because we pulled the same stupid trick you were going to try?" Halloran asked innocently.

"Stupid trick, nothing," Deutsch retorted from the bed next to Halloran's. Only a few bandages graced his form, mute testimony to superior luck or skill. "We were practically on top of the place when you and Ilona made your break, close enough that we were actually inside their temporary picket ring when they all charged out after you. It was perfectly straightforward, tactically—it was just the implementation that got a bit sticky."

"Sticky, my eyeteeth. *Some* of us lost a lot of skin in there." Halloran jerked his head in Deutsch's direction. "Now *him* you're welcome to have sent up. You should've seen the chances he took in there. Not to mention the way he stared down

Borg and got everyone on the streets looking for you."

Which, with a little unconscious help from the Trofts, was what had ultimately saved Jonny's life. He wondered if the aliens had had any idea what Ilona was really doing out there when they'd grabbed her. "I owe you both a lot," he said, knowing how inadequate the words were. "Thank you."

Deutsch waved a hand in dismissal. "Forget it—you'd have done the same for us. Besides, it was pretty much of a group effort, what with half of the Cranach underground taking their share of the risks."

"Including broadcasting the location of that hidden tunnel entrance to us as soon as Ilona phoned in the details," Halloran added. "I don't suppose they mentioned that one to you?—no, I didn't think so. Now *that* was a stupid trick. They're damn lucky the Trofts were too busy to trace the transmission—they certainly had the equipment to do so. I think the whole planet's going to need psychiatric help by the time this is over."

Jonny smiled along with them, hiding the twinge of embarrassment that still accompanied references to Ilona's part in the South Sector underground's counterattack on the Tyler Mansion. "Speaking of Ilona, she's supposed to give me a ride to the new home Ama's moved me to," he told them. "You guys take it easy, and I'll be back to give you a hand when you're ready to move."

"No rush," Halloran told him airily. "These people treat me with a lot more respect than you two clowns, anyway."

"He's definitely on the mend," Deutsch snorted. "Get going, Jonny; no point in keeping Ilona waiting for *this*."

Ilona was waiting inside the building foyer. "All set?" she asked briskly. "Let's go, then—they're expecting you in a few minutes, and you know how nervous we get when schedules aren't met."

She led the way outside to a car parked by the curb. They got in and she headed north . . . and for the first time since their escape two days earlier they were alone together.

Jonny cleared his throat. "So . . . how's the sifting at the mansion going?"

She glanced at him. "Not too bad. Cally and Imel and that East Sector team left a shambles, but we've found a lot of interesting items the Trofts didn't have time to destroy. I'd say that we've gotten far better than an even trade for those records of Jonny Moreau in action."

"No sign of them, huh?"

"No, but it hardly matters. They'd almost certainly have transmitted the data elsewhere as soon as we escaped."

"Oh, I know. But I'd hoped that if we had the original tapes we could figure out exactly how much they'd learned about our gear and be able to estimate the added danger we'll be working under."

"Ah. Yes, I guess that makes sense. I don't think you're going to have anything to worry about, though."

Johnny snorted. "You underestimate the Trofts' ingenuity. Like you very nearly underestimated my kind heart. You could've *told* me you were with the underground, you know."

He was expecting her to come out with some stiff and wholly inappropriate local security regulation; and so her reply, when it finally came, was something of a surprise. "I could have," she acknowledged. "And if you'd looked like you were making the wrong decision I sure would have. But . . . you'd jumped to a rather paranoid conclusion without any real evidence, and I . . . well, I wanted to find out how far you'd go in acting on that conclusion." She took a deep breath. "You see,

Jonny, whether you know it or not, all of us who work and fight with you Cobras are more than a little afraid of you. There've been persistent rumors since you first landed that you'd been given carte blanche by Asgard to do anything you considered necessary to drive the Trofts off—including summary execution for any offense you decided you didn't like."

Jonny stared at her. "That's absurd."

"Is it? The Dominion can't exercise control over you from umpteen light-years away, and *we* sure can't do it. If you've got the power anyway why *not* make it official?"

"Because—" Jonny floundered. "Because that's not the way to liberate Adirondack."

"Depends on whether that's really Asgard's major objective, doesn't it? If they're more interested in breaking the Trofts' war capabilities, our little world is probably pretty expendable."

Jonny shook his head. "No. I realize it's hard to tell from here, but I know for a fact that the Cobras aren't on Adirondack to win anything at the expense of the people. If you knew the screening they put us through—and how many good men were bounced even *after* the training—"

"Sure, I understand all that. But military goals *do* change." She shrugged. "But with any luck the whole question will soon be academic."

"What do you mean?"

She favored him with a tight smile. "We got an off-world signal this morning. All underground and Cobra units are to immediately begin a pre-invasion sabotage campaign."

Jonny felt his mouth drop open. "Pre-invasion?"

"That's what they said. And if it succeeds . . . we owe the Cobras a lot, Jonny, and we won't forget you. But I don't think we'll be sorry to see you go, either."

To that Jonny had no reply, and the rest of the

trip was made in silence. Ilona drove several blocks
past Jonny's old apartment building, stopping finally before another, even more nondescript place.
A tired-eyed woman greeted him at the door and
took him to a top-floor apartment, where his mea-
ger belongings had already been delivered. On top
of the bags was a small envelope.

Frowning, Jonny opened it. Inside was a plain
piece of paper with a short, painstakingly written
note:

Dear Jonny,
    Mom says you're going somewhere else now
and aren't going to be staying with us anymore.
Please be careful and don't get caught anymore and come back to see me. I love you.
                                        Danice

Jonny smiled as he slipped the note back into its
envelope. *You be careful, too, Danice,* he thought.
Maybe you, at least, will remember us kindly.

Interlude

The negotiations were over, the treaty was signed, ratified, and being implemented, and the euphoric haze that had pervaded the Central Committee's meetings for the past two months was finally starting to fade. Vanis D'arl had expected Committé H'orme to pick this point to bring up the Cobras again; and he was right.

"It's not a question of ingratitude or injustice—it's a question of pure necessity," the Committé told the assembly, his voice quavering only slightly. Seated behind him, D'arl eyed H'orme's back uneasily, seeing in his stance the older man's fatigue. He wondered if the others knew how much the war had taken out of H'orme ... wondered whether they would consequently recognize the urgency implied by his being here to deliver this message personally.

From their faces, though, it was obvious most of them didn't, an attitude clearly shown by the first person to rise when H'orme had finished. "If you'll forgive the tone, H'orme," the other said with a perfunctory gesture of respect, "I think the Committee has heard quite enough of your preoccupation with the Cobras. If you'll recall, it was at your insistence that we directed the Army to offer them exceptionally liberal reenlistment terms, and in your place *I* would consider it a victory that over seventy percent chose to accept. We've all heard from Commander Mendro and his associates just how much of their equipment the other twenty-odd percent will take back to civilian life with them, and we've concluded the Army's plans are acceptable. To again suggest now that we force those men to remain in the Army strikes me as a bit . . . overconcerned."

Or paranoid, as the word will be interpreted, D'arl thought. But H'orme had one tacnuke yet in reserve, and as the Committé picked up a magcard from his stack, D'arl knew he was about to set it off. "I remember Commander Mendro's visits quite well, thank you," he addressed the other Committé with a nod, "and I've done some checking on the facts and figures he presented." Dropping the magcard into his reader, he keyed to the first of his chosen sections and sent the picture to the other viewers around the table. "You will note here the percentage of Cobra trainees that were actually commissioned and sent into the war, displayed as a function of time. The different colors refer to the continually updated initial screening tests the Army used."

A few frowns began to appear. "You're saying they never got more than eighty-five percent into the field?" a Committé halfway around the table spoke up. "The number *I* remember is ninety-seven percent."

"That's the number that were *physically* able to go after training," H'orme told her. "The rest of them were dropped for psychosociological reasons."

"So?" someone else shrugged. "No testing method's ever perfect. As long as they caught all of the unacceptable ones—"

"I expect H'orme's point is whether or not they

did catch all of them," another Committé suggested
dryly.

"A simple check of eyewitness accounts from
Silvern and Adirondack—"

"Will take months to complete," H'orme interrupted. "But there's more. Dismiss, if you'd like,
the possibility of antisocial leanings in any of the
Cobras. Are you aware they'll be taking their combat nanocomputers back with them?—with *no*
reprogramming?"

All eyes turned to him. "What are you talking
about? Mendro said . . ." The speaker paused.

"Mendro deflected the question exceptionally
well," H'orme said grimly. "The fact of the matter
is that the nanocomputers are read-only and can't
be reprogrammed, and after being in place even a
short time they can't be removed without excessive trauma to the brain tissue that's subsequently
settled in around them."

"Why weren't we told?"

"Initially, I presume, because the Army wanted
the Cobras and was afraid we'd veto or modify
their chosen design. More recently, the point was
probably not brought up because there wasn't anything anyone could do about it."

All of which, D'arl knew, was only partly correct.
All the data on the nanocomputers *had* been in the
original Cobra proposals, had anyone besides
H'orme deemed it worth digging out. Perhaps
H'orme was saving that fact for future leverage.

The discussion raged back and forth for a while,
and long before it was over the remaining air of
euphoria had vanished from the chamber. But if
the new sense of realism raised D'arl's hopes, the
end result dashed them again. By a nineteen to
eleven vote, the Committee chose not to interfere
with the Cobra demobilization.

"You should know by now that clear-cut victo-
ries are as rare as oxygen worlds," H'orme chided

D'arl later in his office. "We got them thinking—*really* thinking—and at this stage that's as much as we could have hoped for. The Committee will be watching the Cobras carefully now, and if action turns out to be necessary, it'll take a minimum amount of prodding to get it."

"All of which could've been avoided if they'd just paid attention to the Cobra project in the first place," D'arl muttered.

"No one can pay attention to *every*thing," H'orme shrugged. "Besides, there's an important psychological effect operating here. Most of the Dominion sees the military and the government as essentially two parts of a single monolithic structure, and whether they admit it or not the Committee carries a remnant of that assumption in its collective subconscious. You and I, who grew up on Asgard, have what I think is a more realistic perspective on exactly where and to what extent the military's goals differ from ours. They conceived the Cobras with the sole purpose of winning a war in mind, and every bit of their training and equipment—including the nanocomputer design—made sense within those limited parameters. What the Committee should have done, but didn't, was to remember that all wars eventually end. Instead, we assumed the Army had already done that thinking for us."

D'arl tapped two fingers on the arm of his chair. "Maybe next time they'll know better."

"Possibly. But I doubt it." H'orme leaned back in his chair with a tired sigh. "Anyway, this is the situation we have to live with. What do you suggest as our next move?"

D'arl pursed his lips. H'orme had been doing this a lot lately, and whether it was due to simple mental fatigue or a conscious effort to sharpen the younger man's executive capabilities, it was a bad sign. Very soon now, D'arl knew, H'orme's hot seat was going to pass to him. "We should obtain a listing of all returning Cobras and their destinations," he told H'orme. "Then we should set up local and regional data triggers to funnel all government—accessible news concerning them directly to you, with special flags for criminal or other abnormal behavior."

H'orme nodded. "Agreed. Have someone—Joromo, maybe—get started on it."

"Yes, sir." D'arl stood up. "I think, though, that I'll do this one personally. I want to make sure it's done right."

A ghost of a smile flicked across H'orme's lips. "You humor an old man's obsession, D'arl, and I appreciate it. But I think you'll find—you *and* the rest of the Committee—that the Cobras are going to have far more impact on the Dominion than even I'm afraid of." He turned his chair to gaze out the window at the city below. "I just wish," he added softly, "I knew what form that impact was going to take."

Veteran: 2407

The late-afternoon sunlight glinted whitely off the distant mountains as the shuttle came to rest with only a slight bounce. Army-issue satchel slung over his shoulder, Jonny stepped out onto the landing pad, eyes darting everywhere. He had never been all that familiar with Horizon City, but even to him it was obvious the place had changed. There were half a dozen new buildings visible from the Port, and one or two older ones had disappeared. The landscaping around the area had been redone with what looked like newly imported off-world varities, as if the city were making a concerted effort to shake off its frontier-world status. But the wind was blowing in from the north, across the plains and forests that were as yet untouched by man, and with it came the sweet-sour aroma that no cultural aspirations could disguise. Three years ago, Jonny would hardly have noticed the scent; now, it was almost as if Horizon itself had contrived to welcome him home.

Taking a deep breath of the perfume, he stepped off the pad and walked the hundred meters to a long, one-story building labeled "Horizon Customs: Entry Point." Opening the outer door, he stepped inside.

A smiling man awaited him by a waist-high counter. "Hello, Mr. Moreau; welcome back to Horizon. I'm sorry—should I call you 'Cee-three Moreau'?"

" 'Mister' is fine," Jonny smiled. "I'm a civilian now."

"Of course, of course," the man said. He was still smiling, but there seemed to be just a trace of tension behind the geniality. "And glad of it, I suppose. I'm Harti Bell, the new head of customs here. Your luggage is being brought from the shuttle. In the meantime, I wonder if I might inspect your satchel? Just a formality, really."

"Sure." Jonny slid the bag off his shoulder and placed it on the counter. The faint hum of his servos touched his inner ear as he did so, sounding strangely out of place against the gentle haze of boyhood memories. Bell took the satchel and pulled, as if trying to bring it a few centimeters closer to him. It moved maybe a centimeter; Bell nearly lost his balance. Throwing an odd look at Jonny, he apparently changed his mind and opened the bag where it lay.

By the time he finished, Jonny's two other cases had been brought in. Bell went through them with quick efficiency, made a few notations on his comboard, and finally looked up again, smile still in place.

"All set, Mr. Moreau," he said. "You're free to go."

"Thanks." Jonny put his satchel over his shoulder once more and transferred the other two bags from the counter to the floor. "Is Transcape Rentals still in business? I'll need a car to get to Cedar Lake."

"Sure is, but they've moved three blocks farther east. Want to call a taxi?"

"Thanks; I'll walk." Jonny held out his right hand.

For just a moment the smile slipped. Then, almost warily, Bell took the outstretched hand. He let go as soon as he politely could.

Picking up his bags, Jonny nodded at Bell and left the building.

Mayor Teague Stillman shook his head tiredly as he turned off his comboard and watched page two hundred of the latest land-use proposal disappear from the screen. He would never cease to be amazed at how much wordwork the Cedar Lake city council was able to generate—about a page a year, he'd once estimated, for every one of the town's sixteen thousand citizens. *Either offical magforms have learned how to breed,* he told himself as he rubbed vigorously at his eyes, *or else someone's importing them. Whichever, the Trofts are probably behind it.*

There was a tap on his open door, and Stillman looked up to see Councilor Sutton Fraser standing in the doorway. "Come on in," he invited.

Fraser did so, closing the door behind him. "Too drafty for you?" Stillman asked mildly as Fraser sat down on one of the mayor's guest chairs.

"I got a call a few minutes ago from Harti Bell out at the Horizon Port," Fraser began without preamble. "Jonny Moreau's back."

Stillman stared at the other for a moment, then shrugged slightly. "He had to come eventually. The war's over, after all. Most of the soldiers came back weeks ago."

"Yeah, but Jonny's not exactly an ordinary soldier. Harti said he lifted a satchel that must have weighed thirty kilos with one hand. Effortlessly. The kid could probably tear a building apart if he got mad."

"Relax, Sut. I know the Moreau family. Jonny's a very even-tempered sort of guy."

"*Was*, you mean," Fraser said darkly. "He's been

a Cobra for three years now, killing Trofts and watching them kill his friends. Who knows what that's done to him?"

"Probably instilled a deep dislike for war, if he's like most soldiers. Aside from that, it hasn't done too much, I'd guess."

"You know better than that, Teague. The kid's dangerous; that's a simple fact. Ignoring it isn't going to do you any good."

"Calling him 'dangerous' is? What are you trying to do, start a panic?"

"I doubt that any panic's going to need my help to get started. Everybody in town's seen the idiot plate reports on Our Heroic Forces—they all know how badly the Cobras chewed up the Trofts on Adirondack and Silvern."

Stillman sighed. "Look. I'll admit there may be some problems with Jonny's readjustment to civilian life. Frankly, I would have been happier if he'd stayed in the service. But he didn't. Like it or not, Jonny's home, and we can either accept it calmly or run around screaming doom. He risked his life out there; the least we can do is to give him a chance to forget the war and vanish back into the general population."

"Yeah. Maybe." Fraiser shook his head slowly. "It's not going to be an easy road, though. Look, as long as I'm here, maybe you and I could draft some sort of announcement about this to the press. Try to get a jump on the rumors."

"Good idea. Hey, cheer up, Sut—soldiers have been coming home ever since mankind started having wars. We should be getting the hang of this by now."

"Yeah," Fraser growled. "Except that this is the first time since swords went out of fashion that soldiers have gotten to take their weapons home with them."

Stillman shrugged helplessly. "It's out of our hands. Come on: let's get to work."

Jonny pulled up in front of the Moreau home and turned off the car engine with a sigh of relief. The roads between Horizon City and Cedar Lake were rougher than he remembered them, and more than once he'd wished he had spent the extra money to rent a hover, even though the weekly rate was almost double that for wheeled vehicles. But he'd made it, with a minimum of kidney damage, and that was what mattered.

He stepped out of the car and retrieved his bags from the trunk, and as he set them down on the street a hand fell on his shoulder. He turned and looked five centimeters up into his father's smiling face. "Welcome home Son," Pearce Moreau said.

"Hi, Dader," Jonny said, face breaking into a huge grin as he grasped the other's outstretched hand. "How've you been?"

Pearce's answer was interrupted by a crash and shriek from the front door of the house. Jonny turned to see ten-year-old Gwen tearing across the lawn toward him, yelling like a banshee with a winning lottery ticket. Dropping into a crouch facing her, he opened his arms wide; and as she flung herself at him, he grabbed her around the waist, straightened up, and threw her a half meter into the air above him. Her shrill laughter almost masked Pearce's sharp intake of breath. Catching his sister easily, Jonny lowered her back to the ground. "Boy, you've sure grown," he told her. "Pretty soon you'll be too big to toss around."

"Good," she panted. "Then you can teach me how to arm wrestle. C'mon and see my room, huh, Jonny?"

"I'll be along in a little bit," he told her. "I want to say hello to Momer first. She in the kitchen?"

"Yes," Pearce said. "Why don't you go on ahead, Gwen. I'd like to talk to Jonny for a moment."

"Okay," she chirped. Squeezing Jonny's hand, she scampered back toward the house.

"She's got her room papered with articles and pictures from the past three years," Pearce explained as he and Jonny collected Jonny's luggage. "Everything she could get hard copies of that had anything to do with the Cobras."

"You disapprove?"

"Of what—that she idolizes you? Good heavens, no. Why?"

"You seem a bit nervous."

"Oh. I guess I was a little startled when you tossed Gwen in the air a minute ago."

"I've been using the servos for quite a while now," Jonny pointed out mildly as they headed toward the house. "I really *do* know how to use my strength safely."

"I know, I know. Hell, I used exoskeleton gear myself in the Minthistin War, you know, when I was your age. But it was pretty bulky, and you couldn't ever forget you were wearing it. I guess . . . well, I suppose I was worried that you'd forget yourself."

Jonny shrugged. "Actually, I'm probably in better control than you ever were, since I don't have to have two sets of responses—with power amp and without. The servos and ceramic laminae are going to be with me the rest of my life, and I've long since gotten used to them."

Pearce nodded. "Okay." He paused, then continued, "Look, Jonny, as long as we're on the subject . . . the Army's letter to us said that 'most' of your Cobra gear would be removed before you came home. What did they—I mean, what do you still have?"

Jonny sighed. "I wish they'd just come out and listed the stuff instead of being coy like that. It makes it sound like I'm still a walking tank. The truth is that, aside from the skeletal laminae and servos, all I have is the nanocomputer—which hasn't got much to do now except run the servos— and two small lasers in my little fingers, which they couldn't remove without amputation. And the servo power supply, of course. Everything else— the arcthrower capacitors, the antiarmor laser, and the sonic weapons—are gone." So was the self-destruct, but that subject was best left alone.

"Okay," Pearce said. "Sorry to bring it up, but your mother and I were a little nervous."

"That's all right."

They were at the house now. Entering, they went to the bedroom Jame had had to himself for the last three years. "Where's Jame, by the way?" Jonny asked as he piled his bags by his old bed.

"Out at New Persius picking up a spare laser tube for the bodywork welder down at the shop. We've only got one working at the moment and can't risk it going out on us. Parts have been nearly impossible to get lately—a side effect of war, you know." He snapped his fingers. "Say, those little lasers you have—can you weld with them?"

"I can spot-weld, yes. They were designed to work on metals, as a matter of fact."

"Great. Maybe you could give us a hand until we can get parts for the other lasers. How about it?"

Jonny hesitated. "Uh . . . frankly, Dader, I'd rather not. I don't . . . well, the lasers remind me too much of . . . other things."

"I don't understand," Pearce said, a frown beginning to crease his forehead. "Are you ashamed of what you did?"

"No, of course not. I mean, I knew pretty much what I was getting into when I joined the Cobras, and looking back I think I did as good a job as I could have. It's just . . . this war was different from yours, Dader. A lot different. I was in danger—and was putting other people in danger—the whole time I was on Adirondack. If you'd ever had to fight the Minthisti face-to-face or had to help bury the bodies of uninvolved civilians caught in the fighting—" he forced his throat muscles to relax— "you'd understand why I'd like to try and forget all of it. At least for a while."

Pearce remained silent for a moment. Then he laid a hand on his son's shoulder. "You're right, Jonny; fighting a war from a star ship *was* a lot different. I'm not sure I can understand what you went through, but I'll do my best. Okay?"

"Yah, Dader. Thanks."

"Sure. Come on, let's go see your mother. Then you can go take a look at Gwen's room."

Dinner that night was a festive occasion. Irena Moreau had cooked her son's favorite meal—center-fired wild balis—and the conversation was light and frequently punctuated by laughter. The warmth and love seemed to Jonny to fill the room, surrounding the five of them with an invisible defense perimeter. For the first time since leaving Asgard he felt truly safe, and tensions he'd forgotten he even had began to drain slowly from his muscles.

It took most of the meal for the others to bring Jonny up to date on the doings of Cedar Lake's people, so it wasn't until Irena brought out the cahve that conversation turned to Jonny's plans.

"I'm not really sure," Jonny confessed, holding his mug of cahve with both hands, letting the heat soak into his palms. "I suppose I could go back to school and finally pick up that computer tech certificate. But that would take another year, and I'm not crazy about being a student again. Not now, anyway."

Across the table Jame sipped cautiously at his

mug. "If you went to work, what sort of job would you like?" he asked.

"Well, I'd thought of coming back to the shop with Dader, but you seem to be pretty well settled in there."

Jame darted a glance at his father. "Heck, Jonny, there's enough work in town for three of us. Right, Dader?"

"Sure," Pearce replied with only the barest hesitation.

"Thanks," Jonny said, "but it sounds like you're really too low on equipment for me to be very useful. My thought is that maybe I could work somewhere on my own for a few months until we can afford to outfit the shop for three workers. Then, if there's enough business around, I could come and work for you."

Pearce nodded. "That sounds really good, Jonny. I think that's the best way to do it."

"So back to the original question," Jame said. "What kind of job are you going to get?"

Jonny held his mug to his lips for a moment, savoring the rich, minty aroma. Army cahve had a fair taste and plenty of stimulant, but was completely devoid of the fragrance that made a good scent-drink so enjoyable. "I've learned a lot about civil engineering in the past three years, especially in the uses of explosives and sonic cutting tools. I figure I'll try one of the road construction or mining companies you were telling me about that are working south of town."

"Can't hurt to try," Pearce shrugged. "Going to take a few days off first?"

"Nope—I'll head out there tomorrow morning. I figured I'd drive around town for a while this evening, though; get reacquainted with the area. Can I help with the dishes before I go?"

"Don't be silly," Irena smiled at him. "Relax and enjoy yourself."

"Tonight, that is," Jame amended. "Tomorrow you'll be put out in the salt mines with the rest of the new slaves."

Jonny leveled a finger at him. "Beware the darkness of the night," he said with mock seriousness. "There just may be a pillow out there with your name on it." He turned back to his parents. "Okay if I take off, then? Anything you need in town?"

"I just shopped today," Irena told him.

"Go ahead, Son," Pearce said.

"I'll be back before it gets too late." Jonny downed the last of his cahve and stood up. "Great dinner, Momer; thanks a lot."

He left the room and headed toward the front door. To his mild surprise, Jame tagged along. "You coming with me?" Jonny asked.

"Just to the car," Jame said. He was silent until they were outside the house. "I wanted to clue you in on a couple of things before you left," he said as they set off across the lawn.

"Okay; shoot."

"Number one: I think you ought to be careful about pointing your finger at people, like you did at me a few minutes ago. Especially when you're looking angry or even just serious."

Jonny blinked. "Hey, I didn't mean anything by that. I was just kidding around."

"*I* know that, and it didn't bother me. Someone who doesn't know you as well might have dived under the table."

"I don't get it. Why?"

Jame shrugged, but met his brother's eyes. "They're a little afraid of you," he said bluntly. "Everybody followed the war news pretty closely out here. They all know what Cobras can do."

Jonny grimaced. It was beginning to sound like a repeat of that last, awkward conversation with Ilona Linder, and he didn't like the implications. "What we *could* do," he told Jame, perhaps a bit more sharply than necessary. "Most of my armament's gone—and even if it wasn't, I sure wouldn't use it on anyone. I'm sick of fighting."

"I know. But they won't know that, not at first. I'm not just guessing here, Jonny; I've talked to a lot of kids since the war ended, and they're pretty nervous about seeing you again. You'd be surprised how many of them are scared that you'll remember some old high school grudge and come by to settle accounts."

"Oh, come on, Jame. That's ridiculous!"

"That's what I tell the ones that ask me about it, but they don't seem convinced. And it looks like some of their parents have picked up on the attitude, too, and—heck, you know how news travels around here. I think you're going to have to bend over backwards for a while, be as harmless as a dove with blunted toenails. Prove to them they don't have to be afraid of you."

Jonny snorted. "The whole thing is silly, but okay. I'll be a good little boy."

"Great," Jame hesitated. "Now for number two, I guess. Were you planning to stop by and see Alyse Carne tonight?"

"That thought *had* crossed my mind," Jonny frowned, trying to read his brother's expression. "Why? Has she moved?"

"No, she's still living out on Blakeley Street. But you might want to call before you go over there. To make sure she . . . isn't busy."

Jonny felt his eyes narrow slightly. "What are you getting at? She living with someone?"

"Oh, no, it hasn't gone that far," Jame said quickly. "But she's been seeing Doane Etherege a lot lately and—well, he's been calling her his girlfriend."

Jonny pursed his lips, staring past Jame at the familiar landscape beyond the Moreau property. He could hardly blame Alyse for finding someone new in his absence—they hadn't exactly been the talk of Cedar Lake when he left, and three years would've been a pretty long wait even if they *had* been more serious about each other. And yet, along with his family, Alyse had been one of his psychological anchors when things on Adirondack had gotten particularly bad; a focal point for thoughts and memories involving something besides blood and death. Just having her around was bound to help in his readjustment to civilian life ... and besides, to step aside meekly for the likes of Doane Etherege was completely unthinkable. "I suppose I'll have to do something about that," he said slowly. Catching Jame's expression, he forced a smile. "Don't worry; I'll steal her back in a civilized manner."

"Yeah, well, good luck. I'll warn you, though; he's not the drip he used to be."

"I'll keep that in mind." Jonny slid his hand idly along the smooth metal of the car. Familiarity all around him; and yet, somehow it was all different, too. Perhaps, his combat instincts whispered, it would be wiser to stay at home until he knew more about the situation here.

Jame seemed to sense the indecision. "You still going out?"

Jonny pursed his lips. "Yeah, I think I'll take a quick look around." Opening the door, he slid in and started the engine. "Don't wait up," he added as he drove off.

After all, he told himself firmly, he had not fought Trofts for three years to come home and hide from his own people.

Nevertheless, the trip through Cedar Lake felt more like a reconnaissance mission than the victorious homecoming he had once envisioned. He covered most of the town, but stayed in the car and didn't wave or call to the people he recognized. He avoided driving by Alyse Carne's apartment building completely. And he was home within an hour.

For many years the only ground link between Cedar Lake and the tiny farming community to the southwest, Boyar, was a bumpy, one-and-three-quarters-lane permturf road that paralleled the Shard Mountains to the west. It had been considered adequate for so long simply because there was little in or around Boyar that anyone in Cedar Lake would want. Boyar's crops went to Horizon City by way of New Persius; supplies traveled the same route in reverse.

Now, however, all that had changed. A large vein of the cesium-bearing ore pollucite had been discovered north of Boyar; and as the mining companies moved in, so did the road construction crews. The facility for extracting the cesium was, for various technical reasons, being built near Cedar Lake, and a multi-lane highway would be necessary to get the ore to it.

Jonny found the road foreman near a large outcrop of granite that lay across the road's projected path. "You Sampson Grange?" he asked.

"Yeah. You?"

"Jonny Moreau. Mr. Oberland told me to check with you about a job. I've had training in lasers, explosives, and sonic blasting equipment."

"Well actually, kid, I—waitaminit. Jonny Moreau the Cobra?"

"*Ex*-Cobra, yes."

Grange shifted his spitstick in his mouth, eyes narrowing slightly. "Yeah, I can use you, I guess. Straight level-eight pay."

That was two levels up from minimum. "Fine. Thanks very much." Jonny nodded toward the granite outcrop. "You need this out of the way?"

"Yeah, but that'll keep. C'mon back here a minute."

He led Jonny to where a group of eight men were struggling to unload huge rolls of pretop paper from a truck to the side of the new road. It took three or four men to handle each roll and they were puffing and swearing with the effort.

"Boys, this is Jonny Moreau," Grange told them. "Jonny, we've got to get this stuff out right away so the truck can go back for another load. Give them a hand, okay?" Without waiting for an answer, he strode off.

Reluctantly, Jonny clambered onto the truck. This wasn't exactly what he'd had in mind. The other men regarded him coolly, and Jonny heard the word "Cobra" being whispered to the two or three who hadn't recognized him. Determined not to let it throw him, he stepped over to the nearest roll and said, "Can someone give me a hand with this?"

Nobody moved. "Wouldn't we just be in the way?" one of them, a husky laborer, suggested with more than a little truculence.

Jonny kept his voice steady. "Look, I'm willing to do my share."

"That seems fair," someone else said sarcastically. "It was our taxes that paid to make you into a superman in the first place. And I figure Grange is paying you enough money for four men. So fine; we got the first eight rolls down and you can get the last five. That fair enough, men?"

There was a general murmur of agreement. Jonny studied their faces for a moment, looking for some sign of sympathy or support. But all he saw was hostility and wariness. "All right," he said softly.

Bending his knees slightly, he hugged the roll of pretop to his chest. Servos whining in his ears, he straightened up and carefully carried the roll to the end of the truck bed. Setting it down, he jumped to the ground, picked it up again and placed it off the road with the others. Then, hopping back into the truck, he went to the next roll.

None of the other workers had moved, but their expressions had changed. Fear now dominated everything else. It was one thing, Jonny reflected bitterly, to watch films of Cobras shooting up Trofts on the plate. It was something else entirely to watch one lift two hundred kilos right in front of you. Cursing inwardly, he finished moving the rolls as quickly as possible and then, without a word, went off in search of Sampson Grange.

He found the other busy inventorying sacks of hardener mix and was immediately pressed into service to carry them to the proper workers. That job led to a succession of similar tasks over the next few hours. Jonny tried to be discreet, but the news about him traveled faster than he did. Most of the workers were less hostile toward him than the first group had been, but it was still like working on a stage, and Jonny began to fume inwardly at the wary politeness and sidelong glances.

Finally, just before noon, he caught on, and once more he tracked down the foreman. "I don't like being maneuvered by people, Mr. Grange," he told the other angrily. "I signed on here to help with blasting and demolition work. Instead, you've got me carrying stuff around like a pack mule."

Grange slid his spitstick to a corner of his mouth and regarded Jonny coolly. "I signed you up at level-eight to work on the road. I never said what you were gonna do."

"That's rotten. You knew what I wanted."

"So what? What the hell—you want special privileges or something? I got guys who have *certificates* in demolition work—I should replace them with a kid who's never even seen a real tape on the subject?"

Jonny opened his mouth, but none of the words he wanted to say would come out. Grange shrugged.

"Look, kid," he said, not unkindly. "I got nothing against you. Hell, I'm a vet myself. But you haven't got any training or experience in road work. We can use more laborers, sure, and that super-revved body of yours makes you worth at least two men—that's why I'm paying you level-eight. Other than that, frankly, you aren't worth much to us. Take it or don't; it's up to you."

"Thanks, but no go," Jonny gritted out.

"Okay." Grange took out a card and scribbled on it. "Take this to the main office in Cedar Lake and they'll give you your pay. And come back if you change your mind."

Jonny took the card and left, trying to ignore the hundred pairs of eyes he could feel boring into his back.

The house was deserted when he arrived home, a condition for which he was grateful. He'd had time to cool down during the drive and now just wanted some time to be alone. As a Cobra he'd been unused to flat-out failure; if the Trofts foiled an attack he had simply to fall back and try a new assault. But the rules here were different, and he wasn't readjusting to them as quickly as he'd expected to.

Nevertheless, he was a long way yet from defeat. Punching up last night's newssheet, he turned to the employment section. Most of the jobs being offered were level-ten laborer types, but there was a fair sprinkling of the more professional sort that he was looking for. Settling himself comfortably in front of the plate, he picked up the pad and stylus always kept by the phone and began to make notes.

His final list of prospects covered nearly two pages, and he spent most of the rest of the afternoon making phone calls. It was a sobering and frustrating experience; and in the end he found himself with only two interviews, both for the following morning.

By then it was nearly dinner time. Stuffing the pages of notes into a pocket, he headed for the kitchen to offer his mother a hand with the cooking.

Irena smiled at him as he entered. "Any luck with the job hunt?" she asked.

"A little," he told her. She had arrived home some hours earlier and had already heard a capsule summary of his morning with the road crew. "I've got two interviews tomorrow—Svetlanov Electronics and Outworld Mining. And I'm lucky to get even that many."

She patted his arm. "You'll find something. Don't worry." A sound outside made her glance out the window. "Your father and Jame are home. Oh, and there's someone with them."

Jonny looked out. A second car had pulled to the curb behind Pearce and Jame. As he watched, a tall, somewhat paunchy man got out and joined the other two in walking toward the house. "He looks familiar, Momer, but I can't place him."

"That's Teague Stillman, the mayor," she identified him, sounding surprised. "I wonder why he's here." Whipping off her apron, she dried her hands and hurried into the living room. Jonny followed more slowly, unconsciously taking up a back-up position across the living room from the front door.

The door opened just as Irena reached it. "Hi, Honey," Pearce greeted his wife as the three men entered. "Teague stopped by the shop just as we were closing up and I invited him to come over for a few minutes."

"How nice," Irena said in her best hostess voice. "It's been a long time since we've seen you, Teague. How is Sharene?"

"She's fine, Irena," Stillman said, "although she says *she* doesn't see me enough these days, either. Actually, I just stopped by to see if Jonny was home from work yet."

"Yes, I am," Jonny said, coming forward. "Congratulations on winning your election last year, Mr. Stillman. I'm afraid I didn't make it to the polls."

Stillman laughed and reached out his hand to grasp Jonny's briefly. He seemed relaxed and friendly . . . and yet, right around the eyes, Jonny could see a touch of the caution that he'd seen in the road workers. "I'd have sent you an absentee ballot if I'd known exactly where you were," the mayor joked. "Welcome home, Jonny."

"Thank you, sir."

"Shall we sit down?" Irena suggested.

They moved into the livng room proper, Stillman and the Moreau parents exchanging small talk all the while. Jame had yet to say a word, Jonny noted, and the younger boy took a seat in a corner, away from the others.

"The reason I wanted to talk to you, Jonny," Stillman said when they were all settled, "was that the city council and I would like to have a sort of 'welcome home' ceremony for you in the park next week. Nothing too spectacular, really; just a short parade through town, followed by a couple of speeches—you don't have to make one if you don't want to—and then some fireworks and perhaps a torchlight procession. What do you think?"

Jonny hesitated, but there was no way to say this diplomatically. "Thanks, but I really don't want you to do that."

Pearce's proud smile vanished. "What do you mean, Jonny? Why not?"

"Because I don't want to get up in front of a whole bunch of people and get cheered at. It's embarrassing and—well, it's embarrassing. I don't want any fuss made over me."

"Jonny, the town wants to honor you for what you did," Stillman said soothingly, as if afraid Jonny was becoming angry.

That thought was irritating. "The greatest honor it could give me would be to stop treating me like a freak," he retorted.

"Son—" Pearce began warningly.

"Dad, if Jonny doesn't want any official hoopla, it seems to me the subject is closed," Jame spoke up unexpectedly from his corner. "Unless you all plan to chain him to the speakers' platform."

There was a moment of uncomfortable silence. Then Stillman shifted in his seat. "Well, if Jonny doesn't want this, there's no reason to discuss it further." He stood up, the others quickly following suit. "I really ought to get home now."

"Give Sharene our best," Irena said.

"I will," Stillman nodded. "We'll have to try and get together soon. Good-bye, all; and once more, welcome home, Jonny."

"I'll walk you to your car," Pearce said, clearly angry but trying to hide it.

The two men left. Irena looked questioningly at Jonny, but all she said before disappearing back into the kitchen was, "You boys wash up and call Gwen from her room; dinner will be ready soon."

"You okay?" Jame asked softly when his mother had gone.

"Yeah. Thanks for backing me up." Jonny shook his head. "They don't understand."

"I'm not sure I do, either. Is it because of what I said about people being afraid of you?"

"That has nothing to do with it. The people of Adirondack were afraid of us, too, some of them. But even so—" Jonny sighed. "Look. Horizon is all the way across the Dominion from where the war was fought. You weren't within fifty light-years of a Troft even at their deepest penetration. How can I accept the praise of people who have no idea what they're cheering for? It'd just be going through the motions." He turned his head to stare out the window. "Adirondack held a big victory celebration after the Trofts finally pulled out. There was nothing of duty or obligation about it—when the people cheered, you could tell they knew *why* they were doing so. And they also knew who they were there to honor. Not those of us who were on the stage, but those who weren't. Instead of a torchlight procession, they sang a requiem." He turned back to face Jame. "How could I watch Cedar Lake's fireworks after that?"

Jame touched his brother's arm and nodded silently. "I'll go call Gwen," he said a moment later.

Pearce came back into the house. He said nothing, but flashed Jonny a disappointed look before disappearing into the kitchen. Sighing, Jonny went to wash his hands.

Dinner was very quiet that evening.

The interviews the next morning were complete washouts, with the two prospective employers clearly seeing him just out of politeness. Gritting his teeth, Jonny returned home and called up the newssheet once again. He lowered his sights somewhat this time, and his new list came out to be three and a half pages long. Doggedly, he began making the calls.

By the time Jame came to bring him to dinner he had exhausted all the numbers on the list. "Not even any interviews this time," he told Jame disgustedly as they walked into the dining room where the others were waiting. "News really does travel in this town, doesn't it?"

"Come on, Jonny, there has to be *someone* around who doesn't care that you're an ex-Cobra," Jame said.

"Perhaps you should lower your standards a bit," Pearce suggested. "Working as a laborer wouldn't hurt you any."

"Or maybe you could be a patroller," Gwen spoke up. "That would be neat."

Jonny shook his head. "I've tried being a laborer, remember? The men on the road crew were either afraid of me or thought I was trying to show them up."

"But once they got to know you, things would be different," Irena said.

"Or maybe if they had a better idea of what you'd done for the Dominion they'd respect you more," Peace added.

"No, Dader." Jonny had tried explaining to his father why he didn't want Cedar Lake to honor him publicly, and the elder Moreau had listened and said he understood. But Jonny doubted that he really did, and Pearce clearly hadn't given up trying to change his son's mind. "I probably would be a good patroller, Gwen," he added to his sister, "but I think it would remind me too much of some of the things I had to do in the Army."

"Well, then, maybe you should go back to school," Irena suggested.

"No!" Jonny snapped with a sudden flash of anger.

A stunned silence filled the room. Inhaling deeply, Jonny forced himself to calm down. "Look, I know you're all trying to be helpful, and I appreciate it. But I'm twenty-four years old now and capable of handling my own problems." Abruptly, he put down his fork and stood up. "I'm not hungry. I think I'll go out for a while."

Minutes later he was driving down the street, wondering what he should do. There was a brand-new pleasure center in town, he knew, but he wasn't in the mood for large groups of people. He mentally ran through a list of old friends, but that was just for practice; he knew where he really wanted to go. Jame had suggested he call Alyse Carne before dropping in on her, but Jonny was in a perverse mood. Turning at the next corner, he headed for Blakely Street.

Alyse seemed surprised when he announced himself over her apartment building's security intercom, but she was all smiles as she opened her door. "Jonny, it's good to see you," she said, holding out her hand.

"Hi, Alyse." He smiled back, taking her hand and stepping into her apartment, closing the door behind him. "I was afraid you'd forgotten about me while I was gone."

Her eyes glowed. "Not likely," she murmured . . . and suddenly she was in his arms.

After a long minute she gently pulled away. "Why don't we sit down?" she suggested. "We've got three years to catch up on."

"Anything wrong?" he asked her.

"No. Why?"

"You seem a little nervous. I thought you might have a date."

She flushed. "Not tonight. I guess you know I've been seeing Doane."

"Yes. How serious is it, Alyse? I deserve to know."

"I like him," she said, shrugging uncomfortably. "I suppose in a way I was trying to insulate myself from pain in case you . . . didn't come back."

Jonny nodded understanding. "I got a lot of that on Adirondack, too, mostly from whichever civilian family I was living with at the time."

Alyse seemed to wince a bit. "I'm . . . sorry. Anyway, it's grown more than I expected it to, and now that you're back . . ." Her voice trailed off.

"You don't have to make any decisions tonight," Jonny said after a moment. "Except whether or not you'll spend the evening with me."

Some of the tension left her face. "That one's easy. Have you eaten yet, or shall I just make us some cahve?"

They talked until nearly midnight, and when Jonny finally left he had recaptured the contentment he'd felt on first arriving at Cedar Lake. Doane Etherege would soon fade back into the woodwork, he was sure, and with Alyse and his family back in their old accustomed places he would finally have a universe he knew how to deal with. His mind was busy with plans for the future as he let himself into the Moreau house and tiptoed to his bedroom.

"Jonny?" a whisper came from across the room. "You okay?"

"Fine, Jame—just great," Jonny whispered back.

"How was Alyse?"

Jonny chuckled. "Go to sleep, Jame."

"That's nice. Good night, Jonny."

One by one, the great plans crumbled.

With agonizing regularity, employers kept turning Jonny down, and he was eventually forced into a succession of the level-nine and -ten manual jobs he had hoped so desperately to avoid. None of the jobs lasted very long; the resentment and fear of his fellow workers invariably generated an atmosphere of sullen animosity which Jonny found hard to take for more than a few days at a time.

As his search for permanent employment faltered, so did his relationship with Alyse. She remained friendly and willing to spend time with him, but there was a distance between them that hadn't existed before the war. To make matters worse, Doane refused to withdraw gracefully from the field, and aggressively competed with him for Alyse's time and attention.

But worst of all, from Jonny's point of view, was the unexpected trouble his problems had brought upon the rest of the family. His parents and Jame, he knew, could stand the glances, whispered comments, and mild stigma that seemed to go with being related to an ex-Cobra. But it hurt him terribly to watch Gwen retreat into herself from the half-unintentional cruelty of her peers. More than once Jonny considered leaving Horizon and returning to active service, freeing his family from the cross-fire he had put them into. But to leave now would be to admit defeat, and that was something he couldn't bring himself to do.

And so matters precariously stood for three months, until the night of the accident. Or the murder, as some called it.

Sitting in his parked car, watching the last rays from the setting sun, Jonny let the anger and frustration drain out of him and wondered what to do next. He had just stormed out of Alyse's apartment after their latest fight, the tenth or so since his return. Like the job situation, things with Alyse seemed to be getting worse instead of better. Unlike the former, he could only blame himself for the problems in his love life.

The sun was completely down by the time he felt capable of driving safely. The sensible thing would be to go home, of course. But the rest of the Moreau family was out to dinner, and the thought of being alone in the house bothered him for some reason. What he needed, he decided, was something that would completely take his mind off his problems. Starting the car, he drove into the center of town where the Raptopia, Cedar Lake's new pleasure center, was located.

Jonny had been in pleasure centers on Asgard both before and after the tour on Adirondack, and by their standards the Raptopia was decidedly unsophisticated. There were fifteen rooms and galleries, each offering its own combination of sensual stimuli for customers to choose from. The choices seemed limited, however, to permutations of the traditional recreations: music, food and drink, mood drugs, light shows, games, and thermal booths. The extreme physical and intellectual ends of the pleasure spectrum, personified by prostitutes and professional conversationalists, were conspiciously absent.

Jonny wandered around for a few minutes before settling on a room with a loud music group and wildly flickering light show. Visibility under such conditions was poor, and as long as he kept his distance from the other patrons, he was unlikely to be recognized. Finding a vacant area of the contoured softfloor, he sat down.

The music was good, if dated—he'd heard the same songs three years ago on Asgard—and he began to relax as the light and sound swept like a cleansing wave over his mind. So engrossed did he become that he didn't notice the group of teenaged kids that came up behind him until one of them nudged him with the tip of his shoe.

"Hi there, Cobra," he said as Jonny looked up. "What's new?"

"Uh, not much," Jonny replied cautiously. There were seven of them, he noted: three girls and four boys, all dressed in the current teen-age styles so deplored by Cedar Lake's more conservative adults. "Do I know you?"

The girls giggled. "Naw," another of the boys drawled. "We just figured everybody ought to know there's a celebrity here. Let's tell 'em, huh?"

Slowly, Jonny rose to his feet to face them. From his new vantage point he could see that all seven had the shining eyes and rapid breathing of heavy stim-drug users. "I don't think that's necessary," he said.

"You want to fight about it?" the first boy said, dropping into a caricature of a fighting stance. "C'mon, Cobra. Show us what you can do."

Wordlessly, Jonny turned and walked toward the door, followed by the giggling group. As he reached the exit the two talkative boys pushed past him and stood in the doorway, blocking it.

"Can't leave 'til you show us a trick," one said.

Jonny looked him in the eye, successfully re-
sisting the urge to bounce the smart-mouth off the
far wall. Instead, he picked up both boys by their
belts, held them high for a moment, and then
turned and set them down to the side of the
doorway. A gentle push sent them sprawling onto
the softfloor. "I suggest you all stay here and enjoy
the music," he told the rest of the group as they
stared at him with wide eyes.

"Turkey hop," one of the smart-mouths muttered.
Jonny ignored the apparent insult and strode from
the room, confident that they wouldn't follow him.
They didn't.

But the mood of the evening was broken. Jonny
tried two or three other rooms for a few minutes
each, hoping to regain the relaxed abandonment
he'd felt earlier. But it was no use, and within a
quarter hour he was back outside the Raptopia,
walking through the cool night air toward his car,
parked across the street a block away.

He'd covered the block and was just starting to
cross the road when he became aware of the low
hum of an idling car nearby. He turned to look
back along the street—and in that instant a car
rolling gently along the curb suddenly switched on
its lights and, with a squeal of tires, hurtled directly toward him.

There was no time for thought or human reaction,
but Jonny had no need of either. For the first time
since leaving Adirondack his nanocomputer took
control of his body, launching it into a flat, six-
meter dive that took him to the walkway on the
far side of the street. He landed on his right
shoulder, rolling to absorb the impact, but crashed
painfully into a building before he could stop
completely. The car roared past; and as it did so
needles of light flashed from Jonny's fingertip lasers to the car's two right-hand tires. The double
blowout was audible even over the engine noise.

Instantly out of control, the car swerved violently, bounced off two parked cars, and finally crashed broadside into the corner of the building.

Aching all over, Jonny got to his feet and ran to the car. Ignoring the gathering crowd, he worked feverishly on the crumpled metal, and had the door open by the time a rescue unit arrived. But his effort was in vain. The car's driver was already dead, and his passenger died of internal injuries on the way to the hospital.

They were the two teen-aged boys who had accosted Jonny in the Raptopia.

The sound of his door opening broke Mayor Stillman's train of thought, and he turned from his contemplation of the morning sky in time to see Sutton Fraser closing the door behind him. "Don't you ever knock?" he asked the city councilor irritably.

"You can stare out the window later," Fraser said, pulling a chair close to the desk and sitting down. "Right now we've got to talk."

Stillman sighed. "Jonny Moreau?"

"You got it. It's been over a week now, Teague, and the tension out there's not going down. People in my district are still asking why Jonny's not in custody."

"We've been through this, remember? The legal department in Horizon City has the patroller report; until they make a decision we're treating it as self-defense."

"Oh, come on. You know the kids would have swerved to miss him. That's how that stupid turkey hop is played—okay, okay, I realize Jonny didn't know that. But did *you* know he fired on the car *after* it had passed him? I've got no less than three witnesses now that say that."

"So have the patrollers. I'll admit I don't understand that part. Maybe it's something from his combat training."

"Great," Fraser muttered.

Stillman's intercom buzzed. "Mayor Stillman, there's a Mr. Vanis D'arl to see you," his secretary announced.

Stillman glanced questioningly at Fraser, who shrugged and shook his head. "Send him in," Stillman said.

The door opened and a slender, dark-haired man entered and walked toward the desk. His appearance, clothing, and walk identified him as an offworlder before he had taken two steps. "Mr. D'arl," Stillman said as he and Fraser rose to their feet, "I'm Mayor Teague Stillman; this is Councilor Sutton Fraser. What can we do for you?"

D'arl produced a gold ID pin. "Vanis D'arl, representing Committé Sarkiis H'orme of the Dominion of Man." His voice was slightly accented.

Out of the corner of his eye Stillman saw Fraser stiffen. His own knees felt a little weak. "Very honored to meet you, sir. Won't you sit down?"

"Thank you." D'arl took the chair Fraser had been sitting in. The councilor moved to a seat farther from the desk, possibly hoping to be less conspicuous there.

"This is mainly an informal courtesy call, Mr. Stillman," D'arl said. "However, all of what I'm going to tell you is to be considered confidential Dominion business." He waited for both men to nod agreement before continuing. "I've just come from Horizon City, where all pending charges against Reserve Cobra-Three Jonny Moreau have been ordered dropped."

"I see," Stillman said. "May I ask why the Central Committee is taking an interest in this case?"

"Cee-three Moreau is still technically under Army jurisdiction, since he can be called into active service at any time. Committé H'orme has furthermore had a keen interest in the entire Cobra project since its inception."

"Are you familiar with the incident that Mr.—uh, Cee-three Moreau was involved in?"

"Yes, and I understand the doubts both you and the planetary authorities have had about the circumstances. However, Moreau cannot be held responsible for his actions at that time. He was under attack and acted accordingly."

"His combat training is that strong?"

"Not precisely." D'arl hesitated. "I dislike having to tell you this, as it has been a military secret up until recently. But you need to understand the situation. Have you ever wondered what the name 'Cobra' stands for?"

"Why . . ." Stillman floundered, caught off guard by the question. "I assumed it referred to the Earth snake."

"Only secondarily. It's an acronym for 'Computerized Body Reflex Armament. I'm sure you know about the ceramic laminae and servo network and all; you may also know about the nano-computer implanted just under his brain. This is where the . . . problem . . . originates.

"You must understand that a soldier, especially a guerrilla in enemy-held territory, needs a good set of combat reflexes if he is to survive. Training can give him some of what he needs, but it takes a long time and has its limits. Therefore, since a computer was going to be necessary for equipment monitoring and fire control anyway, a set of combat reflexes was also programmed in.

"The bottom line is that Moreau will react instantly, and with very little conscious control, to any deadly attack launched at him. In this particular case the pattern shows clearly that this is what happened. He evaded the initial attack, but was left in a vulnerable position—off his feet and away from cover—and was thus forced to counterattack.

Part of the computer's job is to monitor the weapon systems, so it knew the fingertip lasers were all it had left. So it used them."

A deathly silence filled the room. "Let me get this straight," Stillman said at last. "The Army made Jonny Moreau into an automated fighting machine who will react lethally to anything that even *looks* like an attack? And then let him come back to us without making any attempt to change that?"

"The system was designed to defend a soldier in enemy territory," D'arl said. "It's not nearly as hair-trigger as you seem to imagine. And as for 'letting' him come back like that, there was no other choice. The computer cannot be reprogrammed or removed without risking brain damage."

"What the *hell!*" Fraser had apparently forgotten he was supposed to be courteous to Dominion representatives. "What damn idiot came up with *that* idea?"

D'arl turned to face the councilor. "The Central Committee is tolerant of criticism, Mr. Fraser." His voice was even, but had an edge to it. "But your tone is unacceptable."

Fraser refused to shrivel. "Never mind that. How did you expect us to cope with him when he reacts to attacks like that?" He snorted. "*Attacks.* Two kids playing a game!"

"Use your head," D'arl snapped. "We couldn't risk having a Cobra captured by the Trofts and sent back to us with his computer reprogrammed. The Cobras were soldiers, first and foremost, and every tool and weapon they had made perfect sense from a military standpoint."

"Didn't it occur to anyone that the war would be over someday? And that the Cobras would be going home to civilian life?"

D'arl's lip might have twitched, but his voice was firm enough. "Less powerful equipment might well have cost the Dominion the war, and would certainly have cost many more Cobras their lives. At any rate, it's done now, and you'll just have to learn to live with it like everyone else."

Stillman frowned. " 'Everyone else'? How widespread is this problem?"

D'arl turned back to face the mayor, looking annoyed that he'd let that hint slip out. "It's not good," he admitted at last. "We hoped to keep as many Cobras as possible in the service after the war, but all were legally free to leave and over two hundred did so. Many of those are having trouble of one kind or another. We're trying to help them, but it's difficult to do. People are afraid of them, and that hampers our efforts."

"Can you do anything to help Jonny?"

D'arl shrugged slightly. "I don't know. He's an unusual case, in that he came back to a small home town where everyone knew what he was. I suppose it might help to move him to another planet, maybe give him a new name. But people would eventually find out. Cobra strength is hard to hide for long."

"So are Cobra reflexes," Stillman nodded grimly. "Besides, Jonny's family is here. I don't think he'd like leaving them."

"That's why I'm not recommending his relocation, though that's the usual procedure in cases like this," D'arl said. "Most Cobras don't have the kind of close family support he does. It's a strong point in his favor." He stood up. "I'll be leaving Horizon tomorrow morning, but I'll be within a few days' flight of here for the next month. If anything happens, I can be reached through the Dominion governor-general's office in Horizon City."

Stillman rose from his chair. "I trust the Central Committee will be trying to come up with some kind of solution to this problem."

D'arl met his gaze evenly. "Mr. Stillman, the

Committee is far more concerned about this situation than even you are. You see one minor frontier town; we see seventy worlds. If an answer exists, we'll find it."

"And what do we do in the meantime?" Fraser asked heavily.

"Your best, of course. Good day to you."

Jame paused outside the door, took a single deep breath, and knocked lightly. There was no answer. He raised his hand to knock again, then thought better of it. After all, it was *his* bedroom, too. Opening the door, he went in.

Seated at Jame's writing desk, hands curled into fists in front of him, Jonny was staring out the window. Jame cleared his throat.

"Hello, Jame," Jonny said, without turning.

"Hi." The desk, Jame saw, was covered with official-looking magforms. "I just dropped by to tell you that dinner will be ready in about fifteen minutes." He nodded at the desk. "What're you up to?"

"Filling out some college applications."

"Oh. Decided to go back to school?"

Jonny shrugged. "I might as well."

Stepping to his brother's side, Jame scanned the magforms. University of Rajput, Bomu Technical Institute on Zimbwe, University of Aerie. All off-planet. "You're going to have a long way to travel when you come home for Christmas," he commented. Another fact caught his eye: all three applications were filled out only up to the space marked *Military Service*.

"I don't expect to come home very often," Jonny said quietly.

"You're just going to give up, huh?" Jame put as much scorn into the words as he could.

It had no effect. "I'm retreating from enemy territory," Jonny corrected mildly.

"The kids are dead, Jonny. There's nothing in the universe you can do about it. Look, the town doesn't blame you—no charges were brought, remember? So quit blaming yourself. Accept the fact of what happened and let go of it."

"You're confusing legal and moral guilt. Legally, I'm clear. Morally? No. And the town's not going to let me forget it. I can see the disgust and fear in people's eyes. They're even afraid to be sarcastic to me any more."

"Well . . . it's better than not getting any respect at all."

Jonny snorted. "Thanks a lot," he said wryly. "I'd rather be picked on."

A sign of life at last. Jame pressed ahead, afraid of losing the spark. "You know, Dader and I have been talking about the shop. You remember that we didn't have enough equipment for three workers?"

"Yes—and you still don't."

"Right. But what stops us from having *you* and Dader run the place while *I* go out and work somewhere else for a few months?"

Jonny was silent for a moment, but then shook his head. "Thanks, but no. It wouldn't be fair."

"Why not? That job used to be yours. It's not like you were butting in. Actually, I'd kind of like to try something else for a while."

"I'd probably drive away all the customers if I was there."

Jame's lip twisted. "That won't fly, and you know it. Dader's customers are there because they like him and his work. They don't give two hoots who handles the actual repairs as long as Dader supervises everything. You're just making excuses."

Jonny closed his eyes briefly. "And what if I am?"

"I suppose it doesn't matter to you right now whether or not you let your life go down the drain,"

Jame gritted. "But you might take a moment to consider what you're doing to Gwen."

"Yeah. The other kids are pretty hard on her, aren't they?"

"I'm not referring to them. Sure, she's lost most of her friends, but there are a couple who're sticking by her. What's killing her is having to watch her big brother tearing himself to shreds."

Jonny looked up for the first time. "What do you mean?"

"Just want I said. She's been putting up a good front for your sake, but the rest of us know how much it hurts her to see the brother she adores sitting in his room and—" He groped for the right words.

"Wallowing in self-pity?"

"Yeah. You owe her better than that, Jonny. She's already lost most of her friends; she deserves to keep her brother."

Jonny looked back out the window for a long moment, then glanced down at the college applications. "You're right." He took a deep breath, let it out slowly. "Okay. You can tell Dader he's got himself a new worker," he said, collecting the magforms together into a neat pile. "I'll start whenever he's ready for me."

Jame grinned and gripped his brother's shoulder. "Thanks," he said quietly. "Can I tell Momer and Gwen, too?"

"Sure. No; just Momer." He stood up and gave Jane a passable attempt at a smile. "I'll go tell Gwen myself."

The tiny spot of bluish light, brilliant even through the de-contrast goggles, crawled to the edge of the metal and vanished. Pushing up the goggles, Jonny set the laser down and inspected the seam. Spotting a minor flaw, he corrected it and then began removing the fender from its clamps. He had not quite finished the job when a gentle buzz signaled that a car had pulled into the drive. Grimacing, Jonny took off his goggles and headed for the front of the shop.

Mayor Stillman was out of his car and walking toward the door when Jonny emerged from the building. "Hello, Jonny," he smiled, holding out his hand with no trace of hesitation. "How are you doing?"

"Fine, Mr. Stillman," Jonny said, feeling awkward as he shook hands. He'd been working here for three weeks now, but still didn't feel comfortable dealing directly with his father's customers. "Dader's out right now; can I help you with something?"

Stillman shook his head. "I really just dropped by to say hello to you and to bring you some news. I heard this morning that Wyatt Brothers Contracting is putting together a group to demolish the old Lamplighter Hotel. Would you be interested in applying for a job with them?"

"No, I don't think so. I'm doing okay here right now. But thanks for—"

He was cut off by a dull thunderclap. "What was that?" Stillman asked, glancing at the cloudless sky.

"Explosion," Jonny said curtly, eyes searching the southwest sky for evidence of fire. For an instant he was back on Adirondack. "A big one, southwest of us. There!" He pointed to a thin plume of smoke that had suddenly appeared.

"The cesium extractor, I'll bet," Stillman muttered. "Damn! Come on, let's go."

The déjà vu vanished. "I can't go with you," Jonny said.

"Never mind the shop. No one will steal anything." Stillman was already getting into his car

"But—" There would be *crowds* there! "I just can't."

"This is no time for shyness," the mayor snapped. "If that blast really *was* all the way over at the extraction plant, there's probably one hell of a fire there now. They might need our help. Come *on!*"

Jonny obeyed. The smoke plume, he noted, was growing darker by the second.

Stillman was right on all counts. The four-story cesium extraction plant was indeed burning furiously as they roared up to the edge of the growing crowd of spectators. The patrollers and fireters were already there, the latter pouring a white liquid through the doors and windows of the building. The flames, Jonny saw as he and the mayor pushed through the crowd, seemed largely confined to the first floor. The *entire* floor was burning, however, with flames extending even a meter or two onto the ground outside the building. Clearly, the fire was being fueled by one or more liquids.

The two men had reached one of the patrollers now. "Keep back, folks—" he began.

"I'm Mayor Stillman," Stillman identified himself. "What can we do to help?"

"Just keep back—no, wait a second, you can help us string a cordon line. There could be another explosion any time and we've got to keep these people back. The stuff's over there."

The "stuff" consisted of thin, bottom-weighted poles and bright red cord to string between them. Stillman and Jonny joined three patrollers who were in the process of setting up the line.

"How'd it happen?" Stillman asked as they worked, shouting to make himself heard over the roar of the flames.

"Witnesses say a tank of iaphanine got ruptured somehow and ignited," one of the patrollers shouted back. "Before they could put it out, the heat set off another couple of tanks. I guess they had a few hundred kiloliters of the damned stuff in there— it's used in the refining process—and the whole lot went up at once. It's a wonder the building's still standing."

"Anyone still in there?"

"Yeah. Half a dozen or so—third floor."

Jonny turned, squinting against the light. Sure enough, he could see two or three anxious faces at a partially open third-floor window. Directly below them Cedar Lake's single "skyhooker" fire truck had been driven to within a cautious ten meters of the building and was extending its ladder upwards. Jonny turned back to the cordon line—

The blast was deafening, and Jonny's nano-computer reacted by throwing him flat on the ground. Twisting around to face the building, he saw that a large chunk of wall a dozen meters from the working fireters had been disintegrated by the explosion. In its place was now a solid sheet of blue-tinged yellow flame. Fortunately, none of the fireters seemed to have been hurt.

"Oh, hell," a patroller said as Jonny scrambled to his feet. "Look at that."

A piece of the wall had apparently winged the skyhooker's ladder on its way to oblivion. One of the uprights had been mangled, causing the whole structure to sag to the side. Even as the fireters hurriedly brought it down the upright snapped, toppling the ladder to the ground.

"Damn!" Stillman muttered. "Do they have another ladder long enough?"

"Not when it has to sit that far from the wall," the patroller gritted. "I don't think the Public Works talltrucks can reach that high either."

"Maybe we can get a hover-plane from Horizon City," Stillman said, a hint of desperation creeping into his voice.

"They haven't got time." Jonny pointed at the second-floor windows. "The fire's already on the second floor. Something has to be done right away."

The fireters had apparently come to the same

conclusion and were pulling one of their other ladders from its rack on the skyhooker. "Looks like they're going to try to reach the second floor and work their way to the third from inside," the patroller muttered.

"That's suicide," Stillman shook his head. "Isn't there any place they can set up airbags close enough to let the men jump?"

The answer to that was obvious and no one bothered to voice it: if the fireters could have done that, they would have already done so. Clearly, the flames extended too far from the building for that to work.

"Do we have any strong rope?" Jonny asked suddenly. "I'm sure I could throw one end of it to them."

"But they'd slide down into the fire," Stillman pointed out.

"Not if you anchored the bottom end fifteen or twenty meters away; tied it to one of the fire trucks, say. Come on, let's go talk to one of the fireters."

They found the fire chief in the group trying to set up the new ladder. "It's a nice idea, but I doubt if all of the men up there could make it down a rope," he frowned after Jonny had sketched his plan. "They've been in smoke and terrific heat for nearly a quarter hour now and are probably getting close to collapse."

"Do you have anything like a breeches buoy?" Jonny asked. "It's like a sling with a pulley that slides on a rope."

The chief shook his head. "Look, I haven't got any more time to waste here. We've got to get our men inside right away."

"You can't send men into that," Stillman objected. "The whole second floor must be on fire by now."

"That's why we have to hurry, damn it!"

Jonny fought a brief battle with himself. But, as

Stillman had said, this was no time to be shy. "There's another way. I can take a rope to them along the *outside* of the building."

"What? How?"

"You'll see. I'll need at least thirty meters of rope, a pair of insulated gloves, and about ten strips of heavy cloth. *Now!*"

The tone of command, once learned, was not easily forgotten. Nor was was it easy to resist; and within a minute Jonny was standing beneath his third-floor target window, as close to the building as the flames permitted. The rope, tied firmly around his waist, trailed behind him, kept just taut enough to insure that it, too, stayed out of the fire. Taking a deep breath, Jonny bent his knees and jumped.

Three years of practice had indeed made perfect. He caught the window ledge at the top of his arc, curled up feet taking the impact against red-hot brick. In a single smooth motion he pulled himself through the half-open window and into the building.

The fire chief's guess about the heat and smoke had been correct. The seven men lying or sitting on the floor of the small room were so groggy they weren't even startled by Jonny's sudden appearance. Three were already unconscious; alive, but just barely.

The first task was to get the window completely open. It was designed, Jonny saw, to only open halfway, the metal frame of the upper section firmly joined to the wall. A few carefully placed laser shots into the heat-softened metal did the trick, and a single kick popped the pane neatly and sent it tumbling to the ground.

Moving swiftly now, Jonny untied the rope from his waist and fastened it to a nearby stanchion, tugging three times on it to alert the fireters below to take up the slack. Hoisting one of the uncon-scious men to a more or less vertical position, he

tied a strip of cloth to the man's left wrist, tossed
the other end over the slanting rope, and tied it to
the man's right wrist. With a quick glance outside
to make sure the fireters were ready, he lifted the
man through the window and let him slide down
the taut rope into the waiting arms below. Jonny
didn't wait to watch them cut him loose, but went
immediately to the second unconscious man.

Parts of the floor were beginning to smolder by
the time the last man disappeared out the window.
Tossing one more cloth strip over the rope, Jonny
gripped both ends with his right hand and jumped.
The wind of his passage felt like an arctic blast on
his sweaty skin and he found himself shivering as
he reached the ground. Letting go of the cloth, he
stumbled a few steps away—and heard a strange
sound.

The crowd was cheering.

He turned to look at them, wondering, and finally it dawned on him that they were cheering
for *him*. Unbidden, an embarrassed smile crept
onto his face, and he raised his hand shyly in
acknowledgment.

And then Mayor Stillman was at his side, gripping Jonny's arm and smiling broadly. "You did
it, Jonny; you did it!" he shouted over all the
noise.

Jonny grinned back. With half of Cedar Lake
watching he'd saved seven men, and had risked his
life doing it. They'd seen that he wasn't a monster,
that his abilities could be used constructively and—
most importantly—that he *wanted* to be helpful.
Down deep, he could sense that this was a potential turning point. Maybe—just maybe—things
would be different for him now.

Stillman shook his head sadly. "I really thought
things would be different for him after the fire."
Fraser shrugged. "I'd hoped so, too. But I'm afraid

I hadn't really counted on it. Even while everybody was cheering for him you could see that nervousness still in their eyes. That fear of him was never gone, just covered up. Now that the emotional high has worn off, that's all that's left."

"Yeah." Lifting his gaze from the desk, Stillman stared for a moment out the window. "So they treat him like an incurable psychopath. Or a wild animal."

"You can't really blame them. They're scared of what his strength and lasers could do if he went berserk."

"He doesn't *go* berserk, damn it!" Stillman flared, slamming his fist down on the desk.

"*I* know that!" the councilor shot back. "Fine—so you want to tell everyone the truth? Even assuming Vanis D'arl didn't jump down our throats for doing it, would you *really* want to tell people Jonny has no control over his combat reflexes? You think that would help?"

Stillman's flash of anger evaporated. "No," he said quietly. "It would just make things worse." He stood up and walked over to the window. "Sorry I blew up, Sut. I know it's not your fault. It's just . . ." He sighed. "We've lost it, Sut. That's all there is to it. We're never going to get Jonny reintegrated into this town now. If becoming a bona fide hero didn't do it, then I have no idea what else to try."

"It's not your fault either, Teague. You can't take it personally." Fraser's voice was quiet. "The Army had no business doing what it did to Jonny, and then dropping him on us without any preparation. But they're not going to be able to ignore the problem. You remember what D'arl said—the Cobras are having trouble all over the Dominion. Sooner or later the government's going to have to do something about it. We've done our best; it's up to them now."

Stillman's intercom buzzed. Walking back to his desk, the mayor tapped the key. "Yes?"

"Sir, Mr. Do-sin just called from the press office. He says there's something on the DOM-Press line that you should see."

"Thank you." Sitting down, Stillman turned on his plate and punched up the proper channel. The last three news items were still visible, the top one marked with a star indicating its importance. Both men hunched forward to read it.

Dominion Joint Military Command HQ, Asgard:

A military spokesman has announced that all reserve Cobras will be recalled into active service by the end of next month. This move is designed to counter a Minthisti build-up along the Dominion's Andromeda border. As yet no regular Army or Star Force reserves are being recalled, but all options are being kept open.

"I don't believe it," Fraser shook his head. "Are those stupid Minthisti going to try it *again?* I thought they learned their lesson the last time we stomped them."

Stillman didn't reply.

Vanis D'arl swept into Mayor Stillman's office with the air of a man preoccupied by more important business. He nodded shortly to the two men who were waiting there for him and sat down without invitation. "I trust this is as vital as your message implied," he said to Stillman. "I postponed an important meeting to detour to Horizon. Let's get on with it."

Stillman nodded, determined not to be intimidated, and gestured to the youth sitting quietly by his desk. "May I present Jame Moreau, brother of Cobra-three Jonny Moreau. He and I have been discussing the Reserve call-up set for later this month in response to the alleged Minthisti threat."

"Alleged?" D'arl's voice was soft, but there was a warning under it.

Stillman hesitated, suddenly aware of the risk they were taking with this confrontation. But Jame stepped into the gap. "Yes, *alleged*. We know this whole thing is a trumped-up excuse to pull all the Cobras back into the Army and ship them off to the border where they'll be out of the way."

D'arl looked keenly at Jame, as if seeing him for the first time. "You're concerned about your brother, of course; that's only natural," he said at last. "But your allegations are unprovable and come perilously close to sedition. The Dominion makes war only in self-defense. Even if your claim was true, what would such an action gain us?"

"That's precisely our point," Jame said calmly, showing a self-control and courage far beyond his nineteen years. "The government is trying to solve the Cobra problem, clearly. But this isn't a solution; it's merely a postponement."

"And yet, the Cobras were generally unhappy in their new civilian roles," D'arl pointed out. "Perhaps this will actually be better for them."

Jame shook his head, his eyes still holding D'arl's. "No. Because you can't keep them there forever, you see. You either have to release them again someday—in which case you're right back where you started—or else you have to hope that the problem will . . . work itself out."

D'arl's face was an expressionless mask. "What do you mean by that?"

"I think you know." For just a second Jame's control cracked, and some of the internal fire leaked out. "But don't you see? It won't *work*. You can't kill off all the Cobras, no matter how many wars you put them through, because the Army will be making new ones as fast as the old ones die. They're just too blasted useful for the brass to simply drop the project."

D'arl looked back at Stillman. "If this is all you wanted, to throw out ridiculous accusations, then you've wasted my time. Good day to you." He stood up and headed toward the door.

"It isn't," Stillman said. "We think we've come up with an alternative."

D'arl stopped and turned back to face them. For a moment he measured them with his eyes, then slowly came and sat down again. "I'm listening."

Stillman leaned forward in his chair, willing calmness into his mind. Jonny's life was riding on this. "The Cobra gear was designed to give extra speed, weaponry, and reflexes to its owners; and according to Jame, Jonny told him the original equipment included vision and auditory enhancers as well." D'arl nodded once, and Stillman continued, "But warfare isn't the only area where these things would be useful. Specifically, how about new planet colonization?"

D'arl frowned, but Stillman hurried on before he could speak. "I've done some reading on this in the last few weeks, and the usual procedure seems to involve four steps. First, an initial exploration team goes in to confirm the planet is habitable. Then a more extensive scientific party is landed for more tests; after that you usually need a precolony group to go in with heavy machinery for clearing land and starting settlements. Only then does the first main wave of colonists arrive. The whole process can take several years and is very expensive, mainly because you need a small military base there the whole time to protect the explorers from unknown dangers. That means feeding a few hundred men, transporting weapons and lots of support gear—"

"I know what it involves," D'arl interrupted. "Get to your point."

"Sending in Cobras instead of regular soldiers would be easier and cheaper," Stillman said. "Their equipment is self-contained and virtually maintenance-free, and they can both act as guards and help with the other work. True, a Cobra probably costs more to equip than the soldiers and workers he'll replace—but you've already *got* the Cobras."

D'arl shook his head impatiently. "I listened this long because I hoped you might have come up with something new. Committé H'orme considered this same idea months ago. Certainly, it would save money—but only if you've got some place to use it. There are no more than a half-dozen habitable worlds left within our borders and all have had a preliminary exploration. We're hemmed in on all sides by alien empires; to gain more worlds we would have to go to war for them."

"Not necessarily," Jame said. "We could go *past* the aliens."

"What?"

"Here's what we have in mind," Stillman said. "The Trofts just lost a war to us, and they know that we're still strong enough to really tear into their empire if we decided to invade. So it shouldn't be too hard to talk them into ceding us a corridor of space through their territory, for non-military transport only. All the charts show there's at least *some* unclaimed space on the far side of their territory; that's where we set up the colony."

D'arl was gazing into space, a thoughtful look on his face. "What if there aren't any habitable planets out there?"

"Then we're out of luck," Stillman admitted. "But if there *are*, look at what you've gained. New worlds, new resources, maybe even new alien contacts and trade—it would be a far better return on the Cobra investment than you'd get by killing them off in a useless war."

"Yes. Of course, we'd have to put the colony far

enough past the border that the Trofts wouldn't be tempted to sneak out and destroy it. With that kind of long-distance transport, using Cobras instead of an armor battalion makes even more sense." He pursed his lips. "And as the colony gets stronger, it should help keep the Trofts peaceful—they must surely know better than to start a two-front war. The Army might be interested in that aspect."

Jame leaned forward. "Then you agree with us? You'll suggest this to Committé H'orme?"

Slowly, D'arl nodded. "I will. It makes sense and is potentially profitable for the Dominion—a good combination. I'm sure the ... trouble ... with the Minthisti can be handled without the Cobras." Abruptly, he stood up. "I expect both of you to keep silent about this," he cautioned. "Premature publicity would be harmful. I can't make any promises; but whatever decision the Committee makes will be quick."

He was right. Less than two weeks later the announcement was made.

The big military shuttle was surrounded by a surprisingly large crowd, considering that only twenty-odd people would be accompanying Jonny from Horizon to the new colonist training center on Asgard. At least ten times that many people were at the Port, what with family, friends, and general well-wishers seeing the emigrants off. Even so, the five Moreaus and Stillman had little trouble working their way through the mass. For some it seemed to be fear that moved them out of the way of the red and black diamond-patterned Cobra dress uniform; but for others—the important ones—it was genuine respect. Pioneers, Jonny reflected, probably had a different attitude toward powerful men than the general populace. Not surprising; it was on just those men that their lives would soon be depending.

"Well, Jonny, good luck," Stillman said as they stopped near the inner edge of the crowd. "I hope things work well for you."

"Thanks, Mr. Stillman," Jonny replied, gripping the mayor's outstretched hand firmly. "And thanks for—well, for your support."

"You'll tape us before you leave Asgard, won't you?" Irena asked, her eyes moist.

"Sure, Momer." Jonny hugged her. "Maybe in a couple of years you'll all be able to come out and visit me."

"Yeah!" Gwen agreed enthusiastically.

"Perhaps," Pearce said. "Take care, son."

"Watch yourself, Jonny," Jame seconded.

And with another round of hugs it was time to go. Picking up his satchel, Jonny stepped aboard the shuttle, pausing once on the steps to wave before entering. The shuttle was empty, but even as he chose a seat the other colonists began coming in. Almost, Jonny thought, as if his boarding had been the signal they'd been waiting for.

The thought brought a bittersweet smile to his lips. On Adirondack, too, the Cobras had always taken the lead ... but they'd never really been accepted by the general populace. Would things be different on this new world the survey expeditions had found for them, or would the pattern of Adirondack and Horizon simply be repeated wherever he went?

But in a way, it almost didn't matter anymore. He was tired of being a social pariah, and at least on an untamed planet that kind of failure was unlikely. Out there, the alternative to success was death ... and death was something Jonny had long ago learned how to face.

Still smiling, he leaned back in his seat and waited calmly for takeoff.

Interlude

The haiku garden in H'orme's dome apartment
was a minor miracle of horticultural design, a true
example of the melding of nature with technology.
Somehow, D'arl had never before noticed the har-
mony of the place—the ease, for example, with
which the holographic walls and ceiling comple-
mented the pattern of the walkways to give the
illusion of a much larger garden than was actually
here. The gently shifting winds, the whispered hints
of distant waterfalls and birds, the genuine sun-
shine brought in via mirrors from outside—D'arl
was impressed by the richness of it all. Had H'orme,
he wondered, always kept these sensory distrac-
tions at a minimum whenever the two men had
walked here together in the past? Probably. But
today there were no reports for H'orme to concentrate on. Only small talk . . . and good-byes.

"You'll need particularly to watch out for Committé Pendrikan," H'orme commented as he stooped
briefly to examine a particularly well-textured
saqqara shrub. "He's never liked me and will probably transfer that animosity to you. Illogical, really,
but you know the multi-generational grudges they
like to hold on Zimbwe."

D'arl nodded; he was well aware of Pendrikan's attitude. "I've watched you handle him often enough, sir. I think I know the levers to use on him."

"Good. But don't go out of your way to pick any fights for a while. The Committee's a surprisingly conservative body, and it'll be a bit before they feel at ease with you sitting *at* the table instead of behind it."

"And vice versa," D'arl murmured.

H'orme smiled, the expression becoming wistful as he looked around the garden. "I have no fears for you, D'arl. You have a natural talent for the job of Committé, the ability to see what needs to be done and how to do it. This whole resolution of the immediate Cobra problem showed that: your campaign was masterfully executed, from original concept to final Committee approval."

"Thank you, sir. Though as I've said before the basic idea came from elsewhere."

H'orme waved aside the distinction. "You're not supposed to reinvent the fusion plant every time you need something. It's your staff's job to come up with ideas; it's *your* job to evaluate them. Don't ever fall into the trap of trying to do it all yourself."

D'arl suppressed a smile. "Yes, sir."

H'orme gave him a sideways glance. "And before you savor the irony of that too much, remember how much work *I've* dumped on you alone. Pick your aides well, D'arl—in all too many cases, they're what make or break a Committé."

D'arl nodded silently and the two men continued their walk. Looking around, D'arl found his mind drifting back and forth across his thirteen years as H'orme's aide. It didn't seem nearly long enough to prepare him for the task ahead.

"So . . . what's the latest word from Aventine?"

Startled, D'arl tried to put his brain back on-line. Aventine . . .? Oh, right—the new colony world.

"The first wave of colonists seems to be settling in well enough. No major problems or overly dangerous fauna."

"At least as of three months ago," H'orme nodded.

"True," The communications time lag, D'arl had already realized, was going to be a problem in governing the new colony. Choosing a competent and reliable governor-general was going to be a major Committee task soon.

"And how do the Trofts seem to be taking it?" H'orme asked.

"No trouble at all, so far. Not even any boarding of ships going down the Corridor to check for military hardware."

"Um. Not what I expected. Still, all the ships up to now have been carrying Cobras as well as colonists. They may not have wanted to tangle with them again. But that can't last." H'orme walked for a moment in silence. "Somewhere along the line the Trofts are bound to realize Aventine is a potential threat to them. When that happens . . . the colony has to be strong enough to defend itself."

"Or spread out enough that it can't be taken in a single blow," D'arl suggested.

H'orme sighed. "A less acceptable position, but probably a more realistic one. Certainly in the short run."

They'd come full circle around the garden now, and H'orme paused at the office door for one last look. "If you'll sit still for one final word of advice, D'arl," he said slowly, "I'd recommend you find someone for your staff who really understands the Cobras. Not their weaponry, specifically, but the Cobras themselves."

D'arl smiled. "I believe I can do even better than that, sir. I've already been in touch with the young man who suggested the Aventine colony in the first place. His brother, as it happens, is one of the Cobras out there."

H'orme returned the smile. "I see I've trained you better even than I thought. I'm proud to have you as my successor . . . Committé D'arl."

"Thank you, sir," the younger man managed to say. "May you always be so proud of me."

Together they left the garden, to which H'orme would never return.

Loyalist: *2414*

The boundary between field and forest was as sharp as a laser beam, the giant blue-green cyprenes running right up to the half-meter of orange vegebarrier insulating the tender wheat shoots from native plant encroachment. In his more philosophical moments, Jonny saw a multi-leveled yin/yang in the arrangement: tall versus short, old versus young, native versus man-made. At the moment, though, his mood was anything but philosophical.

Looking up from the note, he found the youth who had delivered it standing in a rigid imitation of military attention. "And what exactly is this supposed to mean?" he asked, waving the note paper gently.

"The message is self-explanatory, sir—" the boy began.

"Yes, I can read," Jonny interrupted him. "And one more 'sir' out of you, Almo, and I'm going to tell your father on you. What I meant was, why did Challinor send you all the way out here just to invite me to a meeting? That's what these things are supposed to be for." He tapped the compact phone resting on his hip.

"Cee-two Challinor didn't want to take any

chances on word leaking out about this, sir—
Jonny," Almo corrected himself hastily. "It's a private meeting, for Cobras only."

Jonny studied the other's face a moment, then
folded the paper and stuck it in his pocket. Whatever Challinor was trying to prove, browbeating
his messenger boy wouldn't do any good. "You
can give Challinor a definite 'maybe,'" he told
Almo. "There's a spine leopard that's been poking
around the edge of the forest lately. If I don't get it
today, I'll have to ride guard with Chin's planter
tonight."

"Cee-two Challinor said I should emphasize the
meeting was very important."

"So's my word—and I promised Chin he could
start his second seedling run by tonight." Jonny
reached for his phone. "If you'd like, I can call
Challinor and tell him that myself," he suggested.

"No—that's all right," Almo said hastily. "I'll
tell him. Thank you for your time." With that he
took off across the field toward where his car was
waiting.

Jonny felt a smile touch his lips, but his amuse-
ment quickly faded. There weren't a lot of teen-
agers in this part of Aventine—the first two waves
of colonists had all been childless, and two suc-
ceeding waves of families hadn't made up the
deficit—and Jonny had always felt a twinge of
pain for the enhanced loneliness he knew Almo
and his peers must feel. The four Cobras assigned
to Almo's town of Thanksgiving were obvious
role models for the teen-aged boys, at least, and
Jonny was glad Almo had found a friend in Tors
Challinor. At least he used to be glad. Now, he
wasn't entirely sure.

Almo's car took off with minimal dust, and Jonny
turned both his face and attention to the towering
trees. He'd worry about Challinor's cloak and laser
later; right now he had a spine leopard to kill.

Making sure all the equipment on his belt was secured, he crossed the vegebarrier and entered the forest.

Even after seven years on Aventine Jonny felt a sense of awe whenever he stepped under the ancient canopy of oddly shaped leaves that turned the day into a diffuse twilight. Partly it was the forest's age, he had long ago decided; but partly also it was the humbling reminder of how little mankind knew about the world it had so recently claimed as its own. The forest was teeming with plant and animal life, virtually none of which was really understood. Clicking on his vision and auditory enhancers, Jonny moved deeper into the woods, trying to watch all directions at once.

The extra-loud snap of a branch above and behind him was his only warning, but it was enough. His nanocomputer correctly interpreted the sound as being caused by a large airborne body, and almost before Jonny's brain had registered the sound, his servos had taken over, throwing him to the side just as four sets of claws slashed through the space he'd vacated. Jonny rolled through a somersault—barely missing a gluevine-covered tree—and came up into a crouch. He got a glimpse of the spine leopard as it leaped toward him, razor-edged quills tucked tightly against its forelegs— and again his computer took over.

Standing flatfooted in the open, the only weapons Jonny could bring to bear were his fingertip lasers; but even as it again threw him to the side his computer used them with deadly efficiency. The twin needles of light lanced out, sweeping across the alien creature's head.

The spine leopard screamed, a full-bodied ululation that seemed to bounce off the inside of Jonny's stomach, and its spines snapped reflexively upright on its legs. The instinctive defensive move proved useless; Jonny was already beyond reach of the spine tips. Again he hit the ground, but this time he didn't roll back to his feet. Looking back over his shoulder, he saw the spine leopard struggling to get up, apparently oblivious to the black lines crisscrossing its face and to the brain damage behind them. A wound like that would have killed a human outright, but the less centralized alien metabolism wasn't as susceptible to localized destruction. The creature rose to its feet, spines still fully spread.

And the brilliant flash of his antiarmor laser caught the spine leopard in the head ... and this time the destruction was more than adequate.

Carefully Jonny got to his feet, wincing at the fresh bruises the battle had given him. His ankle felt warmer than it should have after only a single shot from the antiarmor laser—a heat-sensitization, he'd long suspected, due largely to his overuse of the weapon during the Tyler Mansion escape.

Even on Aventine, it seemed, he couldn't entirely escape the aftereffects of the war.

Taking one last look around him, he pulled out his phone and punched for the operator. "Ariel," the computer's voice said.

"Chin Reston," Jonny told it. A moment later the farmer's voice came on. "Reston here."

"Jonny Moreau, Chin. I got your spine leopard. I hope you didn't want it stuffed—I had to burn its head off."

"Hell with the head. Are *you* okay?"

Jonny smiled. "You worry too much—you know that? I'm fine; it never laid a spine on me. If you want, I'll put a beacon on it and you can come get the pelt whenever you want."

"Sounds good. Thanks a lot, Jonny—I really appreciate it."

"No charge. Talk to you later." Pressing the off switch, Jonny again punched for the operator. "Kennet MacDonald," he told the computer.

There was a moment of silence. "No answer," the operator informed him.

Jonny frowned. Like all Cobras on Aventine, MacDonald was supposed to carry his phone with him at all times. He was probably out in the forest or somewhere equally dangerous and didn't want to be distracted. "Record a message."

"Recording."

"Ken, this is Jonny Moreau. Call me as soon as you get a chance—preferably before this evening."

Switching off, Jonny returned the phone to his belt and unfastened one of the two tiny transponders from the underside of his emergency pouch. A flick of a switch set it in "operate" mode; stepping over the dead spine leopard, he dropped the device on its flank. For a moment he looked down at the creature, his eyes drawn to the foreleg spines. Aventine's biologists were unanimous in the opinion that the spines' placement and range of angles made them defensive rather than offensive weapons. The only problem was that no one had ever found any creature on the planet that a spine leopard might need such weapons to outfight. Personally, Jonny had no desire to be around when the first of that unknown species was discovered.

Reactivating his sensory enhancers, he began working his way back out of the forest.

MacDonald's call came in late in the afternoon, just as Jonny was looking over his pantry and trying to decide what to have for dinner.

"Sorry about the delay," MacDonald apologized after identifying himself. "I was out in the forest near the river most of the day with my phone turned off."

"No problem," Jonny assured him. "Spine leopard hunting?"

"Yeah. Got one, too."

"Likewise. Must be another migration; they don't

usually find the territories we've cleared out quite this fast. We're probably going to be busy for a while."

"Well, things were getting dull, anyway. What's on your mind?"

Jonny hesitated. There *could* be a good reason why Challinor didn't want any word of his meeting going out on the airwaves. "Did you get any unusual messages today?" he asked obliquely.

"Matter of fact, I did. You want to get together and talk about it? Wait a second—Chrys's trying to get my attention." A voice spoke unintelligibly in the background. "Chrys says you should join us for dinner in about half an hour, at her place."

"Sorry, but I've already got my own started," Jonny lied. "Why don't I come over when I've finished eating?"

"Okay," MacDonald said. "About seven, say? Afterward, maybe we can all go for a drive together."

Challinor's meeting was scheduled for seven-thirty. "Sounds good," Jonny agreed. "See you at seven."

Replacing his phone, Jonny grabbed a package at random from the pantry and took it over to the microwave. He would have liked to have joined the others for dinner—MacDonald and Chrys Eldjarn were two of his favorite people—and if Chrys's father hadn't been out of town doing emergency surgery, he would have jumped at the invitation. But Chrys and MacDonald were a pretty steady couple, and they got little enough time to be alone together as it was. With only two Cobras to guard Ariel's four hundred sixty colonists from both Aventine's fauna and, occasionally, each other, spare time was at a premium.

Besides which, he thought wryly, spending more time in range of Chrys's smile would only tempt him to try and steal her away from MacDonald again, and there was no point in making trouble for himself like that. Their friendship was too valuable to him to risk messing it up.

He had a—for him—leisurely dinner and arrived at the Eldjarn's home at seven o'clock sharp. Chrys let him in, treating him to one of her dazzling smiles, and led the way to the living room, where MacDonald waited on the couch.

"You missed a great dinner," MacDonald greeted him, waving him to a chair.

"I'm sure you made up for my absence," Jonny said blandly. Half a head taller than Jonny and a good deal burlier, MacDonald had an ability to put food away that was known all through the district.

"I tried. Let's see your note."

Digging it out, Jonny handed it over. MacDonald scanned it briefly, then passed it to Chrys, who had curled up on the couch beside him. "Identical to mine," he told Jonny. "Any idea what it's all about?"

Jonny shook his head. "The *Dewdrop*'s been out surveying the nearest system for the past couple of months. Do you suppose they found something interesting?"

"'Interesting' as in 'dangerous'?" Chrys asked quietly.

"Possibly," MacDonald told her, "especially if this news is really only for Cobras. But I doubt it," he said, addressing Jonny. "If this were a war council or something we should all be meeting at Capitalia, not Thanksgiving."

"Unless they're passing the news out piecemeal, to the individual villages," Jonny suggested. "But that again drops it out of the 'emergency' category. Incidentally, who brought you the message? Almo Pyre?"

MacDonald nodded. "Seemed awfully formal, too. Called me 'Cee-two MacDonald' about four times."

"Yeah, me too. Has Challinor instituted the old rank system over there, or something?"

"Don't know—I haven't been to Thanksgiving for weeks." MacDonald glanced at his watch. "I suppose it's time to remedy that deficiency, eh? Let's go see what Challinor wants."

"Come back after it's over and tell me what happened," Chrys said as they all stood up.

"It could be late before we get back," MacDonald warned as he kissed her good-bye.

"That's okay—Dad's coming home late, too, so I'll be up."

"All right. Car's out back, Jonny."

Thanksgiving was a good twenty kilometers east-northeast of Ariel along a dirt-and-vegebarrier road that was, so far, the norm in the newer areas of the human beachhead on Aventine. MacDonald drove, guiding the car skillfully around the worst of the potholes while avoiding the occasional tree branch reaching out from the thick forest on either side.

"One of these days a spine leopard's going to jump a car from one of those overhangs and get the surprise of his life," MacDonald commented.

Jonny chuckled. "I think they're too smart for that. Speaking of smart moves, you and Chrys to the point of setting a date yet?"

"Umm . . . not really. I think we both want to make sure we're right for each other."

"Well, in my opinion, if you don't grab her while you've got the chance you're crazy. Though I'm not sure I'd give her the same advice."

MacDonald snorted. "Thanks a kilo. Just for that I may make you walk home."

Challinor's house was near the outskirts of Thanksgiving, within sight of the cultivated fields surrounding the village. Two other cars were already parked there; and as they got out and headed for the house, the front door opened, revealing a slender man in full Cobra dress uniform. "Good evening, Moreau; MacDonald," he said coolly. "You're twenty minutes late."

Jonny felt MacDonald stiffen beside him and hurried to get in the first word. "Hello, L'est," he said, gesturing to the other's outfit. "I didn't realize this was a costume party."

Simmon L'est merely smiled thinly, a mannerism whose carefully measured condescension had always irritated Jonny. But the other's eyes showed the barb had hit its target. MacDonald must have seen that, too, and brushed silently by L'est without delivering the more potent blast he'd obviously been readying when Jonny stepped in. Breathing a bit easier, Jonny followed his friend in, L'est closing the door behind them.

The modest-sized living room was comfortably crowded. At the far end, on a straight-back chair, sat Tors Challinor, resplendent in his own Cobra dress uniform; at his right, looking almost drab in their normal work clothes, were Sandy Taber and Barl DesLone, the two Cobras stationed in Greensward. Next to them, also in dress uniforms, were Hael Szintra of Oasis and Franck Patrusky of Thanksgiving.

"Ah—MacDonald and Moreau," Challinor called in greeting. "Come in; your seats are right up here." He indicated the two empty chairs to his left.

"I hope this is really important, Challinor," MacDonald growled as the two men crossed the room and sat down. "I don't know what things are like in Thanksgiving, but we don't have a lot of time in Ariel for playing soldier." He glanced significantly at the uniforms.

"As it happens, your lack of spare time is one of the topics we want to discuss," Challinor said smoothly. "Tell me, does Ariel have all the Cobras it deserves? Or does Greensward, for that matter?" he added, looking at Taber and DesLone.

"What do you mean, 'deserves'?" Taber asked.

"At last count there were about ten thousand people in Caravel District and exactly seventy-two Cobras," Challinor said. "That works out to one Cobra per hundred-forty people. Any way you slice it, a town the size of Greensward ought to have *three* Cobras assigned to it, not two. And that goes double for Ariel."

"Things seem reasonably calm at the moment in Ariel," MacDonald said. "We don't really need any more firepower than we've got." He looked at Taber. "How are conditions around Greensward?"

"Firepower isn't the issue," Szintra put in before Taber could answer. "The point is that we're required to do a lot more than just guard our villages against spine leopards and falx. We have to hunt down wheat snakes, act as patrollers in domestic squabbles—and if we have any spare time left, we're supposed to help cut down trees and unload supply trucks. And we get *nothing* in return!"

Jonny looked at Szintra's flushed face, then at the other three uniformed men. A cold knot was beginning to form over his dinner. "Ken, perhaps we should get back to Ariel," he said quietly to MacDonald.

"No—please stay a while longer," Challinor spoke up hastily. "Cee-three Szintra was a bit more forceful than necessary, but stuck all alone out in Oasis he perhaps sees matters more clearly than some of the rest of us."

"Let's assume for the present that he's right, that we don't get the respect we deserve," MacDonald said. "What solution are we discussing here?"

"It's not simply lack of respect, or even the way we always seem to be taken for granted," Challinor said earnestly. "It's also the way the syndic's office takes forever to process the simplest requests for equipment or supplies—though they're prompt enough when it comes to picking up surplus wheat and gluevine extract when we have it. They seem to have forgotten that the whole planet isn't as comfortable as Rankin and Capitalia, that when a frontier town needs something we need it *now*. Add to that the mania for making lots of little frontier settlements instead of consolidating the territory we've got—which is why we're spread so damn thin—and you get a picture of a government that's not doing its job. To put it bluntly, we feel something has to be done about it."

There was a long moment of silence. "What do you suggest?" DesLone asked at last. "That we send a petition to the Dominion with the next courier ship?"

"Don't be denser than you have to, Barl," Taber growled. "They're talking about replacing Governor-General Zhu themselves."

"Actually, our thinking is that more than the governor-general needs changing," Challinor said calmly. "It's painfully clear that the centralized system that works so well once a world is established is failing miserably on Aventine. We need something more decentralized, something more responsive to the planet's needs—"

"Governed by those who'd do the best job?" Jonny cut in. "Us, for instance?"

"In many ways, our struggle to tame Aventine is analogous to the guerrilla war we waged against the Trofts," Challinor said. "If I do say so myself, we did a hell of a job back then—don't you agree? Who on this planet could do better?"

"So what are you suggesting?" MacDonald asked, his tone far more interested than it had any business being. "We carve Aventine into little kingdoms, each one run by a Cobra?"

"Basically," Challinor nodded. "It's a bit more complicated than that—there'd have to be a loose hierarchy to settle disputes and such—but that's the general idea. What do you say? Are you interested?"

"How many of you are there?" MacDonald asked, ignoring the question.

"Enough," Challinor said. "The four of us here, plus the three from Fallow, two from Weald, and three more from Headwater and the lumber camps upslope of the Kerseage Mines."

"You propose to take over an entire world with twelve Cobras?"

Challinor's brow furrowed slightly. "No, of course not. But I've talked to a lot of other Cobras, both in and out of Caravel District. Most of them are willing to wait and see what happens with our experiment."

"In other words, to see how hard Zhu comes down on you when you declare independence?" MacDonald shook his head. "Your thinking's got loose connections, Challinor. No Cobra's going to be allowed to stay neutral in something like that— they'll be ordered to come here and restore the syndic's rule, and their answer to that order will put them on one side or the other. With the odds at—let's see; twelve Cobras out of six hundred twenty makes it about fifty to one—which way do you think they'll jump?"

"Which way are *you* jumping, MacDonald?" L'est cut in suddenly from his seat by the door. "You ask a lot of questions for someone who hasn't committed himself yet."

MacDonald kept his eyes on Challinor. "How about it, Challinor? This is going to take more than an ace or two up your sleeve."

"I asked you a question, damn it!" L'est snapped.

Deliberately, MacDonald turned to face the other; just as leisurely he got to his feet. "I stand where I and my family have always stood: with the Dominion of Man. What you're talking is treason, gentlemen; I won't have any part of it."

L'est was on his feet now, too, standing sideways to MacDonald in a Cobra ready stance. "The loyalty of an EarthScot or a fine dog," he sneered. "In case you haven't noticed, EarthScot, this Dominion you're so eager to please is treating you like dangerous garbage. It's thrown you just as far away as it possibly could, with a hundred fifty light-years and two hundred billion Trofts between you and civilization."

"We're needed here for the colonization effort," Jonny interjected, wanting to stand in MacDonald's support but afraid the action might be misinterpreted. In such close quarters an all-out fire fight between the two Cobras would probably be lethal to everyone in the room.

"That's donk dung, Moreau—we're here because it was cheaper than starting a new war just to kill us off," L'est ground out. "The Dominion doesn't care if we live or die out here. It's up to us to insure our own survival—no matter what sort of short-sighted fools get in our way."

"You coming, Jonny?" MacDonald asked, taking a step toward the door.

L'est took a step of his own, putting himself directly in front of the door. "You're not leaving, MacDonald. You know too much."

"Take it easy, Simmon," Challinor said, his tone calm but with steel underlying it. "We're not giving these gentlemen a choice between joining us or death."

L'est didn't move. "You don't know this clown, Tors. He's a troublemaker."

"Yes, you told me that earlier. Cee-two MacDonald, please understand that we're not doing this simply for our own personal gain." Challinor's voice was pure sincerity. "The people of Aventine need strong, competent leadership, and they're not getting it. It's our *duty* to these people—these citizens of the Dominion—to save them from disaster."

"If your friend over there doesn't get out of the way, I'm going to have to move him myself," MacDonald said.

Challinor sighed. "Simmon, step aside. MacDonald, will you at least think about what I've said?"

"Oh, I'll think about it all right." With his eyes still on L'est, MacDonald moved toward the door.

Carefully, his attention on the still-seated Patrusky and Szintra, Jonny got to his feet and followed. "If you'd like to stay, Moreau," Challinor called after him, "we can get you back to Ariel later."

"No, thanks," Jonny said, glancing back over his shoulder. "I have some work I need to finish up tonight."

"All right. But think about what I've said, all right?"

The words were friendly, but something in the tone made the hairs on Jonny's neck tingle. Suppressing a shiver, he got out fast.

The drive back to Ariel was quiet. Jonny, expecting MacDonald to be somewhere on the far side of furious, braced himself for a hair-raising ride on the bumpy road. To his surprise, though, MacDonald drove with a calmness that bordered on the sedate. But the backwash of the car's headlights showed clearly the tension in his jaw and around his eyes. Jonny took the cue and kept his mouth shut.

Lights were still showing in the Eldjarn house when MacDonald brought them to a stop across the street. Parked in front of them was the car Chrys's father had taken to Rankin; obviously, he'd arrived home too late to take it back to the village garage.

As before, Chrys answered the door. "Come on

in," she invited, stepping to one side. "You're earlier than I expected—short meeting?"

"Too long," MacDonald growled.

Chrys's eyes took on a knowing look. "Uh-oh. What happened—Challinor want you to petition for more Cobras again?"

MacDonald shook his head. "Nothing so amusing. They want to take over the planet."

Chrys stopped in mid-stride. "They *what?*"

"You heard me. They want to overthrow the governor-general and set up a warlord system with little fiefdoms for all of the Cobras who join him."

Chrys looked at Jonny. "Is he kidding me, Jonny?" she asked.

Jonny shook his head. "No. Challinor's dead serious about it. I don't know how they hope to do anything but get themselves slagged, though—"

"Just a second," she interrupted, moving toward the door to the bedroom wing. "I think Dad had better hear this."

"Good idea," MacDonald grunted, stepping to the corner liquor cabinet and pouring himself a drink. Holding up the bottle, he looked questioningly at Jonny, who shook his head.

A couple of minutes later Chrys was back, a dressing-gowned man in tow. "Ken; Jonny," Dr. Orrin Eldjarn nodded to them, looking wide awake despite his sleep-tousled hair. "What's this about some kind of cabal being formed?"

They all sat down, the Eldjarns listening intently as MacDonald gave them a capsule summary of Challinor's proposal. "But as Jonny said," he concluded, "there's just no way they can succeed. One Cobra's fighting strength is essentially the same as another's, after all."

"But orders of magnitude higher than anyone else's," Eldjarn commented. "If Challinor announced he was taking over Thanksgiving, there's really nothing the people there could do to stop him."

"Surely there are a few other weapons there," Chrys argued. "We've got at least a half dozen pellet guns here in Ariel, and Thanksgiving's bigger than we are."

"Pellet guns would be essentially useless against a Cobra except in cramped quarters where he couldn't maneuver," Jonny told her. "The firing mechanism has a distinctive click that's loud enough for us to hear, and we'd normally have no trouble getting out of the line of fire. The Trofts on Silvern took forever to learn that lesson."

"But that's not the point," MacDonald said. "To kill twelve rebel Cobras, all it should take is twelve loyal Cobras."

"Unless the rebels manage to target all the others before the battle starts," Chrys suggested suddenly. "Couldn't they kill everyone in one quick volley if they did that?"

MacDonald shook his head. "The optical enhancers we've got now don't have the multiple targeting capability of our old ones. But okay— let's say it'll even take *fifty* Cobras if the rebels are dug in and you want an absolutely sure victory. That's still only a twelfth of Zhu's forces. Challinor has to know that."

"So the question is, what else does he know— that we don't." Eldjarn stroked his chin thoughtfully. "Anything happening elsewhere on Aventine that might be pinning down large numbers of Cobras? Civil unrest in one of the other districts or something?"

Jonny and MacDonald exchanged glances, and the latter shrugged. "Nothing we've heard of," he said. "I suppose it's conceivable that Challinor's organized groups in other towns for a simultaneous declaration, but I don't really believe it."

"The spine leopards are on the move again,"

Jonny suggested doubtfully. "That'll keep a lot of Cobras on patrolling and hunting duty unless the farmers went to stay out of their fields for a few days. I can't see that worrying the governor-general, though. Maybe Challinor's just lost his mind."

"Not Challinor." MacDonald was definite. "He's as sharp and level-headed as they come. And L'est wouldn't have come in on this on the strength of Challinor's sales talk alone, either—that one was a weasel even before we hit Aventine."

"I'm inclined to agree," Eldjarn said slowly. "The timing here is too good for megalomaniacs to have come up with. As you pointed out, Jonny, the spine leopard migration will hinder any official counter-measures, at least a little. Less coincidental, I'm sure, is the fact that the Dominion courier ship left Capitalia just a few days ago, which means it'll be six months before anyone from the Dominion touches down here again."

"Plenty of time to consolidate a new regime," MacDonald growled. "They can present the cou-rier with a *fait accompli* and dare Dome to do something."

"And the *Dewdrop*'s out somewhere in deep space," Jonny said with a grimace.

"Right," Eldjarn nodded. "Until it gets back, there's no way for Zhu to get in touch with anyone—and even then, if the *Dewdrop* can't land some-where secure for fuel and provisions, it won't be able to go for help. No, Challinor's thought this out carefully. It's a shame you couldn't have played along a little longer and found out the rest of his plan."

"I did what I could," MacDonald said, a bit stiffly. "I won't lie about my loyalty to anyone."

"Sure—I understand," Eldjarn said.

For a moment the room was silent. "I suppose *I* could go back to them," Jonny said hesitantly. "I never really stated where I stood."

"They'd be suspicious," MacDonald said, shaking his head. "And if they caught you passing information to us they'd treat you as a spy."

"Unless, of course," Chrys said quietly, "you *want* to go back."

Her father and MacDonald looked at her in surprise, but her gaze remained on Jonny. "After all, we've been assuming Jonny was solidly on our side," she pointed out calmly. "Maybe he hasn't really made up his mind. This isn't a decision that we should be making for him."

Eldjarn nodded agreement. "You're right, of course. Well, Jonny? What do you say?"

Jonny pursed his lips. "To be completely honest, I don't know. I swore an oath of allegiance to the Dominion, too—but the government here really *is* doing some potentially disastrous things, especially the overextending of people and resources. What Challinor said about our duty being to the *people* of Aventine isn't something I can dismiss out of hand."

"But if the legal avenues for political change are ignored—by anyone—you open the way for total anarchy," MacDonald argued. "And if you really think Challinor and L'est would do a better job—"

"Ken." Chrys put a restraining hand on his arm. To Jonny, she said, "I understand your uncertainties, but I'm sure you realize this isn't an issue you'll be able to stay neutral on."

"And you'll need to make your decision soon," Eldjarn pointed out. "Challinor wouldn't have risked telling such a long-shot as Ken about the plot unless they were almost ready to move."

"I understand." Jonny got to his feet. "I think perhaps I'd better go home. If I decide to actively oppose Challinor you can always fill me in later on anything you come up with tonight. At any rate—" he met MacDonald's gaze firmly "—what's been said here already is between the four of us alone. Challinor won't hear any of it from me."

Slowly, MacDonald nodded. "All right. I guess that's all we can expect. You want a ride home?"

"No, thanks; I'll walk. Good night, all."

Like the farming communities Jonny had known on Horizon, Ariel generally closed down fairly early in the evening. The streets were dark and deserted, with the only illumination coming from occasional streetlights and the brilliant stars overhead. Usually, Jonny liked looking at the stars whenever he was out this late; tonight, he hardly noticed they were there.

There had been a time, he thought wryly, when simply gazing into Chrys's eyes would have immediately brought him back onto her side, no matter what the cause or topic at issue. But that time lay far in his past. The war, his failed attempts to reenter mainstream society afterwards, and seven long years of working to build a new world had all taken their toll on the rashness of youth. He had long ago learned not to base his decisions on emotional reasoning.

The trouble was that, at the moment, he didn't have a terrific number of facts on which to base an intelligent decision. So far everything pointed to a quick defeat for Challinor's group ... but there *had* to be more to it than the obvious. Whatever his other irritating characteristics, Simmon L'est was an excellent tactician, his father having been an Army training instructor on Asgard. He wouldn't join any venture that was obviously doomed—and a long, bloody war would be disastrous for the colony.

On the other hand, Jonny's allegiance *was* technically to the government of the Dominion and, by extension, to Aventine's governor-general. And despite L'est's sneers, MacDonald's sense of loyalty had always been something Jonny admired.

His brain was still doing flip-flops when he

reached home. The usual bedtime preparations took only a few minutes; then, turning off the light, he got into bed and closed his eyes. Perhaps by morning things would be clearer.

But he was far too keyed up to sleep. Finally, after an hour of restlessly changing positions, he went to his desk and dug out the tape from his family that had come with the last courier. Putting it on the player, he adjusted the machine for sound only and crawled back into bed, hoping the familiar voices would help him relax.

He was drifting comfortably toward sleep when a part of his sister's monologue seemed to pry itself under a corner of his consciousness. ". . . I've been accepted at the University of Aerie," Gwen's playful voice was saying. "It means finishing my schooling away from Horizon, but they've got the best geology program in this part of the Dominion and offer a sub-major in tectonic utilization. I figure having credentials like that's my best chance of getting accepted as a colonist to Aventine. I hope you'll have enough pull out there by the time I graduate to get me assigned to Ariel—I'm not just coming out there to see what the backside of the Troft Empire looks like, you know. Though Jame ought to be able to pull any strings from Asgard by then, too, come to think of it. Speaking of the Trofts, there was a sort of informal free-for-all debate in the hall at school the other day on whether the Aventine project was really just an Army plot to outflank the Trofts so that they wouldn't try to attack us again. I think I held up our end pretty well—the stats you sent on the output of the Kerseage Mines were of enormous help—but I'm afraid I've ruined any chance I might ever have had of passing myself off as demure or ladylike. I hope there's no ban on letting in rowdies out there. . . ."

Getting up, Jonny switched the player off . . .

and by the time he got back into bed he knew what his decision had to be. Gwen's cheerful tapes to him, full of confidence and borderline hero worship, had helped him over the roughest times out here in a way that the quieter support of his parents and Jame hadn't been able to duplicate. To willingly take on the label of traitor—especially when the situation was by no means desperate yet—would be a betrayal of both Gwen's pride and his family's trust. And that was something he would never willingly do.

For a moment he considered calling MacDonald to tell the other of his decision . . . but the bed felt more and more comfortable as the tension began to leave him. Besides, it was getting late. Morning would be soon enough to join the loyalist cause.

Five minutes later, he was sound asleep.

He woke to the impatient buzz of his alarm, and as he rubbed the sleep from his eyes, the answer popped into his mind. For a moment he lay still, his mind busy sorting out details and possibilities. Then, rolling out of bed, he snared his phone and got the operator. "Kennet MacDonald," he told it.

The wait was unusually long; MacDonald must have still been asleep. "Yes; hello," his voice finally came.

"It's Jonny, Ken. I know what Challinor's up to."

"You do?" MacDonald was suddenly alert. "What?"

"He's going to take over the Kerseage Mines."

Another long pause. "Damn," MacDonald said at last. "That has to be it. Over half of Aventine's rare-earth elements alone come from there. All he'd have to do is use the mine's explosives cache to doomsday the shafts and entrances—Zhu would have to think long and hard about sending a massive force to evict him."

"And the longer Zhu hesitates the weaker he looks," Jonny said, "and the more likely some of Challinor's 'neutral' Cobras will see him as the probable winner and shift sides. If enough do that, Zhu'll either have to capitulate or risk civil war."

"Yeah. *Damn.* We've got to alert Capitalia, get them to send a force up there before Challinor makes his move."

"Right. You want to call them or shall I?"

"It'd be better if we were both on the line. Hang on; let's see if I remember how to do this—"

There was a double click. "Ariel," the operator said.

"The governor-general's office in Capitalia," Mac-Donald told it.

"I'm sorry, but I am unable to complete the call."

Jonny blinked. "Why not?"

"I'm sorry, but I am unable to complete the call."

"Do you suppose the satellite's out of whack?" Jonny suggested hopefully.

"Not likely," MacDonald growled. "Operator: Syndic Powell Stuart's office in Rankin."

"I'm sorry, but I am unable to complete the call."

And Rankin wasn't far enough away to require the communication satellite. "So much for coincidence," Jonny said, feeling a knot forming in his stomach. "How did Challinor get to the phone computer so fast?"

"He could have done this any time in the past few days," MacDonald grunted. "I doubt if anyone's needed to talk to Capitalia or Rankin lately; certainly not since the courier ship left."

"Maybe that's why he sent Almo Pyre with notes instead of calling us from Thanksgiving," Jonny suggested, suddenly remembering. "Maybe all out-of-town contact's been halted."

"Maybe. Listen, I don't like using this phone, all of a sudden. Let's meet at Chrys's shop in, say, half an hour."

"Right. Half an hour."

Jonny clicked off the phone, and for a moment he stared at the little box, wondering if anyone had been eavesdropping on the conversation. Unlikely . . . but if Challinor could fix the computer to block out-of-town calls, why not also set up something to monitor all in-town ones?

Jumping out of bed, he began pulling on his clothes.

One of Ariel's two fully qualified electronics technicians, Chrys shared a two-floor combination office/shop/storeroom near the roughly circular area in the center of town which was known, presumably for historical reasons, as the Square. Jonny got there early and waited nervously outside until Chrys and MacDonald arrived with the keys.

"Let's get inside," MacDonald urged, glancing around at the handful of other people that had appeared on the streets as the village began its preparations for the new day. "Challinor may have hired a spy or two in town."

Inside, Chrys turned on some lights and sank into her workbench chair, yawning prodigiously. "Okay, we're here," she said. "Now would you care to explain what we needed me to do here on five hours' sleep and ten minutes' notice?"

"We're cut off from both Rankin and Capitalia," MacDonald told her. "Challinor's apparently jinxed the phone computer." He went on to describe Jonny's idea about the Kerseage Mines and their attempt to alert the authorities. "Besides the water route up the Chalk River, the only land routes to the Mines are the roads from Thanksgiving and Weald," he explained. "Challinor's in position to block both of them, and if he can control the river here at Ariel, the governor-general won't have any way to move in forces or equipment except by aircar."

"*Damn* him," Chrys muttered, her eyes wide awake now and flashing sparks. "If he's fouled up all the long-distance circuits, it'll probably take a week to repair the damage."

"Well, that answers my first question," MacDonald said grimly. "Next question: can you build a transmitter of any kind here that can bypass the operator entirely and run a signal to Capitalia via the satellite?"

"In theory, sure. In practice—" She shrugged. "I haven't built a high-frequency focused-beam transmitter since my first year at school. It would take at least two or three days' work, even assuming I've got all the necessary equipment."

"Can you use some of your spare telephone modules?" Jonny suggested. "That should at least save you some assembly time."

"Provided I don't overlap one of the regular frequencies and trigger a squelch reaction from the phone computer, yes," she nodded. "Readjusting built-in freq settings may take just as long as building from scratch, but it's worth a try."

"Good. Get to work." MacDonald turned to Jonny. "Even if Challinor didn't set up a flag to let him know when anyone tries to call Capitalia, we should assume he'll be moving against us soon. We'll need to alert Mayor Tyler and organize whatever we can in the way of resistance."

"Which is basically you and me," Jonny said.

"Plus those half-dozen pellet guns Chrys mentioned last night." He saw Jonny's expression and shrugged uncomfortably. "I know—living clay pigeons. But you know as well as I do that our nanocomputers react more slowly when faced with two or more simultaneous threats. It might just give us the edge we'll need."

"Maybe." All the ghosts of Adirondack were rising behind Jonny's eyes. Civilians getting killed in cross-fires . . . "What would we be doing, trying to guard the road from Thanksgiving?"

MacDonald shook his head. "There's no way we can keep them out—they can abandon the road whenever they please if they don't mind having to kill a spine leopard or two on the way into town and don't need to bring in any heavy equipment. No, the best we can hope for is to hold this building until Chrys can finish a transmitter that'll bring help from Capitalia."

"Maybe we should try the innocent approach, too," Chrys suggested, looking up from the book of circuit diagrams she'd been paging through. "As long as they haven't actually invaded yet, why don't we have someone—Dad, for instance—try to drive through Thanksgiving to Sangraal and call Capitalia from there?"

"I doubt if Challinor's letting any traffic travel east from here," MacDonald said, "but it's worth a try. You think your dad would be willing?"

"Sure," she reached for her phone . . . hesitated. "Maybe I'd better just ask him to come over and then explain things once he gets here. Challinor may have put a monitor in the system."

The call took half a minute; Eldjarn asked no questions and said he'd be there right away. As Chrys broke the connection MacDonald started for the door. "I'm going to find the mayor," he said over his shoulder. "Jonny, you stay here—just in case. I'll be back as soon as I can."

Eldjarn had come and gone and Chrys had been working for an hour and a half when they heard the shot.

"What was *that*?" Chrys asked, looking up from her breadboard.

"Pellet gun," Jonny snapped, already moving

toward the door. "You'd better stay here while I—"

"Forget it," she said, setting her solderer down carefully and racing after him. "Ken's out there!"

There was no second shot, but even so they had no problem locating the scene of the trouble. Already thirty or more people had gathered around the edge of the Square; more, like Jonny and Chrys, were hurrying in that direction. Off to the side, at one corner of the building housing the mayor's office, lay a crumpled figure. Kneeling over him was MacDonald.

"Halt!" an authoritative voice barked, as Jonny and Chrys pushed through the clump of spectators and headed for MacDonald. "Stay away from him."

Jonny glanced at the speaker without slowing. "The hell with you, L'est," he said. "The man's hurt!"

The laser blast Jonny had half expected to take in the back didn't come, and they reached MacDonald without further incident. "What can we do?" he asked as they dropped to their knees beside him. The other Cobra, Jonny saw now, was pumping rhythmically on the injured man's sternum with the heel of his hand.

"Ventilate him," MacDonald snapped; but Chrys had anticipated the order and was already beginning mouth-to-mouth. Jonny opened the charred shirt gingerly, wincing as he saw the location of the burn. "What happened?"

"Challinor got here about fifteen minutes ago and told Mayor Tyler they were taking over," MacDonald said tightly. "We weren't in any kind of defense posture yet, but Insley tried to take a shot at him anyway." He swore viciously. "Challinor got out of the way and behind cover. There wasn't any reason to shoot to kill—but L'est apparently felt we needed an object lesson."

Jonny looked over MacDonald's shoulder. L'est

was still standing near the center of the Square, watching them. Glancing around, he noticed for the first time that four more Cobras were also present, spaced more or less evenly around that end of the Square: the two men who besides L'est had been at Challinor's the night before, Challinor himself, and— "Sandy Taber's joined them," he said.

MacDonald grunted. "Chrys?" he asked

She moved her face away from Insley's and shook her head. "There's no pulse in the carotid artery," she said gently. "Hasn't been since we got here. I'm sorry, Ken."

For a long moment MacDonald looked at her, his hands still in position on the dead man's chest. Then, slowly, he stood up and turned back toward the Square, his face like a thundercloud sculpted from stone. "Keep her clear, Jonny," he murmured, and started walking toward L'est.

The action was so casual that he was four steps away before Jonny understood exactly what the Cobra was planning. Simultaneously, a hissing intake of air behind him told him Chrys also had suddenly realized what was going to happen. "Ken!" she blurted, leaping to her feet.

Jonny was faster, standing up and grabbing her in an unbreakable grip before she could get past him. "Stay here," he whispered urgently into her ear. "You can't do anything for him out there."

"Jonny, you have to stop him!" she moaned as she struggled against him. "They'll kill him!"

For Jonny, it was the hardest decision he'd ever made in his life. Every instinct screamed at him to step into the Square and begin shooting, to try and knock out one or more of the Cobras waiting silently in their circle. To him it was obvious that Insley's death had been a deliberate effort on L'est's part to provoke precisely this reaction; to goad MacDonald into a confrontation where all the numerical and tactical advantages were theirs. But equally obvious was the fact that there was nothing he could to change the coming battle's outcome. At five-to-two odds he and MacDonald together would die just as surely as MacDonald alone ... and with both of their Cobra defenders gone, the people of Ariel would have no way at all to fight back against Challinor's fledgling warlords. Even more than it had been the previous night, it was clear where his duty lay.

And so he clung tightly to Chrys and watched as they killed his friend.

It was a short battle. Even burning with rage, MacDonald had enough sense not to simply come to a halt and try to gun L'est down. Halfway through one of his strides he abruptly let his right leg collapse beneath him, dropping straight down onto the ground. Simultaneously, his arms snapped up, fingertip lasers sending fire to both sides. Patrusky and Szintra, at the receiving ends of the two blasts, reacted instantly, twisting aside as their own nanocomputers responded with return fire. An instant later there were twin howls of pain as the renegade Cobras' shots crossed the Square and hit each other ... and from his prone position on the ground, MacDonald brought his left leg to bear on L'est.

He never got a chance to fire. With his own lightning reflexes and servo-augmented muscles, L'est leaped up in a six-meter-high arc that took him almost directly over his opponent. MacDonald moved with desperate speed to get his hands up ... but L'est's leg got to firing position first.

The square lit up for an instant, and it was all over.

Beside him, Jonny felt the tension drain out of Chrys's body. For a moment he thought she would either faint or become hysterical ... but when she spoke her voice was quiet and firm. "Let me go to him, Jonny. Please."

He hesitated, knowing what it would look like. "It'll be pretty bad—"

"Please."

They went together, Jonny with his arm still around her.

It was, indeed, pretty bad. L'est's antiarmor blast had caught MacDonald high in the chest, destroying his heart and probably a good percentage of his lung tissue. His arms lay limply on the ground, indicating that the connections between nanocomputer and arm servos had also been destroyed, denying the Cobra even the satisfaction of one last dying shot.

"Such a terrible waste."

Jonny turned slowly, disengaging his arm from Chrys's shoulders and taking a half step away from her. "Yes, it is, isn't it, Challinor?" he said to the man standing before him, a white-hot anger beginning to burn through his mind. "A shame he didn't try for you and your chief butcher instead of your two dupes."

"He attacked first. You saw that—you all saw that," Challinor added, raising his voice for the benefit of the stuned crowd. "Cee-three L'est was protecting you, as is his duty."

All the possible responses collided deep in Jonny's throat; what came out was an animalistic growl. Challinor regarded him thoughtfully. "I'm sorry about your friend—truly I am," he said quietly. "But we can't allow opposition to our plan. We're going to remake Aventine, Moreau; and the faster and stronger our first stroke, the more likely the governor-general will capitulate without unnecessary bloodshed."

Taber came up to Challinor's side. "Szintra is dead," he reported, avoiding Jonny's eyes. "Patrusky's going to be out of action for a few days, but none of his burns are really dangerous."

Challinor nodded. "I underestimated him rather

badly," he mused. "I thought he was too angry to be thinking tactically. A dangerous man—I wish he'd been on our side."

"I'm going to kill you, Challinor," Jonny ground out. "You set Ken up to be killed, and you're going to die for that."

Challinor didn't move, but his gaze tightened slightly. "You're welcome to try," he said softly. "But you can't stop us. L'est will carry on in my place if I die; would you rather he be in charge? And don't expect you'll get all of us. MacDonald was lucky to do as much damage as he did."

Jonny didn't reply. Like a surfer on a wave, his tactical sense was riding the crest of his rage, calculating odds and possibilities with abnormal speed and clarity. Challinor stood before him, Taber slightly to his left, L'est somewhere behind him. An imperceptible bending of the knees could let him jump high enough to deliver lethal head kicks to the two in front of him, especially if the attack were preceded by a numbing blast from his sonic. L'est was far out of the sonic's outdoor range, but if he was watching the crowd for signs of hostility Jonny might be able to get in the first shot there, too—

"No!" Chrys's unexpected grip on his arm froze his thoughts in mid-stride. "Don't do it, Jonny. I've lost Ken already—I don't want to lose you, too."

Jonny closed his eyes and took a deep, ragged breath. *My duty to Ariel does not include throwing my life away in anger,* he thought at the white heat within him . . . and slowly the bonfire cooled to more controllable embers.

He opened his eyes. Challinor and Taber were watching him tensely. "Dr. Eldjarn had to go to Sangraal this morning," he told Challinor evenly. "You'll need to release our phone system so that we can call him back."

The two renegade Cobras relaxed fractionally.

"No need," Challinor said. "He'll be back at home in a few minutes, if he's not there already. Our roadblock stopped him on the way out of Thanksgiving, of course. You really shouldn't have tried to get a message out like that—you left us no choice but to move in."

There was nothing to say to that. Taking Chrys's arm, Jonny led her away.

"His great-grandfather was the last of six Mac-Donald generations to hold commissions in the Fifty-First Highland Division on Earth—did you know that?"

Jonny nodded silently. Chrys had been curled up on the couch, talking almost nonstop about Mac-Donald, since their arrival back at her home several hours previously. At first Jonny had been worried, wondering whether she was retreating into some sort of personal fantasy world. But it soon became apparent that it was simply her way of saying good-bye.

So he sat quietly in his chair, making verbal responses where necessary, and watched as she purged herself of her grief.

The afternoon was nearly gone before she finally fell silent, and for a long time afterwards they sat together in the stillness, looking out the window at the lengthening shadows. What Chrys's thoughts were during that time Jonny never found out; but his own were a slowly flowing river of bitterness and unreasoning guilt. Over and over the whole scene replayed itself in his mind, nagging at him with unanswered questions. Had MacDonald really been crazy with rage, or thinking perfectly clearly? Had he seen the opportunity to take Szintra and Patrusky out simultaneously and acted accordingly? Had he expected Jonny to back him up in his play? *Could* the two of them actually have defeated Challinor's group?

The sound of the front door broke the cycle of recrimination and guilt. "Dad?" Chrys called.

"Yes." Eldjarn came in and sat down next to his daughter. He looked tired. "How are you doing?"

"I'm all right. What's happening in town?"

"Not much." Eldjarn rubbed his eyes. "Mayor Tyler has basically promised Challinor none of us will make trouble. I don't know, though—I've heard a lot of rumblings to the effect that someone ought to do something."

"That someone being me," Jonny said. "I gather they think I'm afraid to act?"

Eldjarn looked up at him, shrugged uncomfortably. "No one blames you," he said.

"In other words, they do," Jonny said, a bit too harshly.

"Jonny—"

"It's all right, Chrys," Jonny told her. He could hardly blame the others; they didn't know why he'd held back. He wasn't even sure why himself, now. . . . "Orrin, how many men does Challinor have in Ariel? Any idea?"

"At least ten Cobras that we know of, and probably a dozen of those teen-aged arrogants manning roadblocks," Eldjar said.

Jonny nodded. Challinor had said he had twelve Cobras on his side. Add Taber and maybe a couple more, subtract Szintra, and it still looked like nearly all the rebels were now in Ariel. The conclusion was obvious. "They're not ready to move against the Mines yet. So unready that they'd rather try and box up a whole town than move up their timetable. Any guesses as to why?"

For a moment the room was silent. "The miners usually work a two-week shift and then have a week off in Weald, don't they?" Chrys asked. "Maybe Challinor wants to move in during the shift change."

"That sounds reasonable," Jonny agreed. "Depending on how the routine goes, Challinor would hit the mines with either a single shift there or else all three of them. If the former, he has an easier takeover; if the latter, he gets extra hostages, so it makes sense either way." He glanced at his watch. "Three days to go, if they're on a rational system up there. Should be enough time."

"For what?" Chrys asked suspiciously.

"For me to go upriver to the mines and blow the whistle, of course—and I'd better get started right away." He stood up.

"Hold it, Jonny; this is crazy," Eldjarn said. "In the first place, there are forty kilometers of extremely hostile forest between us and them. In the second place, you'd be missed long before you could get there."

Slowly, Jonny sat back down. "I hadn't thought of that last," he admitted. "You really think Challinor will keep such close track of me?"

Eldjarn shrugged. "Despite your . . . um . . . inactivity this morning, you're still the only person in town who can be a threat to him. Your disappearance would certainly be discovered by morning, and I hate to think what desperate steps he might consider it necessary to take. It's a good idea, but someone else is going to have to do it. Me, for instance."

"You?" Chrys looked startled. "That's ridiculous—suicidal, too. Without weapons and with the spine leopards on the move you wouldn't have a chance."

"I have to try," her father told her. "A boat would protect me from all but the most determined spine leopards. And there *is* a weapon still in town that I can take."

"What—Seth Ramorra's machete?" she scoffed.

"No." Eldjarn paused, and Jonny saw a muscle twitch in his cheek. "Ken's antiarmor laser."

Chrys's jaw dropped. "You mean the one in—Dad! You're not serious!"

"I am." He looked at Jonny. "Is it possible to remove the laser without amputating the leg? That would be too obvious for Challinor to miss."

"It was done once before, during out brief foray into civilian life," Jonny said mechanically. All of MacDonald's Cobra gear available—and he'd never once thought about using it. "Have you talked to Father Vitkauskas about the funeral arrangements yet?"

Eldjarn nodded. "It'll be a combined service, for both Ken and Ra Insley, tomorrow at nine in the Square. Most of the town is going to come, I think—and in a crowd that size, Challinor would never realize I was missing."

Jonny stood up. "Then we've got to get that laser out now. Ken's body's back there, isn't it? Good; let's go."

As in most frontier towns on Aventine, Eldjarn's job as Ariel's doctor also required him to act as undertaker when necessary, and the modest office/surgery attached to the house included a small room in the rear for preparation of the dead for burial. Leaving Chrys to stand guard in the office, Jonny and Eldjarn went back there.

Laid out on a table, MacDonald's body didn't look any better than it had sprawled in the street, but at least the odor of burned flesh was gone, either dissipated or artificially neutralized. Jonny looked at the chest wound only once, then turned away, concentrating deliberately on the leg. "The laser lies right here, beneath most of the calf muscle," he told Eldjarn, tracing the position lightly on MacDonald's leg. "There's probably no scar—I haven't got one—but the last time they took it out, the incision line was about here." He indicated it.

Eldjarn nodded. "I see how they inserted it now. All right; I'll get an instrument tray and we'll get started."

The faint sound of footsteps was their only

warning. Jonny looked over his shoulder just in time to see the door swing open as L'est and Taber strode into the room, a white-faced Chrys trailing behind them.

"Good evening, Doctor Eldjarn; Moreau," L'est said, giving the room a quick once-over. "I trust we're not interrupting anything?"

"We're preparing Mr. MacDonald's body," Eldjarn said shortly. "What do you want?"

"Oh, just a little insurance against heroics." L'est glanced over Eldjarn's shoulder. "It occurred to me that perhaps we ought to remove our late compatriot's weapons before someone else took it into his head to do so. If you'll just step aside, this will only take a minute."

Eldjarn didn't move. "No," he said, his tone allowing no argument. "I'm not going to permit you to mutilate the dead."

"You don't have any choice. Move aside."

Eldjarn snorted. "I realize you're new to this warlord business, but if you think you can kill or imprison a town's only doctor and then expect to get even grudging cooperation from the rest of the populace you're in for a very rude shock."

For the first time L'est's confidence seemed to waver. "Look, Doctor—"

"Doctor, would *you* remove the lasers for us?" Taber put in suddenly. "You're a surgeon—you could do it without leaving any marks."

Eldjarn hesitated. "Jonny?" he asked.

Jonny shrugged, trying to hide his disappointment at L'est's rotten sense of timing. "Either you do it or L'est will. I'd rather you did, personally." He impaled L'est with his eyes. "But Orrin's right: we'll have no mutilation. Specifically, we're not going to let you cut off his fingers."

"But the lasers—" L'est began.

"No buts. His hands are going to be in plain sight in the casket."

Taber nudged L'est. "As long as we can confirm the fingertip lasers are still there in the morning, that should do," he murmured. "You can always take them and the power supply out before the actual burial, if you really think it's necessary."

Slowly, L'est nodded. "All right. But if those fingers are missing in the morning, we'll hold you responsible, Doctor."

"I understand. Jonny, perhaps you and Chrys would go over to Ken's house and bring me his Cobra dress uniform?"

Jonny nodded. Bad enough that Chrys had had to stand there and listen while MacDonald's body was discussed like a military bargaining chip; there was no need for her to watch as it was cut up as well. "Sure. I think both of us could use a walk. Come on, Chrys."

"Just be sure and stay where you're supposed to," L'est warned. "The roads out of town are closed—and there are Cobras on each barricade."

Jonny didn't bother to reply. Brushing past them, he took Chrys's arm and left.

MacDonald's house wasn't too far away, but Jonny was in no particular hurry, and the house held a lot of memories for both of them to linger over. By the time they emerged with the carefully folded uniform, it was dark enough for the brightest stars to be visible. "Let's walk for a while," he suggested as Chrys turned in the direction of home.

"That's not necessary," she said tiredly. "Dad will be finished by now."

"But it's such a nice night," he said, steering her gently but firmly toward the center of town.

She resisted only a moment before falling into step beside him. "You have an idea?" she whispered.

Jonny nodded. "I think so. You have the key to your office with you?"

"Yes ... but I hadn't gotten very far on my tight-beam transmitter."

"That's okay. Do you have any of those tiny electrical gadgets you can install in a vehicle's control circuits that let you run it by remote control?"

"Radio microrelays? Sure. The miners at Kerseage use them all the time for boring machines and slave-controlled ore barges going downriver—" She broke off. "A boat going *up*river? With a message in it?"

"Keep your voice down—the guy following us might hear you."

He doubted it, actually; he'd already confirmed that the tail was one of Challinor's teen-agers, who was much too far back to hear anything except a loud scream. But he wasn't at all sure how Chrys was going to react to the plan that was slowly gelling in the back of his mind and wanted to put that explanation off as long as possible.

They were almost to the edge of the Square and within sight of Chrys's shop when she suddenly tugged on his arm. "There's someone standing at the door!" she hissed.

Jonny nudged his vision enhancers up. "It's Almo Pyre," he identified the guard. "With a pellet gun. Challinor's probably worried about you or Nedt putting together something to ungimmick the phone system." Though the fact that Challinor had apparently deployed the bulk of his forces with an eye to keeping anyone from slipping out of town showed how small a threat he considered Chrys's equipment to be. "This shouldn't be too hard."

"What about the tail?" Chrys asked anxiously. "And you're not going to hurt Almo, are you? He's just a boy."

"Who's old enough to face the consequences of his choices," Jonny pointed out. "Oh, don't worry—I like the kid, too. As for the tail, I think a hard right

turn around the drugstore here and a little brisk
walking will lose him without tipping him off that
we were on to him. Then we'll circle around and
come up on your shop from behind. Once we move
there'll be no talking, so I need some information
right now. . . ."

As far as Jonny could tell, the trick worked,
and they reached Chrys's building with Challinor's
spy nowhere in sight. The rear of the shop, with no
door that required guarding, was deserted. Stepping directly underneath the second-floor window
Chrys pointed out, Jonny took one final look around
him and jumped. His leg servos were more than
equal to the task, landing him on the narrow window ledge in a crouched position, knees spread to
the sides to avoid breaking the glass and hands
finding good purchase on the wooden frame. The
window, open a few centimeters for ventilation,
slid all the way up with only token resistance.
Seconds later, Jonny was inside.

The search was short—all the items he sought
were right where Chrys had said they were—and
within two minutes he was back on the ledge,
closing the window behind him. Seconds after that
he was walking away from the building as noncha-
lantly as possible, Chrys, at his side, was breathing harder than he was.

"No problem," he assured her, answering her
unasked question. "No one'll ever know I was there.
Let's get back home—you and your father have a
lot of work yet to do tonight."

L'est and Taber had long since left by the time
they reached the Eldjarn home, but Jonny knew
better than to stay inside too long. Fortunately,
explaining what he wanted them to do took less
than five minutes. Neither Chrys nor her father
was especially happy with the plan, but with obvious reluctance they agreed.

He left immediately afterwards, and as he walked

down the street toward his own house, his peripheral vision caught a glimpse of a shadow detaching itself from a bush near the Eldjarn home and falling into step behind him, somewhat closer than before.

He sighed, and for the first time since MacDonald's death a tight smile flickered across his face. So the gamble had worked: the tail was back on the job, and the absence of nervous Cobras scouring the area indicated the boy had decided that losing his quarry for a few minutes wasn't worth reporting. An understandable reaction, Jonny thought, given the earlier demonstration of Cobra killing power. And as far as he was concerned, the kid was welcome to watch him the rest of the night.

He just hoped Challinor hadn't thought to have someone watch the Eldjarns, too.

The morning dawned crisp and clear, with only a few scaly cirrus clouds to mar the deep blue sky. To Jonny it seemed wrong, somehow, that Aventine's sky should appear so cheerful on the day of MacDonald's funeral and after Jonny's own restless, nightmare-filled sleep. Still, good weather should mean a large turnout at the funeral, and that should draw a lot of Challinor's Cobras. Perhaps Aventine was on his side after all.

Feeling a bit more encouraged, he ate a good breakfast, showered and shaved, and at eight-thirty emerged from his house in full Cobra dress uniform. L'est and Taber, looking as tired as he felt, were waiting for him. "Morning, Moreau," L'est said, looking him up and down. "Neatest I've seen you since the day of the landing."

"You're too kind," Jonny said shortly. "Now if you don't mind, I have a funeral to attend. I'm sure you have somewhere you have to be, too." He stepped between them and stalked down the street.

They fell into step on either side and a pace behind him. "There are about a hundred places I'd rather be going," L'est said, "and about a thousand people whose company I'd prefer. But Tors seems to think you need someone to hold your leash."

Jonny snorted. "Challinor always did have a way with words. What the hell are you afraid of—that I'll start a riot or something at Ken's funeral?"

"There's no point in taking chances," Taber said dully. "So far Ariel's been peaceful, but mass meetings are always potentially explosive. A show of force is the best way to make sure no one gets crazy ideas."

Jonny glanced back at him. "You don't sound thoroughly convinced anymore," he suggested. "Challinor's high-handed methods getting to you?"

Taber was silent for several steps. "I liked MacDonald, too," he said finally. "But Challinor's right: the government here *isn't* working."

"There are ways to improve it that don't involve rebellion—"

"That's enough," L'est interrupted. "The time for talking politics is over."

Jonny clamped his jaw tightly, but he really hadn't expected any other reaction. L'est wasn't just going to stand quietly and let him sprinkle extra water on the seeds of uncertainty that Taber was beginning to show. But maybe—just maybe—there was enough there already for them to sprout on their own. Whether they would do so in time was another question entirely.

Not since the last Landing Day festival had Jonny seen the Square so crowded. In the center, resting on two waist-high stands, were the open coffins; from the edge of the Square, MacDonald's face and folded hands were just visible. Between the coffins, sitting on the only chair in sight, was Father Vitkauskas. Without pausing, Jonny turned to his left, circling the crowd until he was standing in line with the foot of MacDonald's coffin. Looking around, he spotted at least six more of Challinor's Cobras grouped loosely together on the fringes of the crowd near him, their positions obviously having been chosen to take advantage of the slight rise there that would permit a better view of the area. Apparently Challinor really *was* worried about trouble with the crowd.

"Good morning, Moreau," a voice murmured behind him. Turning, Jonny saw Challinor step up next to L'est. "A good turnout, wouldn't you say?"

"Very good," Jonny said coldly. "Ken was a very popular person. Killing him was probably one of your biggest mistakes."

Challinor's gaze flicked over the crowd before returning to Jonny. "I trust you won't be foolish enough to try and take advantage of that," he said, with the faintest edge to his voice. "L'est, Taber, and I will be standing behind you the whole time, and if you even look like you're about to make trouble, it'll be the last thing you ever do. *And* probably the last some of these other people do, too." He glanced significantly at the Cobras standing to either side.

"Don't worry," Jonny growled. "I have no intention of starting anything."

Abruptly, the low murmur of conversation in the Square faded into silence. Turning back, Jonny saw Father Vitkauskas had risen to his feet.

And the funeral began.

Jonny remembered afterwards very little of what was said that morning. He sang mechanically with the other people when necessary, and bowed his head at the proper times . . . but mostly his attention was on the crowd, picking out those people he knew best and trying to gauge their mood. Chrys and her father he found easily, standing in the front row a quarter of the way around the circle from him. Mayor Tyler was near them, looking grimly dignified, a man determined not to show his shock at the sudden inverting of his world. A lot of the people were wearing that same expression, Jonny noted, and he could hardly blame them. The Cobras, their helpers and protectors, had seemingly turned against them, and no one was quite sure how to react. Some showed more uncertainty than others; Jonny noticed Almo Pyre shifting uneasily from foot to foot. Like Taber, the teen-ager seemed to be having second thoughts about the side he'd chosen.

A sudden rustle of cloth brought Jonny's attention back to the priest. The service was drawing to a close, he saw, and the crowd was kneeling for the final prayer. Hastily, Jonny dropped to his knees, glancing around as he did so. Challinor's Cobras were still on their feet, whatever feelings of respect they might have had overridden by the tactical necessity of keeping close watch on the crowd. Out of the corner of his eye he saw Almo hesitate and then, with a glance in Jonny's direction, kneel with the rest of the people around him. Between the coffin stands Father Vitkauskas had himself knelt ... and as he began the requiescat, Jonny's eyes sought Chrys, saw her hand slip under the hem of her long skirt to the device strapped to her leg. . . .

And MacDonald sat up in his coffin.

Behind Jonny someone gasped—but that was all the reaction anyone had time for. MacDonald's hands unfolded themselves, settling smoothly down into what looked like the ready position for a double handshake ... and the lasers in his little fingers abruptly spat flame.

Taber, standing directly in the line of fire, crumpled without a sound. Challinor and L'est, their programmed reflexes finally breaking them free of their astonished paralysis, dodged to either side, raising their own lasers to counterattack. But MacDonald's forearms were already swinging rapidly to his sides, sweeping twin fans of death over the heads of the kneeling crowd. L'est made a choking sound as the beam caught him across the chest and he fell, lasers still firing uselessly at the man he'd already killed once. Challinor broke off his own attack barely in time to duck down—and fell all the way to the ground as Jonny's antiarmor laser flashed. The rest of the Cobras around the Square, their reflexes and targeting locks already keyed to the futile task of avoiding MacDonald's attack, reacted far too slowly to Jonny's entry into the battle; many, in fact, probably never realized anyone else was shooting at them until it was too late. Between MacDonald's wild spray and Jonny's more accurate sniping, they made a clean sweep.

It was over before anyone in the crowd thought to scream.

"We're not going to be able to keep this secret, you know," Mayor Tyler said, shaking his head. His hands were shaking, too. "If nothing else, we— and about a quarter of the towns in Caravel District, for that matter—are going to have to ask the governor-general for new Cobras."

"That's okay," Jonny said, wincing slightly as Eldjarn applied salve to his shoulder, where a near miss had burned him. "No one's going to try and avenge Challinor or pick up where he left off, if that's what you're worried about. All the fence-straddlers he said he had standing by will be moving like crazy to make sure they come down on the right side. The warlord movement is dead." He cocked an eye at the mayor. "You just make sure your report shows that only a very small minority was involved in the plot. We can't have people getting paranoid about us—there's still too much work on Aventine that only Cobras can do."

Tyler nodded and moved toward the door to his private office. "Yeah. I just hope Zhu doesn't take the whole thing wrong. I'd hate for Ariel to get stuck with the blame for Challinor's ambition."

The door closed behind him, and Chrys stood up. "I suppose I'd better go, too—I've got to get busy fixing the phone system."

"Chrys—" Jonny hesitated. "I'm sorry that had to be done at Ken's funeral, and that you had to . . . to see all of that . . ."

She smiled wanly. "That extra damage?" She shook her head. "Ken was long gone from that body, Jonny. He couldn't feel those lasers. *You* were the one I was worried about—I was scared to death you'd be killed, too."

Jonny shook his head. "There wasn't really much danger of that," he assured her. "You, Orrin, and Father Vitkauskas set things up perfectly for me. I just hope Ken's reputation doesn't . . . I don't know."

"It already has," she sighed. "The rumors are already starting to travel out there, to the effect that Ken was faking death so that he could get in one last shot."

Jonny grimaced. Yes, that *would* be what they thought—and within a few days and a hundred kilometers that story would probably be bent completely past recognition. The Avenging Cobra, perhaps, who'd returned from the dead to defend his people from oppression? "A legend like that might not be all bad, though—it ought to at least slow down future Challinors," he murmured, thinking out loud. "I don't think that's something Ken would dislike having attached to his name."

Chrys shook her head. "Maybe. I can't think that far in the future right now."

"You sure you really feel like working?" he asked, studying her strained face. "Nedt could start the phone repairs alone."

"I'm all right." She reached for Jonny's hand, squeezed it briefly. "I'll see you later, Jonny—and thank you."

She left, and Jonny sighed. "The real thanks goes to you two," he told Eldjarn. The reaction was beginning to hit him, and he suddenly felt very tired. "I don't think I could have faced having to wire all those sequential relays to Ken's servos, even if I'd known how to do it. It must have been pretty hard on Chrys, especially."

"We all did what we had to," Eldjarn said obliquely. "You know, though, that it's not over yet—not by a long shot. Zhu's going to react to this, all right. If he's smart, part of his reaction will be to start listening to what Cobras have to say on governmental policies and procedures. You'll need to take advantage of the opportunity to offer some good, concrete suggestions."

Jonny shrugged wearily. "I'm like Chrys: I really can't think that far ahead right now."

Eldjarn shook his head. "Chrys can get away with that excuse; you can't. As long as there are Cobras on Aventine, the threat of something like this happening again will always be with us. We have to act *now* to make sure that possibility stays small."

"Oh, come on, Orrin—you're talking politics now, and that's light-years out of my experience. I wouldn't even know where to start."

"You start by making the Cobras feel that an attack on the government is an attack on them personally," Eldjarn said. "Ken fought Challinor because the rebellion was an attack on his family pride; you probably had similar reasons." He hesitated. "For most of you, I suspect, we'll have to appeal to enlightened self-interest . . . once your self-interest has been properly linked with the government's."

Jonny frowned as understanding began to come.

"You're suggesting we be brought directly into the government somehow?"

"I think it's inevitable," Eldjarn said; and though his voice was firm, his restless hands indicated his uneasiness. "You Cobras have a lot more of the power on this world than the system has taken into account, and one way or another the system has to adjust to reflect that reality. We either give it to you in a controlled, orderly way or risk the chaos of Challinor's method. Like it or not, Jonny, you're an important political force now—and your first political responsibility will be to make sure Zhu understands that."

For just a second Jonny grimaced at the irony. Perhaps, in a small and unexpected way, Challinor had won after all. "Yes," he sighed. "I guess I'll have to."

Interlude

To the trained and observant eye, the signs were all there.

They weren't obvious, of course. An unnecessary phrase in an official Troft message to the Committee, certain small shiftings of both merchant and perimeter guard star ships, comments coming from the Minthisti at obvious Troft prodding—small things, each in itself completely meaningless. But taken as a group, all the tiny pieces pointed unidirectionally to the same conclusion.

After fifteen years of allowing Dominion ships to pass freely through their territory, the Trofts were getting tired of it.

Vanis D'arl scowled blackly as he stared at the nighttime view of Dome visible through his office window. It wasn't exactly a startling development—half the Committee was frankly surprised the Corridor had remained open as long as it had. The Star Force, in fact, had been updating its contingency plans for eleven years now ... and unless something was done, it looked like they'd get the chance to test its strategies within the year.

It went without saying that, win or lose, one of the first casualties of a new war would be Aventine and its own two fledgling colonies ... precisely the worlds the war would theoretically be fought to defend. Which, in D'arl's opinion, made the looming conflict an exercise in near-perfect futility.

But what were the alternatives? The Committee, which had had to be virtually dragged by the nose to accept the colony plan in the first place, had in recent years done a complete turnaround as rare minerals and new pharmaceuticals began flowing the other way down the Corridor. With military ships barred by treaty from entering Troft territory, the Dominion had no way to defend Aventine except by the threat of warfare if the colony was attacked—a threat which had been delivered both publicly and privately over the years.

And if there was one universal rule of politics, it was that a threat that wasn't followed through on would always cost more in the long run.

Reaching over, D'arl touched his intercom. "Yes, Committé?" the young man looked up at him from the screen.

"Have you cross-correlated the Aventine botanical data yet?"

"Yes, sir," Jame Moreau nodded. "It's on your desk, marked 'Aventine Bot/Phys III.' I put it in there while you were at your General Policy meeting."

"Thank you." D'arl glanced at his watch. "You might as well go on home, Moreau; the night staff can help me if I need anything more."

"Yes, sir. Let me mention first that there's one item on that magcard I think might be worth following up, if I understand what you're looking for. It's marked with a double star."

"Thank you," D'arl repeated, and broke the connection. *If you understood what I was looking for?* he thought wryly at the blank screen. *If I understood what I was looking for I'd probably have found it years ago.* The self-sufficiency studies, the deterrent proposal—it all worked, it all made sense, and D'arl was ready at any time to try implementing it. But *something* was missing; a political keystone to insure he could sell the package both here and on Aventine. It *had* to exist ... but at this point D'arl had no idea what it might be.

Sifting through the ordered mess on his desk, he located Moreau's magcard and slid it into his comboard, keying for the double star. It turned out to be an analysis of some reedy plant called blussa that apparently thrived in damp lowland regions on Aventine, busily concentrating one of the strategic metals on D'arl's self-sufficiency list. Growth cycle, ecological niche, biochemistry—he skimmed the overview Moreau had copied directly from the master files.

—biochemical response to climatological changes.

He slowed down and read carefully. Backed up and read it again. Called up the last climatological data Aventine had sent, read those, and contacted the dome's night computer staff for a search/simulation with the colony's fauna records. The chief programmer listened carefully, informed D'arl the task would take several hours to complete, and signed off.

And at that point there was nothing for the Committé to do but wait. If he had indeed found his elusive keystone ... but even then there would be a long way to go, on both of the affected worlds. And on top of that, the scheme might not work even if he succeeded completely in implementing it.

In his early days on the Committee, he would probably have felt the uncertainties as a crushing weight around his shoulders. Now, after more than a decade, the emotional reaction was more reasonable. He would do what he could, to the best of his ability, and leave the rest to the universe.

And in this instance, the universe was kind. Six

hours later, when he awoke from a short night's sleep, the results of the simulation were waiting.

Positive.

He read the entire report through carefully. Yes, the keystone was there. Unexpected; unlooked for, really—but there . . . and now it was time to see if the other pieces he'd assembled would indeed fit together. And if so—

If so, the Dominion was about to see just how the Trofts reacted to a change in the game's rules.

Politician: *2421*

Jonny shook his head. "I'm sorry, Tam, but you'll just have to make do without me. I'm starting my vacation in exactly—" he consulted his watch "—four minutes."

Peering out through the phone's screen, Tamis Dyon's face had already finished the plunge from excitement to shock and was beginning to edge back toward disbelief. "You're *what*? Jonny, that's a *Dominion Committé* out there!"

"I heard you. So what does Zhu want to do, hold a full military inspection of the planet? If the guy wanted pomp, he should've given us more than six hours' notice he was coming."

"Jonny, I realize you and I are new to this politics business, but don't you think it'll be expected that we'll at least be on hand in Capitalia to greet the Committé's ship?"

Jonny shrugged, suppressing a smile. Watching Dyon try to operate in "patient" mode was always an amusing sight. "I doubt seriously that *all* the syndics are going to make it in," he pointed out. "And if it's not going to be unanimous, what difference does one more make?"

"What makes the difference," Dyon ground out, "is that *we* have the honor of the Cobras to uphold."

"So *you* uphold our honor. Seriously, Tam, what's the big deal whether one, both, or neither of us shows up? Unless Zhu's planning a laser light show or something."

Dyon snorted, but even he had to crack a smile at the image of the dignified governor-general pulling a stunt like that. "He's going to be furious, you know, if you're not there. What's so important about this vacation, anyway? Chrys threatening to leave you if you don't take some time off?"

"Don't be absurd," Jonny snorted in turn. Though there *had* been small problems in that area in the past. . . . "In point of fact, the ship that's making orbit just about now has someone more important than a mere Committé aboard: my sister Gwen. I want to give her a tour of the bright lights and then help her settle in with the Molada Mountain geological group in Paleen."

Dyon made a face. "Dawa District, right? Grumf. You're right; she *does* deserve *something* approaching civilization before disappearing into the cultural depths." He exhaled loudly, shaking his head. "You win. Get out of there and forget your phone. You've got half an hour's head start before I notify Zhu's office that you're gone."

"Thanks—I owe you one. And tell Zhu to relax— I'll be back in a week, and the Committé's hardly likely to be gone by then. He'll have plenty of formal dinners left to inflict on me."

"I'll quote you exactly. So long." Dyon disappeared from the screen.

Grinning, Jonny got to his feet, fingering the portable field phone in his belt. He *could* leave it behind, as Dyon had suggested . . . but even though he was no longer on round-the-clock call, he *was* still a Cobra. He compromised, switching the phone off but leaving it in his belt, and left his office.

Chrys was already in the anteroom, chatting with Jonny's assistant. "All set?" she asked as he entered.

"All set," he nodded. "I'm officially off-duty, leaving the fate of Caravel District in Theron's capable hands."

Theron Yutu grinned. "With any luck the district'll still be here when you come back, Syndic," he said. "How off-duty are you?"

"I'm taking my phone, but it's going to be off," Jonny told him. "You reveal the override code to anyone short of a genuine emergency and I'll take you to Dawa District and let the gantuas walk on you."

"A fate worse than debt," Yutu agreed solemnly. "Have a good time, sir; Mrs. Moreau."

Chrys had left the car poised for a quick getaway, and a minute later they were driving through the moderate Rankin traffic, heading for the local aircar field. "Any problem with Corwin I should know about?" he asked Chrys.

She shook her head. "Tym and Sue said they can keep him overnight if we don't make it back by then. How about you? Any problems because of the other ship out there?"

He glanced at her. "You never cease to amaze me, Hon—I just heard about that a few minutes ago myself."

She smiled. "That *is* all I know, though—the bare fact of a second incoming ship was coming through on Theron's net as I got to the office. Is it bad news?"

"Not as far as I know. There's a member of the Central Committee aboard who I gather wants to tour the Dominion's colonies out here. I've included myself out of any ceremonies for this next week."

"I wonder if the Dominion's planning to cut our supply shipments," Chrys mused. "Or whether the Trofts are making trouble."

"If there's anything I need to know, Theron can find me," Jonny shrugged. "Until then, let's assume the visit is just political and act accordingly."

They reached the airfield a few minutes later, and a few minutes after that they were heading for Capitalia at a shade under Mach Two. There had been times—a lot of them, in fact—when Jonny had regretted accepting the position of syndic, of having exchanged the day-to-day problems of a single village for the executive headaches of an entire district. But having an aircar on permanent call was one of the spangles of the job that occasionally made it worthwhile.

Not having to risk his life fighting spine leopards and falx, of course, was another big plus.

The last of the star ship's passengers had been down for some time when Jonny and Chrys arrived at the starfield, but with processing and all the first of them were only then beginning to emerge from the entrypoint building. Taking up a position off to the side, they waited.

But not for long. Suddenly, Gwen Moreau was there ... and Jonny, a corner of his mind still expecting the ten-year-old girl he'd left back on Horizon, nearly tripped over his tongue calling to her. "Gwen! Over here!"

"Jonny!" she smiled, bounding over with an echo of the high spirits he'd always associated with her. For an instant he was tempted to respond by tossing her into the air, as he'd always done back home. Fortunately, probably, he resisted the urge.

The introductions and greetings were a flurry of smiles, hugs, and general giddiness. Chrys and Gwen had known each other well enough through tapes back and forth that the awkwardness Jonny had half feared never materialized. Gwen asked about her nephew, was assured he was like any other two-year-old—except smarter, of course—and Jonny was just turning to lead the way out when she stopped him with a hand on his arm and a mischievous grin. "Before we go, Jonny, I've got a little surprise for you," she said. "Someone I met on the ship who's going to be working in the same town I am." Her eyes flicked over his shoulder.

A ship-met fiancé? Jonny thought. He turned, expecting a stranger . . . and felt his mouth drop open. "Cally!"

Cally Halloran's grin was a thing of truly massive proportions. "Hi, Jonny. *Damn*, but it's good to see you."

"Same to you with spangles," Jonny grinned. "Chrys, this is Cally Halloran, one of my teammates in the Adirondack war. I thought you and Imel were planning to stay in the Army for the rest of your natural lives."

"Imel's still there," Halloran nodded, "but you clowns out here gave the brass too many ideas of what Cobras could be used for. I finally had one Iberiand forest-patrol mission too many and put in for a transfer here."

"If you're expecting palace guard duty work in Dawa District, you can forget it," Jonny warned. "Chances are you'll be doing jungle duty *and* heavy manual labor besides."

"Yeah, but here I'll at least be working more on my own, without some middle-level Army officer looking over my shoulder." He waved a hand skyward. "Or maybe even get to help open up a new world like you did."

"Palatine and Caelian?" Jonny shook his head in mild disgust. "You want Army thinking, there it is in spades. We've barely got a third of Aventine even surveyed, let alone settled, and they open up beachheads on two other worlds. Talk about straining resources and manpower—especially Cobra manpower—"

"Jonny," Chrys interrupted smoothly, "you promised you wouldn't plunge us into Aventine's politics for at least the first hour. Remember?"

They all laughed. Jonny had not, in fact, made any such promise, but the hint was well taken.

"Chrys is right—I *do* tend to go overboard sometimes," he admitted, pointing them all toward the door. "If you're all adequately tired of standing around here, let's go get some dinner. Chrys and I don't get to Capitalia too often, but we know where the best restaurant is."

The meal was a resounding success, the food and atmosphere of the restaurant as good as Jonny had remembered. They spent some time catching up on Halloran's and the Moreau family's recent histories, the conversation then shifting to Aventine in general and Dawa District in particular. Jonny knew relatively little about the latter, Dawa being one of the most recently incorporated parts of the planet, and he was rather surprised to find that he and Chrys still knew far more than the supposedly up-to-date information the colonists had been given.

They were working on dessert and the Aventine version of cahve when Chrys casually mentioned the mysterious Dominion craft coming in fast on the colony ship's wake. "No mystery there," Halloran shook his head. "*I* heard about it back on Asgard; I assumed you'd been told, too. That's Committé Vanis D'arl and some sort of special Cobra project that the Army and Central Committee have cooked up."

"*D'arl?*" Gwen's eyes were wide. "Jonny—that's the Committé Jame's working for."

"You're right." The name hadn't immediately registered, but now he remembered. Jame had been with D'arl's staff for, what, twelve years now? "Any idea who D'arl brought with him, Cally?"

"Boy, you Moreaus really get around," Halloran said, shaking his head in amazement. "No, I don't know who else is aboard—I only know it involves Cobras because Mendro and Bai had Freyr Complex tied up in knots for a month while Committee people crawled all over the place."

"Doing what?"

"All I heard were rumors. But they had a lot of trucks moving in and out . . . and parking by the surgery wing."

"Sounds like they're updating the Cobra equipment," Jonny frowned. "Have the Trofts and Minthisti been behaving themselves?"

"Far as I know. Maybe the Dominion's thinking about really pushing the colonization effort out here and wants to have more Cobras available."

"With D'arl coming here for a final assessment?" Jonny suggested. "Could be."

"Ah-ah," Gwen put in warningly. "That's politics, you guys. Technical foul; Chrys gets a free change of topic."

They all smiled, and the conversation shifted to the sorts of geological and tectonic utilization work Gwen hoped to be doing on her new world. But for Jonny, the relaxed mood of a few minutes earlier proved impossible to totally recapture. Tors Challinor's attempted rebellion seven years ago hadn't been repeated, but Jonny had lived those years waiting for that other shoe to drop, knowing that if Aventine could survive another few decades, the Cobras would all be dead and the society could at last get back to normal. But if the Dominion was planning to send them a new batch . . .

But the evening, if no longer scintillating, nevertheless remained pleasant as Jonny and Chrys gave the others a brief tour of Capitalia's night life. It was odd, though perhaps inevitable, that Jonny found himself mentally comparing everything to their hazily remembered counterparts on Asgard and Horizon; but if Gwen and Halloran found it all quaint and primitive, they were far too polite to say so.

It was after midnight when they finally called it quits, and as there was no point in returning to Rankin at such an hour, they checked into one of Capitalia's small selection of hotels. Gwen and

Halloran had disappeared to their rooms, and Jonny was just starting to undress when he noticed the red "message waiting" light on his phone was glowing. "Uh-oh," he muttered.

Chrys followed his gaze. "Ignore it," she advised. "At least until morning. Theron would've risked waking you up if it was urgent."

"Ye-e-e-s," Jonny agreed, almost unwillingly picking up the instrument. "But he wouldn't have bothered us at all if it wasn't at least important. Might as well get it over with."

The message, as he'd expected, was simply to phone his assistant whenever convenient. Jonny looked at his watch, shrugged, and made the call.

Yutu answered promptly, without any of the grogginess that would have indicated a sound sleep. "Sorry to bother you, Syndic," he apologized, "but something came in on the net a half hour ago that I thought you should know about. Late this afternoon a dead spine leopard was found in the plains a couple of kilometers west of Paleen in Dawa District. It had been mauled pretty badly ... and apparently *not* by scavengers."

Jonny looked up to see Chrys's suddenly tense eyes, felt his own jaw tighten. The elusive predator that even spine leopards needed defenses against had finally made its long-overdue appearance. So to speak. . . . "Any sign of what had killed it?" he asked Yutu.

"There's nothing more yet than what I've told you, sir. The carcass has been taken to Niparin, where I gather they're going to bring some experts in to study it. I just thought you might want to issue some orders immediately."

"Yeah." Caravel District was getting more built up every day, but there were still vast tracts of forest area surrounding the towns ... and if the new predator migrated like the spine leopards did, the region could have unwelcome company at any

time. "Put all the Cobras on alert, and have them
keep an eye out for any unusual tracks or signs if
business takes them into the forest," he instructed
Yutu. "Everyone else is to stay *out* of the forest,
period, and farmers working near the edges are to
keep their cabs sealed."

"Yes, sir; I'll have these on the public net in half
an hour. Uh—Governor-General Zhu also called
this evening. He wants all the syndics at a special
meeting at the Dominion Building tomorrow morning at eleven."

Jonny snorted. "A ceremonial brunch for the
visiting Committé, no doubt."

"I don't think so, actually," Yutu said. "Committé
D'arl will be there, but it sounded a lot more
important than that. The governor-general seemed
preoccupied, for one thing. Anyway, I told him I'd
try to get in touch with you, but I didn't promise
anything."

"Thanks." Jonny glanced at Chrys, mindful of
his promise of a vacation. But her eyes were
worried, and she nodded fractionally. "All right,
I'll try to show up. Start collecting everything that
comes through on that dead spine leopard for me—
we're going to want to ID its killer as fast as
possible."

"Understood, sir."

"Thanks for calling. Good-night." Jonny broke
the connection and again shut off the phone. Looking up at Chrys, he opened his mouth to apologize
. . . but she got in the first word.

"Gwen and Cally are both going to Paleen," she
said quietly. "If something that dangerous is in
the vicinity . . ." She shuddered. "Should I go ahead
and take them back to Rankin in the morning?"

Jonny sighed. "Yeah, probably. No telling how
long that meeting will take. Though on second
thought . . . if I was running Dawa District, I'd
probably cancel Cally's orientation week and hus-

tle him right down to Paleen for guard duty. Maybe you'd better just take Gwen and leave Cally here. If he gets his orders, I can run him down there and get a firsthand look at the spine leopard while I'm at it."

"And maybe join in the hunt?" She held up a hand against his protests. "No, I understand. I don't have to like your risking your life to know that you have to do it. Even middle-aged Cobras are safer out there than younger men."

"Thanks a raft," he snorted. "Thirty-nine is *hardly* middle-aged."

She smiled. "Why don't you quit protesting, then, and come to bed . . . and *show* me just how young you are."

Afterward, they lay side by side in the dark, and Jonny's thoughts drifted back to Adirondack. There, the people he cared for had always drawn back when they feared they might never see him again. Chrys's response to the same situation was far more pleasant . . . though the underlying reality wasn't any easier to face. Still, he'd faced danger a thousand times before. Even Chrys should know by now that he was too lucky to get himself killed.

But his dreams that night were frightening things, centering around a giant creature that walked in haze, killing spine leopards and Cobras and disappearing without a trace.

Seated beside Governor-General Zhu at the conference room table, Committé Vanis D'arl could at first glance have passed for any other Aventine citizen. Middle-aged and reasonably fit, his dark hair cut in a conservative pattern, he gave no immediate sense of his awesome power. But his name labeled his home planet as Asgard, and to Jonny's eyes there were disturbing similarities between him and the failed rebel Cobra Simmon L'est. There was a quiet hardness about his face, the feeling

that he would stop at nothing to get his own way.
And underlying it all was an odd sense of urgency.

Zhu's introduction was a subtle underscoring
to the latter, lasting only a fraction of the time
the occasion should have dictated. "Thank you,
Governor-General Zhu," D'arl said, rising to his
feet as Zhu reseated himself. His voice was heavy
with the subtle accents of Asgard. "I would first of
all like to congratulate you on behalf of the Central Committee on your truly outstanding accomp-
lishment in the development of this new Dominion
world. In barely fifteen years, you've achieved a
solid foothold on Aventine and are even looking
ahead to the future colonization of Caelian and
Palatine. The natural resources for these endeav-
ors are, of course, readily available, and it is obvious as well that you are not lacking in spirit. As
the Committee has studied your progress, in fact,
it has become apparent that the limiting factor in
your expansion has been—and continues to be—
the lack of Cobras to spearhead your efforts."

Jonny felt his breath catch. D'arl's eyes, sweeping the table, shifted to him, and for an instant the
two men locked gazes. "Your reports," D'arl continued coolly, "have from almost the beginning
contained requests for more Cobras, and the Committee has done its best to accomodate you. We've
encouraged Cobra transfers to this colony, to the
point where the Army has barely two companies
left for general Dominion defense. Obviously, this
drain cannot continue indefinitely; and the Committee has therefore come up with the following
solution."

Here it comes, Jonny thought, his stomach tensing.
*A steady stream of Cobras through the Corridor, maybe
forever.*

But even he was unprepared for D'arl's next
words. "Since it seems inefficient for the Dominion to equip and train Cobras only to send them

here, we've decided to shift the entire operation to Aventine instead."

Jonny's jaw dropped. *No!* he shouted . . . though the word never made it past his frozen tongue. But D'arl nevertheless noticed, and his eyes were steady on Jonny's face as he continued. "Aboard my ship is all the necessary surgical and implant equipment, as well as specialists trained in its use. The procedure takes from two to six weeks, depending on how much discomfort you deem acceptable, and training by your own Cobras will probably take no more than four weeks more. This is far better than the seven to nine month response time for getting new Cobras from Asgard, and will in addition put the operation entirely under your control. I could continue . . . but I sense there is a comment waiting impatiently to be made, so I'd like to pause now for at least a brief discussion."

Jonny was on his feet almost before the last word was out of D'arl's mouth. "With all due respect and gratitude, Committé D'arl," he said carefully, "I feel that perpetuating the line of Cobras would be detrimental to the social and political development of Aventine."

D'arl's eyebrows rose politely. "How so, Syndic Moreau? It seems to me your government has adapted remarkably well to the presence of a disproportionate number of Cobras among its citizens. Your own position here would seem evidence of that."

"If you're refering to the Challinor rebellion, yes, we've managed to avoid a repeat of that," Jonny said. "But the cost has been an unnatural distortion of basic Dominion political theory."

"You speak, I presume, of the fact that at all levels of government Cobras have more than the single vote given to ordinary citizens." D'arl's face was expressionless, his voice giving no hint as to his opinion of that practice. "I believe a study of history will show, Syndic, that numerous adjustments of ideal theory have been made when circumstances required it."

Across the table, Brom Stiggur of Maro District rose slowly to his feet. "Perhaps then, Committé, a more concrete objection should be raised," he said. "You speak of perpetuating the Cobra presence on Aventine, and of putting the selection of Cobra candidates under our control. Under *whose* control, though, would it be? The governor-general's? A syndic majority's? Direct vote of the citizens? How do we guarantee, for obvious example, that this Cobra factory doesn't come under the influence of another Challinor?"

"You seem to have a pretty low opinion of the sort of man who'd volunteer to be a Cobra in the first place," Tamis Dyon said stiffly from a few seats down. "You'll notice that the psychological screening methods were perfectly successful with most of us—and as to Challinor, you might remember it was Syndic Moreau and his companions who defeated him, not official paranoia." He shifted his eyes to D'arl. "I, for one, would be delighted to have another dozen Cobras available to station in my outlying villages."

"You're oversolving the problem," Jonny spoke up as murmurs of both agreement and disagreement rippled across the table. "We simply don't *need* full-fledged Cobras for most of the work that's being done. Fitting the lasers Committé D'arl has brought into hand weapons would do perfectly well against falx or wheat snakes. Spine leopards are trickier, I'll admit, but they're a problem only on the very edges of human territory, and the Cobras we have now can control them well enough."

"And how about the spine leopard killers?" Jor Hemner spoke up quietly. "Can you handle *them*, as well?"

All eyes turned to him. "What are you talking about?" Zhu demanded.

"My office put the bulletin on the net late last night," Hemner said. "We found a spine leopard dead yesterday near Paleen, mauled by something as big as a gantua but obviously far more agressive. The leopard's foreleg spines, incidentally, were rigored into their extended, defensive, position."

From the shocked looks around the table Jonny gathered the report was news to nearly all the other syndics. "We certainly don't want to make any decisions on the basis of a single unexplained event," he said quickly, hoping to diminish the shock effect of the incident. "For all we know, the spine leopard might have been poisoned by some kind of snake and killed by extra-bold scavengers."

"The evidence—" Hemner broke off suddenly, and Jonny turned to see D'arl standing with hand raised for silence.

"I must point out that Syndic Moreau is perfectly correct in warning against a hasty decision," the Committé said. "I've given you some of the reasons the Committee is offering you this equipment; there are others which are listed in the complete report I've brought. But the decision is yours, and I expect you to give this issue the careful consideration the Dominion expects from its leaders. I will be here for another few weeks, and you will have that long, if necessary, to determine what course to take." Looking down, he murmured something to Zhu, who nodded and got to his feet.

"I'm declaring a short recess so that we can all have time to examine the information Committé D'arl mentioned," the governor-general announced. "The relevant magcards are down the hall in your offices. Please take some time to study them, and we'll continue this discussion in two hours."

Jonny joined the general exodus to the building's office wing, but unlike the other syndics, he didn't stay there long. Picking up his copy of D'arl's magcard, he made two quick calls and then left.

Twenty minutes later he and Cally Halloran were on an aircar, heading southeast for Dawa District.

The last page flicked from the screen of Jonny's comboard, and with a snort he flicked off the instrument and tossed it onto the next seat. Across from him, Halloran looked up from his own comboard. "Well?"

"Not a single argument that could hold vacuum in space," Jonny growled. "We can answer all the problems D'arl raises without resorting to a Cobra assembly line."

"But your solutions come from an Aventine syndic, while his come from a Dominion Committé?"

"You got it." Sighing, Jonny gazed out the aircar window at the lush Aventine landscape below. "I don't think I've got a hope in hell of pushing a no-vote through unless we can identify this spine leopard killer fast."

"I'm not sure what that'll accomplish, actually," Halloran said, tapping his comboard. "If the stuff in here on spine leopards isn't exaggerated, you may well *need* a Cobra assembly line to fight its killer."

Jonny remained silent a long moment, wondering whether he should give Halloran the rest of it. At best his suspicions were slanderous; at worst they could possibly be construed as treason. "Has it occurred to you," he said at last, "how remarkably handy the timing has worked out for D'arl? Here he is, pushing us to accept a permanent Cobra presence here, and he's barely landed when this mysterious super-predator suddenly decides to pop up. He couldn't have found a better argument for his side if he'd manufactured it himself."

Halloran's eyebrows rose. "Are you implying he *did* manufacture it?"

Jonny shook his head slowly. "No, of course not. Probably not. But I still can't get over the timing."

Halloran shrugged. "That part of Dawa District's undergoing a pretty severe drought right now, with the Kaskia branch of the Ojaante River dried up and all. Could that have hurt the gantuas' food supply to the point where they'd risk taking on a spine leopard?"

"Not a chance. Gantuas are pure herbivores, with no meat-eating capability at all. There are a couple of that type of pseudo-omnivore here, but they're far too small to bother even a sick spine leopard."

"Then maybe the drought drove some other creature down from the mountains," Halloran persisted. "I'm keying on the drought, you see, because that's also an unusual occurrence, at least in the occupied areas of Aventine."

"And you think D'arl's visit just happened to coincide with our first drought?" Jonny said almost reluctantly. "Well . . . maybe. But I still don't like it."

Again Halloran shrugged. "I'll be happy to keep the possibility of foul play in mind," he said. "But until and unless we come up with something approaching hard evidence, we ought to keep such thoughts to ourselves."

In other words, he thought Jonny was making a dangerously big deal out of nothing. And he was probably right. Still . . .

Fifteen minutes later, they landed at the village of Paleen.

A visiting syndic generally called for a minor official fuss, or at the very least the welcoming presence of the local mayor. But Jonny had called ahead with explicit instructions to the contrary, and as he and Halloran left the aircar they found a lone man waiting. "Syndic Moreau?" he said. "I'm Niles Kier, resident Cobra."

Jonny nodded acknowledgment and indicated Halloran. "This is Cally Halloran, your soon-to-be teammate here. What have you got on the dead spine leopard?"

"Not much more than we had yesterday," Kier admitted, leading them toward an open car parked at the edge of the field. "The experts are still studying it up at Niparin, but haven't come to any conclusions yet."

"You're the one who found it, right?"

Kier nodded. "I was out doing a water survey when I spotted the carcass lying in a small hollow."

"Water survey?" Halloran put in. "You were hauling a sounder around by yourself?"

"Here you just measure the diameters of the gluevines that climb around some of the trees," Jonny explained absently. "It gives you a direct reading of the soil moisture and an indirect indication of where the water table is. Any tracks around it?"

"The ground was pretty badly torn up," Kier said as they got into the car. "I spotted some marks nearby that looked like gantua tracks, but if they were the thing was either huge or running faster than any I've ever heard of."

"From the tapes I've seen I can't see any reason a gantua should ever bother to run," Halloran commented.

Jonny nodded. As big as elephants, their bodies armored with snake-patterned horny plates, gantuas were the closest thing to living tanks he'd ever seen. "A dignified trot is about as close as they get," he told Halloran uneasily. "If this thing scared a *gantua* enough to make it run, we *are* in trouble. Let's go to the spot, Niles, and poke around a little. I gather you didn't do much exploring at the time."

"No," Kier said as he turned the car and headed west. His tone sounded more than a little defensive. "I thought my immediate duty lay in sounding the alarm . . . and in *not* leaving Paleen defenseless."

Jonny nodded grimly. It was a rationale he well remembered—and logical though it was, he knew how cowardly it could make a Cobra feel. Perhaps Kier would get the chance later to redeem himself.

They left the car at a section of reasonably dense forest at village's edge and headed into the trees on foot. The forest gave way barely a hundred meters later into a tree-dotted grassland which was the norm for the Kaskia Valley as a whole. Jonny looked around, feeling strangely more exposed and vulnerable than he ever had in the thicker woods back at Ariel. "Which way?" he asked Kier, fighting the urge to whisper.

"Uh . . . over there, I think. It's near a—"

"Shh!" Halloran hissed suddenly. All three men went instantly rigid . . . and in the silence, Jonny's auditory enhancers picked up a strange rustling of grass and a quiet snuffling snort. Turning his head slowly, he located the sound: beyond a wide stand of blussa reeds. Kier had placed it, too. Catching Jonny's eye, he pointed and gave a thumbs-up sign. Jonny nodded; gesturing to Halloran, he moved a few meters to the side and raised his hands in laser-ready position. Halloran did likewise . . . and Kier jumped.

The twenty-meter reconnaissance jump had usually been considered too dangerous to use during the war, leaving the Cobra as it did in a helpless ballistic trajectory for a shade over four seconds. On Aventine, with no Troft gunners around, the trick was often more useful.

"Gantua," Kier said as he hit the ground, knee servos taking the impact. "Looked sort of sick—"

And with a crash of breaking blussa, the brown-gray monster appeared across the plain ... and charged.

"Scatter!" Jonny snapped, his own feet digging into the ground as he sprinted in the general direction of a tall cyprene. He would never have believed a gantua could move so *fast*—

Veering like a hill on legs, the creature shifted to an intercept course.

Jonny picked up his own speed, raising his hands as he did so to send twin bursts of laser fire at the gantua's head. Other flickers of light, he noted, were playing about its side, but if the creature was bothered it gave no sign. Jonny's target tree was seeming less and less likely to be a place of real safety; but on the other hand, if he could get the gantua to blast full tilt into it, the impact should at least stun the beast. Shifting his attention back and forth, he adjusted his speed ... and a bare instant ahead of his pursuer he leaped high into the cyprene's branches—

And lost his grip completely as the tree swayed violently in time with the thunderous crash from below.

The programmed Cobra reflexes included a cat-like maneuver for righting oneself in midair, but Jonny was far too close to the ground for it to be effective. He landed off-balance, crashing down onto his left shoulderblade, the impact driving most of the air out of his lungs.

For several seconds he just lay there, fighting to clear away the spots twinkling in front of his eyes. By the time he was able to force himself to his knees, the gantua had managed to halt its charge and was wheeling around for a second try. From behind Jonny two spears of light lanced out to catch the beast's head—the other Cobras' antiarmor lasers—and this time the gantua noticed the attack enough to emit a bellow in response. But it kept coming. Jonny climbed shakily to his feet, still struggling to get his wind back. He was still too weak to move ... but somewhere along here his nanocomputer should recognize the danger and get him out of the way—

And abruptly he was hurled in a flat dive to the side. Rolling back to his feet, he turned just in time to see Halloran and Kier launch their attack.

For something that spur-of-the-moment, it was as tight a maneuver as Jonny had ever seen. Halloran, waving his arms and shouting to attract the gantua, waited until the last second before leaping to the right, his raised left leg raking the gantua's side with antiarmor laser fire as it swept past. At the same moment, Kier leaped over the beast, directing his own antiarmor blast at the juncture of head and body. Again the creature bellowed, and this time Jonny could see a line of blackened plates when it turned. But even as it paused, he could see its sides pumping rhythmically as it regained its wind, and the barely visible eyes sweeping the three Cobras showed no sign of either fear or imminent death.

Pulling his phone from his belt, Jonny keyed for local broadcast. "Hold your fire," he murmured into it as, across the plain, Halloran and Kier fumbled out their own phones. "We're not going to kill it by brute force alone."

"What the hell is that thing *made* of?" Halloran asked tightly. "That blast would've taken out a Troft APC."

"Gantua plates are highly ablative," Kier told him. "The cloud of vaporized material scatters all but the first couple of milliseconds of beam—and the damn things are *thick*, too. Jonny—Syndic— we're going to have to call Capitalia and see if anyone up there's got a rocket launcher."

"Even if they did, it'd take too long to get it here," Jonny shook his head. "If the gantua bolts, we could lose it for good."

"We go for head shots, then?" Halloran asked.

"Take a long time to kill it that way," Kier said doubtfully. "Gantua central nervous systems are a lot more decentralized than anything you're probably used to. Underbelly and heart-lung would be a better target."

"Only if we can get it to roll over," Jonny pointed out. The gantua's panting, he noticed uneasily, was already slowing down. Another minute or two and it would be ready to either attack or flee. His eyes flicked around the plain, looking for inspiration . . . fell on a gluevine-wrapped cyprene. "Niles, that tree to your left has a long gluevine on it. See if you can ease over and cut us a good length of it."

Moving carefully, attention on the gantua, Kier glided toward the tree. "Cally," Jonny continued, "when Niles gets the gluevine free, he's going to toss you one end. *Don't* touch the cut part; it'll stick like crazy to you. You two will hold it stretched between you at about knee height and I'll try and attract the gantua into it. Clear?"

"Clear," Halloran acknowledged. "Do we slice the vine open in the middle with fingertip lasers?"

"If we have time," Kier told him. "Otherwise we'll just have to hope the impact will open enough of the skin to release the glue."

Kier was at the tree now, judging with his hands the best places to cut the vine. "What happens if it charges one of us instead of you?" Halloran asked.

Jonny was almost in position now, between the other Cobras and perhaps fifty meters behind them. "Wait as long as you can, then throw your end of the vine at its legs and jump," he said. "Niles?"

"Ready." Kier took an audible breath. "Okay, Cally—look sharp."

And with twin flashes of laser fire the vine came loose.

The light, or Kier's sudden movements, triggered

the gantua. With a hoarse roar it lumbered forward.
Jonny yelled at it, waving his arms, and the creature changed direction toward him. At the bottom
of his peripheral vision, Jonny saw the vine snake
over to Halloran ... erupt with laser sparkle along
much of its length ... go rigid just above the
grass—

The gantua hit it full tilt, and with a crash that
shook the area like a minor earthquake, it slammed
headlong to the ground.

Down, but not out. Even as Jonny raced toward
it, the creature rolled to its side, treetrunk legs
straining against the vine wrapped around them.
Lousy leverage or not, the vine was already showing signs of strain. This would have to be done
fast. . . .

And as he raised his antiarmor laser, Jonny
abruptly realized the gantua's legs were blocking
his intended target.

"Uh-oh," Kier muttered as he and Halloran joined
Jonny. "We may have outsmarted ourselves on
that one."

"Let's try wrapping more gluevine around it,"
Halloran suggested. "Maybe we can take it alive."

"Taking a berserk gantua alive is *not* my idea of
a solution," Jonny told him. "There isn't a facility
within a hundred kilometers for a quiet one, let
alone this beast." He gritted his teeth. "Okay; there's
one more thing we can try. Cally, when I give the
word, cut the vine between its front legs. Niles,
you and I'll see what we can do in the half second
or so we'll have. If it doesn't work, scatter and
we'll try to come up with something else. Ready?
Okay, Cally; *now.*"

The vine disintegrated in a flicker of light—and
the gantua's legs, straining against it, flew wide
apart to expose its abdomen.

Afterward, Jonny would shudder at the risk none
of them had quite known they were taking. The

gantua's underbelly was relatively unprotected, the two antiarmor lasers firing their deadly blasts at point-blank range—and still the creature was able to struggle nearly to its feet before they finally penetrated to a vital spot. Even then, its death convulsions nearly caught Kier, saved only by a combination of luck and programmed reflexes.

Halloran summed it up for all of them when the gantua finally lay still. "Good *God*, those things are built tough."

"I don't remember ever hearing of anyone killing one before," Jonny said. "Now I know why."

"I sure hope he was a rogue," Kier agreed, rubbing his shin where the creature's death throes had touched it. "If they've all gone crazy, we'll have to evacuate half of Dawa District alone."

"Or get a whole lot of new Cobras," Jonny muttered. Ignoring Halloran's suddenly thoughtful look, he pulled out his phone.

Governor-General Zhu had the pained look of a man caught between two opposing but equally valid requirements. "But the vote has already been taken," he said. "Committé D'arl's people are already unloading their equipment."

"So negate the vote on the grounds of new evidence," Jonny argued, staring hard at the other through the phone screen. He'd borrowed the Niparin mayor's office specifically for the use of the vision attachment, but so far the face-to-face advantage hadn't gained him a thing. "Or on the grounds that neither I nor the syndics of Palatine and Caelian were present. Come on, Zhu—this vote wasn't even supposed to be taken for a week or so."

"The others were ready to vote—what was I supposed to do? Anyway, you and the other two missing syndics wouldn't have made a difference. The vote was eleven to five, and even with your

Cobra's double vote, the end result would have wound up the same. And as for new evidence, all you've said so far merely reinforces the decision. If one or more gantuas have gone crazy, we certainly *are* going to need more Cobras to defend ourselves."

"Doesn't that depend on *why* they went crazy?"

Zhu's eyes narrowed. "What does *that* mean?"

"I don't know—yet. The scientific people are just starting a biochemical study of the gantua we killed to see if there are any foreign substances in its system."

" 'Foreign substances'? Moreau, it strikes me you're being unnecessarily mysterious. What, in plain language, are you driving at?"

Jonny took a deep breath. "I'm not being mysterious; I simply don't *know* anything for certain. I have . . . suspicions . . . but I'd rather not air them without proof."

Zhu studied his face for a long minute. "All right," he said at last. "I'll tell you what I'll do. I'll call another council meeting for tomorrow morning at ten. Ostensibly it'll be so you can describe your battle with the gantua and present the scientific team's preliminary data. *If* you have whatever proof you seem to expect, we'll listen to your accusations or whatever then; and *if* it seems warranted, I'll call for a new vote. *If*. Is that satisfactory?"

"Yes, sir," Jonny nodded.

"Good. Ten tomorrow, then. Good-bye."

For a moment Jonny stared at the blank screen, trying to form his strategy for the meeting. But there were still too many unknowns. Giving up, he flicked on the phone again and called home.

Chrys answered on the second ring. "Hi," she said, the slight tension lines leaving her face as she saw him. "How are things going?"

"Slow, at the moment," he told her. "I'm just sitting around Niparin waiting for the scientific types to give us something solid to use. Cally went back to Paleen with Niles for the night in case something else happens there. Though there aren't a lot of approaches to the village even a crazed gantua could get through."

"That helps," Chrys nodded. "Is Niles's leg okay?"

"Oh, sure. Bruised, but I'm sure he's had worse."

She smiled faintly. "Listen, Jonny, about a half hour ago we got a call from Capitalia. It was your brother Jame."

So D'arl *had* brought him along. "Well! How was he?"

"Fine, he said. He wanted to know if you and Gwen could meet him at about eleven tonight for a late supper."

Jonny grinned. Imagine Jame Moreau, late of Cedar Lake, Horizon, casually inviting relatives to fly two thousand kilometers for a meal! Life on Asgard had affected him, all right. "What did Gwen say?"

"She said sure, made me promise to call you in plenty of time, and hopped an aircar for Capitalia."

"On my syndic's authority, I presume." He looked at his watch: two hours before he'd have to leave. Well, he could always have the gantua data phoned to him at Capitalia if it wasn't ready before then. "Okay," he told Chrys. "You want to try and scare up a short-notice sitter for Corwin and join us?"

She shook her head. "Jame already asked me that, but I think this one should be for Moreaus only. I'll get to meet him before he leaves Aventine. Oh, Gwen suggested you meet at the restaurant we took Cally and her to yesterday."

"Sounds good." He grimaced. "This is some vacation for you, isn't it? I'm sorry."

"Don't worry about me," she said softly. "You just be careful yourself."

"I will. Love you, Chrys."

"Love you, Jonny. Say hi to Jame for me."

He broke the connection and again glanced at

his watch. Two hours . . . and nothing he could do to help with the gantua autopsy. And whatever they found . . .

Would not in and of itself be proof that D'arl was behind it all.

But at least a part of that proof might still be available. Heading outside, he picked up his aircar and flew back down to Paleen. It was getting dark by the time he and Halloran returned to the place where they'd killed the gantua, but with their vision and auditory enhancers it was unlikely even a spine leopard could sneak up on them. Still, the events of the afternoon had left Jonny a bit jumpy, and he was glad their task took only a few minutes.

An hour and a half later, he was flying over the starlit landscape toward Capitalia . . . with information that would turn the ill-considered council vote on its ear.

Gwen and Jame were already seated at a table when Jonny arrived at the restaurant. "Jonny!" Jame exclaimed, rising for a firm handshake as he joined them. "It's been more than just a couple of years, but you see we *did* finally get here to see you."

It took Jonny a few seconds to track down the reference. "Oh—right. The day I left Horizon. You're looking good, Jame."

His brother grinned. "Hard but useful work. Same prescription you've been following. Let's sit down, shall we? Gwen's been trying to translate this menu for me, but I think we're going to need an expert."

They sat down together and the conversation continued . . . and as they talked, Jonny studied the man his brother had become.

Physically, of course, Jame's transition from nineteen to thirty-five was less of a jolt than Gwen's maturing had been; but like Gwen, there was something about him that all his tapes had left Jonny

unprepared for. Jame's teen-aged self-confidence
had blossomed into an almost tangible air of authority and competence—an air which, almost
paradoxically, had no hint of condescension to it.
Accustomed to dealing with the Dominion elite, he
had nevertheless not forgotten how to talk with
ordinary citizens.

*Or else he's gone beyond even arrogance and learned
how to* fake *sociability*, he thought, and felt immediately ashamed. This was *Jame*, after all; the one
who'd warned *him* not to abandon his ethics. No
matter who or what D'arl was, he could surely not
have corrupted the younger man so thoroughly as
to have left not even a trace of the tampering.

From which it followed that Jame didn't really
know what kind of man he was working for. And if
that was the case . . .

Jonny waited for an appropriate opening, as a
good soldier should, and as the meal drew to a
close it presented itself.

". . . so when I found out Committé D'arl was
going to personally supervise the whole thing here,
I naturally made sure to get my bid in early to
come with him." Jame took a sip of cahve. "He
worked very hard to get the Central Committee to
go along with the plan; I'm glad to see you're
going to accept it, too."

"So D'arl's got his political reputation on the
line here, does he?" Jonny asked casually.

A flicker of uncertainty passed across Jame's
face. "He's got some prestige at stake, but nothing
quite that crucial."

"As far as you know, you mean."

Jame set his mug down carefully and lowered
his voice. "All right, Jonny; you don't have to prod
around the edges like that with *me*. What's on
your mind?"

Jonny pursed his lips. "I expect you've heard by
now that we killed a berserk gantua southeast of

here today." The other nodded. "You may also know that in the fifteen years we've been here no gantua has ever shown even the slightest aggressiveness. All right. What would you say, then, if I told you I have proof the gantua we killed had been drugged?"

Gwen inhaled sharply. Jame's eyes narrowed. "Drugged how?"

"A potent hallucinogen-stimulant chemical had been sprayed over the blussa reeds near where it attacked us. That's all the gantuas ever eat, so it was a perfect way to get the stuff into their systems."

"A perfect way for whom?"

Jonny hesitated. "I don't know, specifically. But I'll point out that it gave D'arl a lot of extra push in the vote today. *And* that it happened right after your ship got in."

Jame leaned back in his seat and regarded Jonny thoughtfully. "I could remind you that I've worked with the Committé and his staff for several years now and that I'm a reasonably good judge of character. I could also point out that unsupported accusations could get you in a lot of trouble. But I'd rather tackle the whole issue logically. Assuming someone aboard our ship sprayed this drug from orbit, why hasn't every other animal in that area gone crazy as well? Even if we dropped a mist bomb or something—and I don't even know if our approach path was anywhere near there—there should've been *some* dispersion."

Jonny exhaled through clenched teeth. "All right, then. Someone on your ship must have had an agent down here with the stuff all ready to spray."

"You only had a few hours' warning, though, didn't you?" Gwen spoke up. "Could something the size of a gantua ingest enough of the drug that fast?"

"It would probably have needed a massive initial dose," Jame agreed. "And in that case, why coat the blussa plants at all?" He frowned. "Though I'll admit the Committé has been very interested in Aventine flora and fauna recently, and I remember blussa reeds showing up in some of the studies I worked on."

"How were they mentioned, specifically?" Jonny asked, leaning forward.

"Let's see. . . ." Jame stared into his cahve. "If I remember correctly, it was part of a strategic minerals study he was having us do. Something about Aventine becoming self-sufficient in case the Troft Corridor was closed. I dug out the fact that your blussa plant is unusually good at concentrating some metal—I forget which one—especially in late autumn."

"And from this study he almost undoubtedly learned that gantuas are the only things larger than insects that feed on blussa plants," Jonny said grimly. "So his agents inject massive doses of hallucinogen into a few gantuas and spray the blussa nearby to ensure they don't come down from their high until they've attracted our attention."

"Jonny, you're edging *very* close to sedition here." Jame's voice was barely audible, his hand rigid as it clutched his mug. "Even if what you're saying is true, you haven't got a shred of evidence to point to the Committé himself."

"Not yet. But maybe you can get that evidence for me."

Jame's face seemed to become a mask. "What do you mean?"

"If anyone aboard your ship is involved in this, they'll almost certainly have had communication with their agents here. You can pull the radio log and look for coded transmissions."

For a long moment Jame locked eyes with his brother. "You're asking *me* to be disloyal now," he said at last.

"Am I? If D'arl's implicated, shouldn't that fact be brought to the attention of the entire Central Committee? And if someone's working behind his back—for whatever reason—shouldn't you find out and let him know?"

"And if the whole thing's some home-grown Aventine plot, wouldn't I be betraying the trust Committé D'arl's placed in me?" Jame retorted.

"Jame, you've got to help me," Jonny said carefully, fighting to keep any hint of his desperation from creeping into his voice. Jame was right: he *hadn't* any proof that D'arl was manipulating Aventine politics, and unless he could get it, the Committé's plan would go ahead unchecked. "Don't you see how the continual presence of Cobras is going to warp our society? I don't want D'arl's Cobra factory set up on Aventine—and I sure as *hell* don't want it here for a fraudulent reason."

He stopped abruptly, embarrassed by his outburst. Jame ran his finger absently around the rim of his mug, then looked up at Gwen. "What are *your* thoughts on this?" he asked her.

She shrugged fractionally. "I've barely been here a day, Jame—I really can't say anything about the benefits versus drawbacks of this so-called Cobra factory. But if Jonny says it'd be bad—" She grinned. "You *know* how everything Jonny says and does is right."

Jame relaxed, smiling back. "That's only because he wasn't around during those critical formative years when you were busy fighting with *me*," he said.

"Jonny was doing a lot for the Dominion during those years," she replied softly.

Jame looked down at his cahve again. "He was, wasn't he?" He took a deep breath, pursed his lips. "All right," he said at last, looking Jonny in the eye. "I guess I can risk the Committé's anger for something that's this important to you. But I won't be able to simply give you any logs I find. I'll analyze them myself and let you know if there's anything out of the ordinary. They're all technically confidential, after all."

Jonny nodded. "I understand. And I wouldn't be asking you to do this if there was any other way."

"Sure." Raising his mug, Jame drained the rest of his cahve and stood up. "I'll call you as soon as I have anything." He nodded to them both and left.

Jonny leaned back with a sigh of relief. If this worked . . .

"I hope you know what you're doing."

He looked over to find Gwen's eyes on him. "If it works, I should have at least enough indirect evidence to get Zhu and the council thinking about what they're doing to Aventine."

"And if it doesn't," she rejoined quietly, "you'll have risked—maybe ruined—Jame's career for nothing."

Jonny closed his eyes. "Don't remind me." He sat like that for a moment, feeling the tension of the day turning to fatigue and soaking into his bones. "Well," he said, opening his eyes and getting to his feet, "what's done is done. Let me get a car to take you to a hotel for the night."

"What about you?" she asked as they headed for the exit.

"I'm staying at the Dominion Building office tonight," he told her grimly. "It occurs to me that I've got information there that someone may think worth stealing. I almost hope they try it."

But the packet from the scientific team in Niparin was untouched when he arrived, and nothing but uncomfortable dreams disturbed his sleep.

It was quickly clear that, whether he'd intended such a result or not, Zhu had given Jonny the best opening he could possibly have come up with. The other syndics listened closely—even raptly—as Jonny described in detail the Cobras' battle with the gantua the previous afternoon. He hadn't had that kind of attention in weeks; and if it emphasized how much Aventine needed Cobra power, it surely also reminded them that Cobra good will and cooperation were equally vital. It was, he decided, a fair psychological trade-off.

"The important question, of course," he said when he'd finished, "is what could cause a gantua to behave like that. As of late yesterday evening we have the answer." He paused, flicking a glance at D'arl. The Committé was as attentive as the others, but if he saw his scheme unraveling, his expression gave no hint of it. "It appears," Jonny continued, "that the gantua was deliberately drugged with a hallucinogenic chemical sprayed directly on its food supply."

He paused again, but the dramatic outburst he'd half expected never materialized. "That's ridiculous," Jor Hemner spoke up into the silence. "Why would anyone do something like that?"

Jonny took a deep breath. This was it. "Perhaps," he said, locking eyes with D'arl, "to persuade us to accept a Cobra presence we don't really need."

D'arl returned his gaze steadily. "Are you accusing *me* of drugging your gantuas, Syndic?"

"And have you got any proof?" Zhu added tartly before Jonny could answer. "Because you'd damn well better not be even *suggesting* Committé D'arl has any connection with this unless you do."

The proof is on his ship, Jonny wanted to say . . . but until and unless Jame contacted him, he didn't dare invite any scrutiny in that direction. "I'm not accusing anyone specifically, gentlemen," he said, shifting his gaze between Zhu and D'arl. "But since it seems obvious a crime has been committed—and since it's unarguable that the drugged gantua's existence had at least an indirect effect on yesterday's vote—I would like to suggest the vote be rescinded and a new vote not be taken until all the facts are in on this case."

"What other facts do you expect to find?" an older syndic put in. "Or should I say *hope* to find? It seems to me you've got nothing but a soap-bubble of—"

"Gentlemen." D'arl's voice was quiet, but there was an edge to it that cut off the syndic in mid-sentence. "If I may make a suggestion, it seems to me you're putting too much emphasis on guarding my honor and too little on solving the genuine mystery Syndic Moreau's uncovered. If there is indeed clandestine activity underway, it must be stopped, no matter who is involved. If, on the other hand, what we have here is a purely natural phenomenon, you should similarly learn all that you can about it, and as quickly as possible."

"Natural phenomenon?" Jonny snorted. "If the Committé will excuse my skepticism—"

"Skepticism is a natural part of science," D'arl interrupted him calmly. "But before you announce your disbelief too loudly, I suggest you check on the following: one, are all the blussa plants in the Kaskia Valley coated by this drug; two, is there any trace of it on the surrounding foliage; three, are there any conditions under which the plants could themselves naturally produce such a drug; and four, are such conditions currently present. The answers to these questions might prove interesting." He stood up and nodded to Zhu. "With your permission, I will continue the equipment setup begun yesterday. If a later vote requires its removal, it can be done easily enough."

"Of course, Committé," Zhu agreed quickly. "Thank you for coming today. Syndics: the meeting is adjourned."

And that was it. In half a minute, D'arl had

completely blunted his attack. An attack the Committé had been remarkably well prepared for. . . .

Tight-lipped, Jonny collected his magcards and left the room.

Halloran, still in Niparin, listened quietly as Jonny described the fiasco over the phone. "He sound awfully sure of himself," he commented thoughtfully. "What chance that he's right about this being a natural phenomenon?"

Jonny exhaled loudly. "It's hard to imagine him going that far out on a purely speculative limb," he admitted. "But if that's what's happening, how come *he* knew about it and we didn't?"

Halloran shrugged. "You've been sending samples and data back to Asgard for a long time, and they've got far better test and computer simulation equipment than you'll ever see here. Or maybe it was something even simpler; maybe some of the live plants got dehydrated during the trip."

"Dehydrated. So you think it's the drought?"

"I don't know what other condition he could have been referring to. It's the only environmental factor that's new to you."

Jonny gnawed the inside of his cheek. "The drought. All right, then. If that's the problem, we'll just have to eliminate it."

Halloran cocked an eyebrow. "You know a rain-maker who specializes in getting clouds over mountains?"

"Actually, I can do better than that. Hang on." He pressed the lock key on the phone and got a connection to Rankin. Chrys answered, the screen splitting to include her image. "Hi, Hon," he greeted her. "Is Gwen there?"

"Hi, Jonny; Cally. Yes, she's in the kitchen. Gwen?"

A moment later Gwen's face replaced Chrys's. "Hi, guys. What's up?"

"Your vacation," Jonny told her. "I've got a little job for you and Cally."

Describing what he had in mind took only a few minutes . . . and it turned out to be the easy part.

"Jonny, that's *crazy*," Gwen told him flatly. "Do you have any *idea* of what you're asking?"

"Syndic Hemner will be furious if he catches them," Chrys put in from off-camera.

"Why?" Jonny countered. "They're both *supposed* to be in his district, remember?"

"But under *his* authority, not yours," Halloran said.

"So you leave your field phones off and plead ignorance," Jonny shrugged. "What's he going to do, bust me back to cee-five?"

"Probably have you arrested and sent to the Palatine beachhead," Halloran said buntly. "Especially if it doesn't work."

"But if it *does* work he won't be able to do a thing without looking like a petty legalist," Jonny said. "And I have confidence in you two."

"Well, *I* don't," Gwen admitted. "Jonny, you can't do something like this on ten minutes' notice. It takes *time*—time for studies, time for mapping and emplacement—"

"Maps we've got—the Molada mountain range has been extensively studied. As to the rest, we can surely risk a little environmental damage."

"Jonny, there's still one major point you're missing." Chrys moved back into camera range, and Jonny was struck by the odd intensity in her face. "What you're doing," she continued softly, "is planning to bypass legal channels, to take a major policy decision away from Zhu and the other syndics and handle it yourself. Don't you see?—that's exactly what you and Ken fought to keep Challinor from doing seven years ago."

Jonny's mouth felt suddenly dry. "No. No, it's different, Chrys. He was trying to take over the whole planet, to totally eliminate the Dominion authority."

"It's different only in degree," she shook her head minutely. "You'll still be setting a precedent that a syndic—or a Cobra who doesn't like a legal governmental decision can simply ignore it and go his own way."

But it's not the same, the words echoed through Jonny's mind. *The government's doing something stupid just because an important outsider wants them to. My responsibility is to the* people *of Aventine—*

To the *people* of Aventine.

Challinor's old argument.

The three faces crowded together in the phone screen were watching him closely. "All right," he said with a sigh. "Gwen, you and Cally will head out for the Kaskia Valley, but to do feasibility studies only. I'll bring it up with the whole council before we take any real action, but I want to be able to at least show them a solid alternative."

Chrys seemed to sag as the tension left her. "Thank you," she murmured.

He smiled tightly. "Don't thank *me*. *You're* the one who was right." He focused on Gwen. "Chrys'll get you in touch with Theron Yutu, my assistant, who'll find you an aircar and pilot and whatever else you'll need. Check with Chrys for anything electronic—if she can't find it, she can probably build it. You can rendezvous with Cally in Niparin and go from there. As for you, Cally—" He held up a finger for emphasis. "No matter what Theron or Gwen tell you, any equipment you take *is* replaceable. If you run into a crazed gantua up there, don't hesitate to grab Gwen and run for it. Got it?"

"Got it." Halloran hesitated. "If it helps any, I think you're making the right decision."

"Not really, but thanks anyway. Chrys?"

"I'll call Theron right away," she nodded, all

business now. "We can probably have Gwen down to Niparin in three hours or less."

"Good. Well . . . keep me posted, everyone, and I'll let you know when you're needed here. And be careful."

They all signed off, and for several minutes Jonny just sat there, feeling oddly alone in the quiet office. As if his own career and Jame's weren't enough, he'd now put Gwen's and Cally's on the target range, too. Could he really be *that* sure he was right about all this?

There wasn't any answer for that . . . but at the moment there was something he needed more than answers, anyway. Flipping on the phone, he called D'arl's ship. "Jame Moreau," he told the young ensign who answered. "Tell him it's his brother."

The other nodded and faded; a minute later the screen lit up with Jame's image. "Yes, Jonny?" he said. His voice was casually friendly, but there was an edge of wariness to his expression.

"I'd like to get together with you later," Jonny said. "Dinner tonight, maybe, whenever you get off duty?"

The wariness deepened. "Well . . ."

"No inquisitions, no favors, no politics," Jonny promised. "I'd just like to be with family for a while. If you've got the time."

Jame smiled faintly, the tension easing from his face. "There's always time for the important stuff," he said quietly. "Let's make it lunch—that same restaurant in half an hour?"

Jonny smiled back. Already the weight around his shoulders was lifting a little. "I'll be there."

It took a week, but at last the results of the various blussa reed tests began to coalesce . . . and they were indeed just as D'arl had suggested.

"It seems to be a response to severe lack of available ground water," the senior botanist told the council, his hand trembling noticeably as he shifted graphs, complex formulas, and photos on the syndics' comboards. He'd probably never before addressed even a single syndic before, Jonny thought, let alone a group of them plus a Dominion Committé. "One of the components in the cutin—that's the layer that protects against water loss—alters chemically from *this* form to *this* one." The two molecular diagrams appeared on the comboards. "It turns out that this makes good biological sense in two complementary ways," the botanist continued. "Not only is the new cutin fifteen to twenty percent better at controlling transpiration, but the chemical reaction involved actually releases two molecules of water, which are then available for the plant to use."

"In other words, the drier it gets, the crazier the gantuas become?" Syndic Hemner asked.

"Basically, yes," the scientist nodded. "There may be a cutoff somewhere where the gantuas switch to a different plant species for food, but if there is, we don't seem to have reached it yet."

Seated beside Gwen against the side wall, Halloran caught Jonny's eye and wrinkled his nose. Jonny nodded fractionally in agreement: if the gantua they'd fought wasn't fully berserk, he had no wish to meet one that was.

"Well, then, our alternatives seem pretty clear," Hemner said grimly. "We either get Committé D'arl's new Cobras into service as quickly as possible or pull completely out of the Kaskia Valley until the drought ends. If it ever does."

"There's one more possibility," Jonny said into the growing murmur of agreement.

"And that is . . . ?" Zhu prompted.

"End the drought now." Jonny gestured to Gwen. "May I present Dr. Gwen Moreau, recently returned from the mountains surrounding the Kaskia Valley."

Gwen stood. "With your permission, Governor-

General Zhu, I would like to present the results of a study Syndic Moreau asked me to make a week ago."

"Concerning what?" Zhu asked suspiciously.

"Concerning a proposal to break a pass in the Molada Mountains that would divert water from Lake Ojaante directly into the currently dry Kaskia riverbed."

Jaw sagging slightly, Zhu waved her wordlessly to the table.

"Thank you. Gentlemen," she addressed the syndics, sliding her magcard into its slot, "let me show you how easily this proposal could be carried out. . . ."

And for the better part of an hour she did just that, punctuating her talk with more charts and diagrams than even the botanist who'd preceded her. She spoke authoritatively and coherently, slipping in enough about the basic methods of tectonic utilization to painlessly educate even the most ignorant of the syndics . . . and slowly Jonny sensed the silence around the table change from astonishment to interest to guarded enthusiasm.

For him the changes went even deeper, as his mentally superimposed image of Gwen The Ten-Year-Old vanished forever from her face. His little sister was an adult now . . . and he was damn proud of what she'd become.

The final picture faded at last from the comboard screens and Gwen nodded to the syndics. "If there are any questions now, I'll do my best to answer them."

There was a moment of silence. Jonny glanced at D'arl, bracing for the attack the Committé would surely launch against this rival scheme. But the other remained silent, his look of admiration matching others Jonny could see around the table.

"We will need more study, if merely to confirm your evaluations," Zhu spoke up at last. "But un-

less you've totally missed some major problem, I
think it safe to say that you can start drawing up
detailed plans immediately for the precise fault-
line charge placements you'll need." He nodded to
her and glanced around the table. "If there's no
further business—" He paused, almost unwillingly,
at the sight of Jonny's raised forefinger. "Yes, Syndic Moreau?"

"I would like to request, sir, that a new vote be
taken on Committé D'arl's proposal," Jonny said
with polite firmness. "I believe the study just presented has borne out my earlier contention that
our problems can be solved without the creation
of a new generation of Cobras. I'd like to give the
council a new opportunity to agree or disagree
with that contention."

Zhu shook his head. "I'm sorry, but in my opinion you've shown us nothing that materially changes
the situation."

"What? But—"

"Governor-General." D'arl's voice was calm as
always. "If it would ease your official conscience,
let me state that I have no objection to a new
vote." His eyes met Jonny's and he smiled. "In my
opinion, Syndic Moreau's earned a second try."

The vote was taken . . . and when it was over,
the tally was eleven to seven in favor of D'arl's
proposal.

Parked at one end of Capitalia's starfield, D'arl's
ship was an impressive sight—smaller than the
big space-only transports, of course, but still more
than twice the size of Aventine's own *Dewdrop*. A
sensor-guard perimeter extended another fifty meters in all directions, and as Jonny passed its
boundary, he noticed an automated turret atop
the ship rotate slightly to cover him. The two Marines at the closed entryway made no such obvious
moves, but Jonny saw that the muzzles of their

shoulder-mounted parrot guns stayed on him the entire way. "Syndic Jonny Moreau to see Committé D'arl," he told them, coming to a halt a few meters away.

"Are you expected, sir?" one of the guards asked. He could afford to be courteous; in full exoskeleton armor he was more powerful than even a Cobra.

"He'll see me," Jonny said. "Tell him I'm here."

The other guard glanced at his partner. "The Committé's quite busy, sir, with the departure tomorrow and all—"

"Tell him I'm here," Jonny repeated.

The first guard pursed his lips and touched a control at his throat. His conversation was brief and inaudible, but a moment later he nodded. "The Committé will see you, Syndic," he told Jonny. "Your escort will be here shortly."

Jonny nodded and settled down to wait; and when the escort arrived, he wasn't surprised to see who it was.

"Jonny," Jame nodded in greeting. His smile was cordial but tight. "Committé D'arl's waiting in his office. If you'll follow me. . . ."

They passed through the heavy kyrelium steel entryway and between another pair of armored Marines. "I was hoping to see you again before we left," Jame said as they started into a maze of short corridors. "Your office said you were on vacation and couldn't be reached."

"Chrys thought it would help me to get away for a couple of weeks," Jonny told him evenly. "Try to come to grips with what your Committé's done to us."

Jame looked sideways at him. "And . . . did you?"

"You mean do I intend to attack him?" Jonny shook his head. "No. All I want is to understand him, to find out *why*. He owes me that much."

Ahead, two more Marines—this pair in dress uniforms—flanked an obviously reinforced door.

Jame led the way between them and palmed the lock, and the panel slid soundlessly open.

"Syndic Moreau," D'arl said, rising from the desk that dominated the modest-sized room. "Welcome. Please sit down." He indicated a chair across the desk from him.

Jonny did so. Jame took a chair by the desk's corner, equidistant from the other two men. Jonny wondered briefly if the choice was deliberate, decided it probably was.

"I'd hoped you'd come by this evening," D'arl said, sitting back down himself. "This will be our last chance to talk—shall we say 'honestly'?—before the tedious departure ceremonies Zhu has scheduled for tomorrow."

" 'Tedious' ? I take it it's not the public acclaim or adoration that makes all this worthwhile to you, then." Jonny took a moment to glance around the room. Comfortable, certainly, but hardly up to the standards of luxury he would have expected in a Dominion Committé's personal quarters. "Obviously, it's not the wealth, either. So what is it? The power to make people do what you want?"

D'arl shook his head. "You miss the whole point of what happened here."

"Do I? You *knew* the gantuas would be going on a rampage just at the time you came dangling your Cobra bait in front of our faces. You knew all along it was the dehydrated blussa reeds, yet you said nothing about it until I forced your hand."

"And what if I had?" D'arl countered. "It's not as if I could be blamed for causing the situation."

Jonny snorted. "Of course not."

"But as you said outside," D'arl continued, as if he hadn't noticed the interruption, "the important question is *why*. Why did I offer and why did Aventine accept?"

"Why the council accepted is easy," Jonny said.

"You're a Dominion Committé and what you say goes."

D'arl shook his head. "I told you you were missing the point. The gantua problem helped, certainly, but it was really only part of a much more basic motivation. They accepted because it was the solution that required the least amount of work."

Jonny frowned. "I don't understand."

"It's clear enough. By placing the main burden and danger of Aventine's growth on you Cobras, they've postponed any need to shift the responsibility to the general population. Given a chance to continue such a system, people will nearly always jump at it. Especially with an excuse as immediate and convenient as the gantuas to point to."

"But it's only a short-term solution," Jonny insisted. "In the long run—"

"*I* know that," D'arl snapped. "But the fraction of humanity who can sacrifice their next meal for a feast two weeks away wouldn't fill this city. If you're going to stay in politics, you'd damn well better learn that."

He stopped and grimaced into the silence. "It's been years since I lost my temper in anything approaching public," he admitted. "Forgive me, and take it as a sign that I'm not any happier than you are that this had to be done."

"Why *did* it?" Jonny asked quietly. Two weeks ago he would have shouted the question, putting into it all the frustration and fury he'd felt then. But now the anger was gone and he'd accepted his failure, and the question was a simple request for information.

D'arl sighed. "The other *why*. Because, Syndic Moreau, it was the only way I could think of to save this world from disaster." He waved his hand skyward. "The Troft threats to close the Corridor have been getting louder and more insistent over the past year or so. Only one thing keeps them from doing it tonight: the fact that it would mean a two-front war. And for Aventine to be a credible part of that two-front threat, you *must* have a continued Cobra presence."

Jonny shook his head. "But it doesn't work that way. We have no transport capability to speak of—we can't possibly threaten them. And even if we could, they could always launch a pre-emptive strike and wipe us out from the sky in a matter of hours."

"But they wouldn't. I once thought that myself, but the more I study the indirect psychological data gleaned over the years, the more I suspect mass destruction simply isn't the Troft way of making war. No, they'd be much more likely to invade, as they did on Silvern and Adirondack."

"But you still don't need *Cobras* to defend against that," Jonny persisted, feeling frustration stirring to life in him again. "You brought in antiarmor lasers—you could just as easily have brought in standard laser rifles and organized a militia or even a standing army. Why can't I make you understand that?"

D'arl smiled sadly. "Because the Trofts aren't afraid of human militias or armies. They're afraid of Cobras."

Jonny blinked. He opened his mouth to disagree . . . but all that came out was a single whispered syllable: "Damn."

D'arl nodded. "And you see now why I had to do all this. Aventine may never have the ability to truly defend itself against an invasion, but as long as a deterrent exists, even a purely psychological one . . . well, you at least have a chance."

"And the Dominion is spared the trouble and expense of a punitive war?" Jonny suggested acidly.

Again, D'arl smiled. "You're beginning to understand the mechanisms of politics. The greatest good for the greatest number, and immediate benefits for as many as possible."

"Or at least for those whose support you need?" Jonny asked quietly. "Those whose objections don't count can be ignored?"

"Jonny, it's *your* safety we're talking about here," Jame put in earnestly. "Yes, it's going to cost you something, but everything in life *does*."

"I know that." Jonny stood up. "And I'll even accept that the Committé had our interests at least somewhat at heart. But I don't have to like his solution, and I don't have to like his method of pushing it on us. You withheld information about the gantuas from us, Committé, maybe for months— and someone could have been killed because of it. If I could see it making a scrap of difference, I'd have that fact on the public net tonight. As it is, I suppose I'll just have to leave you to your own conscience. If you still have one."

"Jonny—" Jame began angrily.

"No, it's all right," D'arl interrupted him. "An honest enemy is worth a dozen allies of expediency. Good-bye, Syndic Moreau."

Jonny nodded and turned his back on the Committé. The door slid open as he approached it and he stepped through, relying on his memory to get him back through the corridors to the ship's exit. Thoughts churning, he didn't notice Jame had followed him until the other spoke. "I'm sorry it had to end that way. I would have liked you to understand him."

"Oh, I understand him," Jonny replied shortly. "I understand that he's a politician and can't bother to think through the human consequences of his chess moves."

"You're a politician now yourself," Jame reminded him, guiding him through a turn he'd forgotten. "Chances are you'll be stuck with a similar no-win situation yourself someday. In the meantime, I hope you have enough wins and losses to be able to handle both a bit better."

They said their good-byes at the entryway—cool, formal words of farewell Jonny would never have envisioned saying to his own brother—and a few minutes later the Cobra was back in his car.

But he didn't drive off immediately. Instead, he sat behind the wheel and stared at the muted sheen of the Dominion ship, his mind replaying over and over again Jame's last words to him. Could he really be reacting so strongly simply because he'd lost a minor power struggle? He *was* unused to defeat, after all. Could his noble-sounding concern for Aventine's future be truly that petty underneath?

No. He'd suffered defeats many times: on Adirondack, on Horizon after the war, even in the opening round of the brief struggle against Challinor. He knew how losing felt, knew how he reacted to it . . . and knew it was often only temporary.

Temporary.

With one final glance at D'arl's ship, Jonny started the car. No, it wasn't over yet. Aventine would survive and grow; and he, not D'arl, would be best in position to guide that growth. And if learning the art of politics was what he needed to do, he would become the best damn politician this side of Asgard.

In the meantime . . . there were a woman, a child, and a district who deserved his full attention. Turning the car around, he headed for home. Chrys, he knew, would be waiting up.

Interlude

The haiku garden had changed over the years, slowly and subtly enough that D'arl no longer remembered exactly how it had been when he had succeeded Committé H'orme. One stretch, however, showed D'arl's hand clearly: a series of blussa reeds, stunted cyprene trees, and other flora from Aventine. As far as he knew, he was the only Committé to incorporate plant life of the Outer Colonies in his haiku garden . . . and it looked very much like no one else would ever have the chance to do so.

Jame Moreau, at his side, correctly interpreted his gaze. "This time they mean it, don't they," he said. It was more statement than question.

D'arl hesitated, then nodded. "I can't see any other interpretation for such a clear-cut demand. We're going to be lucky if the ship we're sending doesn't get stranded on Aventine."

"Or halfway back." Jame squatted down to straighten a blussa reed that was trying to fall over.

"Halfway back *would* be a problem," D'arl agreed. "But we can't let the Trofts close the Corridor without at least giving Aventine a little warning."

"For all the good it'll do." Jame's voice was

284

controlled, but D'arl knew what he was thinking. The younger man's brother and sister were out there; and if the relationships were a bit cooler than they'd once been, Jame still cared deeply for them both.

"They'll survive," the Committé told him, wishing the words could be more than ineffectual puffs of air. "The Troft concept of hostage seems to involve land and property instead of people. If they behave themselves, the Trofts aren't likely to hurt them."

Jame straightened up, brushing bits of dirt from his fingers. "Except that they *won't* behave themselves," he said quietly. "They'll fight, especially Jonny and the other Cobras—and that *is*, after all, just what the Committee and Joint Command want them to do."

D'arl sighed. "That's always been the fate hanging over their heads, Moreau. We knew it when we sent them out—you probably knew it, down deep, when you first came up with the plan. Whatever happens now, it was still worth the risk."

Jame nodded. "I know, sir. But I can't help wishing there was something we could do for them here."

"I'm open to suggestions."

"How about letting the Trofts close the Corridor in exchange for leaving the colonies alone?"

D'arl shook his head. "I've thought of that, but the Committee would never go for it. Impossible to verify, for starters. Besides which, we've put a lot of money, people, and effort into those worlds, and we couldn't simply cut them adrift without a fight."

Jame sighed and nodded in reluctant agreement. "I'd like to request a place on the courier ship, sir, if you can get me aboard. I know it's short notice, but I can be ready before the scheduled lift from Adirondack."

D'arl had suspected the request was coming, but that didn't make his answer any easier to give. "I'm sorry, Moreau, but I'm afraid I can't allow you to go. You've pointed out yourself the danger of Troft capture or destruction on the return trip—and before you tell me you're willing to take the risks, let me say *I'm* not willing for you to do so. You know too much about the internal workings and frictions of the Committee, and I'd hate to have the Trofts using our own most petty politics against us."

"Then let me take a fast recall-blockage treatment," Jame persisted. "It wouldn't delay the lift by more than a day if I can schedule my recuperation period to be aboard ship."

D'arl shook his head. "No—because you could lose it all permanently with a hasty treatment like that, and I'm not risking *that*, either."

Jame exhaled in defeat. "Yes, sir."

D'arl gazed off across the haiku garden. "I'm not insensitive to your feelings," he said quietly, "but such a hurried meeting with your family under these conditions would be bittersweet at best and certainly unproductive. The best thing you can do for them is to stay here and help me hold off the diplomatic breakdown as long as I can. The longer we have before actual hostilities begin, the more time they'll have to prepare."

And the more time—he didn't add—the Dominion would have to prepare its own defenses. Because important as they were, the Outer Colonies represented less than four hundred thousand people . . . and from the perspective of the dome, the Dominion's seventy other worlds and hundred billion other people were vastly more important. In the defense of those people, Aventine and its sister worlds were ultimately expendable. *The greatest good for the greatest number* was still the most stable guidepoint D'arl knew.

He was careful not to spell it all out for Jame
... but then, the other had probably already figured it out. Why else would he have wanted to go
to Aventine and say good-bye?

With a sigh, D'arl continued down the path. One
more curve and he would be back to his office
door. Back to the real world, and to the looming
specter of war.

And to waiting for a miracle he knew wouldn't
happen.

Statesman: *2432*

The bedside phone's signal was a loud, directional buzz scientifically designed to wake even deep sleepers. But it had been months since Jonny slept merely deeply, and his mind barely noticed the sound enough to incorporate it into his current dream. It wasn't until Chrys's gentle prodding escalated to a vigorous shake that he finally drifted up to partial wakefulness. "Um?" he asked, eyes still closed.

"Jonny, Theron Yutu's on the phone," she said. "He says it's urgent."

"Uff," Jonny sighed, rolling heavily onto his side and punching at the hold-release button. "Yeah?"

"Governor, I'm at the starfield," Yutu's voice came. "A Dominion courier ship's on its way in—ETA about an hour. They want you, Governor-General Stiggur, and as many syndics as possible assembled here when they arrive."

"At—what is it, three in the morning? What's the rush?"

"I don't know, sir—they wouldn't say anything more than that. But the starfield night manager said they wanted no more than a twelve-hour turnaround."

"They want to leave in twelve *hours?* What the hell is—? Oh, never mind; I'm sure they wouldn't tell you." Jonny inhaled deeply, trying to clear the ground clutter from his brain. "Have you gotten in touch with Stiggur yet?"

"No, sir. The Hap-3 satellite's still out, and it'll be another half hour before Hap-2 is in position to make the call."

And once he *was* notified it would be another three hours before he could get back from the outland district he was touring. Which meant the whole burden of greeting this mysterious and apparently impatient Dominion representative was going to fall on Jonny. "Well, you'd better get some people calling all the syndics—even the ones who can't get here in an hour should come as soon as they can. Uh . . . any idea of what rank this guy is?"

"No, sir, but from his attitude I doubt he's looking for much in the way of ceremony."

"Well, that's one bright spot, anyway. If it's efficiency he wants, we'll give it to him with spangles. We'll skip the Dominion Building altogether and meet at the starfield's entrypoint building. Can you get us a decently sized office or conference room and set up some security around it?"

"Almo Pyre's already down there—I'll have him find you a room."

"Good." Jonny tried to think of anything else he should suggest, but gave up the effort. Yutu generally knew what he was doing, anyway. "All right, I'll be at the starfield in half an hour. Better get out there yourself—I might need you."

"Yes, sir. Sorry about all this."

"S'okay. See you."

Jonny flicked off the phone with a sigh and lay quietly for a moment, gathering his strength. Then, trying not to groan audibly, he sat up. It wasn't as bad as he'd expected: he felt the usual stiffness in his joints, but only one or two actual twinges of pain. The lightheadedness left quickly, and he got to his feet. The hemafacient pills were on his nightstand, but he technically wasn't supposed to take one for another four hours. He did so anyway, and by the time he finished his shower the last remnants of his anemic fatigue were gone. At least for a while.

Chrys had been busy in his brief absence, finding and laying out his best formalwear. "What do you think it's all about?" she asked, keeping her voice low. The eight-year-olds, Joshua and Justin, were in the next room, and both had a history of light sleeping.

Jonny shook his head. "The last time they sent someone without at least a couple months' warning, it was to stick us with the Cobra factory. I suppose it could be something like that . . . but a twelve-hour turnaround sounds awfully ominous. He either wants to get back home as fast as possible or doesn't want to spend any more time here than absolutely necessary."

"Could some disease have shown up in our last shipment?" Chrys asked, holding his shirt for him. "A lot of those commercial carriers only take minimal precautions."

"If it had, they'd probably have specified that they'd stay aboard their ship while it was being serviced." Jonny grimaced as he backed into the sleeves, trying to keep the sudden pain from showing.

Chrys noticed anyway. "Dad called this afternoon to remind you again about getting that checkup," she said.

"What for?" Jonny growled. "To hear him tell me my anemia and arthritis are still getting worse? I already know that." He sighed. "I'm sorry, Chrys. I know I should go see Orrin, but I truly don't know what good it would do. I'm paying the price for being a superman all these years, and that's all there is to it."

She was silent for a long moment, and in a way her surface calm was more disturbing than the periodic outbursts of bitterness and rage that had occurred over the first months of his condition. It meant she'd accepted the fact that he couldn't be cured and was sublimating her own pain to help him and their three sons handle theirs. "You'll call when you know what's going on?" she asked at last.

"Sure," he promised, relieved at the change of subject. But only for a moment . . . because there was only one reason he could think of for the behavior of that ship out there. And if he was right, progressive anemia was likely to be the least of his worries.

Five minutes later he was driving toward the starfield. Beyond the glow of the streetlights, in the darkened city, the ghosts of Adirondack seemed to be gathering.

Tammerlaine Wrey was the image of the middle-level Dome bureaucrats that had been the favorite target of political caricaturists when Jonny was growing up. Paunchy and soft, with expensive clothes in better shape than he was, he had that faintly condescending air that frontier people often claimed to sense in all mainstream Dominion citizens.

And his news was as bad as it could possibly be.

"Understand, we'll be doing what we can to draw off the bulk of the Troft forces," he said, waving a finger at the curved battle front on the Star Force tactical map he'd brought with him. "But while we'll be keeping them pretty busy, it's unlikely they'll forget about you completely. The Joint Command's best estimate is that you can expect anywhere from twenty to a hundred thousand troops on your three planets within a year."

"My God!" Syndic Liang Kijika gasped. "A hundred *thousand*? That's a *quarter* of our combined populations."

"But you have nearly twenty-four hundred Cobras," Wrey pointed out. "A hundred thousand Trofts shouldn't be too much for them to handle, if past experience proves anything."

"Except that almost seventy percent of those Cobras have never seen any sort of warfare," Jonny put in, striving to keep his voice calm as the memories of Adirondack swirled like swamp vapor through his mind. "And those who have are likely to be unfit for duty by the time the attack comes."

" 'Those who can't do, teach,' " Wrey quoted. "Your veterans ought to be able to whip them into shape in a few months. Gentlemen, I didn't come here to run your defense for you—it's *your* people and *your* world and you'll undoubtedly do a better job of it than I or anyone else on Asgard could. I came here solely to give you a warning of what was coming down and to bring back the dozen or so Dominion citizens that the ban on commercial travel has stranded here."

"We're *all* Dominion citizens," Tamis Dyon snarled.

"Of course, of course," Wrey said. "You know what I mean. Anyway, I'll want those people packed and on my ship within six hours. I have their names, but you'll have to find them for me."

"What's being done to try and prevent the war?" Jonny asked.

Wrey frowned slightly. "It's beyond prevention, Governor—I thought I'd made that clear."

"But the Central Committee *is* still talking—"

"In order to delay the outbreak long enough for you to prepare."

"What do you mean, *prepare*?" Dyon snapped,

rising half out of his seat. "What the hell are we going to do—build antiaircraft guns out of cyprene trees? You're condemning us to little more than a choice of deaths: murder by the Trofts or the slow strangulation of a closed supply pipeline."

"*I* am not responsible for what's happened," Wrey shot back. "The Trofts started this, and you ought to be damned glad the Committee was willing to back you up. If it hadn't, you'd have been overrun years ago." He paused, visibly regaining his control. "Here's the list of people I'm authorized to bring back," he said, sliding a magcard across the table toward Jonny. "Six hours, remember, because the *Menssana's* leaving in—now—eleven."

Slowly, Jonny reached across the table and picked up the magcard. The die was apparently cast . . . but there was too much at stake to just sit and do nothing. "I'd like to talk to Governor-General Stiggur about sending an emissary back with you," he said. "To find out what's really going on."

"Out of the question," Wrey shook his head. "In the first place we stand an even chance of getting hit by the Trofts before we ever reach Dominion space; and even if we get through, your emissary would just be trapped there. The Corridor hasn't a prayer of staying open long enough for him to return, and he'd just be dead weight on Asgard."

"He could function as a consultant on conditions here," Jonny persisted. "You admitted yourself you don't really know us."

"A consultant to what end? Are you expecting the Star Force to launch a backup assault through a hundred light-years of Troft territory?" Wrey glanced around the table at the others and stood up. "Unless there are any more questions, I'm going back to the *Menssana* for a while. Please inform me when Governor-General Stiggur arrives." Nodding, he strode briskly from the room.

"Doesn't care falx droppings for us, does he?"

Kijika growled. His fingertips were pressed hard enough against the tabletop to show white under the nails.

"It's not going to matter much longer what he or anyone else in the Dominion thinks about us," Dyon said grimly.

"Maybe we can postpone that a bit," Jonny told him, handing Dyon the magcard. "Would you give this to Theron Yutu and have him start locating these people? I have an important call to make."

Governor-General Brom Stiggur was still en route to Capitalia, but he was within constant range of the Hap-2 communications satellite now and the picture was crystal clear. Not that it mattered, really—Stiggur's expression was exactly as Jonny had expected it to be. "So that's it, then," the other said when Jonny had summarized Wrey's doomsday message. "The Trofts have finally gotten their courage up for round two. Damn them all to hell." He snorted. "Well, what's it going to take to get us ready for a siege?"

"More time than we've got," Jonny said bluntly. "To be brutally honest, Brom, I don't think we've got an icecube's chance on Vega if the Trofts decide they really want us. The new Cobras are our only defense and they know less than nothing about warfare."

Stiggur grimaced. "Should we be discussing this on a broadcast signal—?"

"We're going to keep all this a secret?"

"Not hardly," Stiggur conceded. "All right, Jonny—you didn't call just to give me advance notice of Armageddon. What do you want?"

Jonny swallowed hard. "Permission to return with Wrey to Asgard and see what can be done to hold off the war."

Stiggur's eyebrows lifted toward his hairline. "Don't you think they've done everything possible in that direction already?"

"I don't know. How can we unless we talk directly to the Central Committee or Joint Command?"

Stiggur exhaled loudly. "We need you here."

"You know better than that. I can't fight worth a damn anymore, and there are a lot of First Cobras with better military and tactical knowledge."

"What about your family, then?" Stiggur asked quietly. *"They* need you."

Jonny took a deep breath. "Twenty-nine years ago I left all the family I had then to fight for people I didn't even know. How can I pass up even the slimmest chance now to save the lives of not only my wife and children, but virtually all the friends I've ever had?"

Stiggur gazed at him for a long minute, his expression giving away nothing of what was going on behind it. "Much as I hate to admit it, I suppose you're right," he finally said. "I'll recommend to this Wrey character that he take you along. Uh . . . another half-hour to Capitalia, looks like. I should have his answer in an hour or so. In the meantime—" He hesitated. "You'd better let Yutu handle things and go discuss this with Chrys."

"Thanks, Brom. I'd already planned to do that."

"I'll talk to you whenever I know something." He nodded and the screen went blank.

Sighing, Jonny carefully flexed his rebellious elbows and punched for Yutu.

They all sat quietly in the softly lit living room as Jonny explained both the bad news and his proposed response to the crisis; and as he gazed at each member of his family in turn, he was struck as never before by the contrasting personalities their expressions revealed. Justin and Joshua, huddled together on the couch, showed roughly equal parts of fear and unquestioning trust, a mixture that was painfully reminiscent of his sister Gwen's childhood hero-worship. By contrast, Corwin's face belied his thirteen years as he clearly struggled to find an adult perspective into which he could submerge his own feelings of dread. Very like Jame, who'd always seemed older than his own biological age. And Chrys . . .

Chrys was as she always was, radiating a quiet strength and support toward him even while her eyes ached with the fear and pain a permanent separation would bring her. An acceptance of his plan based not on submission of any kind, but on the simple fact that her mind worked the same as his did and she could see just as clearly that it was something that had to be tried.

He finished his explanation, and for a few moments the silence was broken only by the soft hum of the air conditioning. "When'll you be leaving, Dad?" Corwin asked at last.

"If I go, it'll be today," Jonny answered. "They'll want to leave as soon as the ship's refueled and all."

"Are you going to take Almo or someone with you?"

Jonny smiled briefly. Almo Pyre had been one of the first volunteers through D'arl's Cobra factory, and with his fierce loyalty toward Jonny and the entire Moreau family, he'd been a natural role model for Corwin to latch onto. "I don't think we'll have any problems on the way back," he told his son. "Besides which, your father's not *that* helpless yet." Steeling himself, he turned to Chrys. Her loyalty toward him deserved at least as much back. "I've explained all of what I know and think, and why I feel I should go," he told her. "But if, after hearing it, you think I should stay, I'll do so."

She smiled sadly. "If you don't understand me better than that by now—"

The abrupt ring from the phone made them all

jump. Getting carefully to his feet, Jonny went to his desk and flipped the instrument on. "Yes?"

It was Stiggur. "Sorry, Jonny, but no go. Wrey steadfastly refuses to clutter his ship with useless colonial officials. His words."

Jonny exhaled slowly. "Did you explain how important it could be?"

"Loudly enough to scare a gantua. He simply refuses to consider anything even marginally outside his orders."

"Then maybe I'd better talk to him again myself. Do I still have *your* authorization to go?"

"I guess so. But it's all academic now."

"Perhaps. I'll get back to you."

He disconnected and started to punch for the starfield . . . but halfway through the motion he paused and turned to look at Chrys.

Her eyes gazed at his, and through them to whatever pain she saw in the future. But though her lips seemed made of wood, her voice was firm enough. "Yes. Try."

He held her eyes another second, then turned back to the phone. A few moments later Wrey's face appeared. "Yes? Oh, it's you. Look, Governor—"

"Mr. Wrey, I'm not going to repeat Governor-General Stiggur's arguments," Jonny interrupted him. "I don't care whether you can't see past your own nose and understand why this is important. The fact of the matter is that I'm coming with you to Asgard, and you can like it or not."

Wrey snorted. "Oh, really? They call that a Titan complex back in Dome, Moreau—the belief that you can go ahead and defy authority any time you want to. I suggest you check on my status here and consider what would happen if you tried to barge past my Marines against my orders."

Jonny shook his head. "I'm afraid it is *you*, sir, who's misunderstanding the legal situation here. Our charter clearly states that the governor-general may requisition a berth on any outgoing ship for purposes of consultation with Dominion officials. The charter makes *no* provision for exceptions."

"I claim an exception anyway. If you don't like it, you can file a grievance with the Central Committee when the war's over."

"I'm sorry, but it doesn't work that way. If you want to claim a legitimate exception, you'll have to present your case here, to Aventine's Council of Syndics."

Wrey's eyes narrowed. "What does that entail?"

Which meant the other had been on Asgard so long he'd forgotten how planet-level politics worked. For an instant Jonny was tempted to spin a genuine horror story, but quickly decided against it. Playing it straight was safer, and the truth was bad enough. "We'll first need to assemble all the Syndics—that's the easy part; they're all on the way here already. Then you'll present your credentials and your case and Governor-General Stiggur will present his. The council will discuss the situation and probably recess to make individual studies of the charter and try to find precedents in whatever Dominion records we have on file. Then they'll reassemble for a full debate, and when that's finished they'll vote. If the law seems to allow both sides of the case, a simple majority will suffice; but if the charter regulation I mentioned seems unopposed, then you'll need a three-quarters vote to grant you a one-time exception. The whole process will take—oh, maybe three to five days, minimum."

From the look on Wrey's face, the other had already added up the times. "Suppose I refuse to cooperate with this little delaying tactic?"

"You're free not to cooperate . . . but your ship doesn't lift until all this is resolved."

"How are you going to stop me?"

Reaching to the phone, Jonny tapped some keys,

and a second later a new voice joined the circuit. "Pyre here."

"Almo, this is Jonny Moreau. How's security setup going?"

"All locked down, Governor," the younger Cobra told him.

"Good. Please inform the night manager that there's no longer any rush to service the Dominion ship. It won't be leaving for a few more days."

"Yes, sir."

"Hold it, soldier," Wrey snapped. "I am a direct representative of the Central Committee, and on that authority I'm countermanding that order. Understand?"

There was a short pause. "Governor, is his claim legitimate?"

"Yes, but this specific action seems to violate a clear charter provision. It looks like it'll be going to the council."

"Understood, sir. Servicing operations will be suspended immediately."

"What?" Wrey barked. "Just a damned—"

"Out, sir."

A click signaled Pyre's departure, leaving the rest of Wrey's outburst to expend itself in thin air. He broke off, fixing Jonny with a furious glare. "You're not going to get away with this, Moreau. You can throw your Cobras against my armored Marines all day without—"

"Are you suggesting a firefight in the vicinity of your ship, sir?" Jonny asked mildly.

Wrey fell suddenly silent. "You won't get away with it," he repeated mechanically.

"The *law* is on my side," Jonny said. "Frankly, Mr. Wrey, I don't see why this is really a problem. You obviously have the room to spare for me, and I've already showed you that you'll be both morally *and* legally in the clear if your superiors become annoyed. And who knows? Maybe they'll actually be glad I came along ... in which case you'll get all the credit for such foresight."

Wrey snorted at that, but Jonny could see in his face that he'd already opted for the simpler, safer course. "All right, what the hell. You want to cut out and spend the war on Asgard, that's none of *my* business. Just be here when the rest of the passengers show or I'll leave without you."

"Understood. And thank you."

Wrey snorted again and the screen went blank.

Jonny exhaled slowly. Another minor victory ... and as emotionally unsatisfying as all such political wins seemed to be. Perhaps, he thought, it was because no opponent was ever fully vanquished in this form of combat. They always got back up out of the dust, a little smarter and—often—a little madder each time. And Jonny would now be spending the next three months heading straight for Wrey's political domain, while Wrey himself had those same months to plan whatever revenge he chose.

So much for victory.

Grimacing, Jonny punched again for Almo Pyre. His order halting the ship's servicing would have to be rescinded.

There was a great deal of work involved in turning over his duties on such short notice, and in the end Jonny wound up with far less time than he'd wanted to tell his family good-bye. It added one more shade of pain to the already Pyrrhic victory, especially as he had no intention of letting Wrey know how he felt.

The worst part, of course, was that there was very little aboard ship to occupy his thoughts. On the original trip to Aventine a quarter century earlier, there'd been fellow colonists to meet as well as magcards of information compiled by the survey teams to be studied. Here, even with the fourteen business passengers Wrey was bringing home, the ship carried only thirty-six people, none of whom Jonny was especially interested in getting to know. And if the ship carried any useful information on the impending war, no one was saying anything about it.

So for the first couple of weeks Jonny did little except sit alone in his cabin, reread the colonies' data he'd brought to show the Central Committee, and brood . . . until one morning he awoke with an unexpected, almost preternatural alertness. It took him several minutes to figure out on a conscious level what his subconscious had already realized: during ship's night they had passed from no-man's space into the Troft Corridor. The old pattern of being in hostile territory evoked long-buried Cobra training; and as the politician yielded to the warrior, Jonny unexpectedly found his helpless feelings giving way to new determination. For the time being, at least, the political situation had become a potentially military one . . . and military situations were almost never completely hopeless.

He began in the accepted military way: learning the territory. For hours at a time he toured the *Menssana*, getting to know everything about it and compiling long mental lists of strengths, weaknesses, quirks, and possibilities. He learned the names and faces of each of the fourteen crewers and six Marines, evaluating as best he could how they would react in a crisis. Doing the same with the passengers actually proved a bit easier: with the same excess of free time he himself had, they were eager to spend time with him, playing games or just talking. More than once Jonny wished he'd brought Cally Halloran along, but even without the other's knack at informal psych analysis, he was soon able to divide the passengers into the old "float/freeze" categories: those who could probably deal with and adapt to a crisis, and those who couldn't. Heading the former were two executive field reps Jonny soon learned to consider friends as well as potential allies: Dru Quoraheim, a pharmaceutical company executive whose face and dry humor reminded him vaguely of Ilona Linder; and Rando Harmon, whose interests lay in rare metals and, occasionally, Dru Quoraheim. For a while Jonny wondered if Dru had latched onto him to use as a partial shield against Harmon's advances, but as it became clear that those advances were entirely non-serious he realized the whole thing was an elaborate game designed to give the participants something to concentrate on besides the mental picture of silent Troft warships.

And when his survey was complete ... it was back to waiting. He played chess with Dru and Harmon, kept abreast of the ship's progress, and—alone, late at night—tried to come up with some way to keep the war from happening, or at least to keep it from happening to Aventine. And wondered if and when the Trofts would move against the *Menssana*.

Twenty-five light-years from Dominion space, they finally did.

It was evening, ship's time, and most of the passengers were in the lounge, grouped in twos and threes for conversation, social drinking, or the occasional game. At a table near the back Jonny, Dru, and Harmon had managed a synthesis of all three in the form of a light Aventine sherry and a particularly nasty round of trisec chess.

A game Jonny's red pieces were steadily losing. "You realize, of course," he commented to his opponents, "that such friendly cooperation between you two is prima facie evidence of collusion between your two companies. If I lose this game, I'm swearing out a complaint when we get to Asgard."

"Never stand up in court," Harmon rumbled

distractedly. His attention had good reason to be elsewhere; Dru was slowly but inexorably building up pressure on his king side and too many of his own pieces were out of position to help. "Dru's the one who's apparently moonlighting from the Joint Command's tactical staff."

"I wish I was," Dru shook her head. "At least I'd have something to *do* during the war. Market developers don't get much work when the market shrinks."

For a few minutes the only sound was the click of chess pieces as Dru launched her attack, Harmon defended, and Jonny took advantage of the breather to reposition his own men. Harmon was a move behind in the exchange and wound up losing most of his cozy castle arrangement. "Tell me again about this collusion," he said when the flurry of moves was over.

"Well, I *could* be mistaken," Jonny admitted.

Harmon grunted and took a sip of his drink. "Going to be the last Aventine sherry anyone back home gets for a long time," he commented. "A real pity."

"War usually is." Jonny hesitated. "Tell me, what does the Dominion's business community think of the upcoming hostilities?"

Dru snorted. "I presume you're not talking about the shipyards and armaments manufacturers?"

"No, I mean companies like yours that've been working with Aventine. Maybe even the Trofts, too, for all I know. Like you said, Dru, you're losing a growing market out here."

She glanced at Harmon. "With Aventine, yes, though I'll point out for the record that neither of our companies deals with the Trofts—Dome is very stingy with licenses for that kind of trade. You're right, though, that the Outer Colonies are going to be missed."

"Anyone who deals with you feels pretty much

the same way," Harmon added. "But there's nothing obvious we can do about it."

"About all we can do is hope our first attack is so brilliant and decisive that it ends the war before too much damage is done." Dru moved a pawn, simultaneously opening Harmon's king to a new threat and blocking an advance from Jonny's remaining rook.

Harmon waved at the board. "And if the Star Force has any brains, they'll put Dru in charge—what was that?"

Jonny had felt it too: a dull, almost audible thump, as if someone had dropped an exceptionally heavy wrench in the *Menssana's* engine room. "We've just dropped out of hyperspace," he said quietly, sliding his chair back and looking around. None of the others in the lounge seemed to have noticed the jolt.

"Out *here?*" Dru frowned. "Aren't we still two weeks inside Troft territory?"

"It may not have been voluntary." Jonny stood up. "Stay here; I'm going to the bridge. Don't say anything to the others yet—no sense panicking anyone until we know what's going on."

He reached the bridge to find Captain Davi Tarvn presiding over a scene of controlled chaos. "What's the situation?" he asked, stepping to the other's command station.

"Too soon to really tell," Tarvn replied tightly. "Looks like we hit a Troft flicker-mine web, but so far the usual spider ships haven't shown up. Maybe they won't."

"Wishful thinking."

"Sure, but that's about all we've got," Tarvn nodded. "If a Troft shows up before the drive's recalibrated, we've had it. You know as well as I do how long our weaponry and plating would hold against attack—you've been studying the ship enough lately."

Jonny grimaced. "About half a minute if they were determined. What can I do?"

"You can get the hell off the bridge," a new voice snapped, and Jonny turned to see Wrey crossing the floor toward them. "Status, Captain?"

"Minimum of an hour before the drive can be fixed," Tarvn told him. "Until then we try to be as inconspicuous as possible—"

"Hostile at ninety-seven slash sixty," the navigator interjected suddenly. "Closing, Captain."

"Battle stations," Tarvn gritted. "Well, gentlemen, so much for staying inconspicuous. Mr. Wrey, what do you want me to do?"

Wrey hesitated. "Any chance of outrunning him?"

"Second hostile," the navigator said before Tarvn could reply. "Two-ninety slash ten. Also closing."

"Right on top of us," Tarvn muttered. "I'd say our chances are slim, sir, at least as long as we're stuck in normal."

"Then we have to surrender," Jonny said.

Wrey turned a murderous glare onto him. "I told you to get lost," he snarled. "You have no business here—this is a *military* situation."

"Which is exactly why you need me. *I've* fought the Trofts; you almost certainly never have."

"So you're an overage reservist," Wrey grunted. "That still doesn't—"

"No," Jonny said, lowering his voice so that only Wrey and Tarvn could hear. "I'm a Cobra."

Wrey's voice died in mid-word, his eyes flicking over Jonny's form. Tarvn muttered something under his breath that Jonny didn't bother notching up his enhancers to catch. But the captain recovered fast. "Any of the passengers know?" he murmured.

Jonny shook his head. "Just you two—and I want it kept that way."

"You should have told me earlier—" Wrey began.

"Be quiet, sir," Tarvn said unexpectedly, his eyes

still on Jonny. "Will the Trofts be able to detect your equipment, Governor?"

"Depends on how tight a filter they put all of us through," Jonny shrugged. "A full bioscan will show it, but a cursory weapon detector check shouldn't."

Behind Jonny the helmsman cleared his throat. "Captain?" he said, his voice rigidly controlled. "The Trofts are calling on us to surrender."

Tarvn glanced at his screens, turned back to Wrey. "We really don't have any choice, sir."

"Tell them we're an official Dominion courier and that this is a violation of treaty," Wrey said tightly, his own eyes on the displays. "Threaten, argue—do your damnedest to talk our way out. Then—" He exhaled between clenched teeth. "If it doesn't work, go ahead and surrender."

"And try to get terms that'll leave all of us aboard the *Menssana*," Jonny added. "We may need to get out in a hurry if we get an opening."

"We damn well better *get* that opening," Wrey murmured softly. "All of this is *your* idea, remember."

Jonny almost laughed. Middle-level bureaucrat, indeed—the operation had barely begun and already Wrey was scrambling to place any possible blame elsewhere. Predictable and annoying; but occasionally it could be used. "In that case, I presume I'm authorized to handle the whole operation? Including giving Captain Tarvn orders?"

Wrey hesitated, but only briefly. "Whatever you want. It's your game now."

"Thank you." Jonny turned back to Tarvn. "Let's see what we can do now about stacking the deck and maybe providing a little diversion at the same time."

He outlined his plan, got Tarvn's approval, and hurried to the Marine guardroom to set things up. Then it was back to the lounge and a quiet consultation with Dru and Harmon. They took the news calmly, and as they all collected and put away the chess pieces, he outlined the minor and—theoretically—safe roles he wanted them to play. Both agreed with a grim eagerness that showed he'd chosen his potential allies well.

He was back in his cabin fifteen minutes later, hiding the most sensitive of his Aventine data on random sections of unrelated magcards, when Tarvn officially announced the *Menssana's* surrender. Obeying the captain's instructions, he went to the lounge with the others and tried to relax. He succeeded about as well as everyone else.

A half hour later, the Trofts came aboard.

The lounge was the largest public room on the ship, but fifteen passengers, thirteen crewers, and four Marines made for cozy quarters even without the seven armed Trofts lined up along the wall. Wrey and Tarvn were absent, presumably having been taken elsewhere; Jonny kept his fingers crossed that anyone who noticed would assume the two missing Marines were with them.

There had been few communications with the Trofts during the war to which Jonny had been privy, but back then he'd gotten the impression the aliens weren't much for social or even political small talk, and the boarding party's spokesman did nothing to shake that image. "This ship and its resources are now possessions of the Drea'shaa'chki Demesne of the Trof'te Assemblage," the alien's translator repeater stated in flat tones. "The crew and passengers will remain aboard as tokens of human consensus-order violations. The so-named Trof'te Corridor has been reclaimed."

So they *were* to be held aboard. That was a stroke of luck Jonny had hoped for but not dared to expect. If Wrey had wangled this concession, perhaps he was good for something, after all—

His thoughts were cut off abruptly as an ar-

mored but weaponless Marine was hauled through
the door by two Trofts and put into line with the
other prisoners. Mentally, Jonny shrugged; he'd
expected the better equipped of his two sleepers to
be found fairly quickly. The other Marine, in shirt-
sleeves and armed only with a knife and garotte,
should withstand the search somewhat better. Not
that his freedom or capture ultimately made much
difference. As long as he drew the Trofts' attention
away from the civilians, he was serving his purpose.
Though Jonny doubted that he realized that.

The prisoners were kept in the lounge another
hour, leading Jonny to wonder whether they would
be staying there until the Trofts were satisfied
everyone had been found. But as they were led
back to the passenger cabin section without the
second Marine making his appearance, he decided
the reason for the delay was probably more prosaic:
that the aliens had been conducting careful sensor
searches of their rooms with an eye toward turning them into cells. The guess turned out to be
correct, and a few minutes later Jonny found himself back in his cabin.

Though not *quite* alone.

The three sensor disks the Trofts had attached to
selected sections of wall and ceiling were rather
conspicuous as such things went, nearly two centimeters across each with faintly translucent surfaces.
A quick check showed that the bathroom and even
the closet were equipped with disks of their own.
What they might pick up besides an optical picture Jonny didn't know, but it hardly mattered. As
long as they were in place, he was unable to act;
ergo, his first task was to get rid of them.

It was probably the first time in twenty-seven
years that his arcthrower might have done him
some good; but then, he hardly could have used it
without announcing in large red letters that he
was a Cobra. Fortunately, there were other ways

to accomplish what he had in mind. Returning to the bathroom, he selected a tube of burn salve from the cabinet first-aid kit. He was in the process of coating the second of the main room's disks with a thick layer of cream when the inevitable Troft charged in.

"You will cease this activity," the alien said, the monotone translator voice editing out whatever emotion lay behind the words.

"I'll be damned if I will," Jonny snarled back, putting all the righteous indignation he could into both voice and body language on the off-chance this was one of those Trofts who could read such nuances. "You attack us, pirate our ship, paw through our cabins—just *look* at the mess you left my magcards in—and now you have the damned nerve to *spy* on us. Well, I'm not going to stand for it—you hear me?"

The alien's upper-arm membranes rippled uncertainly. "Not all of you seem bothered by our security needs."

Not all of you ... which implied Dru and Harmon had followed his instructions to kick up similar fusses. Three wasn't a very big crowd to hide in, but it was better than being blatantly unique. "Not all of us grew up with private bathrooms, either," he retorted, "but those who did can't do without them. I want my privacy and I'm going to get it."

"The sensors will remain," the Troft insisted.

"Then you're going to have to chain me up," Jonny snarled, crossing his arms defiantly.

The alien paused, and Jonny's enhanced hearing caught a stream of high-speed Troft catertalk. It was another minute before the translator came back on-line. "You spoke of privacy in the bathroom. If the sensor is removed from in there, will that satisfy your needs?"

Jonny pursed his lips. It *would*, actually, but he

didn't want to accept the compromise too eagerly.
"Well . . . I could try that, I suppose."

The Troft stepped past him and disappeared into
the bathroom, returning a moment later with the
sensor disk in one hand and some tissues from the
dispenser in the other. He offered the latter to
Jonny. It took the Cobra a second to understand;
then, taking them, he proceeded to wipe clean the
two disks he'd disabled. When he was finished, the
Troft strode to the door and left.

He gave in awfully easily, was Jonny's first
thought. A careful check of the bathroom, though,
showed it was indeed clear of all sensors. Returning to the main room, he sat back down with his
comboard—remembering to maintain an air of
discomfort—and pretended to read.

He waited an hour, ten minutes of which time
was spent in the bathroom to see if the Trofts
would get nervous and send in a guard. But they'd
evidently decided there was nothing dangerous he
could do in there and no one disturbed him. Taking slightly higher than normal doses of his anemia and arthritis medicines, he returned to his
comboard . . . and when the drugs took effect it
was time to go.

He began with the normal human pattern for a
pre-bedtime shower: pajamas carried into the bathroom accompanied by the hiss of water against
tile. But under cover of the sound, Jonny's fingertip lasers traced a rectangular pattern on the thin
metal panel between sink and shower stall, and
within a minute he had a passable opening to the
cramped service corridor behind the row of cabins.
Leaving the water running, he squeezed into the
corridor and began sidling his way forward.

The *Menssana's* designer had apparently felt that
separate ventilation systems for the various service lane levels would be a waste of good equipment and had opted instead for periodically spaced

grilles to connect all of them together. It was a quirk that would ordinarily be of no use to anyone in Jonny's position, as the cramped quarters and high ceilings discouraged vertical movement almost as much as solid floors would have. But then, the designer hadn't been thinking about Cobras.

Jonny passed three more cabins before finding a grille leading to the deck above. Bending his knees the few degrees the walls allowed, he jumped upward, stifling a grunt as a twinge of pain touched the joints. Catching the grille, he hung suspended for a moment as he searched out the best spots to cut. Then, with leg servos pressing his feet against the walls in a solid friction grip, he turned his lasers against the metal mesh. A minute later he was through the hole and sidling down that level's service corridor; two minutes after that he was peering out the corridor's access door at the darkened equipment room into which it opened. Next door would be the EVA-ready room. Beyond that was the main hatch and the probable connection to the Troft ship.

Jonny eased out the equipment room door into the deserted corridor, alert for sounds of activity that weren't there. The main hatch was indeed open, the boarding tunnel beyond snaking enough to block any sight of the alien ship's own entryway. Whatever security the Trofts had set up was apparently at the far end of the tunnel, an arrangement that would be difficult but not impossible to exploit. But any such operation required first that the *Menssana* be under human control again ... and to accomplish *that*, he would have to retake the bridge. Passing the hatch, he continued on forward.

The spiral stairway leading to the bridge had not been designed with military security in mind, but the Trofts had added one of their sensor disks to the spiral in a position impossible to bypass. From a semi-shadowed position down the hall,

Jonny gritted his teeth and searched his memory for a way to approach the stairway from behind. But any such route would take a great deal of time, and time was in short supply at the moment. On the other hand . . . if the Trofts saw an apparently unarmed man approaching their position, they were unlikely to greet him with an automatic blaze of laser fire. They would probably merely point their weapons and order him to surrender, after which they would return him to his cell and find out how he'd escaped. If they followed safe military procedure and called in before confronting him . . . but he'd just have to risk that. *Now*, while the *Menssana* was still in or near the Corridor, was their best opportunity for escape. Gritting his teeth, he started for the staircase.

He moved quickly, though no faster than a normal human could have, and no challenges or shots came his way before he reached the stairs and started up. His catlike steps were small bomb blasts in his enhanced hearing, but between them he could hear the unmistakable sounds of sudden activity overhead. He kept going . . . and when he raised his head cautiously above the level of the bridge floor he found himself facing a semicircle of four Troft handguns. "You will make no sudden movements," a translator voice ordered as he froze in place. "Now: continue forward for questioning."

Slowly, Jonny continued up the stairs and into the bridge, keeping his hands visible. The four guards were backed up by three more at the *Menssana's* consoles, armed but with weapons holstered. Sitting atop the communications board was a small box of alien design. The Trofts' link with their own ship and translator, most likely . . . and in a highly vulnerable position.

"How did you escape from your quarters?" one of the guards asked.

Jonny focused on the semicircle. "Call your

captain," he said. "I wish to speak to him about a trade."

The Trofts' arm membranes fluttered. "You are in no position to trade anything."

"How do you know?" Jonny countered. "Only your captain can make that assessment."

The Troft hesitated. Then, slowly, he raised a hand to a collar pin and let loose with a stream of catertalk. Another pause . . . and the communications box abruptly spoke. "This the Ship Commander. What do you propose to trade?"

Jonny pursed his lips. It was a question he'd been working on since the Trofts first came aboard . . . and he had yet to come up with a really satisfactory answer. Trade back the Trofts aboard the *Menssana?* But the aliens didn't think of *hostage* as a word applicable to living beings. The *Menssana* itself? But he hardly had real control of the ship. Still, if politics had taught him anything, it was the value of a plausible bluff. "I offer you your own ship in return for the humans you hold plus the release of this vessel," he said.

There was a long pause. "Repeat, please. You offer me my own demesne-ship?"

"That's right," Jonny nodded. "From this ship I have the power to destroy yours. For obvious example, a hard starboard yaw would tear out the boarding tunnel, depressurizing that part of your demesne-ship, and a simultaneous blast with the drive at this range would cause extensive damage to your own engines. Is this possibility not worth trading to avoid?"

His captors' arm membranes were fluttering at half-mast now. Either the room temperature had risen dramatically or he had indeed hit a sensitive nerve. "Commander?" he prompted.

"The ability you claim is nonexistent," the box said. "You are not in control of that ship."

"You're wrong, Commander. My companion and I are in full control here."

"You have no companion. The soldier hiding in the dining-area ventilation system has been returned to his quarters."

So the other Marine *had* been found. "I'm not speaking of him."

"Where is your companion?"

"Nearby, and in control. If you want to know any more you'll have to come here and negotiate the trade I've suggested."

There was another long pause. "Very well. I will come."

"Good." Jonny blew a drop of sweat from the tip of his nose. Perhaps it *was* just getting hot.

"You will reveal your companion to us before the Ship Commander arrives," one of the guards said. It didn't sound like a request.

Jonny took a careful breath . . . prepared himself. "Certainly. She's right here." He gestured to his left, the arm movement masking the slight bending of his knees—

And he ricocheted off the ceiling to slam to the deck behind the four guards, fingertip lasers blazing.

The communications box went first, fried instantly by a blast from his arcthrower. Two of the guards' guns hit the deck midway through that first salvo; the other two guards made it nearly all the way around before their lasers also erupted with clouds of vaporized metal and plastic and went spinning from burned hands. A sideways jump and half turn and Jonny had the last three Trofts in sight. "Don't move," he snapped.

With the translator link down his words were unintelligible, but none of the aliens seemed to mistake his meaning. All remained frozen where they stood or sat, arm membranes stretched wide, as Jonny disarmed the last three and then tore the communicator pins from the uniforms of all seven.

Herding them down the staircase, he got them into a nearby water pumping room—spot-welding the latch to make sure they stayed put—and hurried aft toward the main hatch. The Troft commander wasn't likely to come alone, and Jonny needed at least a little advance notice as to what size force he'd have to handle. The possibility that the other would simply veer off, trading his occupation force for two humans, wasn't one Jonny wanted to consider.

He heard them coming down the boarding tunnel long before they actually appeared: ten to fifteen of them, he estimated, from the sound. Hidden in an emergency battery closet a dozen meters down the hall, he watched through a cracked door as they approached. The commander was easy to spot, keeping to the geometric center of his guard array: an older Troft, by the purple blotches on his throat bladder, his uniform fairly dripping with the colored piping of rank. Six guards ahead of him, six behind him, their lasers fanned to cover both directions, the procession moved down the corridor toward Jonny's hiding place and the bridge. The vanguard passed him . . . and Jonny slammed open the door and leaped.

The door caught the nearest Troft full in the back, jolting him forward and clearing just enough room for Jonny's rush to get him through the phalanx unhindered. With one outstretched arm he caught the commander around his torso, the action spinning them both around as Jonny's initial momentum drove them toward the far wall. Slipping between the two guards on that side, they slammed against the plating, Jonny's back screaming with agony as it took the brunt of the impact.

And then, for a long moment, the corridor was a silent, frozen tableau.

"All right," Jonny said as his breath returned, "I know you don't apply the idea of hostage to yourselves, Commander, so we'll just think of this as a matter of your personal safety. All of you—lay your weapons down on the deck. I don't especially want to hurt your commander, but I will if I have to."

Still no one moved, the twelve laser muzzles forming shining counterpoint to the arched arm membranes spread out behind each of them. "I told you to drop your guns," Jonny repeated more harshly. "Don't forget that you can't hit me without killing your commander."

The Troft leaning against him stirred slightly in his grip. "They have no concern for my life," the translator voice said. "I am not the Ship Commander, merely a Services Engineer in his uniform. A crude trick, but one which we learned from humans."

Jonny's mouth went dry. His eyes swept the circle of Trofts, the steadiness of their weapons an unspoken confirmation of the other's words. "You're lying," he said, not believing it but driven to say *something*. "If you're not the commander, then why haven't they opened fire?" He knew the answer to that: they wanted him alive. History—personal history, at least—had repeated itself . . . and even more than on Adirondack, he knew the knowledge he held this time was too valuable to allow the enemy to have. *Chrys*, a detached fragment of his mind breathed in anguish toward the distant stars, and he prepared for his last battle—

"They will not shoot," the Troft in his grip said. "You are a *koubrah*-soldier from the Aventine world, and if killed you would merely fight on until all aboard were dead."

Jonny frowned. "How's that?"

"You need not deny the truth. We have all heard the report."

What report? Jonny opened his mouth to ask the question aloud . . . and suddenly he understood.

MacDonald. Somehow they'd heard about Mac-Donald.

He looked at the circle of Trofts again, seeing their rigidly stretched arm membranes with new eyes. Determination, he'd thought earlier, or perhaps rage. But now he recognized the emotion for what it was: simple, naked fear. *D'arl was right*, that same detached fragment of his mind realized. *They* are *afraid of us.* "I don't wish to kill anyone," he said quietly. "I want only to free my companions and to continue on my way."

"To what end?" the same flat voice came from the direction of the boarding tunnel. Jonny turned his head to see another middle-aged Troft walking slowly toward them. His uniform was identical to the one wrapped in Jonny's arms.

"That of protecting my world, Commander," Jonny told him. "By diplomatic means if possible, military ones if necessary."

The other said something in catertalk, and slowly the circle of laser muzzles dipped to point at the floor. His eyes on the Troft commander, Jonny released his captive and stepped out from behind him. A trick to put the Cobra off-guard, perhaps; but the politician within Jonny recognized the need to respond to the gesture with a good-faith one of his own. "Have we any grounds for negotiation?" he asked.

"Perhaps," the commander said. "You spared the lives of the Trof'tes in your control center when you could as easily have killed them. Why?"

Jonny frowned, realizing for the first time that he had no idea why he'd handled things that way. Too long in politics, where one never killed one's opponent? No. The real reason was considerably less colorful. "There wasn't any need to kill them," he said with a shrug. "I suppose it never really occurred to me."

"*Koubrah*-soldiers were created to kill."

"We were created to *defend*. There's a difference."

The other seemed to ponder that. "Perhaps there *are* grounds for compromise," he said at last. "Or at least for discussion. Will you and your companion come to my bridge?"

Jonny nodded. "Yes . . . but the companion I mentioned won't actually be there. She's an insubstantial entity we humans call Lady Luck."

The commander was silent a moment. "I believe I understand. If so, I would still invite her to accompany us."

Turning, he disappeared into the boarding tunnel. Hesitating only a moment, Jonny followed. The escort, weapons still lowered, fell into step around him.

He was back on the *Menssana* side of the tunnel four hours later when Wrey and Tarvn were brought aboard. "Good evening, gentlemen," Jonny nodded as their Troft escort silently disappeared back down the tunnel. "Captain, if you'll seal that hatch we're almost ready to be on our way."

"What the hell happened?" Wrey asked, his bewildered tone making the words more plaintive than demanding. "No questioning, no demands—no talk, period—and suddenly they're letting us go?"

"Oh, there was talking, all right," Jonny said. "Lots of it. That hatch secure? Good. Captain, I believe the drive repairs are finished, but you'll need to confirm that from the bridge. And make sure we're all ready before you pull away—the other Troft ship isn't in on this and they might try and stop us."

Tarvn's eyebrows arched, but all he said was, "Got it," before heading forward at a fast trot.

"What's going on?" Wrey demanded as Jonny started to follow. "What do you mean, there was lots of talking?"

"The Ship Commander and I had a discussion,

and I convinced him it was in his best interests to let us go."

"In other words, you made a deal," Wrey growled. "What was it?"

"Something I'll discuss only with the Central Committee and only when we reach Asgard," Jonny told him flatly.

Wrey frowned at him, irritation and growing suspicion etching his face. "You're not authorized to negotiate for the entire Dominion of Man."

"That's okay—the Ship Commander wasn't authorized to negotiate for the Troft Assemblage, either." A gentle thump rippled through the deck and Jonny relaxed muscles he hadn't realized he'd had tensed. "But what authority he did have seems to have been adequate to get us away."

"Moreau—"

"Now if you'll excuse me, it's been a long night and I'm very tired. Good-night, Mr. Wrey; you can figure out on your own how you'll write this incident up. I'm sure you'll come out the hero in the final version."

Which was a rather cheap shot, Jonny admitted to himself as he headed aft toward his cabin. But at the moment his body was aching more than Wrey would ever know and he had no patience left for mid-bureaucratic mentality.

Or, for that matter, for illegal business practices and deliberate evasions. Which was why he planned to take a few days to recuperate before confronting Dru and Harmon with the half-truth the Troft Ship Commander had popped. Allies they had been; allies they might yet be . . . and he would like if possible to also keep them as friends.

It was another two weeks' travel to the Troft-Dominion border, fourteen of the longest days Jonny had ever suffered through this side of the last war. The cooling attitude toward him aboard the *Mens-*

sana was part of it, of course, bringing back painful memories of those last months on Horizon. Jonny had all but forgotten the fear mainstream Dominion society felt toward Cobras, and on top of that he suspected Wrey of spitefully dropping hints that he'd made some terrible deal to buy their freedom. Only Harmon and Dru seemed relatively untouched by the general aloofness, and even with them Jonny could tell their friendliness had a large wedge of self-interest mixed in. After the long and painful confession session Jonny had forced them through shortly after their escape, he had the power to bring a fair amount of official flak down on them, and they both knew it.

But the social isolation was only a minor part of the frustration Jonny felt with the slowness of their progress. He had a real chance of sidetracking the war completely, but only if he could get to Asgard before the actual shooting began. To Asgard, and in front of the Central Committee. He hoped Jame would be able to arrange that; Wrey wasn't likely to be of any help.

And at last the *Menssana* touched down on Adirondack, the terminus point for Corridor traffic . . . and Wrey played his trump card.

"I'm sorry for whatever inconvenience it'll cost you to have to find your own ways back to your ultimate destinations," Wrey told the group of passengers as they gathered in the Dannimor starfield's customs building. "Unfortunately, the fast courier I'll be taking to Asgard hasn't room for anyone besides myself and Captain Tarvn."

"And me, I presume," Jonny spoke up.

"Afraid not," Wrey said blandly. "But then, you'll remember I warned you against inviting yourself along."

For a heartbeat Jonny simply stood there, unable to believe his ears. "You can't do that, Wrey—"

"Can't I?" the other retorted. "I suggest you

check the statutes, Moreau—if you know how to look up *real* law, that is."

Jonny gazed at the other's self-satisfied expression, the small gloating smile playing at the corners of the paunchy man's mouth—the small mind having its big moment. And Jonny, his own mind occupied by too many other things, had failed completely to anticipate this move. "Look," he said quietly, "this is foolish, and you know it. The Committee needs to hear what the Troft Ship Commander told me—"

"Oh, yes—the 'secret plan' to stop the war that you won't tell anyone about," Wrey almost-sneered. "Maybe you'd better finally loosen up and give me at least the basic outline. I'd be sure and mention it to the Committee."

"I'm sure you would," Jonny grated. "You'll forgive me if I don't trust you to do the job right. Of course, you realize leaving me stranded here with vital information is likely to land you in very deep water very fast."

"Oh, I wouldn't worry about that." Wrey raised a finger and four men in Army uniforms detached themselves from various walls and stepped forward, halting in a loose box formation about Jonny. "I wouldn't worry about yourself, either," Wrey added. "You're going to be well taken care of."

Jonny glanced at the guards, his eyes slipping from the quietly alert faces to the collar insignia beneath. Interrorum, the Army's crack anti-espionage/anti-terrorist squad. "What the hell is this?" he demanded.

"You'll be getting a first-class military ride to Asgard," Wrey told him. "*After* you've been checked for hypnotic and subliminal manipulation, of course."

"What? Look, Wrey, unless basic citizen rights have been suspended recently—"

"You were alone with the Trofts for several hours,

by your own admission," Wrey interrupted harshly.
"Maybe they let us go because you'd been programmed for sabotage or assassination."

Jonny felt his jaw drop. "Of all the *ridiculous*—
you can't make a charge like that stick for ten
minutes."

"Take it easy, Governor. I'm not trying to make
anything 'stick'—I'm merely following established
procedures. You'll be released in—what were those
numbers? Three to five days minimum? It takes a
three-quarters majority of the examiners to clear
you, of course."

Jonny ground his teeth. Wrey was really taking
his pound of flesh. "And suppose while I'm sitting
around hooked to a biomedical sensor your news
of the Troft hijacking starts a war that could have
been prevented? Or didn't that occur to you?"

For just an instant Wrey's eyes lost some of their
insolence. "I don't think there's any danger of that.
You'll get to Asgard in plenty of time." He smiled
slyly. "Probably. All right, take him."

For a long second Jonny was tempted. But the
soldiers were undoubtedly backed up by plain-
clothesmen elsewhere, and there were lots of innocent civilians in the building who'd be caught in
any crossfire. Exhaling through his teeth, he let
them take him away.

The first part of this kind of testing, Jonny remembered from his Cobra lectures, was to estab-
lish a physiological baseline by giving the subject
several hours of solitary while hidden sensors piled
up data. A side effect, especially for those who
didn't know the procedure, was to raise the subject's
tension level as he contemplated the unknown future awaiting him.

For Jonny, the wasted hours ticking by were
maddening.

A dozen times in the first hour he seriously con-

sidered breaking out and trying to commandeer a
star ship, and each time it was the sheer number
of uncertainties that finally stopped him. By the
end of the second hour the first twinges of pain
began to intrude on his planning. He called the
guard, was politely but firmly told his medicine
would be returned once it had been analyzed. Protests were of no avail, and as he settled back on his
cot to wait, the simmering anger within him began to slowly change into fear. In a very short
time he would lose the ability to function . . . and
when that happened he truly *would* be at Wrey's
mercy.

He'd been in the cell nearly three hours when a
shadow passed across the observation window and
his enhanced hearing picked up a quiet click from
the direction of the door.

He turned his head to see, muscles tensing . . .
but the door wasn't being opened. Instead, a small
hemispherical dome near the floor beside it rotated open to reveal a tray of food.

At the observation window a guard's face appeared. "Thanks," Jonny said, easing from the cot
and retrieving the meal. The old familiar Adirondack cooking, his nostrils told him as he carried
the tray back and sat down.

"No problem." The guard hesitated. "Are you
really one of the Cobras that saved Adirondack
from the Trofts?"

Jonny paused, spoon halfway to his mouth. "Yes,"
he acknowledged. "Are you a native?"

The guard nodded. "Born and raised right here
in Dannimor. Where were you stationed?"

"Over in Cranach." The mesh in the window
made the guard's face hard to see, but Jonny estimated his age in the low thirties. "You were probably too young to remember the war much."

"I remember enough. We had relatives in Paris
when it was destroyed." He pursed his lips at the

memory. "I had an uncle in Cranach then, too. Did you know a Rob Delano?"

"No." Memories flooded back of the people he had known . . . and with the mental pictures came an idea. "Tell me, just how isolated am I supposed to be?"

"What do you mean—visitors or something?"

"Or even phone calls. There are people probably still living nearby who I once thought I'd never see again. As long as I'm stuck here for a while maybe I can at least say hello to some of them."

"Well . . . maybe later that'll be possible."

"Can you at least get me a directory or something so I can find out who still lives in the area?" Jonny persisted. "This dose of solitary isn't a punishment, after all—it's just part of the deep-psych test preparation. I ought to be allowed to have reading material in here."

The guard frowned at that, but then shrugged. "I'm not sure that really qualifies as reading material, but I'll check with the guard captain."

"Be sure to remind him that I *am* a high Dominion official," Jonny said softly.

"Yes, sir." The guard disappeared.

Jonny returned his attention to his dinner, striving to keep his new spark of hope in check. What he could accomplish with a directory—or even with the hoped-for contact with his old allies—wasn't immediately clear, but at least it was somewhere to start. If nothing else, it might give him a feel for exactly how big an official cloud Wrey had put him under.

He had finished his meal and returned the tray to its place by the door, and was considering lying down again, when the guard returned. "The captain wasn't available," his disembodied voice came as the tray disappeared and a small comboard showed up in its place. "But since you're a Dominion official and all, I guess it'll be all right." His face reappeared at the window, and he watched as Jonny brought the instrument back to his cot.

"I really appreciate it," Jonny told him. "The directory's on the magcard here?"

"Yes—it covers Cranach, Dannimor, and the ten or so smaller towns around." He paused. "You Cobras were pretty effective, from all I've read about you."

Something in his tone caught Jonny's attention. "We did all right. Of course, we couldn't have done it without the civilian underground."

"Or vice versa. We're not going to have Cobras for the next war—did you know that?"

Jonny grimaced. "I didn't, but I guess I'm not surprised. The Army just going to set up normal guerrilla teams if war breaks out?"

"*When*, not *if*," the other corrected. "Yeah, we've got a whole bunch of Ranger and Alpha Force groups here now, some of them setting up civilian resistance networks."

Jonny nodded as he finally placed the guard's tone. "Scary, isn't it? War always is ... but this one doesn't have to happen."

"Yes, I heard the Interrorum guys talking about that. They said a Cobra would blow up if he'd been hypno-conditioned."

"No, they took those self-destruct triggers out right after the war. But I *wasn't* hypno-conditioned; by the Trofts or anyone else."

"That Committee man, Wrey, seems to think so."

Jonny smiled bitterly. "Wrey's a short-sighted idiot who's nursing a bruised pride. I had to practically force him to bring me from Aventine in the first place, and then I saved his spangles for him when the Trofts captured the *Menssana*. This is his way of putting me in my place."

"But would you necessarily *know* if your mind had been tampered with?"

"*I* would, yes. That kind of thing requires that the subject be put into an unconscious or semi-conscious state, and I've got internal sensors that would warn me of any chemical, optical, or sonic attempts to do that."

The guard nodded slowly. "Does Wrey know that?"

"I wasn't given the chance to tell him."

"I see. Well . . . I'd better get back to my duties. I'll be back later for the comboard."

"Thanks again," Jonny said; but the other had gone. *Now what*, he wondered uneasily, *was that all about? Information? Reassurance? Or was someone pulling his strings, trying to see how much I'd say?* Maybe Wrey had decided to hang around a few more hours hoping to be spared the trouble of shipping Jonny to Asgard. If so, Jonny knew, it would be a long wait. Balancing the comboard on his knees, he started his search.

Weissmann, Dane, Nunki; the names of a dozen temporary families and twice that many temporary teammates; the names *and* faces of Cobras living and dead—all of them tumbled out together with an ease that belied the twenty-six-year gap. For nearly half an hour he bounced back and forth through the directory as fast as his stiffening fingers would allow; for an hour after that he went more slowly as the flood of names became a trickle and finally ceased entirely.

And none of them were listed.

He stared at the comboard, mind unwilling to accept the evidence of his eyes. Adirondack was still classified as a frontier world, yes, with new areas constantly being developed—but even in twenty-six years how could *everyone* he'd known here have moved somewhere else?

He was still trying to make sense of it all when a movement outside his cell made him look up. The click of multiple bolts being withdrawn gave him just enough time to slide the comboard under his pillow before the cell door opened to reveal a young woman. "Governor Moreau?" she asked.

"Yes," Jonny nodded. "I hope you're someone in authority here."

Something crossed her face, too quickly to identify. "Not hardly. Thank you," she said, turning to the guard hovering at her shoulder—a different one, Jonny noted, than the one he'd talked with earlier. "I'll call when I'm done."

"All right, Doctor." The door swung shut behind her.

"Well, Governor, your medicine's been cleared," she said briskly, reaching into a pouch on her belt and producing the two vials that had been taken from him earlier. "I imagine you'd like to get some into your system before the examination."

Jonny frowned. "Examination?"

"Just routine. Take your pills, please."

He complied, and she sat down beside him on the cot. "I'll be taking some local/gradient readings," she said, producing a small cylinder from her pouch. "Just hold still and don't talk."

She flipped the instrument on and an oddly pervasive humming filled the room. "You've changed a lot," she said, just barely over the noise. "I wasn't sure it was you until I heard you speak."

"What?"

"Talk without moving your lips, please." She moved the instrument slowly across his chest, eyes on the readout.

Jonny felt a cold sweat break out on his forehead. Again, the possibility that this was a test sprang to mind ... but if so the stakes had been jumped immensely. Even passive cooperation with this woman might be worth a conspiracy charge. "Who are you?" he mumbled, lips as motionless as he could keep them.

Her eyes met his for the first time and a strangely

mischievous smile tugged at the corners of her lips. "Don't you remember your star geometry pupil?"

Geometry? *"Danice?* Danice Tolan?"

Her smile widened a bit. "I *knew* I hadn't changed that much." Abruptly, she became serious again. "Now: what are you doing in a Dominion military prison?"

"Officially, I'm here because I've been talking about peace with the Trofts and am therefore considered a security risk. In actuality, I'm here for stepping on a little man's pride."

"Peace." Danice said the word as if tasting it. "Anything come of those talks that could be considered progress?"

"It wasn't exactly a formal negotiation: but yes, I think I can keep the war from happening. If I can get the Central Committee to go along, that is."

"Which you obviously can't do from here." Her eyes were hard, measuring. "How long are you in for?"

"Wrey said three to five days or more. But he's already gone on to Asgard and there's no telling what the Committee'll do when he tells them we were stopped and boarded by the Trofts."

"You think they might declare war right then and there?"

"You tell me—you must know more about Dominion politics these days than I do."

Danice chewed gently at her lip, and for a long minute the only sound in the cell was the hum of her probe. Twice she paused to reset the instrument, and Jonny noticed a worried frown gradually spreading across her face. "All right," she mumbled abruptly. "We'll do it now. I'm registering a possible aneurysm in the hepatic artery—that should buy us a trip to the hospital for a closer look. Just try and play off of any cues." Without waiting for a reply she flicked off the instrument and called for the guard captain.

The captain wasn't wildly enthusiastic about her proposed hospital trip, but it was clear from his tone and worried glances that he considered the Cobra an important prisoner. Barely fifteen minutes later Jonny and Danice were heading under heavy guard through the gathering dusk toward the city's newest and best-equipped hospital.

Jonny's last experience with full mainstream medical care had been just before leaving for Aventine, and he was thoroughly impressed by the added sophistication and power the equipment had achieved in the intervening time. Multiple-layer, real-time holographic displays of his body were available at anything from a quarter- to twenty-thousand-power magnification, with structural and chemical highlighting available. Danice handled the controls with the skill of obvious practice, locating and displaying the alleged aneurysm so clearly that even Jonny could spot it in the holo.

"We'll have to operate," Danice said, turning to the senior guard who'd accompanied them. "I suggest you check with your superiors for instructions—see if there's a particular surgeon they'd prefer to use or whatever. In the meantime I'm going to sedate him and give him a shot of vasodepressor to relieve pressure on that aneurysm."

The guard nodded and fumbled out his phone. A floating table, looking uncomfortably like a coffin with a long ground-effect skirt, was brought up. Jonny was hoisted onto it and strapped down, and from a cabinet in its side Danice withdrew a hypospray and two vials. Injecting their contents into Jonny's arm, she replaced the hypospray and brought out a full-face oxygen mask. "What's that for?" one of the guards asked as she slipped the milky plastic over Jonny's head.

"He needs a slightly enhanced air supply to com-

pensate for his suppressed circulation," she said.
"What room, orderly?"

"Three-oh-seven," the man who'd brought in the
floating table told her. "If you'll all get out of the
way ... thank you."

Danice at his side, Jonny was pushed out into
the hospital's corridor maze, arriving eventually
at room 307, the numbers barely legible through
the mask. "Wait here until he's settled," Danice
told the guards curtly. "There's not enough room
to accomodate spectators in there."

Jonny was maneuvered alongside a bed in a
crackerbox-sized alcove. Stepping to the far side of
his table—the side between him and the guards at
the door—Danice and the orderly reached down—

And he was flipped over into total darkness.

The action was so unexpected that it took Jonny
several heartbeats to realize exactly what had
happened. The flat top of the floating table had
apparently rotated a half turn on its long axis,
concealing him in a hollowed-out part of the table's
upper section. Above him he could hear the faint
sounds of something heavy being lifted from the
table ... felt the table moving away from the bed
... indistinct voices holding a short conversation
... then moving again, through several turns and
a long elevator ride. . . .

When he was finally rotated into the open again,
he and Danice were alone in an underground parking garage. "Hurry," she whispered, her hands shaking as she unfastened his restraints. "We've got to
get you off-planet before they realize that's not
you in that bed."

"Who *is* there?" Jonny asked as they jogged to a
nondescript gray car.

"Fritz—one of the hospital's medical practice
robots." She got behind the wheel, took a deep
breath. "We had a few minutes to touch up his

features a bit, but the minute someone pulls off that mask, it's all over."

"You want me to drive?" Jonny asked, eyeing the tension lines in her face.

A quick shake of the head. "I need to get used to this sometime. It might as well be now."

She drove them through the garage, up a ramp, and out into the bustle of early-evening traffic. Jonny let her drive in silence for a few minutes before asking the obvious question. "Where are we going?"

"There's a freighter leaving for Palm in about two hours," she said, not looking at him. "We've bumped some ungodly number of high-stress plastic whosies to put aboard a yacht and pilot for you—you can tell him exactly where and when to part company with the freighter."

Jonny nodded, feeling slighty dazed by the speed at which this was all happening. "Do I get to ask who I have to thank for all this?"

"Do you really want to know?" she countered.

Jonny thought that one over. It *wasn't* a trivial question. "Yes," he said at last.

She sighed. "Well. First of all, you can lay your worst fears to rest—we're not in any way a criminal group. In fact, in one sense we're actually an official arm of the Dominion Joint Command." She snorted. "Though that may change after this. We're what's known as the Underground Defense Network, an organization that's supposed to do in this war what you and my parents' underground did in the last one. Except that we won't have any Cobras."

"You sound like one of my guards," Jonny murmured. "He the one who told you about me?"

Danice glanced at him in obvious surprise. "You're as quick as I always remembered you being. Yes, he's one of the handful of quiet liaisons between the military and the UDN, though I don't think his immediate superiors know. He's the one who put word of your arrest on our communications net."

"And convinced all of you I was worth defying the authorities over?"

She smiled bitterly. "Nothing of the kind. Everyone helping us thinks this is just another training exercise. Rescuing Prisoner From Under Enemy's Nose 101; final exam."

"Except you." The question was obvious; he didn't bother to voice it.

"I was just a kid in the last war, Jonny," she said quietly, "but I remember enough about it to haunt two or three lifetimes. I don't want to go through it again . . . but if the Dominion goes to war I'll have to."

"Maybe not—" Jonny began cautiously.

"What do you mean, 'maybe not'?" she flared. "You think they're going to all this trouble for the fun of it? They *know* Adirondack's going to be a major Troft target, and they've as good as admitted they won't be able to defend us. The plain, simple truth is that they're writing our world off and preparing us to sink or swim on our own. And for *nothing*."

She broke off and took a deep breath. "I'm sorry, Jonny. I'm sure Aventine means a lot to you. But I just can't see sacrificing Adirondack and maybe Silvern and Iberiand too in what amounts to a war of retribution."

"No need to apologize," he assured her. "No world should have to fight for its life twice in one generation."

Danice shook her head wearily. "You don't know the half of it. The social upheaval alone . . . There were a lot of books written about us after the war, you know, books that listed a lot of the underground people by name. Well, the Joint Command decided those people's lives might be in danger when the Trofts came in again, so five years ago they took everybody mentioned in any of the books and gave them new identities somewhere else on the planet. I was just barely able to find my own parents, and they *still* don't know where half of their oldest friends are."

Ahead, Jonny could see the starfield's control tower silhouetted against the last traces of red in the southwestern sky. "This pilot you've picked out also thinks this is a training exercise?"

"Theoretically. But Don is pretty smart—he may have figured out something else is up. Anyway, you'll have several days to discuss it." She favored him with a thoughtful look. "You really don't like this business of trusting other people with your life, do you? I suppose the habits of being a Cobra die hard."

"Not as hard as you'd think," Jonny shook his head. "You're remembering me with the eyes of a ten-year-old. Even then, I wasn't really any less dependent on other people than you are now."

Which was not, of course, an answer to her question. He *didn't* like depending on others, especially with so much at stake.

But it was something he could get used to.

"Committé Vanis D'arl's office," the bored face in the phone screen announced.

"Jame Moreau," Jonny told her, watching her closely. If she gave even the slightest indication she recognized him . . .

"Who's calling, please?" she asked.

"Teague Stillman—I used to be mayor of his home town. Tell him it's important."

Jonny held his breath; but, "Just a minute, please," was all she said before her face was replaced by a stylized dome. The local "hold" symbol, Jonny supposed, automatically starting his nano-computer clock circuit. He'd give Jame two minutes to answer before assuming the woman had called the cops instead and getting the hell out of the area—

"Hello, Jonny."

Jonny wrenched his gaze back from its survey of possible escape routes. If Jame was surprised to see him, it didn't show. "Hi, Jame," he said cautiously. "Uh . . ."

"The line's secure," his brother said. "You all right?"

"I'm fine, but I need your help. I have to—"

"Yeah, I know all about it. Damn it all, Jonny—look, where are you?"

Jonny felt icy fingers closing around his gut. "Why?"

"Why do you think?" Jame waved a hand in irritation. "Never mind—do it your own way. My neck's stuck far enough out as it is."

Jonny gritted his teeth. "I'm at a public phone on V'awter Street, just north of Carle Park."

Jame sighed. "All right. I'll be there in half an hour or less to get you. And *stay put* this time—understand?"

"Okay. And—thanks."

Some of the steel seemed to go out of Jame's backbone, and a small, guarded smile even touched his face. "Yeah. See you soon."

He was there in twenty minutes flat, and even with Jonny's lack of familiarity with current styles, it was obvious the younger Moreau's car was a top-of-the-line model. "Nice," Jonny nodded as he got in beside Jame and sank into the rich cushioning. "A step or two up from Dader's old limper."

"It won't stay that way long if anyone spots us," Jame replied tartly as he pulled into the traffic flow. "We're just lucky the alert on you was limited to the military and not made public. What did you think you were up to, anyway, breaking confinement like that?"

"What did you expect—that I'd just sit there in Wrey's private limbo while the pompous idiot got a war going?"

"Granted Wrey's a self-centered grudge-holder, credit him with at least the intelligence to guard his own skin," Jame growled. "He wouldn't have left you there more than two days at the most—*and* he'd arranged for a Star Force scoutship to bring you here after you'd been cleared. With the extra speed scouts can make, you'd have been here four days ago—barely a day, if that, behind Wrey."

Jonny's hands curled into fists. Could he really have misread Wrey *that* badly? "Damn," he murmured.

Jame sighed. "So instead of being brought before the Committee to have your say, you're right up there on the military's must-find list. I don't think even Wrey really believed his innuendo about you making a private deal with the Trofts, but the ease with which your friends got you loose has a lot of people very nervous. How'd you organize all that, anyway?"

"I didn't." Jonny sighed. "Okay. I admit I crusked up good. But it doesn't change the fact that the Committee needs to hear what I've brought."

Jame shook his head. "Not a chance. You wouldn't get past the first door of the dome."

Abruptly, Jonny realized that they were heading further *out* of the city instead of inward. "Where are we going?"

"To Committé D'arl's country estate."

Jonny's mouth went dry. "Why?"

Jame frowned at him. "You're the one who just said you wanted to talk to someone. Committé D'arl's agreed to hear you out."

"At his private estate." Where Jonny could quietly and conveniently disappear, if necessary, with no one the wiser.

Jame sighed. "Look, Jonny, I know you don't

like the Committé, but this is the only way you're going to get a hearing. And I'll tell you flat out that you couldn't find a more receptive audience anywhere in Dome." He glanced at his older brother. "Come on—settle back and relax. I know it probably looks like the whole universe is against you right now, but if you can't trust your old pillow-fight partner, who *can* you trust?"

Almost unwillingly, Jonny felt a smile touch his lips. "You may be right," he admitted.

"Of course I'm right. Now: we've got just under an hour for you to bring me up-to-date on the Aventine branch of the Moreau family. So start talking."

D'arl's country estate was at least as large as the entire city of Capitalia; a rich man's version, Jonny thought once, of the Tyler Mansion and grounds of Adirondack. With a rich man's version of security, too. The car was stopped six times by pairs of variously armed guards, and at each roadblock Jonny's enhanced vision picked out hidden remotes and backups lurking near trees or oddly-shaped statues. But the Moreaus were clearly expected, and the guards passed them through without question.

The main house was as impressive as the grounds, its exterior magnificent and imposing, its interior carrying the same underplayed sense of luxury Jonny had noticed on the Committé's star ship so long ago. Personal taste, he'd thought then; but with eleven more years of politics behind him he could now recognize the additional stubtle warning the decor conveyed: its owner was not a man who could be bought.

D'arl was waiting for them in a small study clearly designed for personal work rather than for public or private audiences. He looked up as they entered, waved them silently to the chairs already pulled up to face his. They sat down, and for a moment the Committé gazed at Jonny. "Well, Governor—it *is* Governor, isn't it?" he said at last. "You seem to have made a genuine mess of your little diplomatic trip. I presume your brother has already dragged you through the roasting pit over that asinine escape from Adirondack, so I'll dispense with any further remarks about that. So now tell me why you're worth sticking my neck out."

"Because I have information about the Troft Assemblage I think you don't," Jonny said calmly. "And what may be a good chance to prevent a war. The greatest good for the greatest number— wasn't that the criterion you've always followed?"

D'arl's lip twitched in a brief smile. "Your political skills have definitely improved, Governor. All right. Let's start with why you called the Troft Empire an Assemblage a minute ago."

"Because that's what the Trofts call it, and because that's exactly what it is. There's no centralized government, at least nothing corresponding in authority to Dome or the Committee. The Assemblage is actually nothing more than a loose-knit fraternity of two- to four-planet demesnes."

D'arl frowned. "You'll forgive me if I'm skeptical. A collection of systems working at cross-purposes could hardly have held off the Dominion's military might for three years."

"True—but I never said they always worked at cross-purposes."

D'arl shook his head. "Individual self-interest alone would guarantee disunity among that many demesnes."

"Unless there were some issue of overriding importance to all of them," Jonny said quietly. "Such as an invasion by an alien race. Us."

"Jonny, the Trofts started the war, not us," Jame

spoke up. "That's not just an official line, you know—I've personally seen the records."

"Then perhaps you've also seen the records of the 471 Scorpii exploration," Jonny said. "That, according to the Trofts, is what started the war."

D'arl started to speak, reached instead for a comboard resting on a low table beside his seat. "I don't think I know the reference," Jame said.

"It was a minor double star system the Dominion thought might be worth a mining development," D'arl told him. "But according to this, the initial probe took place almost ten years before Silvern was hit."

"Yes, sir," Jonny nodded. "It took the affected demesnes that long to convince the others a war was necessary."

For a moment D'arl gazed at the comboard, fingers drumming on the chair arm. "You're implying the Committee's been blind for the past thirty years." His tone was less accusing than it was thoughtful.

Jonny shrugged. "The Trofts would hardly have advertised what they probably saw as a major military disadvantage. And any dealings since then on a planetary scale or less really *would* look very similar to how the Dominion does things, too. But the indications were there, if the figures the Troft Ship Commander gave me are correct. Do you have the number of representatives the Trofts sent to the peace talks after the war?"

D'arl busied himself with his comboard. "They had—let's see: twenty-six Senior Representatives. Another eighty-four aides and support personnel came to Iberiand with them."

"Twenty-six. What size team did the Dominion send, about ten?"

"Twelve—and I remember Committé H'orme complaining at the time that that seemed top-heavy." D'arl's eyes met Jonny's. "Twenty-six Troft demesnes?"

Jonny nodded. "One each from the border demesnes, the only ones whose territory would be directly affected by any settlement. But then a year later you began negotiations for the rights to the Troft Corridor, which I estimate affected eighty or so additional demesnes."

D'arl was already punching keys. "One hundred six Senior Representatives," he said, shaking his head slowly. "Eighty more, exactly."

"There were other indications, too," Jonny said into the silence that followed. "The Ship Commander who let us go obviously felt entitled to disobey his orders when he had sufficient reason to do so. And even during the war I was captured by a local officer who kept me alive almost certainly against orders. You may remember me telling you about that one, Jame."

The younger Moreau was frowning. "I remember ... but I don't buy your explanation. This wide-open autonomy between demesnes is bad enough, but if you run it to upper military command level, too, you're going to wind up with complete anarchy."

Jonny shrugged. "I frankly don't understand it myself," he admitted. "The Ship Commander tried to explain how a graduated system of respect or obedience based on an individual's past record kept their society running smoothly, but it still sounds like magic to me."

"All right," D'arl said abruptly. "Assume for the moment all this is true. Then what?"

Jonny turned back to face him. "Then avoiding a war becomes simply a matter of removing the issue the demesnes are uniting over. Specifically, allowing them to close the Corridor."

"Out of the question." D'arl's voice was flat.

"Official Dominion policy says the Corridor stays open or the Trofts pay heavily for closing it."

"Dominion policy isn't carved into bedrock," Jonny countered. "The *purpose* of that threat was to protect Aventine from attack. Fine—but right now we have a better chance of surviving *without* your protection; and if loss of contact with you is the price, we're willing to pay it."

"Are you, now," D'arl said. "And what happens when your machines and electronics start breaking down? Aventine hasn't got an extensive enough technological base to maintain things for long."

"No, but the Trofts do. We can undoubtedly trade with them as well as you do."

"*Our* trade has been extremely minimal, for intelligence purposes only—"

"Oh, come on," Jonny snorted. "We both know what I'm talking about. Practically every one of your licensed carriers routinely stops off for trade en route to Aventine. Why else do you think the Corridor demesnes have put up with the arrangement all these years? They get goods *and* information that they would normally have to buy—with heavy tariffs, no doubt—from their brother demesnes."

D'arl had a sour look on his face. "As it happens, we've been trying to come up with a good way to end that clandestine trade for years."

Jonny spread his hands. "Well, here's your chance."

D'arl sighed. "Governor, you still don't understand the political realities here. The Committee has taken a stand; we can*not* back down without a damn good reason."

"So make one up," Jonny snapped, his patience beginning to fray. "You're a consummate politician—surely you won't let a little matter of truth stand in the way of what you want." D'arl's brow darkened, but Jonny rushed on before the other could speak. "Aventine doesn't want war, the Trofts don't especially want war, your own *people* don't want war. Is the Committee so hell-bent on fighting someone that not even that will stop them?"

"Jonny!" Jame snapped.

"It's all right, Moreau, I'll handle it," D'arl said. "Governor, I'll take your recommendation to the Committee tomorrow. That's the best that I can do."

"A Committé with your experience?" Jonny scoffed. "You can do better than just playing court reporter."

"I can push any solidly-based, politically plausible reason for closing the Corridor," D'arl bit back. "You've yet to give me anything that qualifies."

"You want a good political reason? Fine; I'll give you one right now." Jonny stood up, dimly aware that his anger was near to overwhelming all control over it. "What do you think the Committee would do if a visiting dignitary from Aventine shot down one of its members?"

"Jonny!" Jame jumped to his feet.

"Stay back, Jame." Jonny kept his eyes on D'arl. "Well, Committé? It would mean economic sanctions against the colonies, wouldn't it, which for all practical purposes means closing the Corridor."

"It would." D'arl was glacially calm. "But you wouldn't shoot me down in cold blood just for that."

"Wouldn't I? The greatest good for the greatest number, remember? What does it matter that you and I would be sacrificed? And I've got more than just that, anyway. For what you've done to thousands of Aventine boys alone I could hate you enough to kill. Jame, get *back*."

The younger Moreau ignored the order. Quietly, he walked over to stand squarely between the other two men. For a long moment the brothers locked gazes. Then Jonny reached forward and effortlessly lifted Jame into the air by his upper arms, setting him to the side. The brief burst of anger was gone, leaving only determination and the cold knowledge that he'd come too far to back out now. "Committé, I want you to get on the phone and start calling in all the favors you've undoubtedly been accumulating through the years," he told D'arl grimly. "Now. You *are* going to get the Corridor closing accepted."

D'arl didn't move. "Under threat to my life? No. And certainly not because of your unreasonable feelings about the Aventine Cobra project."

He said the last so casually that Jonny was taken aback. Fury threatened to drown him . . . but abruptly he understood. "You don't know, do you?" he said, more in bitterness than in anger. "I suppose it hasn't happened yet to your own Cobras."

"Know what?"

Jonny dug into his pocket for his medicine, tossed the two vials into D'arl's lap. The Committé frowned at the labels and keyed the names into his comboard. A moment later he looked up to meet Jonny's eyes. "Anemia and arthritis," he almost whispered.

"Yes," Jonny nodded, wondering at the oddly intense reaction. "Every one of the First Cobras in the colonies is coming down with those diseases, as a direct result of our implanted servos and laminae, and there are indications our immune systems are starting to be affected, as well. Best estimates give me barely twenty years left to live, if that long. *That's* the ultimate legacy your Cobra project has left on Aventine."

D'arl stared down at the vials in his hand. "It's starting here, too, Governor. Reports of chronic Cobra illnesses have dribbled in for the past year or so. Statistically inconclusive as yet . . . I'd hoped my suspicions were wrong." He looked up at Jame's stunned expression. "I ran the reports through Alveres, Moreau—I didn't see any point in worrying you about your brother's health."

Jame took a deep breath. "Committé . . . if what Jonny said about secret trade helping to keep the Corridor open is true, then it follows that the whole Aventine Cobra project was indeed unnecessary, or at least premature."

"The Cobras will be needed now."

"No," Jonny shook his head. "We'll be maintaining the trade relationship with the Trofts, and with the Corridor closed we're no longer a military threat. They won't attack us—and *we* won't provoke *them*, either. There's another point for you, Committé: if war starts, you won't be able to count on those hundred thousand Troft troops being tied up on Aventine."

"*My* point, sir—" Jame cut off as D'arl raised a hand.

"Peace, Moreau," the Committé said quietly. "I never said I didn't want to help, just that I needed a stronger case. And now I've got it. Excuse me."

Standing, he brushed by Jonny and stepped to a small desk off to one side. "Starport," he said to the phone screen. ". . . This is Committé D'arl. Number one star ship is to be prepared for travel, under the direction of Jame Moreau. Passenger and cargo lists to be supplied by him; ultimate destination Adirondack. . . . Thank you."

He keyed the phone off and turned to face the two Moreaus. "I'm heading back to Dome to get things started. Governor, you and your brother need to make a list of whatever you'd like as your last shipment of goods to the Outer Colonies. You can go whenever you're ready; I'll contact you on Adirondack before you leave there with any final messages." He turned to go.

"Committé," Jonny called after him. "Thank you."

The other turned back, and Jonny was surprised to see an ironic smile tugging at his lips. "I'll stop the war, Governor. But save your thanks until you see how I do it." He left the room, closing the door gently behind him.

Jonny never saw him again.

It was the end of the road for them, and both men knew it. So for a long moment they stood beside the *Menssana*'s entry ramp and just looked at each other. Jonny broke the silence first. "I saw on the newscast this morning that Aventine's apparently starting to complain about the way Dome's been running the Outer Colonies. The announcer seemed a bit on the indignant side."

Jame nodded. "It's going to get worse, too, I'm afraid. By the time we're finished with you, banning all trade or other contact with the colonies is going to seem like a remarkably restrained response by the Committee."

"In other words, history's going to put the blame squarely on Aventine."

Jame sighed. "It was the only way—the only *political* way—to let the Committee back away from such a long-established stance. I'm sorry."

Jonny looked back across the city, his memory superimposing Adirondack's battered wartime appearance against what was there now. "It's not important," he told his brother. "If vilifying us is what it takes to save face, we can live with it."

"I hope so. You haven't heard yet one of the more secret reasons the Committee accepted Committé D'arl's proposal."

Jonny cocked an eyebrow. "Which is . . . ?"

"A slightly edited version of your confrontation at the estate. He convinced them the Aventine Cobras might get angry enough to seek revenge against them in the near future if contact with the Outer Colonies was maintained." Jame snorted gently. "It's strange, you know. Almost from the end of the last war the Committee's been trying to figure out a safe way to get rid of the Cobras; and now that they've got one, it had to practically be drop-kicked down their throats."

"No one said politics was self-consistent," Jonny shrugged. "But it worked, and that's all that matters."

"So you heard the courier report already," Jame nodded. "The Troft response was very interesting to read—the experts say the phrasing indicated our capitulation on the Corridor issue really caught them off-guard."

"I'm not surprised," Jonny said. "But I wouldn't worry about this setting any precedents. Remember how hard it is for the demesnes to get together on any future demands." He glanced around the visible sections of the starfield, hoping against hope that Danice Tolan would make a last-minute appearance.

Jame followed his gaze and his thoughts. "I wouldn't count on seeing your friend before you have to go. She's probably up to her cloak and laser in the Joint Command's decommissioning procedure—I think they've suddenly decided they don't like having independent paramilitary units running around the Dominion." He smiled briefly, but then sobered. "Jonny . . . you're not condemning your own world to slow death just to prevent a war, are you? I mean, trading with the Trofts is all very well on a theoretical level, but none of you has ever actually done it before."

"True, but we'll pick up the techniques fast enough, and with the *Menssana* to double our long-range fleet, we'll have reasonable capacity. Besides, we're not exactly starting cold." He patted his jacket pocket and the list of Troft contacts and rendezvous points Rando Harmon and Dru Quoraheim had supplied. "We'll do just fine."

"I hope you're right. You haven't got much going for you out there."

Jonny shook his head. "You've been on Asgard

too long to remember how it feels to be a frontier world. Horizon, Adirondack, and now Aventine— I've never lived on anything but. We'll make it, Jame ... if for no other reason than to prove to the universe that we can."

"Governor Moreau?" a voice drifted down from the ship beside them. "Captain's compliments, sir. Control's given us permission to lift any time."

And it was time to say good-bye. "Take care of yourself, Jonny," Jame said as Jonny was still searching for words. "Say hello to everyone for me, okay?"

"Sure." Jonny stepped forward and wrapped his brother in a bear hug. Tears blurred his vision. "You take care of yourself, too. And ... thanks for everything."

Two minutes later he was on the *Menssana*'s bridge. "Ah—Governor," the captain said, attempting with only partial success to hide his bubbling enthusiasm beneath a professional demeanor. The entire crew was like that: young, idealistic, the whole lot barely qualified for the trip. But they were the most experienced of those who'd volunteered for this one-way mission. The last colonists the Dominion would be sending for a long, long time—they, like the *Menssana* and its cargo, a farewell gift from D'arl and the Committee. "We're all set here," the young officer continued. "Course is laid out, and we've got the special pass the Trofts sent already programmed into the transmitter. Whenever you're set, we can go."

Jonny's eyes searched out a ground-view display, watched the tiny image of Jame just disappearing into the entrypoint building. "I'm ready any time," he told the captain quietly. "Let's go home."

Here is an excerpt from Cobra Strike!, *coming in February 1986 from Baen Books:*

The Council of Syndics—its official title—had in the early days of colonization been just that: a somewhat low-key grouping of the planet's syndics and governor-general which met at irregular intervals to discuss any problems and map out the general direction in which they hoped the colony would grow. As the population increased and beachheads were established on two other worlds, the Council grew in both size and political weight, following the basic pattern of the distant Dominion of Man. But unlike the Dominion, this outpost of humanity numbered nearly three thousand Cobras among its half-million people.

The resulting inevitable diffusion of political power had had a definite impact on the Council's makeup. The rank of governor had been added between the syndic and governor-general levels, blunting the pinnacle of power just a bit; and at *all* levels of government the Cobras with their double vote were well represented.

Corwin Moreau didn't really question the political philosophy which had produced this modification of Dominion structure; but from a purely utilitarian point of view he often found the sheer size of the 75-member Council unwieldy.

Today, though, at least for the first hour, things went smoothly. Most of the discussion—including the points Corwin raised—focused on older issues which had already had the initial polemics thoroughly wrung out of them. A handful were officially given resolution, the rest returned to the members for more analysis, consideration, or simple foot-dragging; and as the agenda wound down it began to look as if the meeting might actually let out early.

And then Governor-General Brom Stiggur dropped a pocket planet-wrecker into the room.

It began with an old issue. "You'll all remember the report of two years ago," he said, looking around the room, "in which the Farsearch team concluded that, aside from our three present worlds, no planets exist within at least a 20-light-year radius of Aventine that we could expand to in the future. It was agreed at the time that our current state of population and development hardly required an immediate resolution of this long-term problem."

Corwin sat a bit straighter in his seat, sensing similar reactions around him. Stiggur's words were neutral enough, but something explosive seemed to be hiding beneath the carefully controlled inflections of his voice.

"However," the other continued, "in the past few days something new has come to light, something which I felt should be presented immediately to this body, before even any follow-up studies were initiated." Glancing at the Cobra guard standing by the door, Stiggur nodded. The man nodded in turn and opened the panel ... and a single Troft walked in.

A faint murmur of surprise rippled its way around the room, and Corwin felt himself tense involuntarily as the alien made its way to Stiggur's side. The Trofts had been the Worlds' trading partner for nearly 14 years now, but Corwin still remembered vividly the undercurrent of fear that he'd grown up with. Most of the Council had even stronger memories than that: the Troft occupation of the Dominion worlds Silvern and Adirondack had occurred only 43 years ago, ultimately becoming the impetus for the original Cobra project. It was no accident that most of the people who now dealt physically with the Troft traders were in their early twenties. Only the younger Aventinians could face the aliens without wincing.

The Troft paused at the edge of the table, waiting as the Council members dug out translator-link earphones and inserted them. One or two of the younger syndics didn't bother, and Corwin felt a flicker of jealousy as he adjusted his own earphone to low volume. He'd taken the same number of courses in catertalk as they had, but it was obvious that foreign language comprehension wasn't even close to being his forté.

"Men and women of the Cobra Worlds Council," the earphone murmured to him. "I am Speaker One of the Tlos'khin'fahi demesne of the Trof'te Assemblage." The alien's high-pitched catertalk continued for a second beyond the translation; both races had early on decided that the first three parasyllables of Troft demesne titles were more than adequate for human use, and that a literal transcription of the aliens' proper names was a waste of effort. "The Tlos'khin'fahi demesne-lord has sent your own demesne-lord's request for data to the other parts of the Assemblage, and the result has been a triad offer from the Pua'lanek'zia and Baliu'ckha'spmi demesnes."

Corwin grimaced. He'd never liked deals involving two or more Troft demesnes, both because of the delicate political balance the Worlds often had to strike and because the humans never heard much about the Troft-Troft arm of such bargains. That arm *had* to exist—the individual demesnes seldom if ever gave anything away to each other.

The same line of thought appeared to have tracked its way elsewhere through the room. "You speak of a triad, instead of a quad offer," Governor Dylan Fairleigh spoke up. "What part does the Tlos'khin'fahi demesne expect to play?"

"My demesne-lord chooses the role of catalyst," was the prompt reply. "No fee will be forthcoming for our role." The Troft fingered something on his abdomen sash and Corwin's display lit up with a map showing the near half of the Troft Assemblage. Off on one edge three stars began blinking red. "The Cobra Worlds," the alien unnecessarily identified them. A quarter of the way around the bulge a single star, also outside Troft territory, flashed green. "The world named Qasama by its natives. They are described by the Baliu'ckha'spmi demesne-lord as an alien race of great potential danger to the Assemblage. Here—" a vague-edge sphere appeared at the near side of the flashing green star—"somewhere, is a tight cluster of five worlds capable of supporting human life. The Pua'lanek'zia demesne-lord will give you their location and an Assemblage pledge of human possession if your Cobras will undertake to eliminate the threat of Qasama. I will await your decision."

The Troft turned and left ... and only slowly did Corwin realize he was holding his breath. Five brand-new worlds ... for the price of becoming mercenaries.

**For
Fiction with Real Science In It,
and Fantasy That Touches
The Heart of The Human Soul . . .**

Baen Books bring you Poul Anderson, Marion Zimmer Bradley, C.J. Cherryh, Gordon R. Dickson, David Drake, Robert L. Forward, Janet Morris, Jerry Pournelle, Fred Saberhagen, Michael Reaves, Jack Vance . . . all top names in science fiction and fantasy, plus new writers destined to reach the top of their fields. For a free catalog of all Baen Books, send three 22-cent stamps, plus your name and address, to

*Baen Books
260 Fifth Avenue, Suite 3S
New York, N.Y. 10001*

A giant space station orbiting the Earth can be a scientific boon ... or a terrible sword of Damocles hanging over our heads. In Martin Caidin's *Killer Station*, one brief moment of sabotage transforms Station *Pleiades* into an instrument of death and destruction for millions of people. The massive space station is heading relentlessly toward Earth, and its point of impact is New York City, where it will strike with the impact of the Hiroshima Bomb. Station Commander Rush Cantrell must battle impossible odds to save his station and his crew, and put his life on the line that millions may live.

This high-tech tale of the near future is written in the tradition of Caidin's *Marooned* (which inspired the Soviet-American Apollo/Soyuz Project and became a film classic) and *Cyborg* (the basis for the hit TV series "The Six Million Dollar Man"). Barely fictional, *Killer Station* is an intensely *real* moment of the future, packed with excitement, human drama, and adventure.

Caidin's record for forecasting (and inspiring) developments in space is well-known. *Killer Station* provides another glimpse of what *may* happen with and to all of us in the next few years.

Available December 1985 from Baen Books
55996-6 • 384 pp. • $3.50